PRAISE FOR *FOREVER, ROSE:*

"A sweet, delicious piece of American life. Robin Lee Hatcher's many readers will be delighted!"
—Karen Harper, bestselling author of *River of Sky*

"An enjoyable and romantic slice of Western Americana!"
—Jill Marie Landis, bestselling author of *Past Promises*

"An enchanting love story! Five Stars!"
—*Affaire de Coeur*

"A tender, touching, heartwarming story of a love you won't be able to forget!"
—Kat Martin, bestselling author of *Sweet Vengeance*

"Warm and wonderful, a gem of a book. I loved it so much I stayed up all night reading it!"
—Patricia Potter, bestselling author of *Relentless*

"Rich in detail, *Forever, Rose* is storytelling at its best—imaginative, vivid, and lyrical!"
—*Rendezvous*

A COMPROMISING POSITION

"Michael!"

Rafferty heard Rose Townsend's frightened cry as the bedroom door flew open, banging loudly against the wall. He was instantly awake and out of bed. A second later, she flung herself at him. Instinctively, his arms closed around her.

"Rose?"

She was shaking like a leaf. She was also completely naked.

"Rose?" he whispered again, his arms tightening. Lord, she was tiny—and so obviously afraid.

"What the hell is going on?" Glen Townsend's voice boomed from the hallway.

Lamplight spilled into the room, illuminating the nude girl in Michael's arms. He quickly moved her to stand behind him, putting himself between her and the doorway.

"Rafferty, what the hell are you doin' with my daughter?"

Other *Leisure* books by Robin Lee Hatcher:
MIDNIGHT ROSE
DEVLIN'S PROMISE
PROMISE ME SPRING
PROMISED SUNRISE
REMEMBER WHEN
DREAMTIDE
THE MAGIC

The Americana Series:
WHERE THE HEART IS

Forever, Rose

ROBIN LEE HATCHER

LEISURE BOOKS NEW YORK CITY

To all those who believe in a forever kind of love.

A LEISURE BOOK®

November 1999

Published by

Dorchester Publishing Co., Inc.
276 Fifth Avenue
New York, NY 10001

ISBN 0-8439-4629-6

But to see her was to love her,
Love but her, and love forever.
—from *Ae Fond Kiss* by Robert Burns

Forever, Rose

Chapter One

Homestead, Idaho Territory
May, 1890

"Your pa's coming home."

The soup ladle dropped from Rose's hand into the kettle, splashing an ugly stain onto her apron. She closed her eyes and drew in a deep breath, hoping against hope that when she opened them she would find she'd been imagining her mother's words. But when she looked, she was still standing before the stove in the kitchen of the Long Bow Valley Room and Board.

Rose turned around. Her heart was racing. There was an odd buzzing noise in her ears. She felt choked by the icy panic swelling inside of her. "He's coming *here?*" Her voice was little more than a whisper.

Virginia Townsend nodded as she lifted the letter she held in her hand.

It can't be true. It can't be true. "When?"

"Couple weeks, accordin' to his letter. Doesn't say exactly when they let him out, just when he should get to Homestead."

Rose shook her head, trying to clear her thoughts. "But why's he coming *here?*"

"Where else is he to go? He lost that Denver saloon while he was in prison. Besides, for all he's done, this *is* still his home." There was a brief pause before she added softly, "And I'm still his wife."

Rose's voice sharpened with sarcasm. "This wasn't *ever* a home, not as long as he was here. Ma, you can't let him come back. You *can't.*"

Virginia lifted her shoulders in a helpless gesture. "For better or worse, I'm his wife. That's the vow I took when I married him. He's got a right to come back, if that's what he wants. I can't rightly stop him."

Rose opened her mouth to protest again, then turned abruptly toward the stove. Was there anything she could say to make her mother change her mind? She doubted it. If Virginia had wanted to change things, she would have done it long before now. She would have done it the first time her husband had hit her. Or she would have done it the first time he'd struck one of their children.

No, there was nothing Rose could do to keep her pa from coming back to Homestead and resuming his life in the boardinghouse. And once he was there, there would be nothing

she could do to keep him from hurting Ma—
or from hurting her.

She closed her eyes as her hands clenched
against her stomach. Pa was coming back. Pa
was going to move into the boardinghouse and
stay in the room next to her own. And then
he would drink, and when he got drunk, he
would strike out at them in the black rage Rose
remembered all too well. Mostly he would hit
Ma. He would hit her until she had to hide in
the house so nobody would see her black eyes
or her swollen lips. There wouldn't be anything
Rose could do about it. Everything would be
the way it used to be, before he went away.
Everything would be the same.

No, it won't be the same, she thought angrily.

She wasn't going to let him hurt Ma, and she
wasn't going to let him hurt her either.

Never again! she swore to herself. *Not ever
again.*

Her legs shaking, she opened her eyes and
turned to face her mother a second time. "I've
got almost forty-five dollars saved from workin'
at the restaurant. We could leave Homestead.
We could go to San Francisco . . . or as far as
it'll take us. I could find work. I'd take care of
you, Ma."

Virginia's smile was bittersweet. "You
shouldn't ought to have to take care of your
ma. You're too young to have such worries."

"I'm not a child anymore. I'm goin' on nineteen. Say you'll come with me."

"I can't go, Rose."

"Then I'll go alone," she said, meaning it.

"Rose—"

"I can't stay. I hate him, Ma. I hate him for what he did to you and to me and to. . . ." She felt the old sickness churning in her stomach as a vision of the burning sawmill sprang into her mind. But Rose had never told anyone what she suspected her pa had done the day he'd left Homestead nearly a decade ago, and so she stopped herself before she could speak those suspicions aloud.

Virginia's shoulders sagged. "If you feel you have to go, I'll give you what money I can spare."

"You haven't anything," Rose replied, knowing it was true. Much of what profit the boardinghouse made, her brother, Mark, drank up at the Pony Saloon. "We don't even have any boarders now. You'll need anything you have to see you through." She untied her apron as she spoke, hanging it on a peg near the stove. "I'd better get ready for work." She headed toward the hall.

"Rose?"

She stopped and glanced over her shoulder.

"When will you leave?"

"Before Pa gets here. On the next stage."

Softly, Virginia said, "So soon?"

"I've got to, Ma."

Virginia nodded in resignation. "I'll miss you, Rose."

"I'll miss you, too, Ma."

* * *

Michael Rafferty stopped his horse and stared down the lone street of Homestead. He'd known it wasn't a city like Denver or San Francisco, but he'd hoped it would be bigger than the quaint town that lay before him.

He nudged the roan gelding with his boot-heels and started slowly down the street, his eyes carefully perusing each building, making note of things most folks wouldn't see. For instance, though it was well-maintained and had a fresh coat of paint, the Barber Mercantile had obviously been around longer than any of the other buildings in town, probably twelve to fifteen years. The First Bank of Homestead, in contrast, hadn't been built more than two years ago, judging from the appearance of the red brick walls.

Besides the bank and general store, there were the usual businesses that made up small towns across the West—a church, a school, a livery and blacksmith shop, restaurant, saloon, barbershop and bathhouse, post office, jail. Michael had seen the like in a hundred different places. What was missing, of course, was a hotel.

And that was exactly why Michael Rafferty had come to Homestead.

John Thomas must be getting senile to send me to a town like this.

John Thomas Rafferty had never considered operating a hotel in any but the biggest cities in America. Michael's father had taught him everything about building and running a hotel in cities like San Francisco, Denver, Chicago, and New York. But Michael knew nothing about owning a hotel in a backwater burg.

His mouth thinned.

Of course, that was why John Thomas had chosen it. Because Michael would have to prove himself in unfamiliar territory.

"Since the two of you don't seem inclined to agree on anything," his father had announced several months ago, "there's only one thing for me to do. I'll leave Palace Hotels to just one of you when I'm gone. It'll be up to you to prove who that one will be."

The surprise and betrayal Michael had felt then was just as strong today. He shouldn't have to prove himself. He'd known since the time he was a little boy that the hotels would be his. They should have been his without question. Dillon had no right to any part of Palace Hotels.

Grimly, Michael shoved those thoughts from his mind. He had no time to examine old wounds that continued to fester. He was in Homestead to win what was rightfully his, and unless he wanted to lose to Dillon, he'd better set his plans in motion.

He would need to find a place to stay, but first he meant to get himself something to eat. He stopped his horse before a false-fronted,

wooden building with a sign that proudly
proclaimed it Zoe's Restaurant.

Dismounting, he brushed the trail dust from
his trousers and the sleeves of his shirt, then
stepped up onto the boardwalk and entered
the establishment. He was greeted by delicious
odors coming from the rear of the restaurant,
and his stomach growled in response.

The place was empty of customers. In fact,
if it weren't for the sounds and smells coming from the kitchen, he'd have wondered if
the restaurant was even open for business.
Certainly no one had bothered to answer
the bells that had jingled when he opened
the door.

Assuming someone would eventually check
on the dining area for customers, he selected
a table against a wall, with a view of both the
front door and the entrance to the kitchen,
and sat down, placing his hat on one of the
other chairs. He was untroubled by the wait.
Michael, his stepmother had always stated, had
the patience of Job—and the stubbornness of a
mule. He was willing to act or wait, whichever
was the best means of accomplishing that
which he'd set out to do. His current objective
was to find something to fill the emptiness in
his stomach, and so he waited.

About five minutes later, the front door of the
restaurant swung inward, and a young woman
hurried through the opening. Michael had a
quick impression of shiny, chestnut-colored

17

hair swept smoothly up from her neck, gathered in a bun atop her head, and of a pleasingly female figure compacted into a body barely five feet tall.

As she closed the door behind her, her gaze met his. Michael couldn't be sure from this distance, but he thought her eyes were brown. What he was sure of was the sadness he saw there. He felt a spark of sympathy.

"Rose, is that you?" a voice called from the kitchen.

She looked away. "Yes, it's me, Mrs. Potter."

The door at the rear of the dining room swung open, revealing a middle-aged woman. Michael supposed she was both the Zoe of Zoe's Restaurant and the young woman's Mrs. Potter. The older woman had dark brown hair sprinkled with gray and cheeks bright pink from the heat of the kitchen. "I was just—" Her words broke off abruptly when she saw Michael. "Oh, dear. I didn't know we had a customer."

"No trouble, ma'am," he said politely, nodding in her direction. "I didn't mind the wait."

"Rose, will you take the gentleman's order?" Zoe Potter turned quickly toward the kitchen. "I've got chickens roastin'."

Michael watched as Rose followed Zoe through the swinging door, reappearing a moment later wearing a crisp white apron over her simple blue blouse and skirt. A white cap now covered much of her dark hair. She was carrying a small paper tablet in her left hand and a pencil in her right.

She crossed the room, stopping on the opposite side of the table from him. Pointing toward the door at the front of the restaurant, she asked, "What would you like, sir?"

Her eyes weren't brown. They were hazel, the dark brown centers flecked with gold. He guessed she wasn't more than eighteen or nineteen, but something about her eyes made her seem older, wiser, a little sadder. He wondered why.

"Sir?"

He smiled apologetically. "Sorry." He turned his gaze in the direction she'd pointed. Written on a chalkboard in precise letters was the menu for the day. He considered his choices, then said, "I'll have the corn dodgers, chicken-fixin's, and coffee."

Rose slipped the pencil back into the pocket of her apron. "I'll bring your coffee right out," she said, then moved across the room and into the kitchen.

Before she returned, the front door of the restaurant opened again, admitting two men. One was dressed in a business suit and bow tie, the other in denim trousers and a vest with a badge pinned to it.

There was a look about the first man that almost shouted, "Banker!" Michael knew it was always wise to get on good terms with the town financier as quickly as possible. Such men tended to wield a strong voice in any community. Folks listened to their advice as if it were gospel.

The second man was obviously the sheriff. He had steel-gray hair and eyes to match and was built like a grizzly bear. Michael thought he looked a bit long in the tooth to still be sheriffing, but he seemed hale enough. When the sheriff looked his way, Michael nodded, silently admitting he was a stranger in town.

By the time the two men were settled at a table, the door opened yet again, this time revealing an older couple.

Michael was reminded of the nursery rhyme about Jack Sprat and his wife, which he'd read to his brothers and sister when they were little. Those fictional characters, no doubt, looked like these two—the man was bean pole thin with a shiny bald head, the woman merrily plump with thick gray hair.

They, too, glanced his way. The woman's eyes sparkled with curiosity. It was almost as if Michael could hear her say, *We don't get many strangers in Homestead*.

As with the sheriff, Michael acknowledged her frank appraisal with a slight nod.

Just then, the waitress entered the dining room, carrying Michael's cup of coffee.

"Afternoon, Rose," the other woman called as her husband pulled out a chair for her.

Rose smiled. "Afternoon, Mrs. Barber, Mr. Barber." She set Michael's coffee on the table, then headed toward her new customers. "Sheriff, Mr. Stanford." She pulled her small tablet and pencil from the pocket of her apron. "What can I get for you today? Mrs. Potter's got some mighty good chicken-fixin's ready, and there's beefsteak available. She's also baked up some cider cakes and cherry pies."

Michael sipped his coffee, observing the waitress as she took each of the orders. Now that he wasn't distracted by the sorrow he'd read in her eyes, he could study the rest of her appearance. He found it much to his liking.

She was sweetly pretty with a heart-shaped face and dimples that appeared whenever she smiled. Her mouth was small and pink, her nose dainty. Long lashes—the same dark chestnut color as her hair—framed her expressive eyes.

Sweetly pretty she might be, but Michael didn't fail to appreciate her temptingly rounded figure during this more thorough perusal.

Lillian would scratch my eyes out, he thought as he lowered his gaze to his coffee cup.

He was reminded of Lillian's fury when he'd told her he would be away for a year. "Do you think I'm going to sit around and wait for you while you play out this stupid game?" she'd shouted.

He should have felt guilty, he supposed. After all, everyone expected the two of them to marry. They'd been keeping company for over a year now. Lillian Overhart, who was

21

beautiful, sophisticated, and intelligent, came from one of San Francisco's most distinguished families. There was no reason why he shouldn't marry her. In fact, he was certain he would. It was just he simply felt no urgency to do so at the moment.

He looked up, gazing across the restaurant at the waitress. He wondered what it might be like to be married to someone like her—and then thought of home-cooked suppers and bedroom slippers and long nights spent nestled in a featherbed.

But those things weren't for Michael Thomas Rafferty. He thrived on the bustle of the big city. He loved the challenge of business. He enjoyed nothing more than a night at the theater or a brutal game of cards with the men at his club.

He wasn't interested in a small-town waitress with sad eyes, and he never would be.

"Who's the stranger?" Zoe asked when Rose entered the kitchen, bringing more orders with her.

"He didn't say." Rose glanced down at her tablet. "I need one beef stew, an order of chicken-fixin's, corn dodgers, and a slice of cherry pie, and two orders of ham, mashed potatoes, and coleslaw." She dropped the tablet into her pocket. "I'll serve the coffee."

Rose wasn't as uninterested in the stranger's identity as she pretended to be. It wasn't that plenty of outsiders didn't pass through Homestead on their way to the mining areas or the logging camps. Others came looking for land with intentions of settling in this valley or the next one over. But few of them were as handsome or as well dressed as this particular traveler, and she couldn't help wondering what had brought him to this little town.

As she carried a tray back into the dining room, Rose cast a surreptitious glance in the stranger's direction. She wasn't mistaken about his good looks. He had hair the color of spun gold that brushed his shirt collar, and his eyes were the blue of a summer sky. His masculine features seemed nothing short of perfect, from his straight nose, to his firm mouth, to his beardless jaw. His profile spoke of power and confidence.

Looking at him, she was reminded of the books she'd read in school, her studies of Greek gods of mythology or romantic medieval knights from ancient poetry. But she'd never thought they could be real until she saw this stranger.

But there was something different about this man, she thought, beyond his extraordinary good looks. It wasn't anything she could put a name to, just a sense that the strength she perceived was mixed with a measure of gentleness.

He looked up. Their gazes met. Rose glanced quickly away, but not before she felt an embarrassing flush coloring her cheeks. Had he guessed what she'd been thinking?

"You seem to have an admirer, Rose," Emma Barber said softly as Rose set two cups of coffee on the table. "Who is he?"

"I don't know," she whispered in return. "I never saw him before."

"Stanley, you know who he is?" Emma asked.

Her husband looked across the room, then back at Emma. "Nope." He picked up his coffee and blew on the steamy-hot liquid.

"He must've just arrived in town," Emma continued, undeterred by her husband's apparent lack of interest. "I wonder if he's come to stay?"

Rose had been wondering the same thing, but wasn't about to admit it. Besides, it didn't matter to her, she thought sternly. She wasn't going to be around after a few more days. What did she care if this stranger stayed?

Leaving Homestead. . . .

She felt a tiny flutter in her stomach, a niggle of fear along her spine. She couldn't remember living anywhere but here. What was it going to be like, out there on her own?

Silently, she set the other two cups of coffee in front of the sheriff and Vince Stanford, then returned to the kitchen to help Zoe, trying not to think about how frightening it might be to leave Homestead.

It would be worse to stay, now that her pa was coming back.

*   *   *

Emma could scarcely stand the suspense. Throughout the meal, she kept casting glances in the direction of the handsome stranger. She was dying to know who he was and what had brought him to Homestead. She'd dropped several hints to Stanley to go over and speak to the gentleman before their dinner arrived, but either Stanley hadn't understood her wishes or he'd been ignoring them. More than likely the latter.

Not that she was surprised. There wasn't much her husband did that surprised her.

She watched as Rose cleared the dishes away, thinking that she'd been about the same age as Rose when she'd married Stanley Barber, just eighteen. Thirty-two years later, she wouldn't have changed a single one of those years— or the six children they'd been blessed with. She could honestly say she was as much in love with her husband as she'd been on their wedding day.

But, she thought, turning her gaze once more in the stranger's direction, that didn't mean she always agreed with Mr. Barber. Sometimes, if a woman wanted to find something out, she just had to take matters into her own hands.

When she caught the man's eye again, she smiled and said, "You're new to Homestead."

He nodded as he rose from his chair and picked up his hat. "Yes, ma'am," he replied. He pulled some coins from his pocket and left the payment for his meal beside his empty plate.

"Are you settling in the area?"

"Actually, I'm here on business." He walked toward her table. Turning his eyes on Stanley, he held out his hand and said, "I'm Michael Rafferty."

"Stanley Barber." The men shook hands. "This here is my wife, Emma."

"I'm pleased to meet you, Mrs. Barber." He offered a polite bow. "Perhaps you can help me. I need a place to stay. Are there any rooms for rent in Homestead?"

"There's the boardinghouse down near the church. Long Bow Valley Room and Board. Mrs. Townsend's rates are reasonable, and she's a wonderful cook. You'll be very comfortable there."

"Townsend, did you say?"

"Yes, Virginia Townsend. She's run the place for more than ten years now. 'Course, it used to be called Townsend's Rooming House, but when we started gettin' so many newcomers to the valley, Virginia did some fixin' up and addin' on and changed the name. You can't miss it." She pointed down the street toward the west end of town. "Big, two-story place. There's a sign on the porch."

"Much obliged." Michael Rafferty placed his black Stetson over his golden hair, then touched the brim and nodded before turning and leaving the restaurant.

"Nice young man," Emma said. "What do you

suppose his business in Homestead is?"

"Wouldn't know," was Stanley's only reply.

"Handsome fellow. Perhaps Annalee—"

"Emma." His voice was stern. "Annalee's almost spoke for. Don't go meddlin' in her affairs."

"I'm *not* meddling," she protested. "Besides, Sigmund Leonhardt doesn't seem in any hurry to ask for our daughter's hand in marriage. It wouldn't hurt for Annalee to see there are other fish in the sea. I would think her own father would be more concerned with her welfare. After all, she's twenty-five years old. She should be married and having children by this time. Why when I was her age—"

"Stay out of it, Emma." Stanley rose from the table, then slid her chair back for her. "Believe me, Annalee and Sigmund will get married when they're ready." His fingers slipped beneath her elbow. "Our daughter has a good head on her shoulders. She knows what she's doing."

Emma wasn't so sure, but she knew it would be useless to argue the point. With a sigh of resignation, she bid good afternoon to Sheriff McLeod and Vince Stanford while Stanley paid for their meal; then she and her husband left the restaurant.

Chapter Two

Yancy hadn't figured on ever falling in love, but then he hadn't reckoned he would ever meet a gal like Lark Rider either. Sometimes, he thought he could spend the rest of his life just lookin' at her and be plumb satisfied.

He especially liked the way she looked now, standing beside her bay gelding, her hand on the horse's neck. Behind her, tall mountains loomed, white snow still icing their craggy peaks, their sides thick with green pines. The look in Lark's brown-black eyes—eyes as soft as blackstrap poured on a tin plate—was one of pure serenity. Her soft mouth was curved up in a sweet expression. Her nut-brown skin— the color of shelled almonds—was flawless, revealing the perfect angles of her face. Her straight black hair was pulled into a braid, and a fringe of bangs skirted her forehead. She'd pushed off her hat, letting it hang from its string against her back.

Suddenly, Lark turned her head and looked straight at him. "Yancy Jones, what are you staring at?"

Caught by surprise, the truth popped out of him before he could think of anything else to say. "Just lookin' at you, Miss Lark."

Her smile broadened, and her eyes sparkled mischievously. "Well, you're supposed to be watching the cattle."

As if he didn't know what he was hired to do.

There'd be hell to pay if his boss ever learned how Yancy felt about Lark. Deserved to be, too, he reckoned. After all, the girl was near half his age, her a mere seventeen and him about to turn thirty. Besides, he was just a cowpoke. He owned his saddle and horse, the clothes on his back, and not much else. He had nothin' to offer any woman, let alone someone like Lark Rider, who'd grown up in that fine house and was used to having most everything her heart desired.

Lark was full of life and a fair piece of sass. He supposed she was even a bit spoiled, but it didn't matter to him. She was pretty and smart, funny and educated. She'd been raised to live the life of a real lady, yet she didn't lord it over anyone. Lark was special.

Yancy, on the other hand, was just a saddle bum, and any fool knew you couldn't hitch a horse with a coyote. He'd just have to be satisfied with lookin'.

29

But, Lord, he couldn't help himself from wanting more. From the moment he'd first laid eyes on her, nine months before, she'd had him cinched to the last hole, and there hadn't been a blamed thing he could do about it.

"I love spring, don't you, Yance?" she asked, her melodic voice breaking into his reverie.

"Sure do."

"All the new calves and foals. Birds singing. Trees and flowers blooming." She motioned to him. "Come over here. There's something I want you to see." She started walking along the bank of Pony Creek, leading Dark Feather behind her.

Yancy hesitated a moment. He really should get back to the herd. Will Rider wasn't paying him to stand around talking with Lark. But what else could he do but obey her request? He'd try to move mountains if that's what she wanted him to do.

He stepped down from his saddle and followed her into a cluster of cottonwoods and aspens that lined the creek. She was staring up into the high branches, where tiny buds were just beginning to unfurl into leaves.

She pointed as he stepped up beside her. "Look."

He followed the direction of her arm, but couldn't see anything unusual. "What?"

"Yancy Jones." Her voice had turned low and throaty.

He glanced down and found that she'd moved

closer, her gaze now centered on him.

"Don't you want to kiss me, Yance?"

His mouth went dry. "I don't think Mr. Rider would think much of me kissin' you, Miss Lark."

"My father likes you, and since I like you, too, I think kissing would be a very good idea." She leaned a little closer. The tip of her pink tongue darted out to moisten her lips, and her eyes seemed filled with expectation.

If she kept looking at him like that, his resistance wasn't going to last as long as a boiled shirt in a bear fight.

Her voice dropped even lower as she gazed up at him through a curtain of long lashes. "Yancy Jones, I'm not a little girl. I'm a woman, and I know my mind. My mother—my real mother—was married when she was my age."

"Lark. . . ." he muttered, feeling his resolve slipping fast.

She curled her arms around his neck and stood on tiptoe. "Don't you have sense enough to know I love you, Yancy Jones?" she whispered, and then she pressed her mouth to his.

"Ah, hell," he murmured against her lips before wrapping her in his arms and savoring her as he'd been longing to do all along.

Rose had hoped to speak to Zoe Potter about leaving Homestead when they were alone, but it looked as though such a time just wasn't going to happen. The restaurant stayed busy late into the afternoon, and when Rose finally saw the last customer leave, she went to the kitchen, only to find Doris McLeod and her twelve-year-old granddaughter, Sarah, sitting at the table in the center of the room.

"Hello, Rose," Doris greeted.

"Afternoon, Mrs. McLeod. Hello, Sarah." She carried the tray of dirty dishes over to the counter and set it down.

"How's your mother?"

"She's just fine."

Rose glanced at Zoe. She wondered if it would be rude to ask if she could speak to her alone, then decided against it. Zoe and Doris were close friends and shared every scrap of news and gossip anyway. It wasn't as if Zoe would keep Rose's announcement a secret.

"Mrs. Potter?" She held her head high. "There's something I need to tell you."

The three other people in the kitchen all turned their eyes upon Rose.

She drew in a deep breath. "I'm leaving Homestead, so I won't be able to go on working for you here in the restaurant."

"Leavin'?"

"Yes, ma'am. I'm going to San Francisco to find work there. I'll work for you right up through Tuesday, but I'll be taking the Wednesday stage down to Boise."

"But, Rose, why on ever would you—"

"I've just got to, Mrs. Potter. That's all."

Zoe stepped forward and placed a gentle

32

hand on Rose's shoulder. "I'll be sorry to lose you. If you change your mind, you'll always have a job here. I want you to know that."

She didn't reply. She couldn't do anything more than nod. Telling Mrs. Potter that she was leaving had been harder than she'd expected it to be. Leaving Homestead was going to be harder than she wanted to think about.

She crossed the room and hung up her apron; then with a quick farewell, she left the kitchen and walked toward the front door.

"Rose!"

She turned around.

Sarah hurried toward her. The girl's face was flushed with excitement. "Would you do me a favor when you get to San Francisco?"

"What's that, Sarah?"

"Would you write to me? Would you tell me what it's like there? You're so lucky to be going." Her blue eyes turned soft and dreamy. "It must be heavenly to go somewhere exciting like San Francisco. When I'm old enough, I'm going away, too. I'm not going to stay in a place like this where nothing exciting ever happens. I'm going to go to Chicago and New York and London and Paris. Maybe I'll come see you in San Francisco."

Rose wondered what it would have been like to have a childhood like Sarah McLeod's. Sarah had lost her parents at a tender age, but she had been beloved and pampered by her doting grandparents. Sarah wanted to see other cities simply for the adventure, simply to experience something new. Rose was leaving Homestead because she was desperate to escape the pain that would return with her pa. Would she have gone away if she wasn't forced to? She didn't think so.

"Sure, I'll write to you," she said softly. "I'll tell you just how wonderful it is." She hoped she would be telling the truth.

Rose turned, opened the door, and stepped out on the boardwalk in front of the restaurant. She stood there for a moment, staring at the little town, her heart heavy.

Mrs. Potter's words replayed in her head. *If you change your mind, you've always got a job here.*

Of course, she wouldn't—*couldn't*—change her mind. She couldn't stay, not once her pa was back. She couldn't go back to living the way they used to, seeing Ma hurt, hiding from Pa when he got drunk, pretending that things were okay when they weren't. She couldn't live like that again.

Rose would never forget what she'd felt when she'd heard the news that her pa had been sent to prison in Colorado for that bank robbery. Relief. A relief so great she could scarcely contain it.

From the day Glen Townsend had left Homestead, back in the fall of 'eighty, Rose had worried he would one day return. Even when her ma had learned Pa owned a saloon in

Denver, Rose hadn't stopped worrying. But when he'd been arrested for robbing that bank, then convicted and sent to prison, she had felt that wonderful, blessed relief. He wasn't coming back, she'd thought. He would never come back.

Once again, she'd been wrong.

With a shake of her head, Rose started walking toward the boardinghouse. There wasn't time for wishing that things were different. There was too much she needed to get done before she left next week. She wanted to give the whole place a thorough cleaning so her mother wouldn't have to do it on her own later. At least not right away. Heaven knew, Virginia would get no help from her husband or Mark.

Rose wrinkled her nose at the thought of her brother. If ever a son took after his sire, it was Mark Townsend. Not just in his thick build and brutish features, but in the way he bullied others. She was thankful he spent so little time at the boardinghouse. It made it easier to avoid his bad temper—and his fists.

"Rose! Rose!"

Sne stopped at the sound of the familiar cry and watched as Lark trotted her little bay down the center of the street. Her friend was grinning from ear to ear, obviously about to burst with some sort of exciting news.

Rose felt a sudden wave of nostalgia wash over her as she remembered the first time she'd seen Lark, nearly ten years ago. How had that sad, shy orphan ever grown into this energetic, self-confident beauty? It must have been some sort of miracle.

It was probably just as miraculous that the two of them had become friends. Rose wasn't even supposed to have had anything to do with the little 'breed.' That's what Rose's brother had called Lark because her real father was half Sioux Indian. But despite Mark's attempts to stop their friendship, the two girls had become closer than most sisters. There wasn't a time through all the years since Lark had come to Homestead that she hadn't played an important part in Rose's life.

She was going to miss Lark something fierce when she left. She wondered how she would manage without her.

"You'll never guess what's happened!" Lark exclaimed, pulling Rose's thoughts back to the present. "Wait until I tell you."

I have something to tell you, too, she thought, but she didn't say it aloud. She didn't want to spoil her friend's announcement, whatever it was. She could tell Lark that she was leaving later.

Lark hopped down from Dark Feather's back and grabbed hold of Rose's arms. In a stage whisper, she said, "Yancy kissed me."

"What?"

Lark nodded. "It's true. He kissed me right on the lips. Not more than an hour ago."

"He didn't!"

"He *did!*" Lark threw her arms around Rose and hugged her tightly. "He did, and it was just as wonderful as I thought it would be. He's going to ask me to marry him. I just know he will." She stepped back, her dark eyes sparkling with joy. "Isn't it wonderful? Oh, Rose, I'm so happy, I could burst."

Rose felt a twinge of envy. Everything always seemed to go right for Lark. She had the perfect family. Will and Addie Rider loved Lark as much as they loved their own two children. Eight-year-old Preston and five-year-old Naomi adored their adopted older sister. Lark had a lovely home and beautiful clothes and. . . .

Rose brought her thoughts up short. She didn't have any right to feel jealous. Lark deserved every good thing that had ever happened to her. It wasn't Lark's fault Rose had a mean-tempered jailbird for a father and a shiftless drunk for a brother.

"Then I'm happy for you, too," Rose said, meaning it and hoping Lark hadn't noticed the length of time it had taken her to reply. "But are you sure your pa's going to let you marry Mr. Jones?"

"Of course he will, just as soon as I tell him how much I love Yancy." Lark turned on the boardwalk, threaded her arm through Rose's, and they started walking toward the boardinghouse. Her well-trained bay followed along behind without having to be led. "Have you ever been kissed?" Lark asked Rose, though she already knew the answer.

"*Me?* Why would I want to let a man kiss me?"

"Well, one day you'll have to. You can't very well get married and not let your husband kiss you."

"I've told you before. I'm not ever getting married. I mean to have a say in my life. A woman loses that once she marries."

"You'd change your mind quick enough if you ever got kissed." Lark laughed, the sound husky and mysterious. "It sent tingles clear down to my toes. Made me feel all strange inside."

Rose abruptly stopped walking, pulling Lark to a halt beside her. "Lark, there's something I've got to tell you."

Her friend must have heard a note of warning in Rose's tone, for the look of excited pleasure faded quickly from her face. "What is it? What's wrong?"

"My pa's coming back."

"Oh, Rose. . . . No."

"I'm leaving Homestead. I'm taking next Wednesday's stage."

"But, Rose, you—"

"I have to. I can't stay here and watch it happen all over again. It's been bad enough with Mark, but at least he never—" She stopped. Even though Lark knew the truth about her pa and the way he'd treated her and her mother,

Rose still hated to say it aloud. It was too embarrassing. It always made her feel as if it was her fault, as if had she been different, better, it never would have happened. Perhaps, if she'd been like Lark, her parents might have loved her.

"You could come live at the Rocking R. You know my parents would let you. They care for you as much as I do. They'd be glad to have you come stay."

Rose shook her head. "I can't. I can't stay in Homestead once Pa's here."

"Maybe he'll be different. Maybe prison's changed him."

"He hasn't changed. Unless he's worse."

"You can't be sure. Look how different we are from when he left."

Nonplussed, Rose stared at her friend.

"Well, it's true," Lark persisted.

"We were children."

"Right. And now we're not."

Rose couldn't help her wry smile. "Must you always be so optimistic?"

"You're not a child anymore, Rose," Lark persisted. "He can't hurt you the way he used to."

"But he'll hurt Ma," she replied in a painful whisper, her smile gone, "and I can't stay and see it happen."

Lark was quiet for a long time before asking, "How will I bear it if you go?" As soon as the words were out of her mouth, a horrified expression crossed her face. "Oh, Rose, I'm sorry. Everything's so terrible for you right now, and all I can think about is myself. I didn't mean to be selfish. Really I didn't. Forgive me."

"It's okay." Rose's voice quavered. "I was wondering the same thing a little while ago. I really don't know how I'll manage without you."

They hugged again, Lark unsuccessfully fighting tears. Rose felt the hot burn behind her eyes and in her throat, but she didn't let tears fall. Rose never cried. She wouldn't let herself. But that didn't mean she didn't feel like it.

Rose knew she would never again have a friend as good as Lark—someone who understood her even before she spoke, sometimes before she understood herself; someone who cared about everything in her life, both the joys and the sorrows—and that realization left her feeling as if there was a hole in her chest.

She released Lark and stepped backward. "Listen, I have to get home and help Ma." She took a deep breath. "There's a lot I have to do before I leave."

"Do you . . . do you need money? I'm sure I—"

"No, Lark. I've got to do this on my own. I'm going to be taking care of myself from now on. I might as well start out that way."

Her friend smiled sadly. "You always were a

fighter, Rose. I remember the day you butted Mark with your head and knocked the air clean out of him."

"Which time?" Rose asked, trying to make them both laugh.

It didn't work.

"Ah, Rose. . . ."

She leaned forward and kissed Lark's cheek. "I'll see you in church Sunday. Maybe we can have a picnic or something. We'll spend the day together, just like we used to. Okay?"

"Okay."

"See you Sunday." She hurried toward the boardinghouse, the lump in her throat truly painful.

Michael stared down at the street, watching as the petite waitress from Zoe's Restaurant hurried along the walk. He was mildly surprised when she turned onto the path leading up to the boardinghouse. He'd had the impression he was Mrs. Townsend's only boarder.

He let the curtain fall back into place, then crossed the bedroom and lay down on the bed. Bracing the back of his head on his hands, he stared up at the ceiling and listened to the silence.

What on earth was a year in this place going to be like? He would die of boredom. In the few hours since arriving in Homestead, he'd already decided on the location of his new hotel. Tomorrow he would call on the banker and find out who owned the land, then arrange to buy it. Next week, he would order the lumber and begin construction. In a matter of weeks, the hotel would be open for business. And then what?

You're insane, all of you.

He heard his stepmother's voice as clearly as if she were in the room with him.

John Thomas, have you taken complete leave of your senses? Do you mean to make war between your sons? There must be a better way.

Kathleen had never been one to mince words.

And you, Michael. Isn't it time you quit punishing your brother for how he was born? Have you completely forgotten the friend he's been to you?

There'd been no escaping her Irish temper.

And you, Dillon. Will you never stop trying to prove to the world that you're the same as Michael? Be yourself instead.

She'd glared at them all, her hands on her hips, her green eyes snapping with fury.

You're all daft is what you are.

She was right, of course. About everything.

But there wasn't anything Michael could do about it. He had to play his father's game and play it to win. John Thomas had left him no choice.

Chapter Three

Virginia greeted Rose at the door with the news. "We've got us a boarder."

Rose's gaze flew to the stairway.

"Mr. Rafferty from San Francisco. He came in by horseback this afternoon. I put him in the green room."

The stranger from the restaurant. It had to be.

Unbidden, Lark's question echoed in her memory: *Have you ever been kissed?*

She thought of the handsome stranger with his golden hair and sky-blue eyes and wondered what it would be like. . . .

She shook her head, angered by her own thoughts. Rose didn't believe in Greek gods or medieval knights who rescued fair damsels, and she definitely didn't believe in kissing one if he did exist.

Virginia started toward the back of the house. "I've got a pork shoulder roasting. We'll need some potatoes boiled, and there's some green beans we put up last summer which will do nicely. Will you set the table?" She glanced over her shoulder. "Set it for four. I'm expecting Mark for supper."

Rose followed her mother into the kitchen, her mood darkening at the mention of her brother. "Of course we can expect him," she responded in a foul tone. She knew Mark. It wouldn't take long before he heard they had a boarder, and as soon as he did, he'd show up, wanting whatever money had been paid in advance. It was always the same.

Virginia stopped. "Try not to pick a fight with him. We rarely see him these days. Maybe if we made him feel more welcome—"

"Ma!" Rose's hands balled into fists at her sides. "Do you *hear* yourself?"

"He's my son," Virginia whispered as she turned toward the stove. "I can't turn my back on him."

Rose's fury nearly strangled her, but she couldn't fight with her mother over this. It had all been said before.

Every time Mark came looking for money to pay off his drinking debt at the saloon, Rose objected, but it was always to no avail. Virginia paid no heed to Rose's argument that it was Mark who had turned his back on them. He did nothing to help them in any way. Even though he lived within a stone's throw of the boardinghouse, in a room above the Pony

Saloon, he didn't come to see his mother or sister unless he was looking for a free meal or wanted to dip his hand into the till. And he was *always* in need of money. His own earnings from tending bar at the saloon went for his room and to pay for his constant supply of liquor.

With a sigh of frustration, Rose forced her anger to cool. It was an old debate, and she would change nothing by railing at her mother. "I'll put the potatoes on to boil, then set the table." She reached for her apron.

"Thank you, dear."

The two women worked in silence as they each moved around the spacious kitchen. The routine tasks, performed countless times before, allowed Rose's mind to wander.

At first, she could only think about her brother, which started to make her angry again. Then she thought about her father coming back to Homestead, which was even more distressing. Finally, she forced herself to think about San Francisco.

She'd heard Chad Turner, the blacksmith, talking about his visits to San Francisco to see his sister and her family. She'd always thought it sounded wonderful, so lively and full of people. There must be a world of golden opportunities waiting for a person there, even a woman alone. Maybe she would be able to open her own business in good time. She could run a boardinghouse or she could operate a restaurant. She certainly had plenty of experience doing both. All she needed now was the money to see her through until she found her own personal golden opportunity.

Rose stared at the potatoes, the water in the pan boiling gently. There'd been times, after her pa had left town, when she'd counted herself lucky to have a potato to eat. She had more than a nodding acquaintance with hardship, and it hadn't done her any lasting harm. She could survive whatever difficulties were ahead of her, as long as she didn't have to stay in Homestead with her pa.

She turned away from the stove and went to the dining room. She put a fresh tablecloth over the scarred table, then got the plates out of the cupboard, her thoughts still churning.

She wondered how long it would take her to reach San Francisco by train. Perhaps two days, maybe three? She wasn't really certain how far it actually was. Mr. Turner would know. She could ask him. Maybe she could stay with his sister for a while, just until she got on her feet.

Mr. Rafferty from San Francisco. . . .

She straightened, her gaze turning up in the general direction of the green room. Mr. Rafferty, their boarder, was from San Francisco. At least, that's what he'd told her mother. If it were true, Mr. Rafferty might be able to help her. He could tell her how long a train trip it was, what to expect when she first got there, perhaps even recommend an inexpensive place to stay when she arrived.

Feeling her spirits growing lighter, more confident, she returned to the sideboard and selected the silverware from the drawer.

"So, you do live here."

She whirled to face the doorway.

Standing there, their boarder offered a smile. "I wondered if you did when I saw you coming up the walk earlier." He stepped into the dining room. "I'm Michael Rafferty."

He was truly the most handsome man she'd ever seen. Even Lark's uncle couldn't compare with him. Everything about him was perfect, from the tips of his fancy dress boots to the top of his golden head.

Have you ever been kissed?

No, she hadn't. She'd never wanted to be kissed, and she'd told all the boys so, too.

You'd change your mind quick enough if you ever got kissed.

She did like his mouth. It looked as if a grin must always lurk in the corners, ready to spring to life. She wondered what it might be like to feel his lips pressing against hers. What was it about a man's kisses that could make a girl tingle all the way down to her toes, as Lark had claimed Yancy's did?

Rose forced her gaze away from Michael's mouth, but she found his eyes even more disconcerting, especially when she was certain he'd guessed what she'd been thinking. "I . . .

47

I'm Rose Townsend." She moved over to the table and started placing the silverware beside the plates. "You're a bit early for supper."

"Perhaps I can help you."

"Oh, no," she answered quickly, looking up to find him standing next to her. Her stomach tumbled.

He grinned. The look was warm and friendly. "You think I can't set a table?" He reached for the silverware in her hand.

A shock ran up her spine the moment their fingers met. Her skin felt all prickly, even after he'd moved away.

"I come from a family of five brothers and only one sister. My stepmother never let a one of us boys slack off in our work, just because we were born male." As he spoke, he finished placing the silver around the table.

His family . . . San Francisco. . . .

She forced her thoughts to concentrate on matters of more importance than Michael Rafferty's good looks. She'd been planning to ask him questions about where he came from, seek his advice. "My mother says you're from San Francisco. Does your family still live there?"

"Yes."

"It's always been your home?"

"The only one I remember," he answered, straightening behind one of the cane-back chairs and meeting her gaze. "And has Homestead always been your home?"

"The only one I remember," she echoed him softly.

There was something about his eyes—the unwavering way he watched her—that left her feeling strange inside. It wasn't a truly unpleasant feeling. In fact, she thought she rather liked it.

Lark's comments about kissing and tingling toes returned to taunt her. She found her gaze slipping to his mouth again. Her thoughts became all jumbled and muddled. Her questions about San Francisco seemed to vanish like a whiff of vapor.

"And what about you, Miss Townsend? Do you have family besides your mother?"

"A brother." She couldn't stop the frown from wrinkling the bridge of her nose. "He doesn't live with us. He tends bar at the Pony Saloon."

When she didn't volunteer anything more, he asked, "And your father?"

"He's not here either," she said quickly, specters of her brother and father spoiling the special feeling she'd had only moments before. "I'd better help Ma with supper. You can wait in the parlor if you'd like."

With that, she hurried from the dining room.

She was a mercurial creature, Michael thought as Rose disappeared into the kitchen. One moment she was all friendly smiles, the next she resembled a trapped doe, desperate

49

to escape. He wondered why.

He turned and walked into the parlor, his eyes making a quick assessment of the room. Simple, clean, attractive. It wasn't anything like his own home or the luxurious suites he normally stayed in when on business, but it had a pleasant appeal that surprised him.

Michael moved over to the large window in the front wall of the parlor. Brushing aside the curtain of lace, he stared out at the main street.

A couple of horsemen passed in front of the boardinghouse, their faces shaded by wide-brimmed hats, their postures relaxed, almost lazy. Across the street, the sheriff, whom he'd seen at the restaurant earlier in the day, nodded and spoke to the two men as they rode past. Michael could hear a tune being hammered out on the rinky-tink piano in the saloon a few doors down the street.

All in all, a quiet day in Homestead. He supposed most days were like this. Lord, it was going to be a long, long year.

He wondered how Dillon was getting along in the hamlet of Newton, Oregon, and took some satisfaction in knowing his brother was as miserable as he was, probably more so.

Maybe the two of them should have found some way to compromise. Dillon didn't really want the company. It wasn't in his blood as it was in Michael's. He only wanted it because Michael did.

Maybe, if he sent a wire to Dillon. . . .

He shook his head. Dillon wouldn't call things off. He wouldn't concede the competition. He had as much to prove, as much to gain, as Michael did.

No, like it or not, Michael was stuck in Homestead for the next twelve months.

He was about to step away from the window when he saw a man stride up the street and turn abruptly onto the walkway leading to the boardinghouse. He was a hard-looking fellow, close to Michael's own age, maybe a year or two younger.

A moment later, the man in question appeared in the parlor doorway. He stopped and glared at Michael, his expression surly, his eyes blurry, and his nose red. "You must be Ma's boarder."

Rose's brother?

Michael could smell whiskey from across the room. If this was Rose's brother, it was obvious he did more than simply tend bar at the saloon. He did his share of consuming the liquor as well.

"Name's Rafferty." Michael continued his silent assessment, wondering if pretty little Rose could really be related to someone as repugnant as this.

"Townsend. Mark Townsend." His eyes narrowed. "You plan on stayin' in town long?"

"Until my business is finished."

"What sorta business you in?"

"I'm in the hotel business."

"Hotel?" Mark snorted. "And you got business *here?*"

Michael merely shrugged.

"Well, I sure hope you paid up in advance." Mark seemed to be doing an assessment of his own, carefully judging just how much money he might squeeze out of this boarder before he left. "Ma's not very good about demanding the money up front, and she's had some who's left without payin' their bill."

Michael smiled without warmth. "I assure you, sir, I always pay my debts."

At that moment, Virginia came out of the kitchen, saw her son, and hurried toward him. "Mark, I'm so glad you could join us for supper."

He brushed her aside before she could embrace him. "Is it ready? I'm hungry." Mark headed for the dining room.

Virginia's shoulders slumped and a look of resignation settled over her face. Without looking at Michael, she said, "Please be seated at the table, Mr. Rafferty. Supper will be served in a moment."

Michael thought of his stepmother—the way Kathleen was loved by all of the Rafferty children, whether hers by birth or by marriage—and felt a wave of pity for this woman. Wordlessly, he entered the dining room.

Chapter Four

"Lark, what *is* the matter with you?" Addie Rider looked at her adopted daughter with a raised eyebrow. "That's the fourth time you've checked outside to see if your father's arrived. You know he might not even get home today, and if he does, he'll likely be late."

The girl reentered the parlor, but didn't take her seat in the chair by the fireplace. Instead, she walked over to the window and stared out at the waning daylight.

Addie laid aside her needlework. "Lark, tell me what's troubling you," she encouraged gently.

Without turning around, Lark asked, "How did you know you were in love with Papa?"

In love? Addie felt a shiver of alarm. Lark couldn't be in love. She was just a child.

But as Addie stared at Lark, she admitted to herself that it wasn't true. Lark was seventeen, a young woman standing on the brink of a whole new stage of her life. She hadn't even been a child when she went away to finishing school two years ago. She definitely hadn't been a child when she returned.

Addie was suddenly awash with a flood of memories. She remembered the first time she'd seen Lark, a frightened orphan with large, sad eyes, thrust so tragically into an unknown— and ofttimes cruel—world. She remembered the first time she'd held Lark's hand and the two had begun to build a trust—the lonely child and the lonely schoolmarm—both of them in need of a friend, both of them wanting to be loved. And she remembered the way Lark had looked, months later, in her pretty dress, beaming with happiness while Will and Addie spoke their marriage vows.

Addie had thought of herself as Lark's mother from the moment the minister had pronounced her Will's wife. She hadn't needed to wait for the legal adoption to love and cherish this precious child. One of the proudest moments of her life had been when Lark quit calling her Aunt Addie and started calling her Mother.

So many memories of Lark. . . .

"How *did* you know?" her daughter repeated, louder this time.

Addie blinked, forcing her thoughts to return to the present. "That isn't an easy question to answer," she replied belatedly, avoiding Lark's eyes as she picked up her sewing again.

"Was it when he kissed you?"

Kissed? Unsettled, Addie dropped her sewing a second time, her gaze darting back to her daughter.

Lark nodded. Her smile was like a ray of sunshine, brightening the room with the sheer exuberance of her secret. "It's true. I'm in love." She hurried across the parlor and knelt on the floor beside Addie. She reached forward and took hold of her mother's cool hands, folding them within her own. "I'm in love, and it's the most wonderful feeling. I can't wait to tell Papa."

Addie wasn't certain that was such a good idea. "Just who is this young man who has captured your devotion?"

Lark's dark eyes turned soft and dreamy as she stared off into space. "Yancy Jones," she whispered with the same reverence someone else might use for a prayer.

"Yancy Jones?" Addie freed one hand and placed it beneath Lark's chin, forcing the girl's gaze back to her own. She tried to keep the accusation out of her voice when she asked, "What has that man done to encourage your affections?"

"Absolutely nothing." She sounded thoroughly disgusted and more than just a little disappointed. "Why, you'd think he didn't know I exist, the way he's tried to ignore me. But I wasn't having any of that. Not once I knew I was in love with him." She grinned. "So today I told him so."

"Oh, Lark. . . ." Addie closed her eyes briefly, then shook her head. "What happened?"

The smile faded away as Lark sighed dramatically. "He kissed me." Her eyes turned dreamy again. "It was the most wonderful thing that's ever happened to me. I never imagined it could be so splendid. No wonder you and Papa kiss so often."

"We're married."

"You kissed before you were married," Lark responded teasingly. "I remember. I saw you."

It was true. In fact, Will and Addie had done a good deal more than just kiss before they were married.

Addie felt an uncomfortable warmth flooding her cheeks as she remembered the passion shared inside the old cabin beside Pony Creek all those years ago.

Abruptly, she turned her thoughts back to her daughter. Lark was certainly too young to know of such things. It was Addie's duty to protect her until she was ready for marriage.

She stiffened her back and used her most prim, schoolteacher's tone of voice. "You are only seventeen, Lark Rider. Mr. Jones is thirty if he's a day—"

"He's twenty-nine," Lark interrupted.

"Twenty-nine then. It makes no difference. He's still far too old to be kissing an innocent, unsuspecting young girl. I shudder to think what your father will do when he finds out about this. There's a good chance Mr. Jones

56

will be looking for another job."

Lark jumped to her feet. "That's not fair! I love him! I mean to marry him! Besides, it was *my* fault he kissed me."

"I don't doubt it for a moment." Addie sighed, then continued, "But he should know better. He shouldn't have taken advantage of your infatuation."

Her daughter's eyes filled with tears. "It's *not* an infatuation. I love him. Don't you understand? I've been in love with him for months. If you send him away, I'll die. So help me, I'll die." Those words said, she ran from the parlor and up the stairs.

Addie heard the door to Lark's bedroom slam, and then the house was silent.

Lord, help her. Whatever was she to do?

Rose carried the last of the supper dishes into the kitchen. She gave wide berth to Mark, who was leaning against the cabinet beside the sink. Virginia already had her arms deep in soapy dishwater.

"Beat it, Rose. I need t' talk to Ma."

She tossed him a belligerent look. "Why don't you help with the dishes then?"

He straightened slightly. "I said beat it."

"I won't. I know what you're after. You're going to ask Ma to give you the money Mr. Rafferty paid. Well, you can't have it. Ma needs it."

"This ain't any of your concern, runt."

She hated it when he called her that. She doubled her hands into fists. "Leave Ma be, why don't you?"

"Rose. . . ." Virginia twisted to glance behind her, her hands still in the sink. "Go on and talk to Mr. Rafferty. I don't need your help with the dishes. Mark'll keep me company."

"Keep you company? Ma, he's just looking for money. You can't spare any. You'll need everything you've got—" She stopped before she could say *once I'm gone*. She didn't want Mark to know she was leaving. Besides, it wasn't going to change her mother's mind, and she knew it.

"What're you worried about, runt?" Mark jeered. "You've got your job at the restaurant. You won't go hungry if Ma lends me a few bucks."

"Lend?" She made an unladylike sound in her throat. "I'd like to see the day you repay anything you've taken from us."

Mark drew back his hand, but Virginia stepped between them before he could swing at Rose. Her hands dripping water onto the floor, she turned pleading eyes on her daughter. "Please, Rose. Go on and let us talk."

Unexpectedly, she felt close to tears, her eyes and throat burning. But she didn't let them fill her eyes or trace her cheeks. Rose Townsend never cried, especially not when Mark might see. Not that he would care what she was feeling. No, it was because he might find some way to use it against her. She didn't ever want Mark to see any of her weak points. Not ever.

She left the kitchen through the hall doorway, stopping as soon as she was in the dim passage, giving herself a moment to regain her composure. It was silly to feel this way. It didn't change anything.

Why? she wondered. Why couldn't Ma stand up to Mark just once in her life? Why couldn't she take Rose's side in an argument?

Just once. That's all Rose wanted. Just once to see Ma take her side.

She was disgusted with herself for even wondering why. She'd been silently asking the same questions for years and never yet found an answer. It was always a waste of time.

Drawing in a deep breath, she walked toward the parlor.

Michael was there, sitting in a chair near the window, an open book in his lap. But he wasn't reading. He was staring out the window, obviously deep in thought, his eyes unfocused.

She hesitated, undecided whether to enter the parlor or go upstairs to her own room.

He glanced up then, as if he'd sensed her presence. He stared at her as if she was some sort of puzzle he was trying to solve.

"Am I disturbing you?" she asked.

"No." He closed the book. "I don't feel much like reading."

The last rays of sunshine cut sharply through

the window, spilling over his head and shoulders. The effect was rather like a halo, and for the third time that day, she thought of the Greek gods in Mrs. Rider's old schoolbooks. She wondered if anyone had ever told Michael he resembled a Greek god before. She wondered if he would think her crazy for thinking it.

"Was there something you wanted to say to me?" Michael asked.

The sun settled behind the mountains. The halo effect faded, and she was left feeling embarrassed by her fanciful thoughts.

"Miss Townsend?" He frowned and leaned forward, encouraging her to speak.

Lifting her chin, determined not to give the man's appearance another thought, Rose entered the parlor. "Yes, as a matter of fact, there was something I wanted to say. To ask, really." She sat in the companion chair to the one he occupied. "I would like you to tell me about San Francisco."

He settled back in his chair, his expression relaxing. "Ah, San Francisco. . . . Great city. Good weather. Fine society. Terrific theaters with entertainers coming from all over the world. And one of the finest hotels to be found anywhere. What else would you like to know?"

"Well, you see, I'm going there next week."

"Really. What takes you there? Family?"

Rose thought of her father. "I guess you could say so."

"And where do they live?"

She shook her head. There was no point in pretending. "No, I haven't any family living , there. I'm going there alone. I want to find work and—"

"Alone? Miss Townsend, San Francisco is no place for a young woman alone."

"If you could just suggest a place I might stay. Some place reasonably priced. I haven't much money, you see. But as soon as I get a job. . . ."

He reached forward and touched the back of her hand where it rested on the arm of the chair. Her sentence died in her throat. She looked at his fingers—long, tanned, well-manicured fingers—lying against her small hand, her skin red and rough in comparison. It made her stomach feel peculiar, looking at their hands touching like that.

"Miss Townsend, I hate to disappoint you, but I could never encourage a beautiful young woman such as yourself to go there unescorted."

He thought her beautiful?

"While there are parts of my city that are quite wonderful, we have many undesirable elements living there, too. They would take one look at you and know you were an innocent from the country and unable to take care of yourself. Why, you wouldn't be safe for even one day before—"

"What?" She scrambled to catch up with

what he'd been saying. "Unable to take care of myself?" She pulled her hand into her lap. "You're wrong about that, Mr. Rafferty. I've been taking care of myself for years."

He stared at her for a few moments, then said, "Not in San Francisco." There seemed to be a hint of mockery in his voice.

She felt her temper start to boil. "You're certainly not under any obligation to give me the information I want," Rose said, hating the huffy tone of her voice, but unable to control it. She got to her feet. "However, I assure you, I *am* going. I'm leaving on Wednesday's stage."

Michael placed his book on the table beside him, but didn't rise from his chair. "Then I wish you well, Miss Townsend."

After more than two weeks on a cattle-buying trip to Oregon, Will Rider was dead tired when he opened the front door and entered the house. All he wanted was a good meal, a hot bath, and bed.

That wasn't exactly what he got.

"Will, I'm so glad you're home," his wife called from the parlor before the door was even closed behind him. "I need a moment with you."

In the lamplight, Addie's red hair reminded him of hot coals in a fire that had burned low. Tall and as slender as ever, even after bearing their two children, she had grown more attractive with the passing of time. The years suited her well.

It was good to be home.

"I need *more* than a moment with you," he replied, pulling her into his embrace and giving her a robust kiss. He suddenly didn't feel quite as tired as he had a short time before.

"Will. . . ." Addie pushed against his shoulders, pulling her mouth free. "It's important. It's about Lark."

He stepped back, his hands still closed around her upper arms. "What about Lark? Is she hurt?" His gaze flew to the stairs.

"No. No, she's not hurt. She's upstairs in her room. Asleep, I hope." She took hold of his hand and led him into the parlor. "I think we'd better sit down."

He didn't like the sound of this.

Addie took a deep breath, stiffened her back, and straightened her shoulders. It was a familiar gesture. She always did it before tackling something difficult. "Lark thinks she's in love."

"*What?*" He hadn't meant to shout. That's just how the word came out. "With who?"

Addie chewed on her lower lip a moment, as if considering whether or not to tell him.

"Is it one of the Barber boys?"

"No."

"It's not Paul Stanford, is it? That boy hasn't got enough grit to—"

"It's not Paul Stanford."

63

Will tried to recall all the boys who'd gone to school with Lark, but there wasn't a one of them he could imagine Lark feeling a strong affection for, let alone thinking herself in love with.

"It's Yancy Jones."

"*What?*" He was shouting again.

It was crazy. It was outrageous. It was ridiculous. Of course it was ridiculous. Addie was joking with him. That had to be it. A joke.

He started to chuckle. "You really had me goin' for a second, Addie. Lark in love with Yancy."

Addie wasn't smiling. "It's true, Will. She swears she's in love with him and will die without him. She thinks she wants to marry him." She paused, then added, "She told me he kissed her."

This time he didn't shout. This time he was speechless with rage.

Yancy Jones kissing his daughter. He was going to break him in half.

"Will. . . ." Addie laid her fingers on his arm. "Don't do anything foolish. She *is* seventeen. What she's feeling is real, even if it isn't really love. If we give her some time, she'll grow out of it. As for Yancy—"

He got to his feet. "I'm going out to the bunkhouse."

"Will—"

"Let me handle this, Addie," he said as he strode toward the door and went outside.

Will was thankful for the crisp evening air. He felt hot enough to explode as it was.

Intent upon his destination, he didn't see the man leaning up against the side of the bunkhouse smoking a cigarette until he pushed off from the building and stepped into the moonlight.

"I reckon you're lookin' for me." Yancy tossed the smoke into the dust and ground it with the heel of his boot.

Will had always like this cowpoke, from the first day he had ridden up to the Rocking R looking for work. But he didn't like him now.

Almost of its own accord, Will's fist shot out, connecting with Yancy's jaw and knocking him to the ground. Will stood ready, rubbing his aching knuckles, waiting for Yancy to get to his feet so he could take a second punch.

Yancy didn't get up. He simply stroked his jaw with one hand while he leaned on the opposite elbow. "I reckon I had that comin'."

"You sure as hell did."

"I guess if Lark was my daughter, I'd've done the same. Truth is I'd've kicked you so far it would take a hound dog six weeks just to find your smell."

Will wished he'd get up. He wanted to hit him again. He *needed* to hit him again.

"I don't suppose you'll believe me if I said I didn't do anything to encourage her feelin's for me."

"I don't care what you say or do, as long as

you do it some place other than the Rocking
R. You're fired. Get your gear and get out
of here."

Yancy got up from the ground, dusted himself off, then gave Will a long look. "I reckon I
should tell you how I feel about Lark."

"Don't bother."

"Truth is I love her."

Will hit him again.

This time, Yancy took the punch without
falling. He stiffened, but made no move to
retaliate. "I reckon I had that one coming,
too," he said grimly. He touched the corner
of his mouth and glanced at his fingertips to
see if he was bleeding. "I told Lark you'd be
madder than a peeled rattler when you found
out. I know you don't think I'm any prize. Hell,
I've been tellin' myself that for far too long. Ever
since I first seen her, I suppose."

Will wished Yancy would shut up. He didn't
think he'd heard the cowboy talk this much in
all the months he'd been at the Rocking R, and
right now Will didn't care to hear what Yancy
Jones had to say.

Yancy ran his fingers through his shaggy
hair. "Lark's a thoroughbred, and that's a fact.
I don't know what she sees in the likes o' me.
My family tree ain't no better than a shrub."
He leaned down and picked up his hat from
where it had fallen in the dirt. "But I'd sure
like to prove I can be somethin' better."

Will clenched and unclenched his fists.

"You're not proving it with *my* daughter," he warned. "Now get out." He spun on his heel and started back toward the house.

"Mr. Rider!"

He stopped and turned.

"I figure, if a gal like Lark can see somethin' worth lovin' in me, then maybe I oughta try to live up to it. I know you think I'm just a saddle bum. I reckon you'd feel that way about any man who was makin' eyes at her, no matter who he was. But I aim to prove her right. And if she'll have me, when the time's right, I mean to ask her to be my wife."

If Will had had his gun with him, he'd have shot Yancy Jones right then and there. "Get out," he snarled, "and don't come back."

Turning again, he saw a movement at the window in Lark's room. With a sinking feeling, he knew the fight wasn't over yet.

Chapter Five

Rose waited anxiously for Lark to arrive at church for services. She had so much to share with her friend. She'd had a long talk with Chad Turner the day before about San Francisco, and she was excited about the word pictures he'd painted for her. Of course, she hadn't told Mr. Turner that she was planning to go there alone. She'd learned her lesson with Michael Rafferty. The blacksmith would more than likely have reacted the same way if she'd told him the reason for her questions. It seemed to be most men's opinion that women couldn't take care of themselves.

A lot they knew.

Seated in the church pew beside her mother, she glanced over her shoulder, but the row the Rider family usually occupied was still empty. Rose began to wonder if something was wrong. The Riders almost never missed services.

Before she turned toward the front again,

she noticed Michael Rafferty sitting at the back of the church. He looked even more handsome today, dressed in his black Sunday-go-to-meeting clothes. Most men in Homestead looked uncomfortable in a tie and fancy suit. Not Michael Rafferty. He looked as confident as ever.

He glanced her way. Their gazes met. His nod was infinitesimal and for her alone. A private greeting. Somehow disturbing.

She straightened, turning her eyes toward the pulpit, that odd feeling starting up in her stomach again.

She hadn't seen Michael at all yesterday. Her mother had told her the only meal he'd eaten at the boardinghouse was at noon when Rose was working at the restaurant. She wondered what had occupied his time so thoroughly and why he'd returned to the boardinghouse so late in the day.

Not that it mattered to her whether she saw him or not. She was simply curious.

Reverend Jacobs stepped behind the pulpit. "Let us all stand and sing." He nodded at his wife, Priscilla, who was seated at the pump organ. "A mighty fortress is our God. . . ." The minister's singing was strong and hale—and not quite on key.

Rose missed Reverend Pendroy's beautiful tenor voice. The whole congregation had sounded better back when he was pastoring the church. But Reverend Pendroy had died

two years ago, and Reverend Jacobs had
been sent to fill the opening. She supposed,
to be fair, that Simon Jacobs was a good
preacher and a fine shepherd of his flock.
Still, she often thought he just didn't look
or sound right when he was standing behind
the pulpit. She supposed no one besides Reverend Pendroy would ever seem quite right
to her.

From the corner of her eye, Rose caught sight
of the Riders slipping into the empty pew. She
turned to look at them.

Will Rider led the way, followed by his son,
Preston, then his daughters, Lark and Naomi,
and finally by his wife. As soon as Rose looked
at Lark, she knew something was terribly
wrong. She didn't think she'd ever seen Lark
look so sorrowful, not even when she'd first
come to Homestead.

Lark kept her eyes cast downward. Her hands
were folded in front of her, and her shoulders
drooped dejectedly. Her face looked puffy. Rose
guessed she'd been crying, though her cheeks
were dry at the moment.

Rose's gaze flicked to Will Rider. He was
standing rigidly, his chin up, his eyes straight
forward. He didn't even pretend to sing. Anger
emanated from him.

A glance at Addie Rider told Rose she was
nearly as sad and miserable as Lark. She,
too, was staring toward the pulpit. She was
mouthing the words to the hymn, but Rose

couldn't hear her lovely singing voice as she usually could.

She told them about Yancy.

Rose hurt for her friend. She could only imagine what must have happened when Will and Addie found out about Lark falling in love with one of the hired hands. From the look of things, it had gone even worse than she'd expected.

When the hymn ended, the congregation sat down. Rose turned her eyes toward the front of the church, but she only pretended to listen to the sermon. She wanted the service over so she could talk to Lark.

Michael made it a practice to attend church services, no matter what city or town he was in. His father had taught him that it was a sound business practice, and he knew it to be true. People were more apt to trust a man if he was seen in church on Sundays. Not that Michael wasn't a believer. He was. But he was also a man with plenty of common sense and an understanding of human nature. He had to be. Especially now when so much was at stake.

"You're too serious about things," his step-mother was forever telling him. "Palace Hotels is only a business. You should have more than that. You should find yourself a wife and settle down. Give yourself a chance to find happiness. You've a right to your own life, Michael. Your father is not a saint. No one knows that better than you or I."

Michael felt an old knot of pain in his gut, the same one he always felt when he thought of his father.

John Thomas Rafferty a saint? No, that he wasn't. Far from it.

He remembered Dillon the first time he'd seen him. It had been almost like looking into a mirror, except Dillon's hair was dark while Michael's was fair. He should have known the truth then, but he'd been only ten years old. He'd been too excited at the thought of having a new friend living in the same house with him.

John Thomas had married Kathleen only a few months before, and Michael had been feeling lonely and excluded. For as long as Michael could remember, it had been just him and his father. Then suddenly, there'd been Kathleen, a new center of his father's universe, and Michael had felt left out, no matter how hard his stepmother had tried to make him feel loved and welcome.

But then Dillon had come to the Rafferty home. The two boys had quickly become inseparable, constantly getting into mischief, pulling pranks on the household servants, driving the hotel staffs to distraction when the family traveled. The boys were like shadows of each other, their thoughts somehow intertwined.

It wasn't until just after their sixteenth birthdays, celebrated only three days apart, that John Thomas had told them both the truth.

Michael had never been able to forgive Dillon for who he was, no matter how hard he'd tried. From the moment he'd learned Dillon was more than just an orphan who'd come to live with them, from the moment he'd learned Dillon was his father's illegitimate son and Michael's own half brother, Michael's life had changed.

He closed his eyes and hardened his heart against the memories. He wouldn't allow himself to get caught up in sentimentality or wishing for what could never be. Things were as they were.

He opened his eyes again and looked at those around him. Simple people with simple lives. They would never understand a man like him.

His gaze paused on the two Townsend women—Virginia with her worn, downtrodden expression, Rose with her strange mixture of stubborn determination and haunted sadness.

A grudging smile crept into the corners of his mouth as he stared at Rose's pretty profile, remembering the way her anger had flared the other night when he'd told her she shouldn't go to San Francisco alone. She might be tiny, but it was clear she had plenty of fire and fight in her. She might do all right in San Francisco at that.

* * *

Rose caught up with Lark at the bottom of the church steps. "Lark, wait."

Lark lifted her downcast eyes, then looked at her father. "May I speak with Rose privately?"

"For a moment. We have a long trip ahead of us."

Lark nodded solemnly, then took hold of Rose's elbow and steered her toward the grove of trees that bordered the church property. When they were schoolgirls, this was where they'd come during lunch breaks and recesses to share their secrets and plan their futures.

"Lark, what did your pa mean about a long trip?" Rose asked the moment they stopped.

"He's taking the family to Boise City."

Rose felt a rush of relief, forgetting for a moment that she was planning to go farther away than Boise in just a few days.

Lark turned to face her friend. "Papa thinks I'll forget Yancy if I don't see him for a while." Tears flooded her dark eyes. "He thinks I don't know what love is. He thinks I'm too young." She pulled a handkerchief from her reticule, pressed it to her nose, and sniffed daintily. "He's wrong. I won't ever stop loving Yancy."

"Oh, Lark. . . ." She didn't know what to say. She knew nothing about falling in love. She'd never wanted to know.

"He fired Yancy and ordered him off the Rocking R. All because of me. It's so unfair. Yancy didn't do anything wrong. Just because

74

Yancy's a cowboy and a few years older than me, Papa thinks he's not right for me. He thinks he can treat me like a child."

Rose placed her hand on Lark's arm. "I'm sure it'll all work out." She hated platitudes, but they were the only words she could think to say. "You'll see. It'll be okay."

"Rose, will you do me a favor?"

"Of course."

Lark pulled a piece of paper from the pocket of her gown. "Will you find Yancy and give this to him before you leave town?"

"How will I find him?" Rose asked as she took the folded message.

"I don't know." Teardrops slipped down her cheeks, leaving moist trails on her flawless skin. "I heard Frosty say he was going to look for work at the sawmill. Maybe he was hired on." She dried her cheeks with her handkerchief. "He can't go away without reading my note. What if I were never to see him again?" Her voice broke, and suddenly she was sobbing.

Rose held her, patting her back and murmuring soothing sounds, not knowing what else to do.

"Lark?" Preston appeared through the trees. "Papa says it's time to leave."

"I'm coming," she said without looking toward her brother. She stepped back from Rose. "You'll find him? You won't leave without seeing he gets it?"

"I promise."

"Thank you. Oh, Rose, I'm going to miss you so very much. What'll I—" Without finishing her question, she spun around and hurried after Preston.

Rose didn't move. She stood there, staring at the spot where Lark had disappeared. She felt an overwhelming loneliness as she considered the weeks and months ahead of her. Lark had helped her through so many rough times. And now they wouldn't even get to say good-bye properly. She would be gone before Lark returned from the territorial capital. They might never see each other again.

She felt suspiciously close to tears herself as she walked out of the grove of aspens and headed toward the boardinghouse.

Yancy stared inside the house that was nestled against the mountains at the east end of the valley, not far from where Pony Creek emptied into the river. The old Hadley place had been vacant for three years, Vince Stanford had told him, but it looked as if it had been vacant for more than a decade.

Two of the three glass windows were broken. Leaves and dust lay thick on the floor inside, and the house smelled strongly of forest creatures. The place had obviously provided shelter for a variety of small animals such as raccoons, squirrels, and mice.

It was going to take some elbow grease and plenty of sweat to make the place livable, but

Yancy hadn't ever been afraid of hard work. And he especially wasn't afraid of it now, when he had something to work for. He figured he had a lot to prove, first to himself and then to Will Rider. He'd meant what he'd said the other night. If Lark thought there was something worth seeing in him, then he meant to find out if she was right.

He shook his head slowly. If people had asked Yancy six months ago if he thought he'd be contemplating marriage to a girl like Lark he'd have told them they were plumb loco, clean off their mental reservation. But here he was, planning for just such an event. If it weren't for Lark, he never would have paid that visit to the banker yesterday, and he wouldn't be standing in front of this broken-down place now.

Yancy had been as uncomfortable going into the bank as a camel in Alaska. He'd thought for sure Vince Stanford would tell him he wouldn't even consider lending Yancy money to buy his own spread. Instead, Vince had suggested the Hadley place as a possibility. The price was reasonable, and if Yancy could come up with one hundred dollars within sixty days, the bank would give him a mortgage on the rest.

One hundred dollars. . . . It was a lot of money. He might be able to come up with half of it if he sold his horse and saddle, but that didn't seem like a good solution to Yancy. Without them, he couldn't do much ranching, and he sure as blue blazes wasn't a farmer. The only thing he really knew was horses and cattle. As soon as this place was his, he meant to make a first-rate cattle ranch out of it.

In the meantime, he'd been lucky. Sigmund Leonhardt at Homestead Lumber had been willing to take him on at the mill. That would earn him eight dollars a week. In addition, he'd heard Zoe Potter was looking for someone to make some repairs at the restaurant and around her house, so he'd gone to see her. She had measured him up with one long glance, then had said as how a widow woman with three daughters could always use a man's help in fixing things up, long as he was a hard worker. He'd promised her he was, and she'd offered to pay him fifteen dollars when the work was done. Another job or two like that one, and he'd have his hundred dollars.

Well, this place wasn't going to clean itself up, he decided, bringing his thoughts back to the present. Yancy tossed his hat aside and rolled up his shirtsleeves as he entered the house.

It sure as heck wasn't much of a house. Just three rooms and a loft, but he reckoned a good scrubbing and a bit of whitewash would make a heap of difference. Still, he wondered if it would be good enough for Lark.

As he started picking up pieces of furniture and hauling them outside, he pictured Lark in his mind in her fine clothes, her black hair hidden beneath a pert bonnet, her eyes sparkling with laughter.

Shoot, he'd gone plumb weak north of his ears, thinking this house—or himself, for that matter—would ever be good enough for Lark. Will Rider had been right to throw him off the Rocking R. If Yancy had any sense left, he'd leave this valley, forget he'd ever kissed that pretty little gal and held her close against him and smelled her warm-scented cologne.

But even as he thought how foolish it all was, he kept working. The plain truth was he was in love with Lark Rider, crazy or not, and he'd do whatever he had to do to make her his wife.

Chapter Six

Her money was gone!

Rose stared into her keepsake box with horror and disbelief. Her money had been there last night. She knew it because she'd added the week's wages Mrs. Potter had paid her yesterday when she'd finished her shift. Now all forty-eight dollars were gone.

Mark!

She felt the anger boiling up inside. It took her nearly four months, working six days a week at the restaurant, to earn forty-eight dollars. It had taken her even longer to actually save that much. How dare her brother come into her room, go through her things, and take her money? How dare he do this to her when she needed so desperately to leave Homestead?

She stared at the contents of the box where she'd dumped them on the bed. A hair ribbon her mother had given her when she was ten. A marble she'd won in a game with Loring Barber when they were both eleven. A poem Lark had written and given to her. Bits and pieces of her past. Nothing of real value except to her. Only the money was gone. And with it had gone all hope of escaping Homestead.

Damn him!

Whirling away from the box on her bed, Rose hurried from the room and down the stairs. She headed for the front door, determined to find Mark, even if she had to go into that saloon to do it. But she only had to go as far as the parlor. Mark was seated there, as if waiting for her.

He grinned when she stepped into the room, then reached for a bottle of whiskey and poured some into a leaded glass. "Looking for me, runt?"

She stared at him, rage leaving her momentarily speechless.

"Where's Ma? She gone to the McLeods' for Sunday dinner again?"

Rose still didn't answer.

"Well, then, you'd best fix your brother somethin' to eat."

Cook for him? She'd rather die first. "Give it back."

"Give what back?"

"You know what." Her head pounded, and her breathing came hard and fast.

Mark drained the whiskey. "Ahhh." He set the glass on the table beside him and refilled it. His grin broadened. "Now that's smooth, I tell you.

81

It's some of O'Neal's best stock. Expensive, too. A real pleasure goin' down. I don't usually get to buy whiskey this good. Would you like a sip, Rose? Might make a woman of ya."

"I want my money back, Mark. The money you stole."

He picked up the glass, held it with the fingertips of both hands, and stared at the amber contents, his elbows braced on the arms of the chair. "Stole is a mighty harsh word. I like borrowed myself."

In a flash, Rose was across the room. Her arm darted out and she knocked the glass from his hands before he could react. It broke upon impact with the wall. The whiskey ran down the wallpaper and puddled on the floor.

"How dare you?" she yelled at him. "How dare you take what's mine?" With another swing of her arm, she knocked the whiskey bottle from the table. It rolled across the room, leaving a stain on the rug.

Mark rose to his feet, his face darkening, his eyes narrowed.

Rose paid no heed. She was too angry to care what his reaction might be. "I want my money back," she shouted.

"Well, you sure as hell ain't gonna get it. Besides, you just poured some of it out on the floor. A real waste, Rose. You shouldn't waste good whiskey."

She slapped him.

"Why, you little bitch!"

She reeled beneath his blow, colliding with the divan, bruising her shins on the carved birch legs. She stumbled, trying to catch her balance, then hit the floor. Her ears rang, and black dots appeared before her eyes distorting her vision. Still, she scrambled back to her feet and headed toward him, too angry to exercise caution.

"I want it back." She lunged at him.

He caught her arm, but she managed to scratch one side of his face before his backhand sent her crashing to the floor a second time. She tried to get up, but another slap knocked her head back against the floor. Then he kicked her in the abdomen.

The room lurched and darkened. She thought he spoke, but she couldn't be sure. She swallowed, trying to ignore the pain that spread through her body screaming at every nerve ending for her to lie still. But she couldn't. She had to make him give her back her money. She had to leave Homestead. She had to get away.

Mark's fingers snaked through her hair and yanked her head up from the floor even as his boot pressed harshly against her belly. "You need yourself a good lesson, runt. I shoulda made sure you learned how to behave a long time ago." He jerked on her hair as he removed his foot from her body. "Get up."

She couldn't have stayed on the floor, even if she'd tried. He was lifting her up by the roots of her hair. She cried out in protest, though she knew it would make no difference.

"Don't you ever do that again, Rose." Mark hit her without letting go of her hair. "Not ever."

He lifted his arm to strike again. Rose closed her eyes, trying to prepare herself mentally for the explosion of pain she knew would come. But the expected blow never happened.

"I suggest you let go of your sister."

She opened her eyes, her gaze slowly focusing on Michael. His fingers were closed around Mark's wrist. His face was an expressionless mask.

"This ain't your concern, mister," Mark retorted.

"I'm making it my concern. Let her go."

Mark gave her a shove. She caught herself against the wall, glad it was there to help steady her shaking legs.

She watched as her brother turned and tried to hit Michael, but Michael ducked, then brought his left fist upward, catching Mark under his chin. His right fist followed with a violent punch to her brother's middle. Mark staggered backward, the air whooshing out of his lungs. Michael didn't give him even a second to recover. He followed with four lightning-quick jabs. The fourth one left her brother sprawled unconscious on the floor.

Instantly, Michael turned toward Rose. A couple of quick strides brought him to her. His hands—hands that had dealt so harshly with

Mark moments before—closed gently around her arms.

"Are you all right?" he asked, his voice low and concerned.

"Yes . . . yes, I'm okay."

"I think you'd better sit down. You're shaking like a leaf." He glanced across the room. "Let's get you out of here before he comes to."

She nodded, her gaze following his to her brother's inert form lying in the middle of the floor.

Fear streaked through her, mingling with her pain. She began to shake even harder. It had been a long time since Mark had hit her. She'd been staying out of her brother's way for years, just as she'd always tried to stay out of her pa's way. She'd forgotten just how much pain a man could deliver with one swing of his arm.

She felt a wave of dizziness and leaned against the wall, feeling herself begin to crumple. Before she knew what was happening, she was cradled against Michael's chest, one of his arms behind her back, the other beneath her knees.

She gasped. She clutched her hands together behind his neck in an instinctive move to prevent herself from falling. Her heart hammered, and she felt her throat closing, choking her.

She couldn't recall ever being held like this in her life. She'd never wanted a man to hold her like this. It was terrifying, but she hadn't the strength left to resist.

85

"Don't worry, Rose," Michael said softly. "You're safe with me."

She looked up into his eyes and saw only tender concern. She knew she shouldn't trust him, but for some reason, she did.

Rose closed her eyes and pressed her forehead against Michael's shoulder, hiding from the rest of the world. For a moment, she allowed herself to believe she was truly safe. That she wasn't trapped in a web from which she couldn't escape. She pretended for this moment that her brother hadn't hit her and her father wasn't coming back to Homestead. For this moment, no one could harm her.

With swift, smooth strides, Michael carried her out of the parlor and up to her room.

Mark was gone by the time Michael came back downstairs after leaving Rose in her room. He was sorry. He'd have taken great pleasure in tossing him out into the street. Michael couldn't remember the last time he'd felt such a cold rage as the one that had swept through him at the sight of Mark striking his sister.

Brawling really wasn't Michael's style. Nor was it usual for him to involve himself in another family's squabbles. He had enough problems with his own family. Michael liked to keep a cool and controlled eye on any situation. He liked to think things through before he took action. He tried never to act in haste. Controlled retaliation was more his style.

That had been impossible today.

As he reached for the whiskey bottle on the floor, he discovered his hand had balled into a fist again at the memory of Mark striking Rose. Again, Michael wished Mark were still there so he could hit him a few more times, just to work the rage out of his system.

He picked up the bottle and set it on a table, then crouched to gather the larger pieces of the broken glass.

He gave his head a self-deprecating shake. He couldn't be sure he'd continue to be welcome in the boardinghouse after today. Beating up his landlady's son wasn't likely to endear him in her eyes. Worse yet was the trouble it could cause him if word of this got back to John Thomas. Michael couldn't afford that kind of mistake.

But it was done now. He couldn't change it. Besides, he wasn't sorry for what he'd done. Mark could have broken Rose's neck the way he'd held and hit her.

Michael felt the anger returning and made a conscious effort to control it. What was done was done, but that didn't mean he had to become more involved. He would give Miss Rose Townsend wide berth from now on. If she was as determined to leave Homestead as she'd said she was, then he wouldn't have to worry about her for much longer. A few more days and she would be on the stage bound for Boise. He wished her well.

"Mr. Rafferty, what happened?"

Michael straightened, the broken glass in his hand, and turned to meet Virginia's startled gaze. "Just a little accident. A glass broke."

Her glance flicked to the whiskey bottle nearby. "I don't tolerate liquor in this house, Mr. Rafferty."

"It isn't mine."

She stared at him a moment, then looked back at the bottle. "Mark." She breathed out her son's name on a note of sorrow, her shoulders slumping more than usual.

"Yes."

Virginia was nearly as small as her daughter, but without any of the stubborn strength he'd recognized in Rose. Mousy was the word that came to mind whenever he looked at her. Her face was thin and lined, and he suspected she looked much older than she really was. There was a hopeless air about Virginia that made him feel sorry for her. He realized that, even in those rare moments when she smiled, she managed to look sad.

"Mr. Rafferty." Virginia held out her cupped hands. "I'll not have you cleanin' up my son's mess. You give me that before you cut yourself. Then go on about your business."

He hesitated a moment before carefully placing the jagged pieces of glass in her hands. She was right. He wasn't there to clean up after the Townsend family. He wasn't there to become involved in their problems.

Virginia would just have to work things out on her own—and so would her daughter.

* * *

Rose lay on her side on the bed, curled into a fetal position, her eyes staring blankly at the wall, her arms cradling her bruised ribs. Her body ached, and she could feel the swelling beginning on her bruised face. She could still taste blood. It was a bitter taste. Bitter—like her heart.

How had this happened to her? She had sworn she would never allow anything like it to happen again. Not to her. Not to Rose Townsend.

She closed her eyes, fighting the pain, fighting the fear, fighting the reality of what the future would bring if she couldn't escape soon.

How was she to leave Homestead now? How was she to escape before her pa returned?

A shiver shook her as she recalled the shattering pain of Mark's hand upon her cheek. She knew where he'd learned to hit like that. He'd learned it from their father. And Pa was coming back soon.

She groaned. God help her. What was she to do? She couldn't stay. She couldn't live like that again. Even though he'd been gone nearly a decade, she remembered what it had been like to live with him as if he'd been gone no more than a week.

The pain was real. The fear was real. The hate was real.

Whatever was she to do now?

Chapter Seven

The next morning, Rose stood in front of her dressing mirror and stared at her reflection with her right eye. She couldn't see out of her left. It was nearly swollen shut. The skin around it was black-and-blue. Another bruise marred her right cheek.

Tenderly, she touched the sore flesh, wincing as pain spread from the point of contact.

I can't go to the restaurant like this.

She remembered how often her mother had hidden inside the house so others wouldn't see her bruises, and despair threatened to overwhelm her.

No money. No escape. Trapped. . . .

Moving awkwardly, feeling the stiffness of muscles where her brother had hit and kicked her, Rose shed her nightgown, bathed herself from the washbasin, then put on a faded skirt and white blouse. She found it even more difficult to bend and lace up her shoes.

Discouragement slammed into her with the force of one of Mark's fists. *What am I to do?* It was the same question that had haunted her throughout the night.

She swallowed the hot tears in the back of her throat. Crying solved nothing, she reminded herself. She hadn't shed a tear in years, and she wasn't about to start now. Nor was she going to be beaten down by this setback in her plans.

She had things to do, and she would not cower inside her room all day.

Rose reached for her purse, checking to make certain Lark's note was still inside, then headed for the door. First she would stop by the restaurant and tell Mrs. Potter she wasn't leaving Homestead as soon as she'd thought. She hoped she would still have a job.

After that, she had to find Yancy Jones. She wasn't about to forget her promise to Lark just because she had problems of her own. Lark was counting on her. She wasn't going to fail her dearest friend in the whole world.

If only Lark were here now. . . . She needed her friend more than she'd ever needed her before in her life.

Rose quietly descended the steps. She didn't want her mother to hear her leaving. She had avoided Virginia yesterday by pretending to be tired and just wanting to nap. She wasn't ready yet for her ma to know what had happened. A part of Rose didn't want her ma upset, another part suspected Virginia would just blame Rose for what Mark had done. It was her ma's way. The men of the family were always in the right, no matter what.

Before opening the front door, Rose tied a deep-brimmed sunbonnet over her hair, tugging the edges forward to help hide her face. She knew it was only a temporary disguise, but her pride demanded she try to hide the bruises. Finally, she opened the front door and stepped out onto the porch.

Michael was standing on the bottom step, his back to her. He turned at the sound of the opening door.

Rose stopped, wanting to retreat into the house, yet knowing she had to go forward. She dropped her gaze to the porch, unwilling to meet his eyes.

"Good morning, Miss Townsend," he said, his voice low and gentle.

"Mr. Rafferty." She moved toward him, expecting him to step aside for her to pass.

He didn't.

She waited a heartbeat, then glanced up. With her on the top step and him on the bottom, they were at eye level with each other—and close. Close enough for her to notice that his eyes were the color of robin eggs and circled with rings of indigo. Close enough to see that his lashes were surprisingly long and thick and much darker than the golden-blond hair of his head. Close enough for her to read the tender concern in his eyes.

Did she also see pity? She didn't want his pity.

"Excuse me." Her throat was tight and her words came out in a whisper.

He didn't move from her path. "Listen, about yesterday—"

"I'd prefer not to speak of it," she said quickly with all the dignity she could muster.

He looked as if he would say more, then closed his mouth and stepped back, making room for her to pass.

Rose lowered her gaze and tugged at the brim of her bonnet, trying to shield more of her face. That was when the idea came to her— Mr. Rafferty could help her!

She looked at him a second time. He was still watching her with that thoughtful gaze of his.

He'd helped her yesterday. He'd saved her from Mark. He had been gentle with her, caring, concerned. He was still concerned. Perhaps. . . .

"Mr. Rafferty?" She stopped, not sure how to ask what she wanted to ask.

"Yes?"

She squared her shoulders and tried to stand tall. She even lifted her chin, giving him a full view of her bruised face. "Mr. Rafferty, I . . . I need to ask a favor of you."

"And what is that favor, Miss Townsend?" His expression didn't alter, nor did he seem put off by her forwardness.

A bit more hopeful, she continued, "I would like you to take me with you when you return to San Francisco."

One of his eyebrows arched. "I beg your pardon."

"I need to get to San Francisco, and I don't have the price of a ticket just now." She saw the start of a frown creasing his forehead. She rushed onward. "I wouldn't be any trouble to you. Not a bit. I promise I wouldn't. I eat very little, and I could sleep sitting up. And as soon as I find a job, I would pay you back every cent." She took a quick gasp of air. "Please, Mr. Rafferty. Take me with you to San Francisco."

"I'm very sorry, Miss Townsend, but that's just not possible. My plans don't call for me to return home for quite some time."

The urge to burst into tears and beg was so strong she had to get out of there before she embarrassed herself completely. Whispering a quick apology, she scooted by him and hurried down the walk without a backward glance.

Doris McLeod felt every one of her fifty-eight years this morning. Her lumbago was acting up, and the arthritis in her fingers made holding the coffee cup painful. She watched Zoe bustling about the restaurant kitchen and wished she had half the woman's energy.

"Sit down, Zoe. You're wearin' me out, just watchin' you."

The woman glanced over her shoulder, smiled, then filled another cup with coffee and joined Doris at the table. "You're right. I could use a moment of rest." She ran the palms of her hands over her head, smoothing back the hairs that had pulled loose from her bun. "It's a good thing school is nearly out. I'll be needin' the girls' help during the day now that Rose won't be workin' for me."

"She's really going to leave then? I thought she might change her mind."

Zoe shook her head. "Goin' to San Francisco, she says."

"Alone?"

"I suppose so. Can't imagine how Virginia could go off and leave the boardin'house, not now that summer's almost here, and I sure can't see Rose goin' anywhere with that brother of hers."

Doris sniffed her dismissal of that notion. There wasn't anybody in their right mind that would bother to cross the street with that worthless, no-good drunkard, let alone take some cross-country trip in his company. As far as Doris could tell, Mark was as bad, maybe worse, than his father had ever been. Her husband, Hank, was forever locking Mark up for disorderly conduct, just as he used to have to do with Glen.

Zoe sighed. "I've been feelin' sorry for her

mother ever since Rose told us she was leavin'. Imagine, Virginia tryin' to take care of that place all by herself. She's not a strong woman. And she sure won't get any help outta that boy of hers."

"No, she won't," Doris agreed.

"I guess we can thank our lucky stars. My girls aren't perfect—heaven knows, I wouldn't pretend they are—but they've never caused me the kind of heartache I've seen others suffer. And your grandchildren—why, I've never seen better behaved children than those two."

Doris nodded in agreement. "Tommy's a lot like his father was when he was little. Tom would have been proud of that boy. I wish he'd had a chance to see him just once before. . . ." A lump formed in Doris's throat. It always did when she remembered the day Tommy was born—a solitary joy in the midst of so much tragedy.

Zoe laid her fingers over Doris's hand. "Tom and Maria would be proud of those two children. Real proud. You've done a fine job raising them."

Doris managed a smile. She'd certainly done her best, but she wasn't young like Zoe. It was difficult for her to keep up with a rambunctious nine-year-old boy, even one as basically well behaved as Tommy. Thank heaven, Sarah was easier for an old woman to care for. She was a bit of a woolgatherer, true, but she was a good girl.

The back door to the restaurant opened, and Rose entered the kitchen. She was wearing a sunbonnet over her dark hair, the brim pulled so far forward it obscured most of her face, and her head was tipped forward at an odd angle. Something about the stance reminded Doris of Virginia.

"Mrs. Potter." Rose's voice was soft. "I'm afraid I won't be able to work today. I . . . I had an accident." Her head came up slightly.

Doris gasped. Even with her face hidden in shadows, the bruises could be clearly seen. "Good heavens, Rose! What happened?"

Zoe had risen to her feet and was already hurrying toward the young woman.

Rose dipped her head forward again. "I . . . I tripped and fell down the stairs. I'm all right. Really, I am. But I . . . I don't want folks to see me like this."

"Of course not," Zoe responded. "I understand."

"Mrs. Potter?" Rose hesitated a moment, then said, "I won't be going to San Francisco as soon as I thought. If . . . if you haven't given my job to someone else, I . . . I'd like to stay on."

"The job is yours, Rose. I told you that."

"Thanks. I'll come back to work on Thursday if that's all right." She reached for the door. "Thank you, Mrs. Potter. I . . . I really appreciate it." She slipped out the door, closing it behind her.

Zoe turned and looked at Doris. Each knew

what the other was thinking—Mark Townsend.

"Isn't there something the law can do?" Zoe asked as she returned to her chair at the table.

"Perhaps if Rose asked Hank, he could have a talk with Mark." Doris shrugged her shoulders helplessly. "But when it comes to family. . . ."

Yancy couldn't say he cared much for working in a sawmill. The noise, the dust, the cramped quarters. He much preferred being out under the wide canopy of sky, breathing fresh air and listening to the sounds of nature. But the work was honest and the pay was good. That made his days seem a little more tolerable.

"Jones! There's someone here to see ya."

Yancy turned and looked at the foreman, then followed the man's gesture. He saw a slight, feminine shape silhouetted in the mill doorway, daylight at her back. For just a moment, he wondered if it was Lark and, just as quickly, knew it wasn't.

His gaze returned to Ted Wesley. "Be right back."

It wasn't until he was almost to the doorway that he knew who was waiting for him. He'd met Rose once when she'd come out to the Rider ranch, and he recognized her petite height and woman's figure even though he couldn't see her face. The morning sunlight glared behind her, keeping her face beneath her bonnet in shadows.

"I'm sorry to bother you, Mr. Jones," she said as he approached her, stopping a short distance away. "Lark asked me to give you something before she left Homestead."

He felt a bolt of alarm. "Left Homestead?"

"Her parents took her down to Boise City for a while."

"Oh." The word came out with a sigh of relief.

Rose lifted her chin slightly. Yancy had the distinct feeling she was studying him with an unrelenting gaze. "Mr. Jones, Lark thinks she's in love with you. I guess she is, from the look on her face when she was leavin'. I hope you feel the same, 'cause if you don't, it's going to break her heart." She held a slip of folded paper out to him, dipping her head forward so that the brim of her bonnet obscured her face once again.

"Thanks." He stepped closer and took it from her.

She turned to leave without looking up again.

"Miss Townsend?"

She stopped, but didn't glance back.

"I mean t' see that she's happy. You got my word on it."

Rose nodded, then walked away.

Yancy stared down at the paper in his hand for several heartbeats before he worked up the courage to open it and see what it said.

* * *

My dearest Yancy,

By now you must know Papa has taken me and the rest of the family down to the capital for a spell. He thinks if I don't see you that my feelings will change. That just isn't true.

It's my fault you lost your job at the Rocking R. I never should have told Papa how I felt about you. He doesn't understand. He's too old, I guess, to understand. I'm sure he's never felt this way or he wouldn't have done what he did. He'd have known I would die without you. That's how I'm feeling now. As if I'm going to perish.

Please don't leave Homestead, no matter what happens. I will be back, and when I am, I'll come to you. Papa can't stop me from loving you. Nothing can stop that. I swear it on my life.

Devotedly yours,
Lark

Yancy smiled sadly. He could almost hear Lark speaking the words to him. She was so passionate, so boldly dramatic in the things she felt. He couldn't imagine why she'd given a man like him a second look, let alone why she'd decided he was worth loving.

Chances were she was wrong. Chances were a few days or weeks in Boise would be enough for her to come to her senses, just as her father wanted.

But there was also a chance that she loved him and would keep on loving him, as her letter said, and that was the chance Yancy was hanging his hopes on.

Chapter Eight

Glen Townsend drew his sweat-covered horse to a halt and stared down the street. Homestead had changed in the years he'd been gone—there were new houses, new businesses, even a red-brick bank—but as far as he was concerned this town was still a spot in the middle of nowhere. But that was what made it such a good place to lie low. At least, that's what his old partner, Quinn Tracy, had told him.

He glanced over at the man riding beside him. Mad Jack's face was expressionless, as usual.

Glen and Mad Jack Adams had been released from prison in Colorado at the same time and had just kept on together. It was Mad Jack who'd stolen the horses they were riding now, and it was Mad Jack who'd made sure the men who'd owned them wouldn't be reporting them stolen. Not ever.

"Come on," Glen told him. "My place is at the other end of town."

The two men rode slowly. Glen made note of all the changes, including the new sawmill on Pony Creek. Homestead Lumber, the black letters on the side of the building proclaimed. He wondered who owned it.

Two doors up from the boardinghouse, they passed a saloon. Glen grinned. So, at last Homestead had a place for a man to wet his whistle without having a wife hanging over him, nagging at him for drinking. As soon as he'd had a bite to eat, he was going to pay himself a visit to the Pony Saloon and find out just how good their whiskey was.

Drawing back on the reins, Glen stopped in front of the boardinghouse. "Well, I'll be," he muttered.

There'd been some additions made to the place since Glen left, including a porch, which wrapped around the front and one side of the building. The house was painted a dark blue, and there was a fancy sign that gave the name as Long Bow Valley Room and Board.

Maybe it wouldn't be so bad here after all. Glen hadn't liked the idea when Quinn had told him they wouldn't be going after the money as soon as they were released from prison.

"They'll be watchin' us like hawks," he'd whispered to him as the two men had headed toward the mess hall. "You go back to that wife o' yours an' look like that's where you mean t' stay. I'll meet you there in July an' we'll go for the money together. Then we'll head for Mexico or Brazil."

Again, Glen let his gaze roam over the changes that had taken place during the last decade. His wife obviously had done all right for herself while he'd been away. Maybe it wouldn't be so bad living here again—especially since it was only temporary. That is, it wouldn't be bad as long as Virginia remembered her place. She always had been a woman to get on his nerves.

He dismounted and curled the reins around the hitching post, then headed up the walk, followed by Mad Jack. He halfway wished he hadn't sent that letter telling Virginia he was coming back. It might have been worth it not to, just to see her surprise. But he'd known how she would feel having him come back, and he'd wanted her to squirm a little, not knowing exactly when he would be there.

Glen opened the door and entered the house. The parlor was empty, but he heard sounds coming from the kitchen. He walked down the hall and pushed the door open before him.

Virginia turned at the sound. Her eyes widened. Her face paled.

She'd grown old since he'd last seen her. Her hair was grayer, her face more wrinkled. But then she'd never been much to look at—even when she was young. He'd often wondered why he'd married her in the first place. He supposed it was because she'd been the only female around at the time, and he'd been a young buck with an itch to scratch.

"Yeah, it's me. You got somethin' I can eat? I've been travelin' a long way, and I'm hungry."

Her gaze flicked over his shoulder.

"That's Mad Jack," Glen said. "Fix him a plate, too. He'll be stayin' with us awhile."

She didn't move, only continued to stare at the two men.

"Don't stand there gawkin', woman. I said get us somethin' to eat."

His raised voice set her in action. While Glen and Mad Jack sat down, dropping their dusty hats on the table, Virginia scurried around the kitchen.

When she set the plate in front of Glen, she said, "I wasn't expectin' you back so soon. I don't have anything ready but this stew."

"It'll do," he answered without looking at her. He grabbed the spoon and began to eat.

Rose carried the dishes back into the restaurant kitchen and placed them beside the sink. She let out a long sigh, then drew in another deep breath. She would be glad when this day was over.

She'd stayed home from work for three days, and she'd thought, with the careful use of rouge and powder, she could disguise the bruises. It hadn't worked. Everyone had asked her what had happened. She'd repeated the story about falling down the stairs, but she had the awful feeling no one believed her, that they all knew the truth.

"Are you feeling all right, Rose?" Zoe asked, looking up from the table, where she was dicing onions.

"I'm fine."

"Maybe you should go on home. I can wash up those dishes and Esther and Faith will be here soon to help get ready for the supper crowd."

"I don't mind staying." She went over to the stove and, using a towel to protect her hand from the heat, lifted the kettle filled with water and carried it back to the sink. She filled the washpan, then returned the kettle to the stove.

"Do you know what I heard today? Emma told me that Mr. Rafferty, the fellow staying at your mother's boardinghouse, has bought some land and plans to build a hotel here in Homestead."

Rose set some of the dirty dishes into the washpan and began cleaning them. "A hotel?" she asked, not really listening, only making conversation.

"Well, don't you see? He's obviously a man of some importance. You only have to look at him to know he's wealthy. He wouldn't come all the way to Homestead unless he was sure such a venture would be profitable. Doris says

Mr. Rafferty must know something we haven't heard yet. Something that'll turn Homestead into a real boomtown."

Homestead a boomtown? Rose had a hard time picturing it. But then, she didn't really know what a boomtown could look like. She'd never even been down to Boise City. Imagine . . . thousands of people living in one place.

And San Francisco was even bigger. What would it have been like to live in a city like that? Exciting? Scary? Probably a bit of both. But she would never know, at least not until she could earn back the money her brother had stolen.

For that matter, she didn't know if forty-eight dollars would have taken her all the way to San Francisco. She hadn't really cared. She would have gone as far as possible and then worked until she'd earned enough to take her farther.

But now. . . .

Suddenly, she was afraid. More afraid than she'd ever been before. Her pa was coming back, and she was trapped. She couldn't get away. She remembered him through the memory of a child—a dark, angry man with an iron fist and a gruff voice.

She remembered the day she'd sat in church and thought how much she hated him. She'd known it was a sin to hate one's own pa, but she hadn't cared. She'd hated him, and she'd been afraid of him, and she'd wished he'd go away.

And then he *had* gone away. Like an answer

to a prayer, he'd left Homestead—but not before he'd killed Tom McLeod and burned down the old sawmill.

She knew he'd done it as certainly as she knew her own name, but she'd never told another soul. The child she'd been was afraid they would bring her pa back to Homestead if she shared her suspicions with anyone. Later, when she was told he'd been imprisoned for bank robbery, she'd thought it enough that he'd been locked up, was being punished, was never coming back. At least, that was what she'd told herself.

But now Glen was coming back, and there was nothing she could do to prevent it.

"Rose?" Zoe's hand alighted on her arm. "Rose, you'd better sit down. You're as white as a sheet."

She allowed the other woman to help her to a chair, not realizing until she started to walk that her legs were like rubber.

"Here. Have a drink of water." Zoe pressed a cup into Rose's hand.

She sipped slowly, trying to steady her shaking hands. Finally, when she'd drained the cup, she said, "I think I will go home, Mrs. Potter, if you don't mind."

"Of course, I don't mind. But are you sure you want to go alone? Maybe you should wait for the girls to get home from school. Esther could walk you back to your place, make sure you got there all right."

"No." Rose shook her head. "No, I'll be fine on my own." She rose unsteadily, bracing her thigh against the table. She drew several deep breaths and forced herself to smile at Zoe. "I'll be fine," she repeated as she removed her apron and cap.

Zoe took the articles from her. "Don't you mind these. I'll hang them up. You just get home and get to bed. And don't you come into work tomorrow unless you're feelin' a whole sight better."

Rose hadn't the strength to do more than nod before heading toward the door.

The mid-May sun was hot, the sky an expanse of unmarred blue stretching from horizon to horizon.

At the top of Tin Horn Pass, Michael drew his roan gelding to a halt beneath the shade of a tall pine tree and stared down at the valley below. Freshly turned fields and those already planted with spring crops created a checkerboard of browns and greens. Cattle and horses grazed in pastures of grass. A ribbon of blue—Pony Creek—wound its way across the valley, disappearing into the next range of mountains.

Michael had left the boardinghouse at dawn and ridden over into the next valley. Now, in late afternoon, he was returning to Homestead.

He'd been reluctantly impressed by what

he'd seen and learned today. The farmers and ranchers in these two neighboring valleys were prospering, and the logging and mining interests in the mountain areas were reportedly thriving. With Idaho sure to become a state within the next few months, there would be an influx of people coming to the area. Homestead was bound to see its share of newcomers.

He'd known, of course, of the plans to bring a spur of the Oregon Short Line up this direction. His father had not been so reckless to choose towns where a hotel was guaranteed to fail. No, he'd given both of his sons equal opportunities to succeed. Michael had known that coming in.

But for the first time, he was feeling like he had a chance to *really* succeed at the task set before him. He'd resisted admitting to himself that Dillon just might win this contest, but that was exactly what he'd thought. Now Michael was convinced he really could pull this off. Palace Hotels would be his, just as it was always meant to be.

He couldn't deny, even to himself, that there was a certain increasing excitement inside him at the idea of making a success of this venture—for the sake of success alone. It was so different from anything he'd ever done before. The Palace Hotels had been built to host royalty and dignitaries, not miners and loggers or farmers and traveling salesmen. But who was to say he couldn't make a success of a hotel in a town like Homestead?

Michael lifted his dusty Stetson from his head, wiped his shirtsleeve across his forehead, then set the hat back in place. His gaze swept over the panoramic scenery of the valley and surrounding mountains. It was wild, beautiful, and rugged, yet strangely serene. The sight made him feel some things he hadn't felt in years—a sense of newness, of adventure and challenge, even a sense of peace.

Perhaps, when this year was over, he would have something more to thank John Thomas for than simply control of Palace Hotels.

The two men glanced up as Rose opened the back door of the boardinghouse. She saw him—her father—and froze in the open doorway, her chest growing tight, her knees growing even weaker.

"Well, I'll be damned," Glen muttered, his face suddenly split with a grin. "Look who's all grown up." He pushed his chair back from the table and rose to his feet.

Rose glanced toward her mother standing near the stove. Virginia seemed more faded and wan than ever.

"Come here, girly, and let me have a closer look at ya."

Reluctantly, she moved toward him.

His eyes narrowed, but his grin remained as he studied her face. "What happened?" he asked as he touched her cheek.

She flinched. "Nothing."

"I see you're still as prickly as a porcupine." He grabbed hold of her arm, his face darkening into a scowl. "Now, I asked you what happened."

"Mark happened." Rose jerked her arm away and stepped around to the other side of the table.

Her pa chuckled. "Still scrappin' with your brother, are you? Guess you haven't grown up as much as I thought."

The other man got up from his chair, drawing Rose's attention. He had wild black hair and a grizzled beard. His eyes—such a pale gray they seemed almost colorless—traveled over her.

She shivered but tried to hide her distaste.

"And who might you be?" the man asked.

Her father answered for her. "That's my daughter, Rose. Rose, this here's Jack Adams. Folks call him Mad Jack."

She could see why. She would swear there was madness in his eyes.

Mad Jack continued to stare. "You didn't tell me you had anything like her waitin' for ya, Townsend."

I wasn't waiting for him, she wanted to say, but didn't.

"Been a long time since I seen a gal as purty as this one." His lurid grin revealed a missing tooth near the right corner of his mouth.

Rose felt a sudden need for a bath.

Mad Jack stepped around the table, drawing closer to her. "I think you an' me are gonna become good friends."

"I doubt it," she replied through gritted teeth. She wanted to back away from him, but forced herself to hold her ground.

Glen laughed aloud. "I don't think she cottons to your attentions, Mad Jack."

"She just don't know what she's missin'," he answered without taking his eyes off Rose. "But I mean t' show her."

"Well, if that's what you're aimin' for, you'd better plan to marry her and take her off my hands. That'd be one less female for me to worry about."

Rose whirled toward her father. "Marry? I don't have any intention of marrying this man or any other."

Before she could react, Glen was around the table, his fingers once again squeezing her arm until she involuntarily whimpered with pain. "You seem to forget who's in charge around here, little girly. I been gone a long time, but I'm back and you're damn well gonna do what I tell you to do. You hear me?" He gave her a shove toward her mother. "Come on," he said with a glance at Mad Jack. "Let's go check out that saloon. Time I said howdy to my son. Besides, I need a drink to wash down that lousy stew."

Rose watched them go, pain and fear congealing into a cold knot in her belly.

So this was it then. Her nightmare had begun.

Later that evening, Rose stood at the open window of her room. She could hear laughter and music coming from the saloon, two doors down the street. The saloon noises had never sounded so uninviting as they sounded tonight, since she knew her father was there.

You mustn't provoke your pa.

That's what Virginia had said to her after Glen and Mad Jack had left the kitchen.

Her mind repeated the phrase. *You mustn't provoke your pa.*

Rose sighed. How many times as a child had she heard the same words? Dozens, perhaps hundreds. Always Virginia had defended Pa and Mark. No matter what they'd said, no matter what they'd done, always she had defended the men. Always.

Why?

Rose had been the one who'd stood up for her mother when her pa was still at home. Rose had been the one who had worked so hard in the boardinghouse after Glen had left Homestead. It was she who had helped support the family through the lean times by taking the job at Zoe's Restaurant. Just once, why couldn't her ma. . . .

She stopped herself from thinking about it. It was pointless to wonder. Ma wasn't ever going to change. She believed this was a woman's lot

114

in life and they just had to live with it, no matter how bad it might be.

You seem to forget who's in charge around here, little girly. . . . You're damn well gonna do what I tell you to do. . . . You'd better plan to marry her and take her off my hands. . . .

Rose gripped the windowsill. She had to get away. She had to leave. She couldn't stay here and see it happening all over again to her mother. Even more, she couldn't stay and let it happen to herself. She wasn't going to be forced into marriage to a man like Mad Jack, a man who would use her and beat her and trample her underfoot. She didn't want to become like her mother—broken and beaten down, both by circumstances and by some man. Rose wanted more from life than that.

But how? How did she escape? It would take her many weeks to replace the money Mark had taken. Anything could happen before she earned enough to get her to the territorial capital, let alone beyond.

If only Lark were here, she thought, not for the first time. She could have gone to stay at the Rocking R or she could have borrowed money from her. But Lark wasn't there, and Rose didn't know when she would be coming back.

She turned from the window and walked over to her bed, where she lay down on her back. The evening breeze rustled the curtains, and shadows upon shadows danced across her ceiling.

Her cheeks grew warm as she recalled how she'd asked Michael Rafferty to lend her the money to escape. Never had she felt desperate enough to ask anyone for help, let alone a stranger. Even now she found it difficult to believe she'd done it.

She remembered something Mrs. Potter had said earlier in the day, something about Michael building a hotel here, about him being a wealthy man. Rich enough to take a gamble on a hotel in Homestead when her ma struggled to run a simple boardinghouse. He must be very, very rich to throw his money away like that. He could have helped her if he'd wanted to.

But why should he want to? What reason had he to help someone like Rose?

Suddenly, she remembered the way he'd cradled her in his arms and told her she was safe with him. He'd sounded like he cared, really cared. So why hadn't he helped her?

She refused to let tears form in her eyes. She wasn't going to give in to despair. She wasn't. She could take care of herself. She didn't need Michael Rafferty's help. She didn't need any man's help.

Rolling onto her side, she closed her eyes and tried not to think about anything more. She just wanted to sleep . . . and forget.

In a hotel room in Boise City, Lark also lay on her bed, tears wetting her pillow. She understood now what the poets meant by a broken heart. Surely her own was shattered into a thousand pieces.

It wasn't supposed to be like this. Falling in love was supposed to be the most wonderful thing in the world. She and Yancy should be together. He should be courting her. She should be planning a wedding.

Instead, she was estranged from the father she adored and separated from the man she loved.

A light tapping broke the silence. "Lark," Addie called softly from the other side of the door, "are you awake?"

She swiped at the tears on her cheeks. "Yes."

The door opened.

"May I come in?"

Lark sat up. "Yes."

Addie paused just inside the doorway and turned up the gas lamp. "Are you all right, dear?" she asked as she faced the bed again.

Lark swallowed the lump in her throat. "Yes," she whispered.

Addie approached the bed. She was clad in an evening gown of emerald-green satin. Her red hair was swept high on her head. Unusually tall and as slender as a reed, Addie looked stunning as only she could.

"I wish you had come with us this evening. It was a wonderful play. You'd have enjoyed it."

"I didn't want to go."

Robin Lee Hatcher

Addie sighed as she sat on the edge of the bed. Lightly, she patted Lark's hand with her own. "You can't keep trying to punish your father this way, shutting yourself off from everything and everyone."

"He's being unreasonable."

"Perhaps so are you. You won't change his mind by acting like a child."

Lark drew in a quick, shallow breath. She'd thought her mother was on her side. Addie had been trying to convince Will to take the family back to the Rocking R from the moment they'd left Homestead.

Addie placed her index finger beneath Lark's chin and lifted her head, forcing their eyes to meet. "Darling, you don't seem to understand what it means to a father to have his little girl growing up. Will has taken care of you from the moment you got off that stage all those years ago. In his mind, you'll always be that shy, little orphan who needed his love so desperately. It's hard for him to imagine that you might want another man more than you want him."

"But I'm not a little girl any longer," she protested.

"Then prove it to him. Prove to him that you're an adult." Addie slid closer to Lark and put her arm around her back, hugging her close. "If the love you and Yancy feel for each other is real, it will last through this separation. If it isn't, it's better you find it out now."

"Oh, Mother." Lark turned her face against

118

Addie's neck. "I miss Yancy so terribly much. I honestly sometimes think I'll die if I can't see him soon."

"I know. I know because I've felt that way myself."

She sniffed. "You have?"

"Yes. I have." Addie kissed the top of Lark's head, then stood up. "You get some sleep. Tomorrow, you and I are going shopping for some new frocks. Staying in your room and crying isn't going to change your father's mind, so we may as well make the best use of our time."

"Mother. . . ."

"Yes?"

"I really *do* love Yancy. I *am* old enough to know what I feel."

Her mother simply nodded, then walked across the room, turned down the lamp, and left, closing the door behind her.

Lark lay back on the bed, the room cloaked in darkness. For a while, she mindlessly allowed the silence to wrap around her, not trying to analyze what she was thinking or feeling. Finally, as the minutes ticked away, she admitted to herself that her mother was right. She wasn't proving to Papa that she was a woman by acting like a child.

Tomorrow she was going to change things— starting with herself.

Chapter Nine

Morning sunlight spilled like liquid gold through the open doorway and across the kitchen floor.

Rose leaned her shoulder against the jamb, her eyes closed, feeling the brilliance of the sun upon her face. She listened to robins and sparrows and bluebirds singing their morning hymns of praise. The sharp scent of dew-covered pine trees filled her nostrils as she drew in a deep breath of mountain air.

She loved early mornings. They were nature's promise of fresh beginnings. She loved to watch and listen as the earth came to life. She treasured this comforting interlude before she began the business of living.

For now, the boardinghouse was quiet, the other members of the household still asleep, although she knew her mother would be joining her in the kitchen soon.

She squeezed her eyes more tightly closed,

trying not to think about her father's raised voice coming from the adjoining room late in the night. She tried not to think of the whimpers of protest—her mother's—or the rhythmic thrumming of bedsprings that seemed to go on forever.

Oh, Ma, why didn't we go away from here when we had the chance?

With a sigh, the pleasures of morning forgotten, Rose backed out of the doorway and closed the door, abruptly cutting off the sunlight, plunging the kitchen into layers of gray.

Quickly, she busied herself, stoking the stove with wood and lighting the fire, then organizing the ingredients for pancakes on the worktable. In a large bowl, she mixed the milk, sugar, and eggs. Then she added a teaspoon of dissolved pearl ash, spiced with cinnamon, a dash of salt, and a bit of rose water. Finally, she stirred in the flour, adding it slowly until the mixture was just the right texture.

She did it all by rote, not needing to think about it. She'd been helping her mother in the kitchen for as far back as she could remember. When she was little, Virginia had let her stand on a stool and stir ingredients in a bowl, much as she was doing now.

Maybe that's why she liked mornings so much. It had been a time when the house was quiet and safe, just she and her mother alone in the kitchen with no one to bother them.

A sudden string of loud curses interrupted

her musings. She turned just as the kitchen door flew open and her father stumbled, barefoot, into the room. He jerked a chair out from the table and sat down, then lifted his foot and examined his toe.

He swore again. "Don't just stand there, girly. Get your old man something cold. 'Bout tore my foot clean off on that table in the hall. Fool place for it."

Rose pumped the handle beside the sink until a stream of cold water poured from the spout. She held a rag beneath the water, then wrung it between her hands, squeezing out the excess moisture before carrying it over to her father.

Glen didn't bother to look up as he took the rag from her hand and held it against his toe, muttering another sequence of vile curses.

She didn't move away at once. Instead, she looked at him and felt her stomach turn at the thought that his blood was somehow tied to hers. Would that blood tie follow her no matter where she went? Could she ever escape who she was or where she'd come from?

Glen glanced up and caught her staring at him. "What you gawkin' at? Get back to your cookin'."

She was only too happy to obey. She busied herself, cutting slices of bacon to fry in the skillet on the stove.

"Mad Jack took a real shine to you, Rose." The anger was gone from his voice. In fact, he sounded almost amused. "Couldn't stop talkin' about you the whole time we was at the saloon last night."

The knife stilled in Rose's hand. Her breath caught painfully in her chest. He was baiting her, much as Mark liked to do. She tried to tell herself to ignore him, to stay silent. It would be better for her if that's what she did.

"I think he just may want a roll in the hay with you bad enough to marry you, just like I suggested." Her father laughed. "Can you believe he'd be fool enough for that?"

She couldn't stay silent. She couldn't ignore it.

Rose set the knife aside and clasped her hands together. She held herself stiffly as she turned to face him. Determinedly, she kept her voice from quavering when she spoke. "I don't know about your friend, but *I* am certainly not fool enough for that."

"Don't be takin' on airs with me, girl. You'll do whatever I tell you to do. Even marryin' Jack, if that's what I want."

"No," she whispered tightly. She cleared her throat, then repeated, "No, I won't."

Glen frowned as he leaned forward, resting his arms on the table. "I don't think I heard you right."

"Yes, you did. I won't marry Mad Jack or anybody else. I don't mean to end up like Ma."

He came to his feet so suddenly the chair fell over backward. "Your brother told me you needed to be taken down a notch or two, and by heaven, I mean to do it." He took a step toward her.

Rose pressed herself against the counter. Her gaze darted toward the door. She wondered if she could get there in time. She wondered if she could escape before he bruised the other side of her face.

The kitchen door swung open, and Michael Rafferty stepped into the room. His gaze found her first. "Good morning, Miss Townsend." Then he turned his intense blue gaze upon her father, who had stopped just a few strides away from her. "And you must be Mr. Townsend. Your wife told me you'd returned to Homestead yesterday. I'm Michael Rafferty, your boarder." He held out his hand.

He'd saved her again. Like one of those dashing medieval knights in books and fairy tales, he'd come to her rescue—even if he didn't know that was what he'd done.

Michael's gaze didn't waver as he stared at Glen Townsend and the two men shook hands. He wondered if Mark had told his father about the fight they'd had. Glen's handshake was friendly enough, which made him think Mark had kept the altercation to himself.

Michael was glad when the contact with Glen broke. He'd heard the raised voices as he'd descended the stairs, and he suspected he'd come into the room just in time to prevent Rose from taking another beating. It made his blood run hot to think how she was treated by her brother and father.

Damn, there he went again, letting himself worry about something that wasn't his concern. He had to stop before it became a habit. He wasn't there to protect Rose Townsend.

"My wife tells me you're lookin' at buildin' a hotel here in Homestead." Glen picked up the chair that had toppled onto the floor.

"That's right."

"Seems like a fool thing to do, if you ask me." He sat down and propped his bare feet on the table, ankles crossed. "Shoot, you're the only boarder we've got. What makes you think this town needs a hotel?"

Michael shrugged. "Instinct. This area's going to continue to grow."

"Well, I think you're crazy, but I guess it's your money."

"Yes, it is." He grinned and shrugged. Let the man think him a fool. He was anything but.

Rose stared at Michael from across the kitchen.

Michael Rafferty was rich. Very rich. And he wasn't afraid of her father.

He'd come to her rescue, not once but twice. He'd treated her with kindness. He'd refused her request before because he wasn't going to San Francisco right away. She could see it all so clearly now. But if she didn't ask him to take her with him, if she simply asked to borrow the money, surely he wouldn't turn her down a second time.

She couldn't wait for breakfast to be over and done with. Then she could talk to Michael privately. This time he wouldn't refuse her. She just knew he wouldn't.

It was afternoon before Rose finally managed to catch Michael alone. He'd left the house right after breakfast and hadn't returned until noon when she was working at the restaurant. When she came home, she found him in the parlor reading some official-looking documents.

He glanced up when she appeared in the hallway.

She hesitated briefly before stepping into the room. "May I speak with you a moment?"

"Of course." He set the papers onto the divan beside him. "What can I do for you?"

Suddenly she wasn't so sure he would help her. Why should he? Why should he help someone he didn't know? She was nothing to him. She felt her panic rising, choking off her ability to speak.

"What is it, Rose?"

Strange how hearing him call her by her given name left her feeling comforted. The panic started to recede. She drew in a deep breath and lifted her chin. "Mr. Rafferty, I understand now why you turned me down when I asked you to take me to San Francisco. Since you're planning for a hotel here in

Homestead. . . . Well, it'll keep you busy for some time, and you won't be going home right away." She clenched her hands before her waist. Her words came out in a rush. "But, you see, I don't need you to take me with you. I . . . I'd just like you to lend me the money. After all, you must have lots of it, being rich and all. I'd pay you back. I promise." The panic was back. "Please, Mr. Rafferty. I've got to get out of here. I've just got to."

She was so small and pretty and helpless looking. He stared at her beautiful, gold-flecked eyes and her bruised face and felt like a knife was turning in his gut. How could he turn her away? How could he not help her? He was, after all, just as rich as she thought he was. Giving her the money would take no more effort than scribbling a bank draft. It wouldn't even matter to him if she never repaid it.

But why should he help her? He didn't owe her anything. He had enough to worry about without adding Rose Townsend to the lot.

He saw the anxiety so clearly in her wide eyes, in the way she was wringing her hands. Yet she had plenty of pride, too. It was hard for her to ask for help. He could see that.

He should let someone else help her. If it weren't for Dillon and John Thomas, if it weren't for Michael's own determination to win control of Palace Hotels, he would never have met her, would never have known of her existence, let alone her problems.

Yet, he couldn't leave her here. He couldn't let Glen or Mark hit her again. He couldn't.

"Sit down, Rose," he said gently, then waited while she complied.

She was really extraordinarily beautiful, even with the bruises marring her face. He wondered why she had turned out so differently from the others in her family. She was like a single flower—a beautiful rose—in a patch of weeds. She belonged with other roses.

"As I said before," he began, "San Francisco is no place for a young woman alone. It's dangerous."

He heard her sharp intake of breath, saw her disappointment.

"I can't, in all good conscience, simply give you money and send you off to make your own way."

The corners of her mouth quivered. Her body stiffened, and he suspected she was about to cry, but wouldn't allow herself to do it. He wondered if he'd ever met anyone as strong as Rose Townsend.

"However," he continued and saw hope return to her eyes, "if you will allow me some time to make proper preparations, I think I can arrange for a position for you in San Francisco. I . . . have some contacts with . . . with some of the hotels there, and I'm sure I can find someone who will agree to take you on. I also know a woman who runs a respectable boardinghouse for young working ladies. I'll see if she has an opening for you in her establishment."

"Oh, Mr. Rafferty. . . ."

He raised his hand to stop her thanks. "I also will want to arrange for you to have a proper escort to San Francisco. It's a long journey, and not one to be made by a woman alone."

"Tell them I'll be a good employee, Mr. Rafferty. And I promise I'll pay you back every cent it costs for me to get to San Francisco. I swear it."

He nodded, thinking he must be going daft to have involved himself in Rose Townsend's private affairs. "I'm sure you will." He reached for the papers he'd received from the bank that morning.

She rose quietly and hurried across the room. At the entrance, she glanced back at him and softly said, "You'll never know what this means to me, Mr. Rafferty. You won't ever regret it. I promise you."

He already regretted it, he thought as she disappeared.

Just how, exactly, *was* he going to accomplish all he'd promised her? He wasn't supposed to contact anyone in San Francisco. Not anyone at the hotel. Not anyone at the bank. Not the company attorney or any personal friends.

Of course, the intent of that stipulation was to prohibit him from using his family name or position with Palace Hotels to gain an unfair advantage, and that wasn't what he was doing now.

Still, his father was a stickler for details. He'd said no contact, and he'd meant no contact.

He would have to write to Kathleen. John Thomas hadn't said his sons couldn't correspond with their stepmother. Kathleen would, of course, read more into Michael's relationship with Rose than what existed, but he could deal with that later.

Chapter Ten

As she worked in the kitchen that evening, preparing supper, Rose felt enveloped by a euphoric cloud. Michael was going to help her. She'd be leaving for San Francisco soon. Maybe just a week or two. She wouldn't need to be afraid of her father or brother ever again. She didn't need to worry about being forced to marry someone like Mad Jack Adams. She would be free.

Michael had set her free.

She didn't realize she was smiling until she caught her ma looking at her with a quizzical gaze. Rose shrugged and continued slicing the carrots for their supper, not wanting to spoil her secret thoughts with conversation.

Michael was the nicest man she'd ever met. She wasn't sure even Lark's father would have helped her this way, for all that he'd always seemed a kind man. She only had to remember how Will Rider had used his control and authority to whisk Lark away just because he disapproved of the man she loved. No, not even Lark's father would have helped Rose this way.

But Michael had. He'd done even more than lend her the money. He was going to see that she had a job and a place to live.

Yes, he was nice—and attractive, too.

You'd change your mind quick enough if you ever got kissed.

Her hand idled over the raw carrots as she stared off into space, Lark's words replaying in her mind.

Kissed by Michael Rafferty. . . . She imagined herself standing in the middle of the parlor. She pictured Michael putting his hands on her shoulders and drawing her toward him as he lowered his head. She would have to stand on tiptoe, and he would have to bend low. He was so very tall.

Was Lark crazy or could a kiss be as wonderful as she'd said?

Just before Rose could envision Michael's lips touching hers, she shook off the thought and began chopping carrots with a vengeance. Perhaps Lark could indulge in such fantasies, but Rose couldn't. Rose knew there weren't really any chivalrous knights, riding in to rescue fair damsels. A man, no matter how wonderful he might seem at times, was still a man. He had the superior strength—and the legal right—to make a daughter or a wife do whatever he wanted. She didn't ever intend to give a man that sort of authority over her once she escaped her father. She wanted no part of marriage or anything that went with it.

And yet, there lingered the memory of Michael's strong arms wrapped around her as he carried her up the stairs to her room. Strong, yes, but gentle also. What might it be like—

"Rose? Is something troublin' you?"

She glanced across the worktable at her mother. "No. Nothing's troubling me."

"Is it—" Virginia broke off her sentence.

Rose could almost see the thoughts going through her mother's head. Virginia was probably wondering if Rose had had more trouble with Mark. She was probably wondering why her brother had hit her. She'd never come right out and asked Rose what had happened between them. It wouldn't have occurred to her mother to question it, Rose thought. Virginia had always accepted a thrashing as a woman's due.

I can't be like you, Ma. I don't want to be like you.

Mad Jack leaned back in his chair, his gaze following Rose as she moved back and forth between the kitchen and the dining room, carrying serving dishes to the supper table. He felt the hot stirring in his groin as she leaned over to place a platter of sliced beef across from him. Her blouse was pulled tautly across her generous breasts, and he ached to rip the fabric off so he could view them fully.

Damn, if she wasn't the prettiest thing in skirts he'd seen in a good long while. Of course, he'd had to do without women for the three years he was in prison, and he and Glen hadn't had much time to dally in Colorado once he'd killed those two men for their horses. He'd bedded one of the hurdy-gurdy girls over at the Pony Saloon last night, but she hadn't begun to satisfy the lust he'd been feeling since first laying eyes on Glen's daughter.

Young and virginal. That was how Mad Jack Adams had always liked his women. Whores knew too much. Either they tried to take over and run the show or they pretended to feel something they didn't or they lay in bed like a cold, dead fish. But a frightened virgin—especially one as petite, yet lushly developed as Rose. . . . Now that was the makings for a night of pleasure.

The swelling in his groin became almost painful.

He meant to have Rose Townsend before he moved on, and that would have to be soon. He wasn't about to get stuck in this two-bit town. Mad Jack belonged in a city where the pickings were easy. He'd only come here because he'd heard Townsend had stashed the money from the bank holdup, and he'd hoped to share in the bounty. The rumor was obviously false. Townsend had nothing besides this boardinghouse . . . and his lovely daughter.

He followed Rose with his eyes as she returned one last time, carrying a basket piled high with steaming hot rolls. This time he looked at her face. He didn't know if he'd ever seen a gal look so good, even with a bruised eye and cheek. It was a shame her brother had knocked her around. Mark needed to learn how to inflict pain without leaving signs, just as Mad Jack knew how to do.

He grinned to himself. They didn't call him Mad Jack for nothing.

He glanced down the length of the table, his gaze stopping on Glen. He didn't like the man, didn't trust him. He sensed Glen would turn tail on anyone to save his own hide.

His gut told him to get the hell out of Homestead, and he meant to do just that—his gaze shifted back to Glen's daughter—right after he spent a few hours in Rose's bed.

"Sorry I'm late," Michael said as he entered the dining room.

Everyone turned to look at him as he took his place at the table.

"You're not late, Mr. Rafferty," Virginia said. "We just sat down ourselves." She held a platter of sliced roast beef toward him. "Help yourself."

Michael poked a fork into a juicy piece of meat.

"Tell me somethin', Rafferty." Glen leaned forward over his empty plate. "You been in the hotel business long?"

He paused for a fraction of a second before meeting Glen's gaze and replying, "My family has."

"You ever been in the Palace Hotel in Denver?"

Michael didn't allow his expression to change, despite his surprise. Did Townsend know about Michael's association with Palace Hotels? Had Townsend guessed the truth about his identity? Knowing what an unsavory character Glen Townsend was, Michael couldn't help wondering if he might try to contact John Thomas, try somehow to use this information to get money from his father.

He didn't reveal any of his private concerns as he answered evenly, "I've been there."

"Thought you might have, you being in the business and all." Glen's smile could have warmed the room in a blizzard. "Quite the place, ain't it? I was there once, before they sent me to prison. Never seen anything like it in all my born days. I guess a man could live out his life on just what one of them fancy chandeliers cost." He leaned back in his chair. "Folks who own that hotel must be as rich as Midas. Got money to waste, I'd say. You suppose they throw their money away, building hotels in towns like this one, same as you?"

"I don't believe I'm throwing my money away, Mr. Townsend." He deliberately began cutting his meat, acting as if the conversation meant little to him.

"But you're rich enough not to care if you lose it, right?"

Michael glanced up again. "No one is ever so rich he doesn't mind losing it."

"No, I suppose they ain't." Glen's grin broadened. "You a married man, Mr. Rafferty?"

"No."

Glen glanced at his daughter. "Ya oughta be. Man oughta have a wife t' keep his bed warm at night and fix him his meals. Take my Rose. She's of an age to be gettin' herself a husband. You interested, Rafferty?"

"Pa!"

"Not that she don't need herself set straight now and agin, just like her ma does. Virginia wasn't able to keep the girl in line while I was away. But now I'm home, I'll be seein' that she learns the proper way to treat a man."

Michael didn't so much as blink, but inside he was seething. So that was Glen Townsend's game. He suspected—as did, apparently, everyone in town—that Michael was wealthy, and he intended to strike it rich by marrying off his daughter to him. Never mind what her feelings in the matter might be.

It gave Michael no small measure of satisfaction knowing how furious Glen would be when

Rose left Homestead. In fact, he meant to see what he could do to expedite her departure.

Glen helped himself to a generous serving of potatoes, then smothered them with gravy. "All those years I was gone, I'd never've guessed she'd turned out so pretty, 'specially when her ma's no pleasure to look at. Even Mad Jack here's taken notice. But if you're interested, I'd give you first chance."

Michael glanced at Rose in time to see her face pale. He wished he could do something to help her, but he couldn't. Not for the moment. Tomorrow, he would write to Kathleen.

Rose lifted her eyes toward him. He tried to offer her encouragement with his gaze. He hoped she understood and would take heart.

Later that evening, Rose sat before her dressing mirror as she brushed her hair. Clad in her white nightgown, she stared at her reflection without seeing it, her thoughts returning to the supper table.

Imagine her pa suggesting Michael consider her for a wife. Didn't Pa understand she had no intention of marrying anyone, no matter what he did or threatened to do?

Then she remembered the way Michael had looked at her, and her stomach somersaulted.

She had already tried to envision what it would be like to be kissed by Michael, but now other, more disturbing thoughts tried to form in her mind. What about a wife's duties? Once, her mother had obliquely explained what a woman was expected to endure in order to have children, but Rose still didn't truly understand what happened between a man and a woman. She'd never wanted to know. But perhaps, with Michael. . . .

She gave her head a hard shake, glaring into the mirror now. *I don't want anything from Mr. Rafferty except a loan,* she thought furiously, disturbed that she would contemplate such thoughts even for a moment.

Rose set the brush on the dressing table and quickly plaited her long hair into a thick braid. Then she rose from the stool and walked over to her bed. Once there, she put out the lamp, bathing the bedroom in darkness.

Nothing was going to trap her into marriage, she thought as she crawled into bed, pulling the covers up to her chin. Nothing. She would never allow a man to rule over her the way her pa had ruled over her ma. The way he was ruling over her again. She didn't care how handsome or kind the man might be. She would never allow it.

Maybe Michael. . . .

No. There were no maybes. Rose would never gamble with a perhaps.

She closed her eyes and rolled onto her side, facing the wall. She would be leaving Homestead soon. Once she was in San Francisco, she would make a new life for herself. A life that was all her own.

Sleep began to tug at the edge of her musings. She sighed, allowing herself to drift toward unconsciousness.

A hand over her mouth jerked her back to reality. She felt the man's stubbly cheek near hers. She tried to scream, but the sound caught in her throat.

"It's damn cold out on that window ledge of yours," Mad Jack whispered in her ear. " 'Bout time you turned out the light so I could come in and get warm." His free hand began to grope at her breasts through her nightgown. "Don't you worry none. I'm gonna show you one helluva good time."

She tried to get away, but only succeeded in winding up on her back. She could see Mad Jack's shadow looming over her. His fingers closed over the opening at the front of her gown. With a sudden yank, he rent the fabric down the front. The cool night air rushed over her bare skin.

His hand on her mouth seemed to be cutting off her air supply. She thrashed her head from side to side, trying to escape, trying to draw just one more deep breath. Then his hand grabbed one of her breasts, squeezing the nipple between his thumb and forefinger, and her heart stopped. Her body stilled.

"You go on an' fight me if you want, Rose." He straddled her with his legs. "I like to know what a girl's feelin'."

Panic flowed into rage. She started pummeling his arms with her fists. She barely heard his throaty chuckle. He leaned forward as if to kiss her, and she dug her nails into his face. As he reared back, she drew her knee up sharply, catching him in the groin.

He cursed and fell off to one side. That was all she needed to send her scrambling out of bed. He caught hold of her nightgown, slowing her escape.

"No!" she cried, fighting against the tattered gown as panic returned.

In the shadows of her darkened room, she saw him sliding toward the edge of the bed. Another moment and she would never escape him.

She shoved at the gown, pushing it the rest of the way off her shoulders, then put her left foot through the tear in the front of the nightgown. His hand reached for her, touching her wrist.

"No!" she cried again.

She stumbled, her right ankle caught in the fabric. She pitched forward, and the nightgown tore free. She heard her attacker bump into the nightstand as she crawled toward the door.

Up on her feet again, she yanked the door open and ran, naked, into the hall, racing toward the only place of safety that existed in this house. . . .

Michael's room.

"Michael!"

141

He heard Rose's frightened cry as the bedroom door flew open, banging loudly against the wall. He was instantly awake and out of bed. A second later, she flung herself at him. Instinctively, his arms closed around her.

"Rose?"

She was shaking like a leaf. She was also completely naked.

"Rose?" he whispered again, his arms tightening. Lord, she was tiny—and so obviously afraid.

"What the hell is going on?" Glen Townsend's voice boomed from the hallway.

Lamplight spilled into his room, illuminating the nude girl in his arms. He quickly moved her to stand behind him, putting himself between her and the doorway.

"Rafferty, what the hell are you doin' with my daughter?"

Michael would have sworn he could see a delighted gleam in Glen's eyes. "It's not what it appears."

"I'll just bet it ain't." Glen turned toward his wife, standing not far behind him. "Virginia, fetch the sheriff."

"Glen—"

"Fetch him! I'm not lettin' this fella rut with my daughter an' get off without marryin' her. Look at him standin' there in his underdrawers and her without a stitch. He'll marry her in the mornin' or I'll see him in jail. One or the other."

Rose looked out from behind him. "Pa, you don't—"

"Shut up. I mean to deal with you later."

"Listen, Townsend." Michael's voice was firm, controlled. "I don't know what happened to Rose, but I had no part in it. If you'll give her a second to explain, I'm sure we can find out the truth of what's happened."

Glen moved forward. "Well, then, let's just have a look at the truth." He grabbed Rose's wrist and yanked her out from behind Michael. "Tell me what you was doin' in here, girly. Tell me why you were standin' naked in this fella's arms, actin' like a common strumpet. You just give me one good reason."

"Pa. . . ."

The word came out in a pleading whisper. Her head hung forward, the thick plait of chestnut hair trailing over her shoulder. She tried to cover herself with her free arm, but there was no escaping her humiliation. Either Glen was unaware of the embarrassment he was causing or he was causing it on purpose.

Angered, Michael turned and pulled the bedspread from the bed, then laid it over her shoulders.

She glanced up at him, her eyes glittering with tears of gratitude. She mouthed the words, "Thank you," as she closed the blanket around her, but no sound was heard. Her face was as white as a sheet, and her lips looked blue. He knew it was fear, not cold, that caused her to shiver, and he wished he could help her. But there was nothing more he could do.

Finally, she turned to look at her father.

Michael waited with the others to hear her explanation, waited to learn what had sent her running into his room in the dead of night. He knew she must have had a good reason, and he believed her reply would sort things out.

Rose opened her mouth to speak, then stopped as Mad Jack appeared in the doorway behind her mother. With his eyes, he dared her to tell everyone what had happened in her room. He taunted her with his presence.

What if Pa made her marry Mad Jack because of what had happened? It was Mad Jack who had torn her nightgown, who had fondled her breasts, who had meant to do more.

The truth stuck in her throat. Quickly, her gaze dropped to the floor.

Pa was determined to make her marry someone for what had happened tonight. Wouldn't it be better if she were forced to marry Michael? At least Michael wouldn't hurt her. He wouldn't handle her roughly as Mad Jack had. He wasn't cruel. No, he had always been kind to her. He had rescued her more than once.

Her father's fingers pinched her jaw, forcing her head up, making her look at him. "Speak up, Rose. What happened?"

She couldn't marry Mad Jack. She would rather die than let him touch her again.

"I just wanted to see him," she whispered. "Nothing happened."

"Get back to your room." Glen gave her a shove toward the door. "You're gettin' married in the mornin'."

She wanted to look back at Michael, but she couldn't. She wanted to explain why she hadn't told the truth, but she couldn't do that either. She'd had no choice. None at all.

Chapter Eleven

Michael stood stiffly before Reverend Jacobs, repeating his lines in a monotone. Never once throughout the brief ceremony did he glance to his left at his bride.

His bride. . . .

He wondered if he was crazy for allowing this to happen to him. He could have let Sheriff McLeod lock him up. He could have sent to San Francisco for his attorney, Christian Dover. A week or two in jail wouldn't have done him any permanent harm. He didn't doubt that he'd have gone free, given a little time, Christian's legal expertise, and a handsome portion of the Rafferty fortune.

But requesting help from Christian would be a violation of his father's terms. Michael would lose all hope of ever getting control of Palace Hotels. He would be conceding the contest to Dillon. He wasn't going to do that. Not even if he had to take a dozen wives.

146

Besides, he'd be damned if he'd let Glen Townsend get one red cent of Rafferty money.

A grim smile twisted the corners of his mouth. Townsend obviously thought he would be profiting from this union. He probably thought he could get money from his daughter's husband whenever he asked. If so, he was sorely mistaken.

"And now, by the power vested in me by the church and the Territory of Idaho, I pronounce you man and wife. What God has joined together let no man put asunder." Reverend Jacobs's solemn demeanor disappeared the moment he stopped speaking. He leaned back on his heels, looking thoroughly pleased as he gazed at the couple before him.

For the first time, Michael glanced at Rose. Her face was pale, her eyes circled with dark shadows. The bruise on her cheek had faded to a sickly yellow shade, marring—but not hiding—her natural beauty. She looked tiny and helpless and more than a little frightened.

He felt a stab of bitter regret. He'd felt sorry for her. He'd wanted to help her. And this was how she'd repaid him—with treachery. She'd helped her father set him up. She'd fooled him completely.

Well, she was about to be fooled, too. He had no intention of making this a real marriage. When his year of exile in Homestead was completed, he would arrange for an annulment. Or a divorce if that's what he was forced to do. He

147

would leave this town—and Rose—and never see either of them again.

Rose glanced up at him, and he caught a glimmer of sorrow in her eyes. Good. He hoped she *did* regret what she'd done. If she didn't now, she soon would.

The reverend cleared his throat. "Mr. Rafferty, you may kiss your bride."

He'd be damned if he'd kiss her.

Michael took hold of Rose's elbow, turning her around. Without a word, he guided her past her parents and out the back door. He strode quickly away from the church. She had to almost run to keep up with him, but he didn't slow down to make it easier for her. He wasn't about to make any of this easy for her.

Once inside the boardinghouse, he said, "Pack your things. We're leaving."

"Where are we going?"

"Not to San Francisco, if that's what you were hoping. We're going to find us another place to live right here in Homestead."

"But—"

"Get your things and don't argue with me," he snapped, feeling his frustrations boiling to the surface.

Her eyes widened, and her chin lifted almost imperceptibly. For a moment, she looked as if she might come to life, might even defy him. Then, just as quickly, the light in her eyes died.

"It won't take me long," she said softly before climbing the stairs to her room.

*   *   *

Michael hated her.

Could she blame him?

No, she couldn't blame him. After all, it was she who had raced naked into his room in the middle of the night. It was her fault they had been forced to marry. He had done nothing more than try to protect her, and look what it had gotten him—a wife he didn't want.

Rose sagged onto the bed and hid her face in her hands.

She should have told the truth.

But she knew why she hadn't. When she considered what her pa might have done if she'd told him what had really happened, she knew she couldn't have done anything differently. She couldn't have risked being forced to marry Mad Jack. Being married to Michael Rafferty was bad enough.

Married. . . . The word was ominous in its finality.

She hadn't been going to marry. Not ever. She hadn't wanted to place herself under a man's rule. Now her worst fears had come true. Married only a matter of minutes, and already her husband was ordering her around. He hadn't asked if she wanted to go on living at the boardinghouse or move elsewhere. He hadn't cared what her wishes might be. As quickly as the vows had been spoken, he had become like all men—dictatorial.

To honor and obey. . . . That was what she

had promised. Until the day she died, she was to honor and obey a man who hated the sight of her.

This was the darkest moment of her life.

She wasn't certain how long she sat on the edge of the bed, her hands over her eyes, letting the waves of despair wash over and consume her, crying in her heart, but shedding no tears. She wished now—as she had during the long, sleepless night—that she could simply curl up and die. Death would be preferable, she was certain, to marriage.

"Rose?"

She looked up, surprised to find her mother standing inside the bedroom doorway.

"It's not as bad as it seems." Virginia moved forward.

"Isn't it?" Rose asked morosely.

Her mother shook her head as she sat down beside Rose: "He'll be good to you. He's different from. . . . He's just different. You'll be better off with him than here with your pa."

It was the closest her mother had ever come to admitting that Rose's father was less than kind, less than a husband should be.

"Oh, Ma," she whispered, sliding closer and resting her head on Virginia's shoulder. "If only we could've left Homestead before he came back."

Her mother stroked Rose's hair. "You've got a chance for somethin' better. Don't lose it just because you're off to a poor start." She held Rose away from her, forcing their gazes to meet. "You've always been made of sterner stuff than me. Don't give in now, Rose. Maybe this is God's way of helpin' you escape. Your marriage doesn't have to be what mine's been."

Her mother's words brought back the memory of Michael's arms wrapped protectively around her.

Was there hope?

Virginia rose from the bed. "I'll help you pack. Your husband'll be waitin' for you."

Her husband. . . . Michael. . . .

She had a funny feeling in her stomach, half fear, half anticipation. She wondered if her mother could possibly be right.

When Michael opened the bank door a few minutes later, he found Vince Stanford bent over his desk, intently studying columns of figures. It wasn't until Michael stopped before the desk that the banker glanced up to see who had entered his financial domain.

Vince's eyes widened as he met Michael's gaze. His eyebrows arched in obvious surprise. Then he removed his glasses and rose to his feet.

"Mr. Rafferty, this is unexpected." Smiling warmly, Vince held out his hand. "I understand congratulations are in order."

Michael returned the handshake, wondering all the while just how much the other man had heard. Too much, he was sure. He imagined the whole town was gossiping about the reasons behind the hasty marriage of Michael Rafferty and Rose Townsend.

His jaw clenched. He detested gossip—especially when he was at the heart of it. He hated it even more knowing what could happen if John Thomas got wind of it. His father wouldn't stand for the Rafferty name to be blackened by scandal. He'd have Michael's hide.

But marriage had been his only real choice, so there was no point belaboring it.

"Thanks," he responded at last, certain he sounded less than grateful.

"So, what brings you to the bank today, Mr. Rafferty? Surely not business."

"Actually, it is business that brings me. I was hoping you might know of a place I could lease or buy. My . . . my wife"—it was difficult to call her that—"and I don't wish to impose on her parents any longer than necessary."

Vince nodded. "Of course not. I understand. And as a matter of fact, I *can* help you. There's a house just west of town that's been vacant for almost a year now. Even comes with some furnishings. Belonged to the Reverend Pendroy and his sister. Reverend Jacobs and his family let it when they first came to Homestead, but they wanted something bigger, having children and all, so they built that big house of theirs. But the Pendroy place would be just right for a young couple starting out." He returned to his desk, pulled open a drawer, and began shuffling through the files. "Miss Pendroy is quite anxious to sell it. The price is most reasonable." To himself, he muttered, "Now where did I put those papers?"

"The price doesn't concern me."

The banker looked up, clearly appalled by Michael's pronouncement. How could anyone *not* be concerned with price? his expression asked.

"Can we move into the house at once?"

"Well. . . ." Vince cleared his throat. "It hasn't been cleaned or aired since last fall and—"

"We can see to the cleaning ourselves. You draw up the papers. I'll be in tomorrow to sign them." Michael held out his hand, palm up. "Do you have the key?"

"Why, yes, I do." Vince opened another drawer and withdrew a key, then dropped it into Michael's hand. "Are you sure you don't want to look at the place first before deciding—"

"No." Impatience made his voice sharp. Deliberately, he softened his tone when he added, "I'm sure we'll be more than satisfied."

As Michael turned to leave, the door to the bank opened and a lanky fellow dressed in dusty denims and a battered Stetson stepped inside.

The cowboy paused when he saw Michael, then nodded at Vince as he removed his wide-brimmed hat. "Mornin'."

153

"Good morning, Mr. Jones," the banker returned as he skirted his desk, coming to stand near Michael. "Have you met Mr. Rafferty?"

"Haven't had the pleasure." The cowboy looked back at Michael, a friendly grin curving his mouth. "Yancy Jones," he said, holding out his hand.

Michael's impatience surged to life, but he subdued it. Years of experience had taught him to meet everyone as a potential business ally or opponent. This day shouldn't be any different.

"Michael Rafferty," he said and returned the handshake.

"Mr. Rafferty and Rose Townsend were married this morning," Vince interjected.

"Is that a fact?" Yancy's grin widened. "You're a lucky man, Mr. Rafferty. Your wife's as pretty as a little red heifer in a flower bed, if you don't mind me sayin' so."

His wife. . . .

Michael felt his impatience turn to irritation. He didn't much feel like standing around the bank, discussing the attributes of the woman he'd been forced to marry that morning. She could be more beautiful than Helen of Troy—and probably was—and it wouldn't have made any difference in the way Michael felt about her.

He returned Yancy's smile, although his felt tight and false. "Thank you. Now" —he glanced from the cowboy to the banker— "if you'll both excuse me, I must be on my way."

"Of course. Of course," Vince replied jovially. "Don't keep the little woman waiting on account of us. It's your wedding day after all." The man did everything but wink and poke Michael in the ribs.

Michael felt it was a sign of his excellent self-control that he managed to keep silent. Grinding his teeth, he made a hasty departure.

Rose had packed all of her personal belongings into two carpetbags and was waiting on the front porch for Michael's return. She sat on the wooden porch bench, her back pressed against the siding of the house, her hands clenched tightly in the folds of her skirt. She stared across the street, too lost in her own thoughts to notice the golden beauty of the spring day.

She wasn't sorry Michael had decided against remaining at the boardinghouse. She had no desire to live under the same roof as her father.

At least she needn't worry about seeing Mad Jack again, she thought with an odd combination of relief and anger. He'd left Homestead that morning—while she was standing in front of the minister, losing what freedom she'd ever had.

She turned her head to the left and her eyes came into focus just as Michael stepped through the doorway of the First Bank of

Homestead. She saw him pause and glance up the street in her direction. Her pulse quickened.

Suddenly, Lark's words returned to taunt her. *You can't very well get married and not let your husband kiss you.*

Maybe Lark couldn't, but it hadn't been any problem for Rose. It was clear Michael didn't *want* to kiss her.

She wished he would.

At the unexpected thought, Rose's stomach turned over.

No. It wasn't true. It couldn't be. She didn't want him to kiss her. She didn't want to be his wife. She was as trapped by this marriage as he was, perhaps more, just because she was a woman.

Now it was the memory of her mother's words that flitted through her mind. *You've got a chance for something better. Don't lose it just because you're off to a poor start.*

Was it possible Ma was right? Was it possible to find happiness with Michael?

She rose to her feet as he drew closer to the boardinghouse. He moved with such power and confidence, his long strides chewing up the distance that separated them. She'd never met anyone like him before, never known a man who could make her feel safe. But Michael could.

With sudden clarity, she knew that the choices she made in the coming hours and days would set the course for her entire future. She prayed she would make the right ones.

The Pendroy house wasn't half bad, considering. Dust lay thick on the white sheets that covered the furniture and the windows needed a good washing, but all in all, it would be a suitable home for the short time Michael planned to be in Homestead.

He walked from room to room, looking things over.

Downstairs, there was a modest-sized parlor and a small but adequate kitchen. Upstairs, there were two bedrooms. He dropped Rose's two carpetbags on the floor of the first bedroom, then carried his things into the second one. When he turned around, he found Rose watching him from the top of the narrow staircase.

"I gave you the room overlooking the grove," he said gruffly. "I hope that's satisfactory."

"Michael. . . ." His name on her lips was little more than a whisper. Her knuckles whitened as she clung to the banister. "Michael, I'm sorry about what happened last night. I never meant for this—"

His self-control shattered unexpectedly. In a voice laced with contempt, he said, "Listen, we'd better get something straight between us right now. I don't want your excuses. I wasn't looking for a wife, and if I had been, I wouldn't have chosen a scheming, fortune-hunting—"

"That's not true," she retorted, her docile demeanor vanishing. "I didn't want a husband any more than you wanted a wife. I *definitely* didn't want you!"

"Good. Then we're agreed this marriage is a sham and shall be temporary."

"Nothing could please me more." The gold flecks in her hazel eyes seemed to spark, and color rose in her cheeks. She raised her head in haughty dismissal, turned, and descended the stairs.

"Wait just a minute," he shouted. "I'm not through with you yet." Quickly, he followed after her, taking the steps two at a time.

She stood waiting for him in the center of the parlor. Her fists were clenched at her sides. Her body was tense, her eyes wary.

There was something about the way she looked that caused him to pause at the bottom of the stairs. In a flash of insight, he knew she expected him to express his anger in more physical terms. She could have run out the door, but she didn't. She stayed to face him, to fight him if necessary.

Michael drew in a deep breath and carefully brought his anger under control. He was appalled by his show of temper. He'd always prided himself on never letting anyone have the advantage of reading his emotions. He'd faced wilier—and more dangerous—opponents than Rose Townsend, yet it was this slip of a girl who had caused him to lose control of his temper, who had shattered his patience.

He ran his fingers through his hair in a gesture of frustration, then calmly walked toward his bride. "Sit down," he told her.

Rose's chin shot up a notch.

"Please."

She hesitated a moment longer before doing as he'd asked, sitting on the edge of the sheet-covered sofa, her back ramrod straight, her head held high, her gaze vigilant. He wondered if she still feared he would beat her.

He winced internally at that thought. It would never have occurred to Michael to strike a woman, and it wasn't pleasant to have Rose think he might do so.

Not that she hadn't given him enough cause.

As the silence stretched between them, he noticed a slight tremble in her lower lip, though she was doing her best to control it. Her fear and sorrow were almost palpable. He felt the urge to sit beside her on the sofa and comfort her.

But he'd be damned if he would! She'd already fooled him once. She wasn't going to do so again.

Quickly, before he could fall prey to her helpless pretense, he worked up his righteous indignation.

Oh, he was willing to admit she had plenty of reasons for wanting to get away from her father and brother, maybe even plenty of reasons for wanting to get away from Homestead. But he'd

159

already promised to help her do just that. For whatever reason, she'd decided she wanted more than just a job and a place to live in San Francisco. She'd decided she wanted a wealthy husband.

"I think we'd better come to an understanding," he said harshly.

She flinched at the sound of his voice, but her gaze never wavered from his.

"My business will keep me in Homestead for the next year, and I have no intention of jeopardizing things by divorcing you now. I can't afford the scandal. But when this year is up, that's exactly what I intend to do. And if you think you're going to walk away with any of my money, you can forget that right now."

"I don't want your money."

"This marriage will be in name only. You'll have your room, and I'll have mine. You'll keep the house and prepare the meals, and I'll give you the funds to keep the household properly. We'll keep up the pretense of marriage for appearance's sake. And when the year is up, we'll each go our separate ways."

"That's fine with me."

Damn! There was a glitter of sorrow in her eyes, and her lip was quivering again.

"Well, then. . . ." He cleared his throat and turned away from her, looking out the window toward town. "Since we seem to be in agreement about how this marriage will work,

I suppose we'll be able to get along until we can end it."

He heard her breath catch. She made a tiny sound in her throat. He was certain she was crying now, and knew, if he turned and saw her tears, he would be overwhelmed by sympathy for her. And he wasn't about to let that happen.

Heading toward the door, he said, "I've got some business to see to."

Then he marched out of the house, slamming the door behind him.

Chapter Twelve

Men! They were all the same.

Rose attacked the kitchen floor with the scrub brush and soapy water.

What had ever possessed her—even for the briefest of moments—to think Michael Rafferty was different from any other man? Dictatorial. Stubborn. Domineering. Imperious. Rude. So what if he didn't hit her? Maybe being hit would be better. At least it was more honest. He'd pretended that he cared enough to help her get away from Homestead, offering her help in finding a job and a place to live, but it had all been an act. He didn't care a whit what happened to her.

Maybe it would have been better to take the risk of her father marrying her off to Mad Jack. Chances were it wouldn't have happened. Chances were he'd have run off in the night, and she wouldn't be stuck here in this house with a man who despised the sight of her.

162

Men!

She shoved the brush into the bucket, sloshing water over the sides, then inched forward on her knees as she continued to scrub the floor.

What on earth had possessed her to tell him she was sorry? It had given him the wrong impression. She hadn't cried, but somehow she knew he'd thought she had. She'd been sad, yes. Even frightened. But she hadn't felt like crying.

She'd felt like *throttling* him!

She'd been so angry. Accusing her of marrying him for his money. As if money would make marriage worthwhile. As if she were willing to give up her independence so she could have a pretty party frock or something. Ha! She wasn't about to sell herself so cheaply. She wanted more from life than a husband, especially one who couldn't stand the sight of her.

Such gall!

She sat back on her heels and shoved damp curls away from her forehead with the back of her wrist, a heavy sigh escaping her lips.

This is some wedding day.

She wondered where Michael had gone when he'd left the house.

Oh, no, you don't, Rose Townsend, she scolded silently. *You're not going to start acting like a nagging wife. He can go where he darn well pleases, and you're not going to say one single word about it. Not one.*

163

She lifted her gaze from the floor and stared around the kitchen. She had spent the last two hours scrubbing it from top to bottom. She'd venture to guess it had never been this clean, not even when Ellen Pendroy lived there.

Well, at least she was holding up her side of the bargain. She was keeping his household for him.

She dropped the brush into the bucket and got to her feet. There were still the parlor and two bedrooms to go, she reminded herself. And she was determined to have it all done before he returned.

Pressing her fingertips against the small of her back, she stretched her aching muscles.

Maybe this wasn't such a bad arrangement, she thought. Maybe a few months, pretending to be Michael's wife, wasn't such a terrible price to pay for the freedom she would gain later, once they were divorced. She could keep house and cook for him as easily as she'd done it at the boardinghouse for the last ten years. And she *was* out from under her father's roof. Pa couldn't threaten or hurt her again. She could be thankful for that.

Rose picked up the bucket and carried it out the back door. She followed the path toward the outhouse, stopping when she reached the grove of trees. Then she dumped the soapy water into the underbrush.

Turning around, she saw three women approaching the Pendroy house. Emma Barber

164

led the way, followed by Zoe Potter and Doris McLeod.

Rose glanced down at her water-stained dress. She felt her damp hair sticking to the sides of her face and knew she must look a sight. But there was no time to do anything about it. The women had already spotted her and changed their direction.

"Rose!" Zoe exclaimed as she hurried forward and grabbed Rose's arms. "My dear girl, what a stir you've caused. To think you would marry so quickly and not tell a single, solitary soul. Why, Mr. Rafferty must have fairly swept you off your feet. It's so very romantic, don't you think?"

Emma interrupted Zoe's effusive exclamation. "We've come to see what we can do to help." Her gaze took in Rose's appearance. "Land o' Goshen, you shouldn't have to be working so hard on your wedding day. What on earth was that husband of yours thinking about, moving you into this house without giving it a proper cleaning first?" She shook her head and *tsked, tsked.* "Sometimes, I don't think there's a man alive with as much common sense as God gave a goose." Emma took hold of Rose's arm and led her toward the back door. "You just leave things to us."

Michael returned late in the afternoon.

He'd left without saying a single word to Rose about where he was going or when he'd be back. The truth was he hadn't known. He'd just wanted to get away, to have some time to think. He'd spent the day up on a ridge overlooking the valley, pondering the fix he'd gotten himself into and wondering what he was going to do to get out of it. He hadn't come up with any solutions—only more questions.

Out of all the small towns in the West that John Thomas could have chosen for this ridiculous contest, why had he selected Homestead, Idaho. Why did Michael have to end up in Mrs. Townsend's boardinghouse? And why did he have to be so susceptible to the sorrow in a young woman's eyes?

A grim chuckle escaped him. Kathleen had been after him for a long time to get married. He supposed she would find his current situation amusing if she were to find out about it. Thank goodness he hadn't written to her already.

Dillon would find it amusing, too, especially after their rivalry for the fair Lillian Overhart. His half brother would most likely think Michael deserved whatever happened to him. In his most honest moments, he would probably agree with Dillon.

And then there was Lillian herself. Saints preserve Michael should *she* ever find out about this . . . this mishap. She would never understand why Michael had married a girl he'd known little more than a week when Lillian herself hadn't been able to entice him to the altar after more than a year.

Michael cursed, his anger at his own stupidity surging back to life. How could he have been so naive? Why hadn't he seen through Rose's helpless little act? How on earth was he going to tolerate the next twelve months?

When he opened the door to the Pendroy house, he was greeted by the tantalizing aroma of onions and roasting beef. His appetite sprang instantly to life, reminding him that he hadn't eaten all day. A quick glance around the parlor made him wonder if he'd walked into the wrong place. Everything was spotless. All signs of dust and neglect had disappeared completely.

Then Rose stepped into the doorway. She paused when she saw him standing there.

She was wearing a dark yellow dress with short, puffy sleeves and a scooped neckline. Her chestnut-colored hair fell in a smooth cascade down her back, caught back from the sides of her face with tortoiseshell combs.

She looked entirely too lovely.

"Hello," she said softly. "I'm glad you're back."

Wordlessly, he removed his hat and hung it on a peg near the door.

"Dinner will be ready soon."

He glanced over the parlor a second time. What trick was she up to now? he wondered.

She drew herself up, as if she'd heard his silent question. Her voice was cool and laced with wounded pride. "I know you don't believe

I didn't set out to trap you into marrying me, Mr. Rafferty, but the truth is still the truth. I didn't want *or* plan to marry you or anybody else. But here we are, like it or not." She drew in a quick breath while further stiffening her shoulders. "You were real clear about what you expect of me for the next year, and I mean to do just as you said. I'll give you that comfortable house you want, and I'll cook your meals for you. And I'll make sure there's no scandal to hurt your business. I won't be causin' you any embarrassment. I've got only one favor to ask in return. When your business here is done, you help me leave Homestead before gettin' that divorce. Then you'll never have to see me again." She glared at him a moment, then added, "If you'd care to clean up, dinner'll be ready in a few minutes." She stepped back into the kitchen, disappearing from view.

Damn! He couldn't figure her out. One minute she was as fragile as spun glass, the next she was as rigid as iron.

Why, Mr. Rafferty must have fairly swept you off your feet. It's so very romantic, don't you think?

Rose leaned against the back of the kitchen chair and drew in a deep breath.

Oh, yes, Mrs. Potter. It's all very romantic. My husband simply adores the ground I walk on.

She glanced down at the lovely new dress Emma Barber had given her for a wedding gift. She'd never had a dress this pretty before, but Michael hadn't even noticed. And as much as she hated to admit it, she'd wanted him to notice.

That's what she got for letting her head be filled with silliness. Emma and Zoe and Doris all chattering on about love and how wonderful marriage was and how handsome her new husband was and how romantic it all was. That was what she got for allowing her mother to give her hope, telling her she could have a wonderful marriage and not to lose the chance for happiness just because they were off to a poor start. Making her believe this was God's way of giving her something better.

It was all stuff and nonsense. She didn't want to be married to Michael Rafferty and he didn't want to be married to her. They were both caught in an unbearable situation. She, at least, was trying to find a way for them to live together in some measure of peace. Michael, on the other hand, was acting just as she'd expected him to—like an unreasonable, bullheaded male.

She heard his footfall on the stairs and turned to face him.

Michael paused just inside the doorway. While upstairs, he'd put on a clean shirt and his hair had been slicked back with a comb and water.

Zoe Potter was right. He was wonderfully handsome.

He cleared his throat. "Rose...." A frown furrowed his brow. "Let's sit down, shall we?" He motioned toward the kitchen chairs, then pulled one away from the table and waited for her to be seated.

She didn't want to think about how handsome he was. It made her feel strange inside. It confused her thoughts.

"Please sit down, Rose. We need to talk."

She sat, but only because she suddenly felt as if her legs wouldn't hold her up.

Michael rounded the table and sat down across from her. Then he leaned his forearms on the table and looked straight into her eyes.

"You keep saying you didn't want to marry me. Then why didn't you tell your father the truth?"

"I couldn't." She looked down at the table.

"Why?"

"I . . . I was afraid of what he would do . . . of what he would make me do."

"What would he have made you do, Rose? Tell me."

She swallowed the lump in her throat as she looked up and met his gaze. Finally, she answered, "I couldn't say anything because he would've made me marry Mad Jack. He was already mad enough to make me marry you for doing no more than holding me in your arms. If he'd known what'd happened with Mad Jack. . . ."

Michael's frown turned to a dark scowl. "And

what *did* happen with Mad Jack?"

"He came to my room. He snuck in through the window." She couldn't meet his gaze any longer. For a second time, she looked down at her hands, folded on the table before her. "He tried. . . . He was going to. . . . When I ran from him, he ripped my nightgown. I was afraid he was going to. . . ." The back of her throat was burning. "I swear I never meant for this to happen."

"Did he hurt you?" His voice was harsh and filled with anger. "Did he. . . ."

She shook her head as shame flooded her face with color.

The room grew silent except for the sound of boiling water on the stove.

A long while later, she heard his sigh and glanced up. He was holding his face in his hands. He sat that way for several more moments, not moving at all. Then he raked his fingers through his hair as he straightened. His blue gaze found and captured her own, holding it as the silence lengthened between them.

It was just his luck to believe her.

He slid his arm across the table, reaching out to cover her folded hands with one of his own. "I'm sorry, Rose. I judged you unfairly."

Once again, her mouth quivered, this time in a tremulous smile. Her eyes were filled with that same heart-wrenching sadness. He imagined he also read regret in their depths and perhaps a little fear, too.

171

If he wasn't careful, the next thing he'd be doing was taking her in his arms and telling her he'd take care of her, promising her a bright and happy future. If he wasn't careful, he would lose sight of what was important to him.

He pulled back his hand. "I think we can agree to work together to make this next year tolerable for us both. Do you agree?"

Wordlessly, she nodded again.

"As for a divorce. . . . Well, I'm sure we'll be able to get a quiet annulment instead. That way, there'll be no stigma for you. No one need ever know we were married. When you finally find the right man—"

"That's very kind of you, Mr. Rafferty, but I don't intend to ever marry again." Her tears had vanished, and she held herself erect with a quiet dignity and an iron fortitude.

Still, Michael felt a strong desire to comfort her, to protect her from those who would cause her harm. He couldn't shake the feeling that beneath that strong veneer lay a vulnerable and tender heart.

"Well. . . ." Once again he cleared his throat. "All the same, it will be better for you."

"And you," she said softly.

At this particular moment, he wasn't certain it would matter to him. Not while he was gazing at the beautiful young woman across from him.

Chapter Thirteen

Lark leaned forward to better hear what the commissioner's son was saying. She found him and his conversation mildly amusing, and she laughed in all the appropriate places. Still, she wished herself any place but this glittering assembly.

"Does your father intend to remain in Boise City for the summer? Idaho is certain to be admitted to the union soon. You'll want to be here when it happens."

She glanced away from her handsome supper companion, looking down the length of the table to where her father sat. "I'm not sure what Papa intends to do, but I can't imagine we will be able to remain here much longer. There is a great deal of work involved in operating a successful ranch like the Rocking R. His time is often not his own."

She hoped against hope that she was right. Surely her father would have to return to

Long Bow Valley and the Rocking R soon.
Though the family had only been in Boise City
for eleven days, it already seemed a lifetime
to Lark.

"Miss Rider. . . ." A second male voice interrupted her thoughts.

She pulled her attention away from her
father, looking at the elegant gentleman seated
across the table from her.

Edward Patton was a professor from a uni-
versity in the East. He was on sabbatical, using
the time to travel and study the Western states
and territories. In his thirties, single, and quite
dashing in appearance, he was a popular guest
at any social gathering.

Lark found him dreadfully boring.

"Statehood is a landmark occurrence, Miss
Rider, and the heart of the celebrations will be
right here in the capital city. You should do
your utmost to convince your father to remain
until then."

His smile reminded her of a cat that had just
finished off a bowl of cream.

He leaned forward, and his voice lowered,
suggesting intimacy. "I had hoped to celebrate
with you."

There were layers of meaning in his words
and the look he gave her. She might be only
seventeen, but she understood a man like
Edward well enough.

"As I said before, I'm afraid only my father
can decide how long we can stay. A rancher's

life is ruled by matters other than social occasions. I'm sure we'll need to leave Boise soon. You had better plan to celebrate with someone else, Mr. Patton."

"If what you say is true, Miss Rider, I shall be an unhappy man. Unhappy, indeed."

A thrumming started up in her temples, and she wished for the evening to come to an end.

After her talk with her mother a week ago, she hadn't refused a single invitation. She had gone shopping with Addie in the afternoons, and now had a trunk full of new frocks and bonnets and gloves and shoes. She had been excruciatingly polite to all the men, both young and not so young, who had made overtures toward her. She had promised herself she would act like an adult rather than a petulant child, and she thought she had succeeded quite well at it all.

But inside, her heart was still breaking. When she looked into Edward Patton's dark eyes, she longed instead to be gazing into a pair of gray ones—eyes that were crinkled in the corners, eyes that were warm and open, eyes without pretense or subterfuge. When she laughed at the sophisticated humor of the commissioner's son, she wished instead to be listening to Yancy's colorful speech. When she gazed at the fancy evening attire of those around her, she wanted nothing more than to see a tall, lanky man in a dusty pair of jeans, a plaid shirt, and a battered Stetson shading his eyes.

She wondered how long she could go on pretending.

Rose glanced surreptitiously at the man across the table from her. The only sounds in the kitchen were the clinking of utensils on plates as the couple ate their supper. It had been the same all week long.

Being married to Michael had proven to be easier—and more difficult—than she'd anticipated. With the exception of church last Sunday, the only time she had spent with him during the past week had been during meals. And meals were mostly a silent affair with only an occasional word exchanged between them.

Each morning she arose in her solitary bed to wash in the basin, then dressed and went downstairs to prepare breakfast. Michael would join her in the kitchen, eating quickly before excusing himself, saying he had a great deal of work to be done. Then he would leave the house, usually not to return until suppertime.

Evenings, after they'd eaten, Michael would sit in the corner of the parlor, reading a book or studying sheaves of paper while Rose sat nearby, pretending to sew, but getting nothing accomplished.

The silence was torture, yet she didn't know how to broach it. Her husband had apparently made the decision that the best way for them to survive the coming year was to say as little as possible to each other. She hated to admit it, even to herself, but she wished he would share just a small portion of himself with her.

"Wonderful meal, Rose."

She nearly jumped out of her skin at the unexpected sound of his voice. Her fork clattered onto her plate. She flushed, feeling his eyes upon her.

"Sorry. I didn't mean to frighten you."

She glanced up.

He stared at her for a long while before saying, "I haven't been making things easy for you, have I, Rose?"

She shrugged.

"No, I haven't." He tilted his head slightly to one side. "I'll try to do better. We'll *both* try to do better. Agreed?" A gentle smile tipped the corners of his mouth. "Tell me, Rose, what is it you hope to do, once you are able to leave Homestead?"

Her heart was doing some crazy flip-flops inside her chest. Her mouth felt dry. She'd been longing for conversation with him, and now that he was willing, the words seemed to be stuck in her throat.

He placed his elbows on the table, his fingers laced at about chin level, and continued to wait for her response.

"I . . . I thought I might open a restaurant one day."

"A restaurant?"

She nodded. "I've learned an awful lot,

working for Mrs. Potter. And from Ma, too. Not just about cooking, but on how to run a business. I know I could do it, if I just had a chance."

"Are you still determined to go to San Francisco?"

Again she shrugged. "It doesn't have to be San Francisco. I don't care if it's a big city or a small town, just so long as it's away from here."

She glanced toward the window and the direction of town. She'd only seen her ma once in the week since the wedding. There'd been a nasty bruise just below the hairline on her forehead. Virginia had insisted she'd done it herself on a kitchen cupboard. Rose knew better.

"Just away from here," she repeated in a whisper.

Michael watched the emotions play across Rose's face, and he'd have sworn he could read her thoughts. He couldn't blame her for wanting to get away from Homestead and her father and brother.

Once again he thought how she was like a solitary rose in a garden of weeds. It was a miracle she had survived at all, considering her family. He couldn't help thinking she deserved better than she'd gotten.

It had to be darned hard for her, married to him but not married. She had little to do except clean house and cook meals for the two of them. She spent her days alone. Zoe Potter had assumed Rose would no longer want to work, now that she had a husband to take care of her, and so Rose no longer went to the restaurant every day. And Michael had been so involved with his plans for the hotel that he'd scarcely spoken more than a dozen words to her in the evenings.

When this year was over, she would need a way to support herself until she found a husband, no matter where she chose to live. Getting work wouldn't be easy, especially if it was learned she was a divorced woman. Perhaps running a restaurant wasn't a bad idea. He could help her out, once she decided where she wanted to live. It wouldn't be any particular hardship for him to give her some financial assistance, to make sure she was reasonably safe and secure in her new location.

"Maybe you'd like to run my hotel restaurant when it opens."

Damn! He couldn't believe he'd actually said that. He didn't need to complicate his life by having Rose work in his hotel.

Her hazel eyes widened, filled with hope. "Really?" she asked softly. "You would let me do that?"

Despite his misgivings, he said, "It would be a good way for you to find out if it's what you really want to do when you leave Homestead."

"Oh, Michael, I would love to." She smiled.

179

Maybe that's why he'd said it. Maybe he'd wanted to see that look of hope spring to life in her lovely hazel eyes. Maybe he'd wanted to see the appearance of her dimples when she smiled at him. He hadn't seen her smile since the day before he'd married her. He'd almost forgotten just how beautiful it was.

He picked up his knife and fork as he lowered his gaze to his plate. "After supper, I'll show you the plans for the hotel. Maybe you'll have some ideas for the restaurant."

An hour later, the couple knelt on the floor of the parlor, the blueprints of the Rafferty Hotel spread out on the floor between them.

Michael had spent the first half hour answering Rose's many questions about the blueprints themselves. It hadn't taken him long to discover she had a quick mind that easily grasped details. He couldn't help but be impressed with the way she assimilated information.

Rose straightened, sitting back on her heels. With one hand, she tossed her thick braid over her shoulder. "I'm bothered about one thing," she said, her brows drawn together in a frown. "Can Homestead really support two restaurants? I'd hate to see Mrs. Potter suffer. She's been running her restaurant since right after Mr. Potter died. It's her only means of support and . . . and it just wouldn't seem right if your restaurant caused her hardship."

"You don't need to worry about that. There'll

be plenty of business for both of us."

Her eyes narrowed slightly. "You *do* know something we don't. Mrs. McLeod said you did. She said you must expect Homestead to become a boomtown. Is it true?" She leaned forward, pressing the heels of her hands against her thighs. Her braid fell forward over her shoulder again. Their heads were only inches apart. "Please tell me."

He laughed. "Do you want me to give away trade secrets?"

"Yes!"

"How can I be sure you won't tell anyone?" he whispered, as if concerned someone else might be listening.

She drew herself up and offered a mock-serious expression. "Because, sir, I am your wife."

As quickly as the words were out of her mouth, the room became thick with tension. The twinkle in her eyes faded, and the somber expression on her face was no longer just pretend.

His wife. . . . And a very beautiful one at that.

Michael's gaze seemed to caress her face, lingering longest on her mouth.

Have you ever been kissed?

She could hardly breathe. It was horrible, wanting him to kiss her while fearing he would do just that.

It sent tingles clear down to my toes. Made me feel all strange inside.

She wondered if the feeling Lark had described was anything like what was happening in her stomach right now, the topsy-turvy, spinning sensation just looking at him gave her. She felt as if a spell had been cast over her, over the entire room. It pulled and tugged, urging her to lean forward, to offer herself to him.

A tiny gasp slipped between her parted lips.

Michael straightened abruptly. "Well. . . ." He glanced down at the blueprints between them. "Did you have any other questions? About the hotel restaurant, I mean? If not, I think I'll call it a night. I've got a full day ahead of me tomorrow."

"Questions? No . . . no, I don't have any more questions."

"Good." He began rolling up the plans.

Rose scrambled to her feet. She could still feel the crazy racing of her heart and wondered if she might be ill. She felt so flustered and disoriented, as if she'd just awakened from a dream.

"You go on up," Michael said. "Don't wait for me. I'll put out the lights."

"Thank you." She hurried up the stairs without a backward glance.

Once inside her room, the door closed behind her, she shed her clothes, donned her nightdress, and crawled quickly beneath the covers.

Did you have any other questions?

Yes. Yes, she did have more questions. What would it be like to kiss him? What would it be like to have someone cherish her? What would it be like to have someone care what she thought, how she felt, someone to share her hopes and dreams?

What would it be like to fall in love?

Chapter Fourteen

Doris leaned against the railing and called up the stairs, "Sarah Marie, for the last time, come help me set the table."

When there was still no answer, she let out an exasperated sigh and began climbing the steps leading to the second floor of the McLeod home. She didn't bother to knock when she reached Sarah's room. Experience told her the girl wouldn't hear her even if she did.

She turned the knob and pushed the door open. Sarah was seated beside the window, gazing off into space, an open magazine in her lap.

"Sarah. . . ."

No reaction.

Doris stepped into the room, walking over to stand behind her.

"Sarah. . . ." She laid a hand on the girl's shoulder.

Sarah started, her eyes opening wide in surprise. "Gramma, you scared me."

Doris shook her head. "I've been callin' for you for the last ten minutes. I need your help with the dinner table. Your grandpa will be home for his noon meal, and you know how he hates to be kept waitin' when it comes to food."

Sarah nodded, then looked down at the magazine. "Look, Gramma. Have you ever seen anything like this?" She pointed to an illustration of an odd-looking structure. "It's called the Eiffel Tower. They built it for the World Exhibition in Paris last year. Oh, Gramma. Wouldn't you love to go see it in person?"

"Sakes alive! I should say I would not," Doris responded as she gazed over Sarah's shoulder at the drawing, thinking that the tower looked none too safe. "I'm more than happy to stay right here at home where I know folks. And you will be, too, once you're grown and know how well off you are."

Sarah closed the magazine and set it aside. "You just don't understand." She sighed. "Why do you suppose Rose didn't go away like she planned?"

"I reckon she fell in love and decided it was better to marry and stay with her husband than to traipse off to parts unknown. You'll know what I mean when you're older."

"I know what you mean now, Gramma, but I

won't let anything keep me in Homestead once I'm old enough to go off on my own. Not even love. Rose'll never go anywhere now. I feel sorry for her."

Doris shook her head. "There's no call to feel sorry for Rose Rafferty now."

Another sigh escaped Sarah. "Gramma, you just don't understand."

Doris didn't fail to hear the frustration in her granddaughter's voice. As the girl rose from her chair, Doris placed her arm around Sarah's shoulders. "Maybe I don't, my dear. Maybe I don't. But I sure hope you'll come to understand what I'm sayin' someday . . . or I'm afraid you're in for a powerful lot of disappointment."

"Oh, but I won't be disappointed, Gramma," Sarah responded fervently, "because one day I *am* going to go see all the wonderful places in the world, just like I've said. I'm going to go to Paris and to London and to New York and lots of other places, too. You'll see, Gramma. I'll do it."

Doris sighed as she leaned over to kiss Sarah's golden hair. "Maybe you will, child. Just maybe you will." Her arm still around the girl's back, she headed toward the door. "But for now, we're in Homestead, and we'd better be gettin' dinner on the table for your grandpa and brother."

Sarah glanced longingly over her shoulder at the magazine, then went quietly from the room with her grandmother.

186

*   *   *

Carrying a lunch pail filled with cold chicken, biscuits and honey, and some canned beans, Rose walked toward the site of the Rafferty Hotel.

She was surprised to see the tall stacks of lumber and the many stakes pounded in the ground, indicating where the building would be. Just yesterday the ground had been vacant except for the long field grass and a couple of trees. Now, with the stakes marking the outline of the building, combined with the memory of the blueprints Michael had shown her last night, she could actually envision what the hotel would look like when it was finished.

Homestead with its own hotel. . . . It was hard to imagine. And Michael had said she could run the restaurant. It was too good to be true. If she made a success of it, she would be able to get employment no matter where she went after she left Homestead. She would be able to support herself and she wouldn't ever again have to let a man have any say in her life. She could be truly independent.

At that moment, Michael stepped into view, and she felt the quickening of her pulse.

She would be independent just as soon as Michael allowed her to leave Homestead. Just as soon as he got the annulment. Just as soon as she no longer had a husband. She couldn't wait to be free.

"Hello," he called to her. His smile added warmth to his greeting.

Honestly, she couldn't wait to leave.

"What brings you here?"

Feeling awkward and uncomfortable, she held up the lunch pail. "I thought you might be hungry. It's just some cold chicken. Leftovers from last night."

"I like cold chicken." His smile broadened. "And I *am* hungry." He motioned toward a long plank placed atop two sawhorses. "Care to join me?"

She shook her head, but moved to stand near one end of the makeshift bench.

"This was really thoughtful of you, Rose. I've grown rather tired of skipping lunches." Michael took the lunch pail from her outstretched hand.

Rose shrugged. "It wasn't any bother. I was on my way to the mercantile anyway."

"You sure you won't stay? Just for a minute or two?"

"Well. . . ." She felt her cheeks begin to flush. Why did he always make her feel so flustered? "I suppose I can spare a minute."

"Good." He sat down on the wooden plank and lifted the white cloth covering the top of the lunch pail. "I hired on my crew this morning. There's five of us. We start work on Monday." He pulled out the chicken and laid it on the cloth. "I wasn't able to get as many workers as I'd hoped. All the farmers are busy planting their crops and tending their livestock." He set the can of beans next to the chicken. "But I still think we'll be able to open the hotel this summer, maybe by July, autumn at the latest."

"That soon?" She looked at the lumber stacked nearby. How could this be turned into a hotel in so few months?

As if reading her thoughts, he said, "I ordered the furnishings before I left San Francisco. It should all start arriving in the next couple weeks." He picked up a chicken breast and bit into it.

She watched him, noting how the sun glistened on his golden hair. A lock fell forward, curling over his forehead and brushing his eyebrow. She liked the way it looked, the way it made him look. It brought attention to the handsome lines of his face, that long, straight nose, the firm jawline.

Her gaze drifted downward to his broad shoulders beneath his blue work shirt. She could see the strength of his biceps through his rolled up sleeves.

He was so extraordinarily handsome.

He was her husband.

An odd feeling tumbled in her stomach.

Her husband. . . .

Michael set aside his chicken and wiped his hand on the checkered napkin as his gaze locked with hers. He seemed to be looking beyond her eyes and into the secret corners of her mind and soul.

189

She felt warm, a warmth that went far beyond the heat of that beautiful spring day. The way he watched her was unsettling. It summoned too many unwanted feelings, too many unanswered questions. She wished he would stop, wished he would look away, but she was powerless to make herself do so, let alone make him obey.

Then he lifted his hand. She watched it drawing closer to her face and found it impossible to breathe. When he touched her cheek—a touch as light as butterfly wings—she felt a quiver run through her and barely managed to stifle a surprised gasp.

"The bruise is gone," he said softly as he pulled his fingers away.

Her own hand flew to the place he had touched. She wanted to ask him why he'd done it, but the words were trapped in her throat.

"You're very lovely, Rose. Has anyone ever told you that before?"

She shook her head, her fingertips still lingering on her cheek.

"That's a shame. Someone should have told you."

Rose felt a sudden panic, a fear that turned her blood to ice in her veins. She rose quickly from the wooden seat. "I'd better get my shopping done." She turned away. "Don't forget to bring the pail home." With those words, she hurried toward the mercantile.

Michael watched his wife's retreat with a sense of regret. He hadn't meant to startle or frighten her. He'd never known a woman who didn't like being told she was lovely.

He thought of Lillian Overhart. Lillian expected to be told how beautiful she was on a regular basis. Of course, her expectations were not so plainly stated, but they were there, all the same.

But not Rose. She didn't expect anyone to say anything nice to her. And if he were to believe her, she didn't want anything more than for him to leave her alone for the next year and then let her go her own way.

That's what he wanted, too. Just to get through this next year so he could put his life back in order, make everything normal once again.

But maybe. . . .

His thoughts were interrupted by the appearance of a man striding toward him, coming from the direction of the sawmill. By the time the fellow was across the street, Michael had recognized him as the man he'd met in the bank a week ago. Jones. Yancy Jones.

Yancy stopped and bent his hat brim in greeting. "Mr. Rafferty, I hear you're hirin' a crew to build this here hotel."

"That's right."

"I was wonderin' if you'll be needin' any more help? I put in four days a week at the mill, but I could sure use the extra work. I can't say I've done much carpenterin', but I'm not afraid to work up a sweat and I'm a quick learner. I don't have a family to go home to, so I can keep workin' as long as there's light. I'm willin' to work when I'm done at the mill, and I got two full days besides. Three if you want me t' work on Sundays."

"I imagine work on Sunday would be frowned upon in Homestead," Michael answered, wondering why the man was so eager for work. He hadn't even asked what Michael was paying for wages.

"I guess so," Yancy agreed, "but I'm willin' to put up with a bit of talk if it'll get me the money I need."

Michael raised an eyebrow in question.

"I'm buyin' me a ranch, and I mean to take me a wife just as soon as I can get her pa to agree, and that won't happen till the place is mine." He grinned. "I'd guess you can understand the hurry I'm feelin' about gettin' hitched."

Michael didn't tell Yancy that he hadn't the foggiest idea why any man would be in a hurry to get married. The cowboy obviously wouldn't have understood.

"I'm a hard worker, Mr. Rafferty. You won't be sorry you took me on."

Michael rose from the bench, studying Yancy Jones a little longer. He'd always been a fair judge of character, and something told him Yancy would work just as hard as he'd promised. Finally, he nodded and held out his hand. "Pay's sixty-five cents an hour. We start Monday morning. You tell me when I can expect you, and you can work as many hours each week as you're willing and able."

"That's plenty generous, Mr. Rafferty." Yancy grasped Michael's hand and shook it, grinning the whole while from ear to ear. "Plenty generous."

"Call me Michael."

A few minutes later, Yancy headed back to his job at the sawmill, leaving Michael to finish his lunch of cold chicken, biscuits with honey, and beans. But Michael's thoughts remained on his newest crew member.

Buyin' him a ranch and meanin' to take himself a wife, and in a hurry to do so besides. In a hurry, and he thought Michael would understand.

But Michael didn't understand. He couldn't. He couldn't understand why a man would be in a hurry to get married.

An image of Rose flashed in his head, but he mentally shoved it aside.

Michael Rafferty was not the sort of man to be swayed from his appointed course by a pair of expressive hazel eyes.

Chapter Fifteen

"Rose! Rose Rafferty!"

Both Michael and Rose stopped and looked at each other, as if the sound of her name tied with his had never occurred to either one of them. Then they turned in unison and watched Rachel Henderson hurry toward them.

"My goodness, you two left services so quickly folks couldn't hardly say a word to you." Rachel waved her hand in front of her face to indicate how winded she was from racing after them. "I haven't even had a chance to say congratulations to you, me not being in town for church last Sunday. Truth is I haven't even been introduced to your husband yet, Rose."

Rose wasn't sure how Michael felt, being reminded of his marital status. Quickly, she said, "Rachel Henderson, this is Michael Rafferty. Michael, Rachel is Emma Barber's daughter. She's married to Norman Henderson."

"It's a pleasure to meet you, Mrs. Henderson." Michael tipped his hat brim.

"And mine, Mr. Rafferty. I was so excited when I heard about your wedding. Most of the married women in the valley are older than Rose and me. It'll be nice to have a married friend close to my own age." She looked at Rose. "I'm having a quilting bee at my house tomorrow. In the afternoon. I'd like you to come. Priscilla Jacobs will be there and so will Ophelia Turner. Please say you'll come."

"Well, I. . . ."

"Don't disappoint us. I know Ophelia and Priscilla would enjoy your company."

Rose couldn't think of any reason to refuse. She wasn't even sure she wanted to, but it did feel strange, being invited to a quilting bee with these women. Rose had never been included in much of anything. Lark had been her only real friend in school. Rose had always felt a little like an outsider, always looking at other families and wondering what it would be like to have a father who loved her, a brother who stood up for her. Even after her father went away, she still hadn't had a family like anyone else, and so she'd kept to herself, just like her ma.

But then, Rose had never had time to spend with other girls anyway. She'd always needed to work, first in the boardinghouse and then at the restaurant.

"Please?" Rachel prompted, drawing Rose's thoughts from the past.

"Yes," she answered softly. "I'll be there."

"Oh, good." Rachel grabbed her hand and squeezed it warmly. "Why don't you come at noon? We'll have lunch together before the others arrive."

"All right."

Rachel turned a grin up at Michael, then walked back toward the church.

"Old schoolmates?" Michael asked.

"No." Rose shook her head. "Not really. I knew her in school, of course, but she's a couple of years older than me."

"Well, she seems nice. You should have a good time tomorrow."

"Yes, I suppose so."

Together, they started walking past the grove of aspens that separated the Pendroy house from the church.

Rose continued to think about Rachel's invitation. She couldn't help wondering what made her so different now from before. No one, other than Lark, had ever invited her to any sort of party or intimate gathering, not since she was a small child. Why did a wedding change her? What made the difference in her this week from a month ago?

She glanced up at the man at her side. *He* made the difference, she supposed.

Rose Rafferty. . . .

That awful fluttering started up in her stomach, like a wild bird in a cage. She looked back down at the ground.

Rose Rafferty. . . .

Michael's wife. . . .

What did it really mean to be a man's wife? she wondered. Rachel Henderson was ready to include her into that special circle of married women, but Rose felt like an impostor. She wasn't really and truly Michael Rafferty's wife. She was more like his housekeeper. She fixed his meals and washed his clothes and cleaned his house, and in return, she got room and board. And in a year, she wouldn't even be that to him.

She thought of the night when he'd shown her the plans for the hotel. She remembered the moment when she'd thought he might lean forward and kiss her.

Rose Rafferty. . . .

Michael's wife. . . .

Just what would it be like to be kissed by him, to really be his wife? What would it be like to share his thoughts, his hopes and dreams . . . his bed?

Those thoughts were far too disconcerting to pursue any longer, she decided, and she was eager to reach the house, knowing she could escape up to her room for a while before starting dinner, knowing she would have a few minutes to organize her thoughts.

Then she saw her father rise from the swing on the front porch and step toward the porch railing. Her stomach sank and twisted into a knot.

Michael's hand cupped her elbow. She looked at him. For a moment, their gazes met and held. There was something about the way he looked at her that made her feel strong and unshakable. She half expected him to smile at her, but he didn't.

" 'Bout time you two showed up," Glen said. "I been waitin' near on a half an hour. Preacher must've been long-winded today."

"We didn't expect you, Pa," Rose said as she stopped at the base of the steps leading up to the porch.

"Well, haven't seen my girly since her weddin' day. Thought it was time I come callin' t' see how you're gettin' along."

"We're getting along quite well, Mr. Townsend," Michael responded, his fingers tightening slightly on her elbow.

"Good. That's good. You don't mind if me and Rose have a few minutes, just t' talk."

Michael glanced down at her, one eyebrow raised in question.

She didn't want to be alone with her pa, of course. She'd never liked being alone with him. She couldn't think of a time when being alone with him hadn't been unpleasant, if not downright painful.

But she nodded at Michael, agreeing to her

father's request. "We'll just sit on the porch a spell."

Michael hesitated before guiding her up the steps. After another glance down at her, he left her at the porch swing and went inside.

She hated the sound of the closing door.

Glen leaned his backside against the porch rail and crossed his arms in front of his chest. "Seems your old pa did all right by you, ain't that right, Rose? Look at you. Rich husband. House all your own."

"What is it you want, Pa?"

He frowned. "That don't sound like a grateful daughter should."

Rose clenched her hands together in the folds of her skirt. "Just *what* should I be grateful for?"

"Just what I said." He stepped closer to her. "I saw to it that you got yourself a rich husband."

"You forced me to marry a man I didn't even know."

"Well, it didn't look that way to me. You standin' there in his room without a stitch on."

She felt the heat of anger and embarrassment coloring her cheeks. She didn't want to be reminded of that night. "What is it you want?" she asked again.

"Well, I'll tell you. The boardin'house ain't doin' no business, and your ma don't seem to have the money she should. There's things we're needin' from the mercantile, just to see us through this dry spell. Just until we get us some strangers comin' through town."

"I can't help you. Mark stole every last penny I saved before you ever came back to Homestead."

Glen chuckled. "I'm not talkin' about a few dollars put back in a tin box. Just ask your husband for—"

"No."

"Listen, don't you go sassin' me, Rose. That's no way to show your gratitude for what I've done for you. You just smile pretty and tell that man o' yours that you—"

"*No!*"

He grabbed her arms so quickly she had no time to prepare for the pain as his fingers bit into her arms. He jerked her up from the swing. "I've told you before not t' talk back to me." He swung her around, pushing her back toward the railing. He gave her a harsh shake. "Now, I'm not askin' anything unreasonable. If you don't help, what do ya think's gonna happen to your ma?"

"Ma's done just fine without you all these years. If you'd never come back, we'd all be happier."

He raised his hand to slap her, but before it could strike, it was stopped in midair.

Michael pulled Glen Townsend away from Rose, letting go of his wrist only so he could grab the man by his shirt collar with both hands. He yanked Rose's father toward him until they stood almost nose to nose, Michael leaning down toward the shorter man.

"Let me explain something to you," he said in a low, threatening voice. "You ever lay a hand on my wife, I'll break every bone in your body. Is that perfectly clear, Townsend?"

"A pa's got a right—"

Michael's grip tightened, lifting the other man's feet off the floor. "You gave up your rights the day she married me. Now get off my porch." He gave him a shove.

Glen stumbled backward, catching his balance with a hand on the post beside the steps.

Michael didn't waste a moment on the man's furious glower. He moved toward Rose, placing his hands gently on her upper arms. Her face was chalk white. "Are you all right?"

She nodded.

"Let's go inside."

She glanced toward her father. From the corner of his eye, Michael saw Glen descend the steps and walk away, but he concentrated on the woman before him.

He could sense her fear. For some reason, it surprised him. Maybe because he'd seen how fearlessly she'd faced her brother. He'd known the father and son were cut from the same cloth, and he supposed he'd expected her to be as dauntless with Glen as with Mark. That wasn't the case.

"Come here," he said softly as he pulled

her toward him, pressing the side of her face against his chest. With one hand, he stroked her hair. With the other, he stroked her back, making small circles with his fingertips. "There's nothing to fear. I'm here."

Rose let out a shaky sigh. For some crazy reason, she did feel the fear leaving her.

Michael's arms around her felt so strong, so sure, so . . . so safe. With her ear pressed against his chest, she could hear the steady rhythm of his heart. It, too, sounded strong and sure and . . . and safe.

She had no idea how long they stood like that, there on the porch, his arms holding her close. Time didn't seem to matter. Nothing in the world mattered beyond the circle of Michael's arms. She was safe and secure here. No one could ever hurt her again.

Her heart skipped a beat.

Did she really believe that? Was it possible?

She pulled her head away from him, tipping it back so she could gaze up into his eyes. They were so wonderfully blue. She didn't think she'd ever seen eyes as blue as Michael's. Or eyes that looked at her with such tenderness.

You'd change your mind quick enough if you ever got kissed.

Rose couldn't seem to breathe.

His hands moved to the sides of her face, cupping her head gently, tipping it backward. She felt more than saw him bending toward her. It seemed to take forever for his mouth to draw near.

When his lips touched hers, her knees lost all strength. To keep from falling, she was forced to wrap her arms around his neck and hang on for dear life.

The kiss didn't last long, but when it was over, Rose felt as if the world and everything in it had changed. Above all, *she* had changed.

Michael lifted his head. His hands still cradled her face with infinite gentleness. His eyes stared down, questioning eyes, looking deep into her soul. She felt more naked now than she had the night she'd run into his room at the boardinghouse.

And in that moment, fear returned. She was more afraid of Michael than she'd ever been with her father or her brother, because she knew Michael had the capacity to hurt her far more than anything those two had ever done. Pa and Mark had left bruises on her skin, but Michael, if she let him, could bruise and break her heart.

She stepped back from him, grasping the porch rail behind her with both hands. "I don't think we should have done that," she whispered in a raspy voice. Then, a bit stronger, she added, "We won't do it again."

Michael watched her, the silence hanging thick and tense between them. Finally, he nodded. "You're right. We won't do it again."

Twelve months would surely be an eternity.

Chapter Sixteen

Michael was gone from the house when Rose awakened the following morning, much to her relief. Sunday afternoon and evening had been uncomfortable for them both, their kiss seeming to linger between them whenever their gazes met. She wasn't certain she could have faced it again this morning. She was certain he felt the same, and that was why he'd left so early, just so he could avoid her.

Remembering her invitation to join the quilting at Rachel Henderson's home that afternoon, Rose took extra care with her toilet, donning her prettiest dress, the one Rachel's mother had given her for a wedding present, and brushing her hair until the chestnut mane gleamed with warm undertones. She arranged it carefully in a bun atop her head, knowing it made her look slightly older than her actual age. She hoped it would also add a measure of confidence.

She didn't know why she felt so nervous about today. She wasn't a complete stranger to them, after all. She knew both of the other women who were going to be there. Priscilla Jacobs was the reverend's wife and Ophelia Turner was married to the blacksmith.

No, she had no call to be nervous. Still, she was.

Promptly at ten o'clock, Rose left the house and began the walk out to the Henderson place. She figured, if she moved briskly, it would take her just shy of two hours to reach her destination. Yesterday, Michael had offered to hire a buggy from the livery, but she'd declined. She'd told him she enjoyed walking. The truth, however, was she hadn't the foggiest notion how to drive a horse and buggy. Her ma had never owned one. There'd been no reason. Virginia had never gone anywhere.

The bad thing about walking was it gave her plenty of time to think. Unfortunately, her thoughts inevitably turned to Michael.

Michael saw her walk through town on her way to Rachel Henderson's place. She was wearing that pretty new dress of hers, the one that matched the gold flecks in her eyes. It had been a gift from Emma Barber on their wedding day. He wished he'd given it to her.

There were lots of things he'd like to give Rose Rafferty. He'd like to give her fancy dresses and glittering jewels and outrageous hats with ostrich plumes and fabric flowers. He'd like to give her the freedom to smile more often. He'd like to give her laughter. He'd like to give her more than just one brief solitary kiss. He'd like to take her into his bed and make love to her. He'd like. . . .

"Well, I'll be damned," he muttered as he watched Rose disappear from view.

When was it, exactly, that he'd fallen in love with his wife?

Rose had never been an expert with a needle, and at first, she felt terribly awkward, sitting around the quilt, watching the other women so confidently working, their needles seeming to fly in and out of the fabric. But before long, she began to relax and enjoy the easy camaraderie that pervaded the parlor of the Henderson house.

The conversation centered on familiar, comfortable topics—Homestead and the families they all knew. They talked about crops and about calving. They talked about who had been ill and who was moving away and who had just arrived in the valley.

Although Rose added very little to the conversation, the other women made her feel as if her opinions and comments mattered. As the afternoon progressed, Rose felt less and less like an outsider.

"Tommy McLeod broke his arm yesterday," Ophelia announced as she threaded her needle again. "He fell out of a tree by Pony Creek." She bit off the thread with her teeth. "Chad had to carry him over to Doc Varney's office."

"That boy is a caution," Priscilla returned. "I don't know how Doris McLeod manages. I'm thirty years younger than she is, and I can scarcely keep up with my two."

Rachel nodded. "My mother used to say she hoped I'd have a daughter just like me one day, and then I'd know what she went through." A warm smile spread across her face. "I just might do that, come next winter."

"Rachel!" Ophelia dropped her needle on the quilt and leaned over to grab Rachel's hand. "Really? A baby? You and Norman are going to make me an aunt?"

Rachel nodded again. Her eyes looked suspiciously moist.

"What a joy," Priscilla added. "I pray you'll have an easy confinement."

"If I'm anything like my mother, I'll have no hardship at all. She always said there wasn't anything to childbearing for her but lying still and letting nature take its course."

"And my mother always said childbearing is both a blessing and a curse for women." Ophelia picked up her needle and began to take slow, careful stitches. "But I wouldn't care how terrible it was, if only I could give Chad a son."

The other two women murmured sympathetically. Rose simply listened and observed.

207

"Not that being Chad's wife isn't wonderful, mind you," Ophelia continued. "I've loved him almost from the moment I first laid eyes on him at that barn dance all those years ago, but he was so stuck on Addie Rider he didn't even notice me." She sighed.

Rachel nodded. "I know exactly what you mean, Ophelia. It wasn't easy for me to catch your brother's eye."

"When Chad and I were first married, I didn't think I cared if I ever had to share him, even with our own children. I thought it would be enough for me to live out the rest of my life right there in his bed. That anything so wonderful could also make a baby. . . ." A blush brightened her cheeks.

Rose saw the knowing look that passed between the other two women. Rachel tittered and Priscilla clucked.

Although her face was beet red by this time, Ophelia continued, "Well, it's true. It is wonderful, and you all know it." Her gaze moved from woman to woman, looking last at Priscilla Jacobs. "Even the Holy Bible says how wonderful the union of a man and a woman is. Right there in the "Song of Solomon." I don't know why we're never supposed to talk about it, as if it was some terrible secret. We talk about having babies all the time. Why should this be any different? We're all married."

Rachel leaned forward, her voice little more than a whisper. Her own cheeks were flaring with color. "I don't know *why* it's different. It just *is*."

Rose felt as if she were eavesdropping on a conversation spoken in a secret code. Oh, she knew what it was they were talking about. She just didn't know it firsthand. She hadn't ever wanted to know. She'd always suspected it was something a married woman just had to endure. That was the way it was for her ma. She'd thought that was the way it was for all women.

But Ophelia didn't seem to think so. She thought it was wonderful.

Unbidden and unwanted, the memory of Michael's embrace, his lips upon hers, returned to taunt her. She thought of the strength of his arms, the steady pounding of his heart inside his chest. She thought of the way he'd smelled, like soap and water and a dash of bay rum.

Would it be wonderful to lie in Michael's bed?

Her own face felt warm. Glancing up, she found Rachel watching her. She smiled, somehow communicating that they shared a special knowledge.

Once again, Rose felt like a fraud.

For what his crew lacked in experience, they made up for in enthusiasm. The men were quick to follow Michael's instructions, and by late afternoon, they'd made a lot of headway on the foundation. It wouldn't be long before the framing of the Rafferty Hotel was up.

Michael stepped back and stared at the building site. With his practiced eye, he envisioned the hotel, its board siding painted a pristine white, its name in black letters emblazoned above the awning.

There would be ten bedrooms. Most, he realized, would remain empty at first, but he'd planned the building so that an addition could be made later, expanding the number of sleeping rooms. The lobby would be airy without wasting too much space. The dining room would be the largest individual room by far. It was where the money would be made initially. Even before the influx of newcomers to the area, brought by the train that would soon begin its way up from Boise City, the restaurant would be important to his profits. Later, miners and loggers, ranchers and farmers would all pass through Homestead on their way north, filling his hotel to capacity.

He shook his head, silently mocking himself for the inordinate pleasure he felt thinking about the success of this little venture. When he'd dreamed of one day running a Rafferty-owned hotel, this certainly hadn't been what he'd had in mind.

He thought of the Palace Hotel in San Francisco. Built on the grand scale of a European palace—with its sweeping staircases, its glittering chandeliers, its Turkish carpets, its gilded-and-mirrored assembly halls and ballroom, and its expansive dining room, which featured foods prepared by some of the best chefs in the world—the San Francisco Palace made his plans for the Rafferty Hotel in Homestead seem paltry, if not downright pathetic.

And yet, he reminded himself, for the people of Homestead, Idaho Territory, this hotel *was* important. It meant progress for them. And for travelers through these parts, it meant a comfortable place to stay and a chance for a decent meal.

Gads, what was he thinking? That he could actually be content in a place like this? Not a chance. He belonged in San Francisco or New York. Just because he'd fallen in love with a small-town girl didn't mean they had to stay there. After all, Rose was looking forward to leaving Homestead just as much as he was. She'd be willing to go anywhere else, once this year was finished.

Of course, she thought she'd be leaving here alone. It was going to take some work, convincing her that an annulment wasn't what she wanted after all.

He remembered the way she'd felt in his arms and grinned. Maybe it wouldn't be so hard to convince her at that. Maybe. . . .

"Hey, Mr. Rafferty."

The shout pulled him from his reverie.

"What do you want us to do with this rock pile?"

211

He started walking toward Paul Stanford. "We'll have to cart them away. Bring the wagon over here and we'll toss them in."

"Yes, sir."

Michael waited as the young man jumped up onto the wagon seat, picked up the reins, and guided the team of horses over to the tall stack of rocks that stood close to what would be the back door of the hotel kitchen. He supposed the rocks had been dumped there from some other building site, back when no one had dreamed the town would spread out this far. But where they'd come from didn't matter. They just needed to be moved.

He began grabbing the large stones and tossing them into the back of the wagon. As he worked, he could feel trickles of sweat beginning to streak the sides of his face and the back of his neck. The day had turned hotter than he'd expected. Still, he was rather enjoying the physical labor. It had been a long time since he'd rolled up his sleeves and actually taken part in the construction of one of the Rafferty hotels.

Several smaller rocks tumbled from their high perch, rattling their way to the ground. At least, he thought that was what caused the commotion.

He reached in with both hands to grab a large rock at the base of the pile. The strikes happened so quickly he scarcely knew what had happened until he heard Paul's shout of alarm.

"Get back, Mr. Rafferty. It's a whole nest of rattlers."

He stared down at his bare right arm. He'd been bitten several times from the look of it.

"Mr. Rafferty's been bit by a rattler!" Paul shouted to the other crew members. "Go get Doc Varney!"

He could see the snakes now.

Damn, his arm burned like the devil.

Most of them were just babies. They couldn't be all that dangerous. The burning would stop soon. They were just baby snakes.

"My pa says rattlers are poisonous soon as they hatch," Paul said as he pulled Michael farther from the nest of coiled snakes.

Had he spoken his thoughts aloud? He glanced at the young man, then back at his arm.

It was as if someone had jabbed him several times with a hot needle. Unpleasant, but it probably wasn't all that serious. Just baby snakes.

"You'd better sit down in the shade here, Mr. Rafferty. Best thing to do is stay calm. Doc'll probably cut the bites and suck the venom out."

His arm felt slightly numb.

A bottle of whiskey appeared before him. "Have a swig of this, Mr. Rafferty," someone said. He wasn't sure who. "They say it's best for snakebites."

He heard some gunshots. His heart jumped,

racing madly in his chest. He looked toward the rock pile. Several men were shooting at the snakes. The noise started a severe pounding in his head.

He took a swig of the whiskey, just as he'd been told.

"Let's get him over to his house."

His vision was starting to blur, but he thought he saw the town doctor standing near him. When had he arrived?

"How long ago did it happen?"

"Ten, maybe fifteen minutes."

So long?

No, that wasn't right. It had just happened. Just now. They bit him. He sat down. Somebody gave him the whiskey.

No, they shot the rattlers first, then gave him the whiskey.

No . . . no, he was right the first time. Whiskey, then shooting.

"Easy now, Mr. Rafferty. We're going to put you in the back of the wagon. Get you inside where I can work on you."

Lord, he was thirsty. Where had that bottle of whiskey gone? He needed a drink. He'd give a silver dollar for a drink, even just a glass of cold water.

"That's right, Mr. Rafferty. You just lie still on the bed. Let me have a look at that arm."

Bed? Where had his bed come from? How had he arrived in his room? He couldn't remember.

214

He was covered with sweat. His body was drenched. Was May always so hot in this country?

No, it wasn't the heat of day. It was the work he'd been doing. Moving all those rocks. That's why he was sweating. That's why he felt so tired, so dizzy, so strange.

"Not good. . . ."

Was that Doc's voice?

"Two bites. Maybe three. I'm afraid they may have hit a vein."

Doc sounded so far away.

"We'll have to wait and see."

Michael thought he was going to be sick. Waves of nausea hit him as he spiraled into darkness.

"Michael? Michael, it's Rose. I'm here. Can you hear me?"

Rose. Sweet, little Rose. He'd wanted to tell her he loved her.

Chapter Seventeen

An accident at one of the logging camps to the north took Doc Varney away before sunset. If Yancy Jones hadn't stayed to help Rose care for Michael, she didn't know what she would have done.

"You're no bigger than a mite, Mrs. Rafferty. You wouldn't have the strength to lift him if he needed it. If you don't mind, I'll just stay over, just in case you need me."

"Thank you, Mr. Jones. That's very kind of you."

"I'll make my bed on the couch. You holler if I can be of help."

The violent vomiting started just after midnight. Seated in a chair beside Michael's bed, Rose had drifted off to sleep some time before. The ugly sounds brought her instantly awake.

Michael rolled onto his side, his head hanging over the edge of the bed, and began to retch. Rose shoved the washbasin beneath him on the floor, then grabbed his shoulders and tried to keep him from falling out of bed as the wrenching spasms hit him.

"Yancy! Yancy, help me!"

She wondered if a man could survive such fierce torture. It felt as if his own body was trying to rip itself into separate pieces. He flailed the air with one arm, nearly striking the side of her head.

"Yancy!"

"I'm here, ma'am."

Yancy's hands replaced hers on Michael's shoulders. Rose stumbled backward, her heart racing as she stared at her husband.

Michael was going to die.

"Why don't you go get some cool water?" Yancy asked. "He's gonna need it when he's through here."

"Yes. Yes, I'll get some water," she whispered, then hurried from the room.

In the kitchen, she leaned her hands against the table and let her head drop forward. She drew in a deep breath, trying hard to quiet the rapid beating of her heart. It was ridiculous to be this frightened or upset. The doctor had said it wasn't good, but he'd also said there was hope. Michael wasn't necessarily going to die. Not if she took proper care of him.

And if he *did* die? Well, she would be sorry, of course. He hadn't been unkind to her. But it would simplify her life, wouldn't it? She would be a respectable widow instead of a scorned divorcee. She would be a *wealthy* widow, if all she'd heard was true. She would be able to move away and start her own business. Her mother could come and live with her if she wanted. Everything would be perfect.

She closed her eyes. *God, forgive me.*

She couldn't believe she'd thought such things. It wasn't true. She wasn't that mean and small and cruel. She wouldn't wish a man dead just to simplify her own life.

Michael wasn't going to die. She wouldn't let him.

Pushing away from the table, Rose went to the sink and began pumping the handle until water streamed from the spout. Then she grabbed a pitcher and filled it to the brim.

He wouldn't die. She would make sure he lived. She owed him that. He *had* helped her— more than once. He'd protected her from her brother and her father. He'd been kind to her. He'd even kissed her.

She would see that he got well . . . and then she would make sure she got as far away from Michael Rafferty as she could.

"It's not right, Father. The Palace Hotels belong to me. You told me so when I was only six years old."

"I didn't know about Dillon then."

"But I'm your legitimate son."

"Dillon is not at fault for his birth. I am. If I'd known—"

"If you'd known, you'd never have married my mother, and I'd have never been born. That's how you'd prefer it, isn't it? Answer me. Isn't it?"

"No. No, Michael, I have always been enormously proud of you. But I'm proud of Dillon, too. If only the two of you would learn to compromise. . . . You were friends once. You could make Palace Hotels—"

"It's too late for that. You've made your decision. I'll go off to that godforsaken town you've chosen, and I'll make certain that what's mine stays mine."

"Michael. . . ."

"You'll hear from me in a year."

"Michael. . . ."

Rose drew the cool rag across Michael's fevered brow. He lay with absolute stillness, his face pasty white, his lips nearly blue, his breathing so shallow it was nearly nonexistent. The spells of vomiting had passed, replaced by moments of delirium, excessive thirst, and cold sweats.

After two days with little sleep, Rose was exhausted, but she refused to leave Michael, not even at night when Yancy was there. She wanted to be with him if he needed her. She had to make certain he got well. If he were to die, she knew she would always feel guilty because of the terrible thoughts she'd had.

Michael was dreaming a great deal. She knew because he talked and mumbled so much of the time. Sometimes, he talked to his father, other times to a man named Dillon. Once, he called for Lillian.

Who was Lillian?

Today, when the doctor had finished examining his patient, he'd said he thought Michael was through the worst. Rose wished she could believe him, but it was hard to believe when Michael still looked so pale and drawn.

Michael, you must get well.

In her mind, she could see him as he'd been the day he'd kissed her. He'd been dressed in his Sunday best: dark suit jacket, white shirt and collar, black tie. No hat. The hat had been removed while he was in the house. She remembered how the sun had glinted off his golden hair. She remembered the strength of his arms and the strong pounding of his heart beneath her ear.

Now, she reached forward and swept that same golden hair off his brow, her fingers lingering on the crown of his head as she stared at him.

He was so handsome, even with two days' growth of stubble on his face. So very handsome. Everything about him was wonderfully, perfectly made.

Rose felt her cheeks grow warm as she allowed her eyes to travel to his bare chest and the sheet that laid across his abdomen. She'd never seen a man's chest before yesterday. Since then, she had seen much more. She had seen everything about Michael that made him so different from her.

Of course, she'd pretended not to notice those differences as she'd bathed his fevered body. He was, after all, a very sick man, and she was his wife, merely doing what any wife would do. How he was made was of no consequence to her.

But she *had* noticed the differences, and they frightened her because suddenly she'd found herself wondering what it would be like to lie beside Michael in his bed, to have him do more than just kiss her. The oblique references her mother had made to a wife's duty, coupled with those comments made by the women at the quilting, made more sense to her now. They also raised more questions.

What would it be like with Michael?

She closed her eyes and drew back her hand from his head. It must be terribly sinful to be wondering the sort of things she was wondering when her husband could be dying.

And besides, she wanted no part of such intimacies. She was leaving Homestead and Michael Rafferty, just as soon as this year was over. Nothing could induce her to remain any longer than she had to. Absolutely nothing.

Kathleen put her arms around him. "Michael, this is Dillon. He's going to live with us. I hope you'll treat him like your own brother."

221

"Why is he going to live with us? Where's his own family?"

"His poor mother died of the influenza. His . . . his father. . . . Dillon never knew his father, but that isn't his fault. He's a good boy. Be kind to him, Michael. He's not been as privileged as you."

"We'll be great friends. I promise."

"Great friends," Michael said softly, turning his head on the pillow. "I promise."

Rose leaned forward. "Michael?" She brushed her fingertips across his forehead. "Michael?"

"I promise. . . ."

"Michael, can you hear me?"

She thought she saw his eyelids flutter.

"Michael, please wake up." She leaned closer.

He did as she asked. He opened his eyes and looked straight at her.

"He was my friend," he said in a voice made husky by illness and lack of use. "Why did I do it?"

And then his eyes closed again.

"Michael?"

But he had slipped away from her once again.

"Have I ever told you you're the loveliest young lady in all San Francisco, Miss Overhart?" He asked the question as they waltzed around the ballroom of the Palace Hotel. "Why waste your

222

time on someone like Dillon when you know I'm
the better man?"

"I know no such thing, Michael Rafferty. And
what have you against your brother?"

"You know that Palace Hotels will come to
me, not Dillon. He'll probably have to leave San
Francisco, make his fortunes elsewhere."

"They're true then, the rumors I've heard?
Dillon's adopted?" Her eyes widened. "But the
two of you look so much alike. I never believed
it."

He could have said more, but he did more
damage by saying less.

"He's going to be all right, Rose," Doc Varney
said as he shoved his stethoscope into his black
leather bag. "You keep spooning broth into him
and cooling him with sponge baths. Best thing
for him now is rest while the poison works its
way out of his system."

"But shouldn't he be awake by now?"

"He's been a mighty sick man. A snakebite
isn't anything to make light of. Three of them
should have killed him. If they'd hit that
vein as I thought at first, he would never
have made it. He's mighty lucky to be alive.
Sleep is most likely the best medicine for
him now."

Rose stared down at Michael, wishing he
would wake up and thankful he was going to
survive. At least she had nothing more to feel
guilty about.

"And what about you, Rose? Are you getting any sleep?"

"Enough."

Doc Varney lifted her chin with his index finger. "You let Mr. Jones watch over your husband tonight while you get some sleep. There's no point him being here to help you if you won't let him lift a finger."

She shrugged her shoulders. "I'm all right. Really, I am."

"I mean it, young woman. You get some sleep tonight."

"All right. I will."

She followed the doctor from the bedroom, down the stairs, and out onto the front porch. She watched as he descended the steps and walked over to his buggy, tossing his bag onto the seat, then climbing up beside it.

"I'll stop by again tomorrow morning. I want to see you rested by then."

"I will be."

He picked up the reins and turned his horse toward his home and office at the opposite end of town.

Rose let out a weary sigh as she sank onto the porch swing. She closed her eyes, allowing herself a moment to enjoy the fresh air and the warm touch of the morning sun as it peeked beneath the porch awning. She was soothed by the sound of bees buzzing over the morning glories that twined around the porch railing.

Doc was right. She did need some sleep. She

Thrill to the most sensual, adventure-filled Historical Romances on the market today…
FROM  LEISURE BOOKS

As a home subscriber to the Leisure Historical Romance Book Club, you'll enjoy the best in today's BRAND-NEW Historical Romance fiction. For over twenty-five years, Leisure Books has brought you the award-winning, high-quality authors you know and love to read. Each Leisure Historical Romance will sweep you away to a world of high adventure…and intimate romance. Discover for yourself all the passion and excitement millions of readers thrill to each and every month.

SAVE AT LEAST *$5.00* EACH TIME YOU BUY!

Each month, the Leisure Historical Romance Book Club brings you four brand-new titles from Leisure Books, America's foremost publisher of Historical Romances. EACH PACKAGE WILL SAVE YOU AT LEAST $5.00 FROM THE BOOKSTORE PRICE! And you'll never miss a new title with our convenient home delivery service.

Here's how we do it. Each package will carry a 10-DAY EXAMINATION privilege. At the end of that time, if you decide to keep your books, simply pay the low invoice price of $16.96 ($17.75 US in Canada), no shipping or handling charges added*. HOME DELIVERY IS ALWAYS FREE*. With today's top Historical Romance novels selling for $5.99 and higher, our price SAVES YOU AT LEAST $5.00 with each shipment.

AND YOUR FIRST FOUR-BOOK SHIPMENT IS TOTALLY FREE!

IT'S A BARGAIN YOU CAN'T BEAT! A Super $21.96 Value!

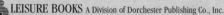 **LEISURE BOOKS** A Division of Dorchester Publishing Co., Inc.

GET YOUR 4 FREE* BOOKS NOW— A $21.96 VALUE!

Mail the Free* Book Certificate Today!

Get Four Books Totally
F R E E* —
A $21.96 Value!

(Tear Here and Mail Your FREE* Book Card Today!)

PLEASE RUSH
MY FOUR FREE*
BOOKS TO ME
RIGHT AWAY!

Leisure Historical Romance Book Club
P.O. Box 6613
Edison, NJ 08818-6613

AFFIX
STAMP
HERE

would let Yancy Jones sit with Michael tonight. He'd been trying to tell her to let him do that from the very first, but she hadn't wanted to leave Michael's side.

Yes, just a little sleep would do her a world of good. And she could do that, now that she knew Michael was going to be all right.

The morning sun caressed her cheek, and she imagined it was Michael's hands, cradling her face. A breeze brushed across her lips, and she thought of Michael's mouth, how gently it had pressed against hers.

Perhaps, when he was well, he might cradle her face and kiss her mouth once again. What could it hurt?

She opened her eyes and jumped up off the swing as if propelled from a slingshot, alarmed at how easily her thoughts had been lulled into thinking such things would be harmless.

Michael's kisses *weren't* harmless. They were dangerous. More dangerous than anything she'd ever known. She would do well to remember that.

Chapter Eighteen

Will looked across the elegant drawing room, his gaze pausing when it came to rest upon his daughter. Lark was staring out the window into the dark, moonless night. Her expression caused his heart to pinch.

If she knew he was watching her, she would be smiling, laughing up into the face of one man or another, but Will wasn't fooled. Lark's heart was breaking, and because of it, so was his.

It wasn't an easy thing for Will to do, but it was time he admitted that he'd been wrong. At least about coming to Boise. It was time he took his family back to Homestead, back to the Rocking R. He would find another way to deal with Lark's ridiculous infatuation with Yancy Jones. He wasn't ready to admit he'd been wrong about him, too. Didn't think he was wrong.

He felt a light touch on his arm. The sweet

fragrance of Addie's cologne—light and barely there, but still recognizable—caused him to smile before he turned his head to meet her gaze.

"You always did have to study things awhile before you could see them clearly," she said, mirroring his smile.

"And you could always see through me," he returned.

"Not always."

"Just about."

"When do we leave for home?"

"Monday morning. No point putting it off."

Addie squeezed his arm. "Go tell Lark now. Don't make her wait."

"What if I'm wrong?" His smile faded, turning into a frown. "What if she doesn't get over Yancy?"

"Would it be so terrible? If she truly loves him, wouldn't you want her to marry him rather than someone you chose for her?" Addie's apple-green eyes were filled with love. "I know you want Lark to find what we've had all these years. It just may be she's already found it."

"She's so young," he said softly, his gaze returning to his daughter.

"Yes, she's young, but that doesn't mean she can't know her own heart." She gave him a little push. "Go on. Tell her."

Reluctantly, Will made his way through the crowd of guests.

227

Lark glanced up as he stepped to her side, then looked away just as quickly. "Is it time to leave?" Her voice sounded hopeful.

"Yes, it's time to leave."

"I'll get my wrap."

"No." He placed a hand on her shoulder before she could move away. "I didn't mean leave the party."

She turned a puzzled look in his direction.

"I meant it's time we leave Boise City. We're returning to the Rocking R."

Lark's face lit up with joy—a look he hadn't seen in weeks.

"We're going home?" she asked. "When, Papa? When are we going?"

"Monday morning."

She grabbed his hands. "Oh, Papa, thank you."

He felt that same painful pinch in his chest. He was going to miss her when the day came for her to leave him. He only hoped he could postpone that leaving for at least a short while longer.

He suddenly had a vision of Lark as she'd been that day back in 1880. The little orphan in a plain brown dress two sizes too large. A slip of white paper pinned to her bodice. A calico bonnet, also too large, obscuring her face from view. Two black braids hanging down her back.

And he'd been just as frightened as she. He hadn't known a single thing about raising a little girl.

He hadn't done half bad by her, he told himself. She was healthy and bright, sensible and sensitive. He'd taught her sound values, and luckily, she hadn't picked up any of his bad habits. He could thank Addie for that.

He pulled his daughter into his embrace, pressing the side of her face against his chest with a large, callused hand. "I love you, Lark," he whispered.

"I love you, too, Papa," she returned in a choked voice. "I love you, too."

Yancy leaned back in the chair, his long legs stretched out before him, crossed at the ankles. His watchful gaze was fastened on the man in the bed. Michael's chest rose and fell in a steady rhythm, and it seemed to Yancy that there was a bit more color in the sick man's face.

He figured he wouldn't be staying at the Rafferty house after tonight. Michael was obviously on the mend, and Rose wouldn't be needing him once her husband regained consciousness. He'd lay odds that would happen by sunup.

He'd be glad when it happened, too. Not that he'd minded helping out, what little Rose had let him do. But now it was time for him to get back to his own place. He still had plenty of fixin' up to get done on the house, and with working two jobs in town, the repairs were taking far longer to get done than he'd expected.

Yancy crossed his arms over his chest and closed his eyes as he laid his head back against the wall behind him. He could use a few winks himself.

Guess if nothing else, he was proving that Will Rider wrong about him. Yancy Jones wasn't just a saddle bum. He already had thirty-nine dollars put back, and he still had fifteen dollars in wages coming from Michael for the work he'd done this week.

Michael's crew of workmen had decided to keep going while their boss was laid up. Yancy had become sort of the unofficial foreman, he supposed because he was helping out at the Rafferty house each night. He figured the others saw that as a sign he knew what he was doing.

Little did they know.

He grinned. Actually, he'd surprised himself by how easily he'd been able to read the blueprints. He hadn't made it much past the flyleaf of a first-grade primer, and he'd often felt as if his brain capacity wouldn't make a drinkin' cup for a hummingbird. But once he'd set his mind to it, reading the blueprints hadn't been hard at all.

He reckoned Lark would be plenty proud of him.

Lord, but he missed her. He wondered if she was still feeling as if she'd perish without him.

He smiled again. He could almost hear her impassioned statement.

. . . . I would die without you. That's how I'm feeling now. As if I'm going to perish. . . .

There wasn't much Lark Rider did without flair and passion. He'd have loved her anyway, of course, but it didn't hurt that he thought she'd be just about the finest blanket companion a man could find. He was plenty ready to let her hog-tie him with matrimonial ropes.

Shoot! He wasn't so sure he wasn't the one who would perish if she didn't come back before long.

Rose awakened in the middle of the night, her skin covered with a light sheen of sweat, her heart hammering at an alarming rate. She'd been dreaming about Michael and rattlesnakes. She'd been dreaming about sickness and death.

She reminded herself that the doctor had said Michael would be all right, that he was out of danger. She told herself he'd been sleeping peacefully when she'd retired for the night. She silently made note that Yancy would have called her if there'd been any change.

None of it mattered. She couldn't shake the images of her nightmare. She had to see Michael. She had to make certain he was all right.

Grabbing her robe from the chair beside her bed, she slipped into it and tied the belt around her waist. Then she picked up the lamp and, with the flame turned low, hurried across the hall to the other bedroom.

Yancy was asleep in his chair, his chin resting on his chest. She spared him only the quickest of glances before turning her attention to the man in the bed.

She leaned over him, holding her lamp so she could study his face. He didn't look at all as he'd appeared in her dream. In fact, he looked better than she'd seen him look since the accident. His coloring was almost normal. His breathing was deep and restful.

She let out a tiny sigh of relief.

As if he'd heard her, Michael opened his eyes and looked directly into hers. Startled, Rose straightened, her heart quickening with joy. She'd never seen anything so wonderful as the blue of his eyes.

"Don't go," he whispered.

She leaned forward again. "I wasn't leaving." She brushed his hair off his forehead. "How are you feeling?"

A frown puckered his brow. "Not great. What. . . ." He paused a moment, then answered his own unfinished question. "Rattlers."

Rose nodded. "Yes. You've been very ill."

Yancy sat up in his chair. "Mrs. Rafferty. . . ."

She looked across the bed. "He's awake, Mr. Jones."

The cowboy stood and leaned toward Michael. "You had your wife clean worried, Mr. Rafferty. Fact is whole town's been askin' about you."

"How long?"

"Five days ago," Rose answered. She set the lamp on the washstand, then filled a glass with water from the pitcher that stood there. "Here. Drink this." She lifted his head off the pillow with one hand as she held the glass to his lips with the other.

For a moment, he simply stared at her. Then he raised his hand and placed it over hers on the glass, lowered his gaze, and drank. When he was finished, he lay back, as if that small bit of activity had completely drained him of energy. He couldn't seem to keep his eyes open.

"Stay . . . Rose. . . ." he said softly, then drifted off to sleep.

What else could she do? She glanced at Yancy, who nodded and left the room. She sat in the chair he had vacated and watched as her husband slept.

The next time Will awakened, sunlight was streaming through the window. He lay still, staring up at the ceiling, trying to recall all that had happened. Piece by piece, the memories fell into place.

The final memory was of Rose, standing over his bed, her dark hair woven into a loose braid and hanging over her shoulder as she gazed down at him.

Don't go. . . .

I wasn't leaving. . . .

He turned his head on the pillow and found

233

her. She was sitting on the chair, her arms resting on the bed beside him, her head cradled in her arms. She was sound asleep, and he took advantage of the moment to study her.

He always had been attracted to her heart-shaped face and her small, pink mouth. Come to think of it, he was equally partial to her dainty nose and the stubborn cut of her chin. He loved the way her long eyelashes curved against her cheeks as she slept, too.

She looked tired, and somehow he knew she had been with him throughout his illness. Five days? Wasn't that what she had said? And she'd been there all the while.

You must care for me at least a little, he thought, *to have stayed with me all that time. What would you say if I told you I love you?*

He loved her. He didn't know why it had taken him by surprise. He always had been a sucker for poor orphans and underdogs who fought against the odds.

And look what that had gotten him in the past. Trouble mostly. Look at the mess he was in with Dillon because of it. If he hadn't grown to love his brother, if he hadn't trusted him, none of this would have happened. He wouldn't be fighting now for what rightfully belonged to him.

Yes, he'd loved Dillon. For six years, they'd been as close as any two people ever had. For the next ten years, they'd been rivals in everything they'd done.

Trouble. . . .

He focused his eyes on Rose again. She stirred, rubbing her cheek against the backs of her hands.

Falling in love with her wasn't the smartest thing he could do. He had enough trouble in his life. He didn't need another complication.

But he did love her. Wrong or not, trouble or not, he loved her. And somehow, he was going to have to make her love him, too.

Chapter Nineteen

It was the boredom that was driving Michael mad. Stark raving mad. For two days, he'd done nothing but eat broth and stare out the window at a blank blue sky and think about things he'd rather not think about. His father for one. Dillon for another.

"Damn it! Can't you fix me anything to eat but soup?" he groused as he looked at the lunch tray Rose had brought into the bedroom.

She glared down at him. "Mr. Rafferty, has anyone told you that you're as surly as a grizzly bear just out of hibernation?"

She was right, and he knew it. But at the moment, he couldn't care less.

"I need to get out of this bed. I've work to do."

"You know Doc Varney said rest was the best thing for you, and you're going to stay right there till he says otherwise."

"I'm *rested!*" He started to toss the covers

aside, then remembered he was bare-assed naked beneath the sheet.

A smile tugged at the corners of Rose's mouth when she saw his aborted movement. Her amusement didn't do anything to improve his foul mood.

"Bring me my trousers."

She held her chin at a lofty angle. "They're on the dresser. Get them yourself."

"I will. Just as soon as you leave the room."

"Not until you promise to eat your lunch."

It was a standoff, and Michael knew she had won this round. He wasn't about to get out of bed in front of her, not when he wasn't at all sure his legs would support him. It was one thing to be naked with a woman he was making love to. It was entirely something different to have a woman see him naked when he was too weak to do much more than feed himself. He didn't even want to think about how she'd cared for him while he was unconscious.

"Hand it here," he ordered, his mood darkening.

She actually grinned at him as she moved the tray onto his lap. "I'll check later to see how you're doing."

"Don't bother," he snapped. "I'll be over at the building site."

"Of course you will," she sallied back as she left the room, laughter in her voice.

He ground his teeth together. If he was just strong enough, he'd. . . .

He stopped stock-still as he stared at the empty doorway. Blast her, she was right. He *was* too weak to get dressed, let alone go over to the building site.

A wry smile curved the corners of his mouth. She was right about something else. He *was* as surly as an old grizzly bear.

This sure wasn't the way to make a woman love him, especially not one who was just as stubborn as he was.

He lifted the bowl of barley-and-beef soup off the tray. He supposed she was right about this, too. He needed to eat if he wanted his strength back. And he had to admit, it *did* smell good.

Before he set the bowl down some time later, he'd eaten every last bite. He was just sliding the tray onto the washstand when Rose reappeared.

She hesitated inside the doorway. "Michael, I'm sorry."

She did look contrite. She also looked pretty. Maybe being laid up wouldn't be so bad with Rose for company. He'd enjoy just looking at her.

"No, it's me who's sorry," he said, meaning it. "I was being unreasonable. You were right. You were right about everything."

Rose shook her head. "I feel so guilty over the way I acted."

"*You* feel guilty?" *He* was the one who was as surly as an old grizzly.

"I swore to myself I would take good care of

you, make sure you got well. It's the least I can do after everything that's happened, you being forced to marry me and all."

He winced inwardly. Guilt and obligation weren't exactly what he wanted Rose to be feeling toward him.

Michael patted the side of his bed. "The problem is I'm bored. Why don't you sit down and talk with me awhile? That would cure my boredom."

She looked surprised that he would ask it. "I really shouldn't. I've got laundry to do."

"It can keep."

"Well, I. . . ."

"Please."

Rose's instincts told her to turn and leave the room and ignore the pleading look in his blue eyes. She owed Michael Rafferty plenty, but keeping him company just because he was bored wasn't part of their bargain. And she knew how dangerous it was to be this close to him. He made her think things she shouldn't be thinking. He made her feel things she shouldn't be feeling. The smart thing would be to turn and go.

She sat down on the chair beside the bed.

"I can't stay long," she said. "There's work to be done."

He wasn't smiling at her, yet he seemed to be. The way he looked at her was like a tender caress. "Tell me, Rose. If you had no work awaiting you, what would you do for a whole day of fun?"

No work awaiting her? She couldn't recall a day when that had been true. Not even on Sundays. There'd always been too much that needed doing.

She shook her head. "I don't know."

"Come on. There must be something."

She shrugged. She didn't know how to respond to him. Besides, the way he was looking at her made her nervous. She felt as if he were drawing her closer to him, not physically but emotionally, and that frightened her.

He observed her silently for what seemed a long time, then said, "Tell me one of your favorite memories. From when you were a little girl."

The mental picture popped into her head instantly. She saw herself scrambling up onto Lark's horse. She was laughing with excitement as she listened to all of Lark's instructions. Oh, it had been a glorious day.

"Tell me," Michael urged gently.

"My ninth birthday." She couldn't help but smile as she remembered that day. "Lark's gift to me was a ride on Dark Feather, her horse. It was the nicest gift I ever had. I didn't do much but go in a tight circle, but I thought it was wonderful. Then Lark got up with me and we went round and round the churchyard." She thought of her friend riding up the street to tell her Yancy Jones had kissed her. "Lark still rides that same horse today."

"And did you ever get a horse of your own?"

The question yanked her thoughts abruptly back to the present. "No."

"But you wanted one."

She shook her head, hating it that he'd read her so well. She *had* wanted a horse of her own. For several years after, she'd remembered that birthday and wished her ma could buy her a horse. But money had never been plentiful in the Townsend house, not before her pa left and certainly not after. Even during the times when the boardinghouse had done well, there'd been too many other things that were needed, too many improvements to the house itself—a porch to build, the siding to paint, new curtains for the windows. There'd been nothing left over for Rose's childish desires.

Eventually, the wish for a horse of her own had been forgotten, tucked away with other wishes and dreams that would never come true.

"Did you ever ride again?"

"A few times with Lark." *But that was a long, long time ago,* she finished to herself.

Michael wanted to give her things she'd never had before. He wanted to give her days with nothing to do but lie beneath the sky and find funny shapes in the clouds. He wanted to take her horseback riding and watch her dark, chestnut hair fly out behind her like Pegasus's wings.

241

Her happiness meant more to him than his own.

Rose stood. "I really must get back to the laundry. It won't do itself."

He looked at her, surprised by the depth of his feelings. It was true. Her happiness *did* mean more to him than his own.

"Just holler if you need anything." She picked up the tray from the washstand and left the bedroom.

All his life, at least ever since his sixteenth birthday, there had been only one thing he'd truly wanted—Palace Hotels. Not even his love for his family had come before it. The business had been his single obsession, from the moment he'd awakened in the morning until the moment he'd retired for the night. He'd expected to marry and have children of his own, but he'd always known that the business would come first. That was natural and right. It was the way of the world.

It seemed impossible and totally improbable that a woman could become more important to him than his father's business. He'd known Rose less than four weeks, but he'd grown up in the grand hotels John Thomas had built. Twenty-six years worth of memories were of suites and ballrooms and kitchens and laundry rooms in Palace Hotels. The hotels were his life.

Or, at least, they had been.

Kathleen had told him he'd know when he'd

met the right woman. He'd always thought it was because she disapproved of Lillian Overhart.

I knew the moment I met your father that he was the man for me. When you meet her, you'll know. She'll mean more to you than your own life, if you truly love her.

He'd thought that was a woman's foolishness, simply female sentimentality. But now. . . .

If he had to choose, would he choose the hotels or Rose?

Michael closed his eyes. What was he thinking? He didn't have to choose. Rose was *already* his wife. He could accomplish the work he'd been sent here to do and still earn her love.

Glen settled back in his chair on the porch of the boardinghouse and took another swig from the whiskey bottle. His gaze moved west along Main Street.

He could see the corner of Rose's front porch from this vantage point. He wondered how his son-in-law was faring. He'd heard he was going to make it. A shame is what it was. Rose could've been a rich widow. That would have suited Glen just fine.

He took another swig of whiskey.

Ungrateful girl. Wouldn't lift a hand to help her own pa. She could have found some way to help him out. That bastard of a husband of hers deserved to die. If just one more of them snakes had sunk its fangs into him, he'd probably be six feet under by this time.

"Maybe I'll just have to help him along," he muttered as he raised the bottle to his lips. "There's other ways a man can die besides snakebite."

He drained the last of the whiskey, then wiped his mouth with his shirtsleeve as he cursed silently. He never should have agreed to come back to Homestead, even if Quinn did think it was for the best.

"We'll just lie low for a while," Quinn had said. "When we don't make a move, they'll get tired of watchin' us an' figure we don't have it. Then I'll come for ya in Homestead an' we'll go after the loot together."

Restlessly, Glen rose from his chair and paced the length of the porch. So help him, if Quinn didn't show up in July as they'd planned, Glen would find him and kill him with his bare hands. All those years in prison paying for that bank robbery, and here he was in Homestead, without a penny to spare. Thinking about all that money—a small fortune—hidden safely away in the mountains of Wyoming was how he'd kept himself sane in that tiny jail cell all those years. Now thinking about it was about to drive him crazy.

Of course, Mad Jack—just like every other inmate at the penitentiary—had heard the rumors about the bank loot never being recovered. That was why he'd accompanied Glen all the way to Idaho. He thought he could cash in on an easy thing. Glen had understood the reasons for Mad Jack's company on the journey to Idaho, but he hadn't cared. He'd known Mad Jack would leave empty-handed (although he hadn't expected him to slink off in the middle of the night as he had) and that was just what had happened. Mad Jack had left Homestead without ever knowing for sure whether or not there was any money to be had, let alone knowing where it was.

The same couldn't be said for Quinn Tracy. Quinn knew exactly where the money was hidden. What if he'd already gone there himself? What if he'd taken the money and left the territory, maybe even headed for South America or something?

Once again Glen's gaze swept to the west end of town and the glimpse of his daughter's house. Blast her! She could have helped her old man if she'd wanted to. Selfish little bitch. He was the one who'd made sure she had a husband. He was the one who'd made certain her reputation hadn't been sullied by allowing a man to take for free what most had to pay for, either by marriage or money. She owed him. She owed him plenty.

With another string of vile curses, Glen turned and went into the house. Virginia had to have some money someplace, and he meant to lay his hands on it or know the reason why.

Chapter Twenty

Lark had never been so happy to see anything in her entire life as she was to see Homestead. She wanted desperately to stop, to go and ask Rose about Yancy, whether or not he'd gotten her letter. At the same time, she was dreadfully afraid that she would find out he'd left Homestead, that she might never see him again.

But her father had no intention of stopping until they reached the ranch, and so Lark had to be satisfied with a quick glance as they passed through town. They waved at the people they saw on the street and called greetings to a few, but Will never slowed the team of horses for a moment. Everyone—even five-year-old Naomi—noticed the large, new building going up between the church and Sigmund Leonhardt's house, and discussions of what it might be filled up most of the time until the family arrived at the Rocking R.

Preston and Naomi hopped out of the carriage the moment it stopped. Lark wanted to do the same, but she waited for her father to help her down, not because she needed it, but because she wanted to impress upon him that she was a woman grown. She'd learned a few things during her weeks in exile. One was that she had to restrain her more enthusiastic nature if she wanted to convince her father she was old enough to know her own mind and heart.

Without being asked, Lark herded her brother and sister up to their rooms and told them to change out of their traveling clothes. She then went to her own room to do the same.

Freshly washed and clad in clean chemise and open-leg drawers, she was just reaching for a pink-and-fawn tartan gown when she heard a light rapping on her door.

"Lark?"

"Come in, Mother."

Addie opened the door. "Frosty wasn't expecting us back," she said, referring to the cook, "and we are sadly lacking in supplies. Would you mind going back into town with me?"

"Now?" Lark's heart started racing. Was there a chance she might see Yancy?

"Yes."

Suddenly, she knew that her mother was doing this just for her. They didn't need supplies so badly that Addie needed to return to town after a long journey. Frosty could have found plenty to feed the family until tomorrow. But her mother understood how anxious Lark was to see Yancy again, and this was her way of helping.

Lark stepped forward and clasped Addie's hands in hers. She squeezed them, silently thanking her mother for understanding all that was in her heart.

Her mother smiled gently, then said, "I told Frosty to have the buggy hitched up for us. As soon as you're ready, we'll go."

"I'll be ready in less than five minutes."

She turned away and immediately slipped her arms into the sleeves of the tartan gown. Her fingers clumsily fought with the hooks and eyes that fastened the bodice closed in the front. They were equally clumsy a few moments later when she tried to tie a satisfactory bow behind her waist with the skirt sash.

But she was as good as her word. She was downstairs in under five minutes, her face flushed with excitement as she hurried out to the buggy and climbed onto the seat beside Addie.

Glancing toward the house, she wondered if her father had objected to the ruse. Surely he, too, had seen through the flimsy excuse for the trip back to town.

"Your father and Mr. Simpson are looking over the cattle in the west range," Addie offered, as if reading Lark's thoughts. "I don't expect them back until late."

Lark glanced at her mother. "Will he be terribly angry with you when he finds out?"

"Maybe for a short while." She grinned, her eyes on the road before her. "But he'll come around. He wants you to be happy, Lark. That's all he's ever wanted."

"Mother. . . ."

Addie looked at her.

"Papa's a lucky man."

Her mother took hold of Lark's left hand. "So is Yancy Jones."

Rose was just leaving the Barber Mercantile, her basket holding the flour, cornmeal, and sugar she'd purchased, when the black buggy drew to a halt by the hitching post.

"Rose!"

She glanced toward the buggy in surprise. "Lark?"

Her friend jumped out of the buggy and fairly flew toward her, throwing her arms around Rose and hugging hard. "Oh, I'm so glad to see you. It seems like I've been away forever." She released her hold on Rose and stepped back. "I was going to walk down to the boardinghouse to see you. Now we can walk together."

"I. . . ." Rose's gaze darted from Lark to Addie, who was just stepping up onto the boardwalk.

"Hello, Rose. How is your mother?"

"She . . . she's fine, Mrs. Rider."

"Good. Tell her hello for me, would you?" She looked at her daughter. "You two have a pleasant visit. I'll come by the boardinghouse for you in about half an hour."

"Mrs. Rider," Rose said quickly, "I . . . I wasn't going to the boardinghouse."

Addie raised an eyebrow and waited for Rose to explain her meaning.

"I . . . I don't live there any longer."

"You don't live there?" Lark asked with surprise. "For heaven's sake, where do you live?"

Rose felt a flush rise in her cheeks. "With my husband."

It wasn't often, in Rose's personal experience, that Lark Rider was caught speechless, but this was apparently one of those times. Her friend simply stared at her with wide brown eyes, her mouth slightly agape.

Before either women could ask, she said, "My . . . my husband's name is Michael Rafferty. He's come to Homestead to build a hotel."

"My goodness," Addie said softly. "We've been away longer than I realized."

"He bought the Pendroy house. That's where we're living now."

Addie's expression was thoughtful as she looked at Rose, making the younger woman feel uncomfortable. She felt too much like the little girl being questioned by the schoolmarm. She was afraid Addie Rider would be able to

250

guess her thoughts as she'd often done when Rose was one of her students.

Finally, Addie relented, moving her gaze to her daughter. "It seems you two have a great deal more to talk about than you expected. I'll come by Rose's home in half an hour." She started to open the mercantile door, then turned, reached out, and touched Rose's cheek. "I hope you'll be very happy, Rose."

"Thank you," she replied, her throat thick with sudden emotion.

Without another word, Addie went inside the store, the door swinging closed behind her.

"Tell me!" Lark said immediately. "Tell me everything."

"There's not much to tell actually." Rose started walking along the boardwalk.

"Not much to tell. Criminy! Rose, you're *married!*" Her friend caught her by the elbow, drawing her to an abrupt halt. "I'm going to bust clean open if you don't tell me what happened. How did you meet? Who is he? Was it love at first sight?"

Rose stared down at the wooden planks of the walkway. What was she supposed to say to Lark? It wasn't romantic or poetic or anything like what her dearest friend expected.

"Rose?" Lark's voice had softened. "Rose, what's wrong?"

She took in a deep breath, then looked at Lark. "Nothing's wrong. There just isn't much to tell. Mr. Rafferty came to Homestead to build his hotel and stayed at the boardinghouse. That's how we met. He's a very nice man. It all happened quickly, and I'm quite happy."

Lark didn't look convinced. "When can I meet this wonderful Mr. Rafferty? We saw the men building over near the church. Is that where the hotel will be? Is he there now? You can take me over and introduce me."

"He's not there now," she replied with sudden inspiration, "but maybe Mr. Jones is."

"Yancy?" Lark turned to stare up the street. "He's here? He's still here in Homestead?"

Rose nodded, glad to have the conversation turned away from her. "He's working for Mr. Rafferty a few days a week and at the sawmill the rest of the time. Mrs. Barber says he's buying the old Hadley place, over near Pony Pass."

"Would you mind if we went by the hotel, just in case he's there?"

"No, I don't mind." As they started walking, Rose wondered if she should ask her friend about Boise City, but decided against it. She could see by the longing expression on Lark's face that she wasn't interested in anything except seeing Yancy Jones.

What would it be like to love someone the way Lark loved her cowboy? Did it happen to ordinary people or was Lark one of the special few?

She shook her head, wanting to rid herself of such thoughts. They served no purpose. Love wasn't for the likes of Rose Townsend Rafferty.

She wanted nothing to do with emotions that would tie her to someone else. Especially not to a man. It was too dangerous. It was too easy to get hurt.

No, she wanted nothing to do with Lark's romantic fantasies.

Out of the blue, she imagined herself standing on the porch of her new home. She felt Michael's arms embracing her, felt his lips brushing softly against her own. She recalled all the crazy, careening sensations that had raced through her at the time, feeling them as intensely now as she had then.

"There he is." Lark's hand gripped Rose's arm. "There he is."

As soon as the words were out of her mouth, Lark stepped away from Rose, hurrying toward the man on the ladder.

"Yance?"

At the sound of her voice, his heart turned over like a flapjack in a frying pan. He glanced down toward the ground, and there she stood, looking even prettier than he'd remembered.

Slowly, he descended the ladder. When he reached the ground, he resisted the urge to pull her into his arms and kiss her until she was breathless.

"You're back," he said. Lord, she was a sight for sore eyes. He'd never seen anything prettier than Lark Rider.

"Just today. Mother's at the mercantile getting some supplies. I've only got a moment."

He nodded, understanding. "I've got work to do. Can't stand around jawin'."

"I've missed you, Yance," she whispered.

He wished he was better at words. Right off the top of his head, he couldn't think of one thing that'd tell her the way he felt. He wasn't too sure there were any words that would say what he wanted.

"I was afraid you'd go away." Her words were barely audible. There was even a glimmer of tears in her big brown eyes.

"I'm not aimin' to go anywhere, Lark. I've got plenty of reasons to stay." Shoot, the way she was lookin' at him made him feel soft as bear grease inside. It was gettin' mighty hard not to hold her.

"Am I one of those reasons?" she asked haltingly.

She was the only reason that mattered, but here wasn't the place he meant to tell her and now wasn't the time. When he got around to tellin' her just how he felt, he didn't mean to do it standin' in front of a bunch of carpenters, and he didn't mean to do it when he still didn't own much more than his saddle and a good horse.

"You're one of 'em," he answered, knowing it wasn't the sort of response she'd been hoping for.

"I heard you're buying your own place."

"I'm tryin'. And I'd best get back to work so I earn my day's pay."

"Will you . . . will you come see me at the ranch?"

Yancy shook his head. "I don't reckon I'd be welcome just yet."

She dropped her head forward. He saw a quiver pass through her; then she took a deep breath and looked up at him again. "Then when will I see you?"

"Church on Sunday, most likely." Hell, if she kept lookin' at him that way, he'd have Will Rider gunnin' for him before sundown. "And maybe when you come to town to call on Mrs. Rafferty."

"Mrs. Raff. . . . Oh, you mean Rose." Her face brightened, a smile curving her mouth. "Of course. I'll be in town often to see Rose. I suppose we would be apt to run into each other then, wouldn't we?"

"I reckon so."

She glanced over her shoulder, and he followed her gaze to where Rose Rafferty stood waiting near the street. "I suppose I should be going." She looked at him again, then stepped closer to the ladder. "Yancy Jones, I love you," she whispered before turning and walking away.

Watching her go, seeing the gentle sway of her pretty plaid dress, tempted him to go after her, throw her across the saddle of his horse, and light out for parts unknown. But then, that wouldn't exactly prove he was the right kind of man to be askin' for her hand in marriage.

No, when Yancy married Lark Rider, it was going to be with her pa right there and the whole town knowing Lark and Yancy belonged together.

He chuckled softly as he climbed the ladder. Who'd've ever thought Yancy Jones would get domesticated by a pretty little filly named Lark?

Chapter Twenty-One

Fishing pole in hand, Hank leaned back against the trunk of a pine tree and watched his grandchildren scampering along the bank of the river. Their laughter drifted to him on a soft breeze.

This was Hank's favorite getaway. Often, over the years, he'd told Doris he'd like to retire to this stretch of river along the road to Boise City. At this point, the water was wide and deep and slow moving. A perfect fishing spot. A half mile down, it narrowed and became frothing white water.

Yessiree, this would be the perfect place for a man to spend his last days. And it was about time he retired, too. He was too old to be sheriffing, even in a quiet town like Homestead. One day they just might need a sheriff to do more than toss one of the Townsend men into jail to sober up.

He frowned, remembering the telegram he'd

received yesterday from Colorado, advising him to keep an eye on Glen Townsend, more information to follow. He didn't have to know what it was about to know it meant trouble. Glen Townsend always meant trouble.

Yes, he thought with a nod of his head, it was time for him to retire. The job needed a younger man. He'd outlived most of his old friends as it was. Now it was time to enjoy life a little. It was time to lay back on a riverbank and fish and watch his grandkids.

"Grampa, look!"

He followed the direction of Tommy's outstretched right arm. He saw the stag with its mighty set of antlers just seconds before it bounded back into the cover of trees. Tommy cried his dismay as the deer disappeared.

Once again, he turned his gaze on the children. They were growing up faster than a wink. Before he knew it, Sarah was going to have young men calling on her. And Tommy. . . .

His chest tightened as he looked at the boy. Tommy was the spitting image of his father when Tom was that age. Hair as black as ink and eyes the same lead gray as all the McLeod men had had for more generations than Hank could remember. Tommy was lively and bright, full of monkey business, and prone to accidents. It was a wonder he hadn't broken more than his arm in his fall from that tree just over a week ago.

Tommy's father had been like that, too.

Always running hell-bent for leather into situations. Hank tried to imagine his son as he would have been had he lived. His hair would probably be starting to turn gray, just like Hank's. He would have developed crow's-feet around his eyes by this time, but age wouldn't have dimmed his smile.

It was hard to believe Tom would have turned forty-two this year. And if Maria hadn't died giving birth to Tommy, she'd have been thirty-seven.

Hank blinked away his suddenly blurred vision. No point gettin' womanish in his old age. It wouldn't change things, wouldn't bring Tom and Maria back. Besides, he still had more than most folks to be thankful for.

The thunder of horses' hooves drew his attention to the road that followed along the opposite side of the river. "She's late today," he said to himself as the stage rumbled past, disappearing quickly into the narrowing canyon above Hank's fishing spot. He checked his pocket watch. "Yep. She's late."

"Grampa, you've got a bite!" Tommy shouted, yanking Hank's thoughts back to the river and his fishing pole.

He rose to his feet and began reeling in his line as his grandson ran toward him.

"He's a whopper!" Tommy jumped up and down on the bank in front of his grandfather.

For several minutes, Hank was deeply engrossed in bringing in his catch while still not cutting the experience short. That was something a man his age had learned, to savor the good moments in life. Fishing was one of those things a man shouldn't rush.

By the time he lifted the large trout out of the water, he was smiling as broadly as his young grandson.

"You're right, Tommy. He's a whopper. Your grandma's going to have a hard time fittin' him into one fryin' pan." He watched as the boy struggled to remove the hook from the fish's mouth with his good hand, but didn't try to help, knowing his assistance wouldn't be wanted. "You ready to drop in your pole now?"

"Yeah."

Hank turned to ask Sarah the same question, but she wasn't beside them as he'd thought. A hasty glance found her seated on an outcropping of rocks, her eyes staring dreamily off into space.

"She's thinkin' about some silly-lookin' tower in a magazine or somethin'," Tommy muttered disparagingly. "Gramma says she's got her head in the clouds."

"I don't suppose it hurts to have dreams of your own," Hank replied, dropping his hand onto the boy's head and ruffling his hair. "Now, let's you and me catch some more fish for supper."

Michael was exhausted by the time he was fully dressed. He sat down on the chair beside

the bed and drew in several slow, steady
breaths. If Rose were to catch him sitting
there looking pale and winded, she would
order him right back to bed.

And if she ordered him back to bed, he was
likely to say something he'd regret later. He
didn't want to do that. They'd been getting on
too well to let his temper spoil it for them.

Michael was a lousy patient; there was no
getting around it. He hadn't been sick more
than a few days in his life and those back
when he was a youngster. He wasn't used to
doing nothing for days at a time.

With nothing to do but lie in bed and think,
he'd spent too much time reminiscing about
his father and his brother, about the anger and
rivalry. He didn't want to think about them. He
didn't want to think about any of it. Not now.
Not when he was starting to doubt.

And he *was* starting to doubt. He'd always
been so sure he was in the right, always
thought he knew exactly what he wanted, yet
suddenly nothing seemed so cut-and-dried. He
kept remembering things he'd done of which
he was less than proud. He was seeing things
in a new light, and that new light made him
feel uncomfortable.

He shook his head, trying to drive off the
thoughts that plagued him. He got up from
the chair and walked to the door. Leaning
against the jamb, he listened for sounds coming
from the kitchen. The house was completely

silent. Rose still hadn't returned from the mercantile.

Good. He wanted to be out on the porch before she got back.

He made his way slowly down the stairs, gripping the handrail the entire way. He paused again at the base. He was feeling a little light-headed, but it wasn't as bad as he'd expected. He moved on.

Being outdoors felt even better than he'd imagined it would. He drew in a long breath of air as he sank onto the porch swing. He'd made it. His knees were shaky and his palms clammy, but he'd made it.

He closed his eyes and allowed himself to relax, breathing deeply. He listened to the breeze rustling the leaves in the nearby trees, heard the chirping of robins in the branches. The sounds were soothing. He'd had no idea how good nature could sound.

Slowly, he felt his strength returning.

When he opened his eyes several minutes later, he saw Rose round the gentle bend in the road. Another young woman was with her. Their heads were nearly touching as they walked. They looked to be deeply engrossed in conversation. Michael gave the stranger a cursory glance, then returned his gaze to Rose.

She looked very pretty in her dark pink gown. It was a color she wore regularly.

Come to think of it, it was the dress itself that was familiar to him. He'd seen it often since first meeting her. It dawned on him that his wife must have only a few dresses to choose from.

Suddenly, he knew something he could do for Rose. He would have Emma Barber order several new ones for her. Tomorrow he would walk down to the mercantile, and he would order Rose a dozen new gowns.

He grinned, pleased with himself. He could just imagine her surprise when the packages arrived.

He was still smiling when Rose looked his way. He saw her eyes widen with surprise, then narrow with displeasure. He was in for a scolding. Rose had warned him not to get out of bed until the doctor had said it was all right. She would be fit to be tied to have him disobey doctor's orders this way. If the other young woman wasn't with her, he didn't doubt Rose would have given him a thorough tongue-lashing.

That thought made him smile even more. He would never tell her so, but he rather liked her feistiness.

He rose from the swing as the two women climbed the steps onto the porch.

"Michael, I didn't expect to find you out." Her tone was mildly censuring and very wifelike.

Wifelike. Damned if he didn't enjoy the sound of it.

"You know Doc Varney wanted you to stay in bed a few more days."

"The doctor is wrong." He shifted his gaze to Rose's friend. "How do you do? I'm Michael Rafferty."

She was an attractive young woman with golden skin, dark brown eyes, and black hair. She was taller than Rose by a good four inches and without Rose's generous, womanly curves. From the look of her clothes, Michael guessed she could go a month and never wear the same dress twice. Pretty and spoiled? Perhaps, but instinct told him there was more to her than that.

She gave him an equally thorough once-over with her eyes before saying, "I'm Lark Rider." She paused. "I trust you intend to make Rose happy."

"Lark!"

"I intend to do my level best, Miss Rider."

Lark smiled. "Good. Then we can be friends, too." She held out her hand.

Michael took it and shook it firmly.

"Please sit down, Michael," Rose admonished softly.

He heard the tender concern in her voice, and that alone made him feel stronger. Without a word of objection, he did her bidding.

"Oh, look. There's Mother already." Lark glanced from the road to Michael. "Don't get up, Mr. Rafferty. You can meet my mother another time. Rose told me about your accident. I'll explain to Mother." She gave Rose a quick hug. "I'll come back to town as soon as I can."

Lark hurried down the steps and out to the road before the buggy could draw closer to the house. A moment later, the women and buggy disappeared from view.

"She must be a close friend," Michael said, his gaze returning to Rose.

"Yes."

"Then I'm glad she decided she could be my friend, too."

His blue gaze was as warm as a summer day. She felt that wonderful-terrible trembling in her stomach, and her breathing seemed to slow down until she felt starved for air.

"It's Lark's nature to be friendly with everyone," she said softly.

He smiled that wonderful, slow smile of his. "I see. Well, then I'm glad I didn't make her go against her nature."

She heard the teasing tone of his voice. It made her heart feel funny.

"Sit down and join me, Rose."

She shook her head. "I've got baking to do."

"Just for a moment."

Why was it so difficult to tell him no?

"You can spare a minute or two."

She still hadn't finished the laundry because he'd wanted her to sit with him yesterday. It was already too late in the day to bake her bread, but she'd planned to make corn muffins and an apple pie for supper. Their agreement was for her to keep his house and cook his meals. No one had said anything about sitting on a porch swing and wasting away an afternoon.

Despite herself, she set down her basket, then joined him on the swing.

He smiled at her a moment before turning his gaze toward the mountains. "It must have been nice, growing up in this valley. It's beautiful here."

He needed a haircut. Was that something a wife was expected to do, too?

"More quiet than the city. Peaceful. San Francisco is all noise and bustle, people rushing from here to there."

Who cut his hair when he was in San Francisco?

"I didn't think I was going to like it here, but I was wrong."

She couldn't stop herself from asking, "Why *did* you come to Homestead, Michael?"

"To build a hotel."

"But why?"

A shadow passed over his blue eyes. "To prove something."

"What?"

"I'm not sure anymore."

She felt he was about to say something more when the rattle of a wagon disturbed the silence. She turned to see who was passing by their house.

But the wagon wasn't going to pass. It

was headed straight for them. She recognized Norman Henderson, but the woman beside him wasn't Rachel.

"Lillian. . . ." Michael uttered, clearly surprised.

She glanced at her husband as he rose from the swing; then she looked back at the gorgeous woman on the wagon seat. No wonder he'd called for her in his sleep.

Michael stepped toward the porch rail as the wagon halted below him.

"Here you go, Miss Overhart," Norman said, hopping down from the seat, then offering his hands to help her to the ground.

Lillian Overhart's striped lavender-and-white satin dress looked brand-new, and Rose couldn't detect a trace of dust on the expensive fabric. She certainly didn't look as if she'd just had an arduous journey up from Boise City. There wasn't even a strand of her silvery-blond hair out of place beneath her pretty lavender bonnet.

She held on to Norman Henderson's hand and leaned toward him. "Thank you so much for bringing me here, Mr. Henderson. It was very generous of you to offer. I should have been lost without you."

She needed a ride from the stage office?

"My pleasure, miss." He grinned at her, then touched his hat brim in the direction of the porch in a silent greeting to Michael and Rose.

Rose just bet it had been his pleasure. She wondered what Rachel would think of Norman's gallant behavior if she were to hear about it.

"Michael, they told me in town that you'd had a serious accident." Lillian approached the porch, not bothering to look behind her as Norman drove away. "They said you'd been deathly ill. I was so worried I left my trunk at the station and came right over."

"I'm all right, Lillian."

It was at that precise moment that Lillian noticed Rose, still seated on the porch swing. Her eyes widened as she swung her gaze back to Michael.

"I wasn't expecting you," he said as if he couldn't see the question in the look she gave him.

"I wanted to surprise you."

"You did."

Lillian arched her eyebrows. "Have you forgotten all your manners, Michael Rafferty?" She held out a hand, clearly a signal that he should come forward and assist her up the four steps to the porch.

Rose's anger came out of nowhere. She rose from the porch swing and stepped up to Michael's side, effectively keeping him from moving away from the rail. "This is Michael's first day out of bed, and he's still much too weak. You'll have to climb the steps on your own."

"Wha. . . ." Lillian's lavender-gloved hand fluttered to her breast.

At another time, Rose might have found the woman's expression humorous. Not today. She turned her gaze up toward her husband. "I think you should sit down, Michael."

He looked every inch as shocked as did Miss Lillian Overhart.

"I think you *really* should sit down," she repeated, more forcefully this time. She took hold of his elbow and steered him back to the swing.

Holding her skirt and petticoats out of the way, Lillian stomped up the steps. "Michael, who *is* this girl?" She made *girl* sound like an insult.

Rose lifted her chin and glanced over her shoulder, trying to mimic the look of disdain she'd seen in Lillian's own eyes. "I am Mr. Rafferty's wife. Who are you?"

Chapter Twenty-Two

This was just the sort of scene that Dillon would probably have paid money to see. If it were happening to someone else, Michael himself might have found some amusement in the situation. But it wasn't happening to someone else. It was happening to him.

"Michael?"

He turned toward Lillian. "Miss Overhart, may I introduce you to Rose Rafferty. Rose, this is Lillian Overhart, a . . . friend of mine from San Francisco."

Rose's fingers tightened on his arm. "Sit down, Michael. You look ghastly."

He *felt* ghastly. His legs were shaky, and there was a sick knot in his stomach that had nothing to do with snakebite. Gratefully, he complied with her request.

"I don't . . . I don't believe it." Lillian moved over to the porch rail and grabbed hold of it as if it were a lifeline. Her cheeks had lost all their color.

Michael glanced over at Rose. The spark that had lighted the gold flecks in her eyes had died, leaving her with that sad, haunted look he'd seen so often before they were married. He'd thought he'd seen the last of it. Now, he was responsible for its return.

"I think I should leave you two alone to talk. When you're ready to go up to your room, just call for me." Rose turned abruptly and disappeared inside the house.

He continued to stare at the door long after it had closed behind her.

"Michael?"

Reluctantly, he turned toward Lillian. He was responsible for the hurt, confused look on her face, too. It wasn't Lillian's fault he didn't love her. She was spoiled and a bit self-centered, but she was also beautiful and intelligent. She was much the same as many of the other debutantes he'd escorted since his own coming of age, but he'd selected Lillian for special attention because of Dillon's feelings for her.

And unlike his previous harmless romances with young women of good breeding and social standing, he'd been unfair to Lillian. He'd allowed her to think they would marry one day. Everyone in both families—including, he supposed, himself—had expected it. Everyone except for Kathleen. His stepmother had told him time and again that he had yet to

271

meet the right woman. She had been correct once again.

But that didn't solve things now. It didn't excuse him for what he'd done. It didn't lessen Lillian's disappointment.

"It's true, isn't it?" she asked in a whisper. "You've married her?"

"Yes, it's true."

"Why ever would you do it?"

He sighed. "It's a long story, Lillian. I would have written to you, but I had no idea you would come to see me. I wouldn't have expected your father to allow it."

"Father doesn't know I'm here. I came because . . . I came because. . . ." Tears pooled in her eyes. "Oh, Michael, why?" She turned away from him, pulling a handkerchief from her handbag to wipe away her tears.

Michael rose from the swing and walked to stand beside her. Rather than looking at Lillian, he stared at the rugged mountains that ringed the valley. "The truth is I'm the *real* bastard in my family. Not Dillon."

She gasped.

He shook his head. "No, I don't mean by birth. I mean by actions." He closed his eyes for a moment, then looked at her. "Lillian, I'm sorry. You have every right to hate me. I wish there were words to say, something I could do. . . ." He shook his head again.

She grabbed his arm. "Come back to San Francisco with me, Michael. Mr. Dover will be able to help you. You can get an annulment. Surely a marriage made so quickly can be easily broken."

"I don't need Christian's help." He covered her hand with his own. "Lillian, I love her."

With another gasp, she jerked her hand away. "I don't believe it. You can't love her. You love me."

"No. I love Rose."

She slapped him.

He knew he deserved it. It didn't matter that he hadn't intended to hurt or betray her. There wasn't anything he could say that would change the truth. Still, he had to try.

"Lillian, let me explain."

Her head held high, she said, "I'm listening."

"There's no excuse for what I've done. While I never told you I loved you or asked you to marry me, I know it's what everyone thought would happen. I knew it was what you thought. The truth is I thought it would happen, too. We were quite suited to each other." He took a deep breath, then said, "But you wouldn't be suited for the man I am now, Lillian."

"What do you mean?"

"I mean the hotels and society balls and everything that was my life in San Francisco are no longer as important to me."

"You don't mean to stay *here*, do you?"

He shrugged. "That will be up to Rose." He reached for her arm. "Come on. I'll see you to the boardinghouse. Tomorrow I'll make plans for getting you back to San Francisco where you belong."

She jerked away from him. "You needn't see me anywhere, Mr. Rafferty. You're *far* too weak, and your *wife* would be worried about you." She glared at him with all the pride she could muster. "I'll find it myself." She whirled about and quickly descended the steps.

"Lillian!"

She paused and glanced back at him.

No matter how hard he tried to find them, there didn't seem to be the proper words. Finally, he said, "I'm truly sorry." It was the best he could do.

Rose waited for him to call for her, but he never did. Finally, unable to keep herself from doing so, she went to the parlor window and glanced out between the curtains. Michael was sitting alone on the porch swing, his elbows resting on his knees, his head held between his hands.

She hurried to the door. "Michael?" She stepped onto the porch. "Michael?" He didn't answer, and she felt a sting of alarm. She knelt beside him, placing her hand on his shoulder. Softly, she said his name once more. "Michael?"

He looked up at her. "Did you ever take a good long look at yourself and hate what you see?" he asked gruffly.

"It's all right, Michael," she whispered, helping him to his feet. "It won't seem so bad once you've rested. You're just tired. Everything seems worse when you're tired." Rose put her arm around his back and pulled one of his around her shoulder. "Come on. Let's get you upstairs."

They moved slowly and without speaking. It seemed a very long time before they reached his bedroom and she eased him down on the side of his bed. She started to back away, but he grasped her wrist and held her there.

"Sit down, Rose. I owe you an explanation."

"No, you don't. You don't owe me anything, Michael. I understand." Her chest and throat felt tight, so tight it hurt to speak.

And she *did* understand. She'd have to be an idiot *not* to understand. Lillian Overhart was the reason he'd wanted no scandal, the reason he'd wanted a divorce at the end of a year. Except now he'd be wanting it sooner.

"Please, Rose." He tugged her toward the bed.

Unable to keep from it, she sank onto the bed beside him. She didn't want to hear about the woman he loved, the reason why he didn't want a scandal, the woman for whom he would divorce Rose. She didn't want to think about the perfect beauty who had followed him all the way from San Francisco and whom he would follow back.

"Have I told you about my brother, Dillon?"

She glanced at him, surprised. It wasn't what she'd expected him to say.

He shook his head. "No, I know I haven't. I never talk about Dillon to anyone." He raked the fingers of one hand through his hair. "Dillon loved Lillian once. I took her away from him. Not because I wanted her. Not because I loved her. It was just for spite."

Rose stared at him, wondering what he was trying to tell her, yet afraid to hear it.

"I've done a lot of thinking since I've been laid up here," he continued. "Thinking about my father and my brother and me and how we've lived these last ten years. I guess I was even dreaming about it while I was sick. Something's been gnawing at me, but I didn't know what it was until I saw Lillian."

When he turned his gaze in her direction, Rose felt a piercing pain in her chest that equaled the pain she saw in his eyes. She longed to comfort him. "I'll tell her how it happened, Michael. It was my fault, not yours. She'll forgive you. I know she will. We can get that annulment at once. You'll be free to marry her."

The distraught look left his eyes, replaced first by confusion, then by tenderness. "I don't want to marry Lillian. I don't love her." He paused, then added, "It's you I love, Rose."

It felt as if her heart had stopped beating. She was starved for air.

"Marrying you is the only right thing I've done in a very long time."

She jumped to her feet. "You should lie down and rest, Michael. I'll bring up your supper later."

She fled from the room, rushing down the stairs and out the front door. She kept walking until she'd reached the banks of Pony Creek. Once there, she turned and followed the stream away from Homestead, trying not to think, trying not to feel.

It's you I love, Rose.

No! No, she didn't want to hear it. She didn't want him to say such a thing. Love was something that happened to other people, not to her. No one had ever truly loved her. Certainly not her father or brother. Even her mother had always seemed to prefer Mark, no matter how hard Rose had tried to be a good daughter, no matter how hard she'd tried to earn Virginia's love.

A cry tore from her throat as she sank to the earth, hiding her face in her hands.

She fought the tears. She *wouldn't* cry. Crying showed weakness, and Rose wasn't weak. She was strong. She'd had to be. She didn't need anybody else. She could make it on her own. That was the way she liked it. That was the way she wanted it.

Was it? Was it really what she wanted?

She strangled a dry sob in her throat, but the questions persisted.

What would it be like to be loved? To be really loved?

Did she dare try to find out?
Was it worth the risk?

Lying on his back, Michael stared up at the ceiling of his room. What a mess he'd made of everything, he thought, and what a fool he'd been.

It wasn't pleasant, looking at himself and finding so little of which to be proud. It wasn't pleasant to realize how he'd allowed himself to be twisted by jealousy and greed.

Oh, he knew everything about business and industry, about building and operating a successful hotel. He was a master at making deals, and he was a shrewd judge of character. He commanded respect from his employees. He could be a charming escort and popular host. He was benevolent to those in need. A pillar of society.

But his private life, he'd realized belatedly, was somewhat less than a stellar achievement. He'd failed the people who should have been most important to him. He'd turned his back on Dillon, the brother he'd loved from the moment the boy had come to live in the Rafferty mansion until the moment Michael had learned the truth of Dillon's heritage. From that moment on, he'd fought his brother. He'd fought his father, too. He'd opposed his father at every turn, the father who'd been his idol as far back as his first memories.

Fought him for what? Pieces of real estate?

The question now was, how could he make amends? How did he go about undoing ten years of misspent anger against a brother who had done nothing more wrong than being born John Thomas's illegitimate son? How did he become worthy again in his father's eyes? How did he become the son and brother he should have been this past decade?

So many questions and so few answers.

And Rose. . . .

What about Rose?

He closed his eyes. Loving her was the first completely unselfish, uncalculated thing he'd done in many a year. Without her, he doubted he would have seen how shallow his life had become. Somehow, he had to prove himself to her.

More than anything he'd wanted in his life, he desired to earn the love of Rose Townsend Rafferty.

Chapter Twenty-three

Michael slept little that night. He spent the hours between dusk and dawn taking a long, hard look at his life, at the boy he'd been, at the man he'd become. He discovered some things about himself that he wished weren't true. Some were unflattering to his ego; a few merely surprised him.

By morning, he knew what he had to do. His decision would change his life, but he believed he would be a better man for it. He hoped he would be the kind of man Rose could love, now and forever.

Before noon, Michael posted two letters—one to Dillon Rafferty in Newton, Oregon, the other to John Thomas Rafferty in San Francisco, California. Then he walked to the boardinghouse and asked to speak to Miss Lillian Overhart.

Virginia Townsend eyed him suspiciously. "She's not here, Mr. Rafferty. She left this morning. Hired a rig and a driver to take her down south. Said she was gonna take the Oregon Short Line out of Nampa. Go back to California."

"I see. Thank you, Mrs. Townsend." He placed his hat back on his head, preparing to leave.

"Mr. Rafferty? I don't know what this is all about, but I hope you're not gonna hurt my Rose. Life's been hard enough for her."

He offered an encouraging smile. "I promise you, Mrs. Townsend, that I have no intention of ever hurting your daughter."

"I'm glad to hear it." She stared at him hard for several more heartbeats, then said, "I think I believe you, too."

"You *can* believe me, ma'am." With a nod, he turned and walked away from the boardinghouse.

His next stop was the hotel site. He'd scarcely given it a glance as he'd walked by on his way to the post office, but now he had to admit that he was pleased with the headway his crew had made while he was ill. Yancy had told him how things were progressing, but he hadn't really believed it until now. Seeing it with his own eyes brightened his spirits considerably.

He spoke briefly with the men, then excused himself and returned home, his pace much slower than when he'd left the house. He was glad for the chance to sit down on the porch swing. The outing had left him drained of energy. Still, he could tell his health was much improved. Tomorrow, he would be even better.

The front door opened suddenly, and Rose stepped onto the porch. He turned his head and met her worried gaze. Neither of them spoke.

She had avoided him last evening. When she'd brought his supper tray, she hadn't given him an opportunity to speak, even if he'd known what he wanted to say. He hadn't seen her this morning before he left the house.

How do I win you, Rose? he wondered as he looked at her. *How do I make you believe I love you? How do I reach that heart of yours? You guard it so closely.*

It wasn't that he didn't know how to woo a woman. But never before had the woman's response to his wooing mattered as it did now.

He rose from the swing. "I had to post some letters," he said, as if she'd asked him to explain. He stepped forward, wanting to be near her. He wanted to be able to see her expressive, gold-flecked eyes. He wanted to touch her soft skin and take her into his arms and kiss her sweet, pink mouth.

Her eyes widened, as if she'd guessed what he was thinking. She looked like a wild filly that was boxed into a narrow space and ready to bolt.

He stopped still. He would have to go slowly. He would have to win her trust before he could win her love.

"I know you have good reason to question what I tell you, Rose, but I hope you'll give me a chance to prove myself. I love you, and I plan to be here for you, whenever you need me."

"Michael, don't."

Unable to stop himself, he reached forward and gently touched her cheek with the tips of his fingers. "Just give me a chance. I won't let you down."

Rose could feel her skin tingling beneath his touch. There was a terrible wanting inside her, one she'd never felt before. Her heart ached for things she knew she couldn't have. She told herself she couldn't have them because they weren't real. Not for her. Never for her.

"You know what I would like, Mrs. Rafferty? I'd like to go on a picnic up on the ridge." Michael removed his fingers from her cheek and pointed toward the mountains to the north. "There's a spectacular view of the valley from up there. Would you join me tomorrow? I'll borrow a rig. I'm not up to a horseback ride just yet."

There were at least a hundred reasons why she should say no. Instead, she said, "I'll pack a lunch."

He smiled down at her, and she felt wonderful and confused and warm and scared all at the same time.

"I'm rather partial to your fried chicken," he said, ending with a wink. "Real partial."

She smiled in return. She couldn't seem to

help herself. "Then that's what we'll have." For a moment, she thought he just might lean down and kiss her. Alarmed that she seemed to be waiting for him to do so, she took a step back from him. "I'd better get on with my chores." Quickly, she turned and went inside.

Riding astride, Lark galloped Dark Feather toward the east. Her destination was a section of land known as the old Hadley place. She knew Yancy wouldn't be there. He would either be working at the mill or at the site of the new hotel. Of course, she would have liked to have seen him again today, but she wasn't going to press her luck. She didn't want to give her father more reason to oppose her love for Yancy.

She saw the small house, set tight against the mountainside, and slowed her mount to a gentle canter as they drew closer. She reined in the mare when they reached the yard.

She stared at the log house. It was a single story with two, maybe three rooms, judging from the size. There were three windows, but two of them were covered with shutters. It was just a simple, ordinary place in the mountains of Idaho Territory, the kind of house young families lived in everywhere.

She smiled as she looked at it. Yancy had done this for her. He'd taken the jobs at the mill and with Mr. Rafferty in order to buy this house and land. And he wanted to buy this house and land because he wanted to marry her. Of course, he hadn't proposed. He hadn't even told her he loved her. Not in so many words. But she knew it all the same.

She nudged her mare forward with her heels, stopping when she was close enough to peer inside through the only unshuttered window.

She looked in upon the sitting room. The room was clean but nearly vacant. Beyond the sitting room was a kitchen. A wall separated the first two rooms from the bedroom. She could tell it was the bedroom because she could see a bed through the open door.

It wasn't a very big bed, she thought, imagining herself and Yancy lying in it, snuggled beneath several blankets, their bodies touching, arms wrapped around each other.

Prickles of excitement shivered up her spine. She wasn't entirely certain what went on beneath those blankets, but she had a fairly good idea. And her body told her, whenever she was close to Yancy, that it must be something very enjoyable.

Her face flushed by her scandalous thoughts, she backed Dark Feather away from the house.

She would make pretty curtains for the windows, and the rug in her bedroom at home would fit quite well in the sitting area of the log house. There were some paintings her mother had put up in the attic that she supposed her parents wouldn't care if she used. They would make the place seem less rustic.

As for the kitchen. . . . Lark screwed up her mouth. Cooking was not one of her talents. Frosty, the Rocking R cook, had tried on more than one occasion to teach her some culinary skills, but she'd always preferred to be out riding her horse rather than standing in a stuffy old kitchen. She supposed, if she didn't want Yancy to starve, she would have to learn to cook. For that matter, she didn't want to go hungry either. Griff Simpson, the ranch foreman, had always teased her, saying she had a very unladylike appetite. He'd often told her she was going to be fat when she got to be an old woman with a dozen children and two dozen grandchildren.

Suddenly, she smiled again as she pictured Yancy holding her in that bed.

She sure hoped he hurried up and changed her father's mind about him being the right man for her to marry. She didn't know how long she could wait to find out what went on under those covers.

Addie stared at the fashion plate in her most recent issue of *Harper's Bazaar*, then glanced at the description beneath the illustration.

White peau de soie is the material of this bridal gown, which is made with a full-trained untrimmed skirt and a short seamless bodice that is draped with lace on the front, and has a lace jabot carried

*diagonally across. The tulle veil, which is
hemmed at the edge, is fastened on with
orange blossoms, and a small cluster of the
flowers ornaments the corsage.*

The dress would be perfect for Lark. If she
ordered the material immediately, she could
probably have the wedding gown ready for a
fall wedding. Naturally, Will would want to
make the young couple wait longer, but Addie
saw no point in delaying the inevitable. Lark
and Yancy were in love, and lovers ought to be
together.

Good lord! she thought. *I could be a grandmother by next summer.*

She set the fashion magazine aside and
walked to the mirror hanging in the entry
hall. Critically, she studied her reflection.

Did she *look* like a grandmother? she wondered.

Addie had never been a beauty, of course,
but she didn't seem to have aged badly. At
thirty-seven, her face was still unlined, and
the freckles that had once made her nose so
objectionable had disappeared entirely. Her
hair was still the same flaming shade of red
and just as curly and unruly as when she
was a girl.

She stepped back slightly from the mirror
and inspected her figure. Still as slender as
she'd been ten years before, her shape had
changed, filled out, after she'd given birth to

Preston and Naomi. Will hadn't seemed to mind that change.

She nearly laughed aloud as a new thought crossed her mind. If she would be a grandmother, Will would be a grandfather.

Oh, dear. She'd better not mention that to him or he'd forbid Lark to marry for another ten years.

The door burst open at that moment, and her two youngest children raced inside. Preston dropped his schoolbooks on the table beneath the mirror and headed toward his room.

"Mama," Naomi announced, tears in her eyes, "Preston says I can't hold any of Starbright's puppies when she has 'em. He says I'd make 'em die."

Preston stopped, then slowly turned to face the music. He had the decency to look ashamed of himself.

Addie frowned at her mischievous son. Her friends told her that older brothers thrived on teasing little sisters, and it wouldn't have any lasting effects on Naomi. She hoped her women advisers were right, because she'd nearly given up on getting Preston to stop.

"I know," her son said with an exaggerated sigh, as if he were the one who'd been put upon. Glancing at his sister, he added, "I'm sorry, Naomi." Then, before Addie could say anything, he dashed away, disappearing into the kitchen and, more than likely, out the back door.

Addie gave her five-year-old daughter a warm hug. "Don't you pay any attention to Preston. You can hold the puppies whenever you like, as long as Starbright doesn't object. That's what puppies like best. Lots of holding and hugging. And it won't hurt them at all." She kissed the crown of Naomi's head. "Now, let's see what Frosty's got in the kitchen for a snack. You must be hungry."

As she straightened and took hold of her daughter's hand, she dismissed all thoughts of being a grandmother. She hadn't time to worry about it. She was too busy being a mother—and loving absolutely every moment of it.

Chapter Twenty-Four

Summer was in glorious bloom. As the borrowed horse and buggy trotted along the road, Rose took note of the season for the first time. Wildflowers—purple and yellow and white—dotted the gently rolling floor of the valley. The air was fresh. The sky was an unmarked canopy of blue stretching from mountaintop to mountaintop.

It was a beautiful day for a picnic.

"Have you ever been to that ridge up there?" Michael asked, pointing toward their destination as the horse started up the steady slope of the mountain.

Rose shook her head. Except for visits to the Rocking R, she'd rarely been outside of town, let alone exploring the surrounding mountains.

"Quite a view from up there. It's a good place to think. Sort of look at your future."

She cast a sidelong glance at him. What had he meant by that?

"I'm famished," he continued. "I could smell that chicken frying all morning."

She relaxed slightly. Perhaps there wasn't any real danger in going on a picnic with Michael. They would sit on a blanket and have their lunch, and then they would go back to Homestead. It was a harmless way to spend an afternoon. Why not savor it? When was the last time she'd taken an afternoon off, just to relax and enjoy herself? There'd always been things to do at the boardinghouse or at the restaurant. Since marrying Michael, she'd had plenty of household chores to fill her days, even before he'd been bitten by the rattlers. She deserved a holiday as much as the next person.

She took a deep breath of air. Yes, she *did* deserve a holiday, an afternoon to not worry about anything, a few hours to simply enjoy herself.

She glanced once again at the man at her side. Would it be so awful to take pleasure in being with him for a short while? She already knew she had no future with him, but she had agreed to stay for one year from the day of their marriage. It was only good sense that they be on friendly terms during that year. Then, come next summer, she would be a free woman. She could go anywhere she wanted, thanks to Michael. The least she owed him was some amiable companionship.

Robin Lee Hatcher

Above the rattle and jangle of the harness and the clipping of the horse's hooves against the hard earth, she became aware of some sort of whining sound. She glanced around, trying to figure out what it was or where it was coming from, but she couldn't see anything.

She shook her head, as if to clear it, but the whining didn't go away.

Michael grinned at her. "When I borrowed the rig from Mrs. Barber, she warned me to keep an eye out for bears up here. Have you ever had trouble with bears?"

"Occasionally, they come down out of the mountains, but they usually come at night and are gone before morning."

"Hmmm. I sure wouldn't want to see one. Not when I'm having a picnic with such a beautiful lady. Good thing I brought something to scare bears away."

She was about to ask him what he meant when the road they'd been following through the pines suddenly burst into the open.

Michael pulled back on the reins, bringing the buggy to a halt, then hopped down to the ground. He turned and offered his hand to Rose. "Come on. Let's have a look at the view."

She took his hand and allowed him to help her down. Side by side, they walked to the edge of the table-flat ridge.

Below them, Long Bow Valley stretched out for miles. Long and narrow, fields of green

292

dotted with cattle and horses, smaller sections in shades of brown, the earth tilled and planted with crops. Pony Creek wound like a blue ribbon from one end of the valley to another. In the distance, Homestead looked even tinier than she knew it was.

She heard the whining sound again. "What *is* that?" she muttered, more to herself than to Michael.

"Our bear protection," he answered.

"What?" She frowned up at him.

He grinned. "Come have a look." Taking her hand, he pulled her toward the buggy. When they reached it, he dropped her hand and reached beneath the seat, pulling out a wicker basket.

Again, she gave him a questioning look.

He slipped the closing loop from its button and opened the lid. There inside was a gold-and-white puppy.

"Mrs. Barber assured me she would be great at keeping away bears with all the racket she makes." He pulled the puppy from the basket, then held her out toward Rose. "She's yours."

"Mine?" She took the furry bundle from his hands.

"I wanted to give you something special, and the mercantile was fresh out of diamond necklaces. I thought Duchess might be a good choice."

"Duchess," Rose whispered, unaware of her own smile.

The puppy's whines grew louder. Rose held Duchess close and nuzzled her with her chin. The puppy immediately licked Rose's face.

Rose was enchanted. She'd always wanted a pet, but they'd never even had a mouser at the boardinghouse. Mark had driven away any stray cats that had come around.

"Do you like her?" Michael asked softly.

"She's wonderful." Rose glanced up, meeting his gentle blue gaze. Her heart skipped, as it so often did when she looked at him. "She's perfect," she whispered, her throat suddenly tight with emotion.

"Perfect," he said, without ever moving his eyes from her face. "My thoughts exactly."

They sat on the blanket spread in the shade of tall ponderosa pines and ate their picnic of fried chicken, biscuits with honey, canned green beans seasoned with bacon and onions, and rhubarb pie, all the while trying to keep Duchess from grabbing food from their plates. They laughed often and said little, making the puppy the center of their attention, yet never more aware of each other than they were right then.

Occasionally, they would reach for something at the same time, and their hands would touch for an instant. Only an instant. Yet the sensations lingered between them long after they'd pulled back their hands.

Time melted away. Place became unimportant. Homestead seemed on the opposite side of the world rather than simply in the valley below. Problems and worries and fears and disappointments belonged to others, not to them.

Or at least, that was how it seemed for now.

Michael lay on his back on the blanket, the puppy curled into an exhausted ball beside him. Idly, he stroked her satiny coat. "My little sister has a dog that looks a lot like Duchess."

"You have a sister?"

He turned his head to look at Rose. She, too, was lying on her back on the blanket. She wasn't looking at him, however. Instead, she was staring up at the sky.

"Yes. Her name's Fianna, and she's ten years old. I also have four brothers. Sean is eleven. Colin is twelve. Joseph is thirteen." He paused, then added, "And then there's Dillon. He's . . . closer to my age than the others."

Michael rolled onto his side, cupping the side of his head with his palm while bracing his elbow on the ground.

"Fianna looks like Kathleen, my stepmother. Dark auburn hair and green eyes. Very beautiful." He smiled. "Kathleen's the reason I have so many younger siblings. The moment my father laid eyes on her, he was smitten. I never knew a man could lose his head so thoroughly over a woman until I saw John Thomas with

Kathleen." His voice softened. "Now, I know it for a fact."

Rose met his gaze.

Michael sat up and carefully lifted the sleeping puppy out of the way before taking hold of the blanket and easing it toward him, pulling Rose along with it. She didn't sit up, didn't protest. She simply watched him with that same vigilant gaze.

"I never had time . . . or the inclination . . . to learn any love poems, Mrs. Rafferty, but right now, I wish I had." He braced himself with his elbow and forearm. Their faces were mere inches apart. "I wish I could tell you how beautiful I find your hair, that it's like the richest furs." He touched her hair with his free hand. "I wish I could tell you how the gold in your eyes has a special light of its own, and how I can see your joy and your sorrow so clearly in them." He moved his fingers to trace the curve of her mouth. "I wish I knew the words to describe what I feel when we kiss."

Her lips parted, and he heard her tiny gasp.

"Maybe," he said as he leaned toward her, "you feel it, too."

Their mouths touched. Michael didn't try to hold her, didn't try to draw her closer, didn't try to keep her from pulling back. And she didn't pull back.

Desire warmed his loins, but he forced himself to proceed slowly. With infinite care, he slid his hand around to the back of her head. His tongue traced her lips. She tasted of honey.

He leaned closer, pressing the length of his body along her side. He waited, half expecting her to try to push him away. She didn't.

While his tongue gently urged her lips to open, his fingers deftly pulled the pins from her hair. He wanted to see her dark chestnut locks spread across the blanket, glimmering in the sunshine, but he dared not break the kiss for fear she would remember to shove him away, to resurrect the wall between them.

With a tiny sigh, her lips parted. Lightly, he ran his tongue over her teeth. He heard the catch of her breath and felt a corresponding surge of desire.

She rolled toward him so slightly he suspected she didn't know she'd done it. He felt the softness of one breast pressed against his chest. He longed to touch that breast with his fingertips, longed to cup it with the palm of his hand, but he sensed to do so would shatter the fragile trust she'd placed in him. It was too soon. When she was ready, she would let him know.

Perhaps that subtle signal would have come that afternoon, if not for a puppy named Duchess.

Michael was happily surprised when Rose's tongue tentatively invaded his mouth. His kiss deepened as his fingers tangled through her thick hair.

And at that precise moment, Duchess scrambled over his back, landing on their faces.

Startled, the couple drew back from one another. There was a moment of absolute silence, and then the puppy lunged toward Rose, licking and nipping in her endearing, aggravating puppy manner.

Rose laughed. "You silly thing," she said as she sat up, holding Duchess in her arms like a beloved child.

Michael wasn't feeling quite so fond of the pet at the moment, but he gave a halfhearted smile when Rose glanced at him.

He rose from the blanket and walked toward the edge of the grassy plateau to stare down at the valley below. Not that he needed to look at it. He simply wanted a moment to bring his raging desire under control.

"Michael?"

He turned around.

She was standing at the edge of the blanket, her thick, tousled hair spreading in a dark mass over her shoulders and down her back, the puppy cradled against her breast. Her blouse was twisted in the band of her skirt. Her cheeks were flushed with color. She looked entirely too fetching, and the sight of her wasn't helping him to cool the passion that still burned hot inside him.

She took a step forward. "It's been a beautiful day, Michael. I'm glad you brought me here." She looked down. "Thank you for giving me Duchess."

He drew in a deep breath and let it out slowly

before saying, "I'm glad you enjoyed yourself, and I'm glad you like the puppy."

"Perhaps it's time we went home now?"

He smiled tenderly. She was so frightened of her feelings for him, so unsure of herself and what she wanted. But Michael had time. He had a lifetime.

I plan to love you forever, Rose. I can wait a little longer to earn yours in return.

"Yes," he said, walking toward her, "it's time we went home."

Chapter Twenty-Five

Virginia listened to the rising voices coming from the parlor and shivered. Her husband and son had been arguing the better part of the evening. It had something to do with the bank robbery that had sent Glen to prison eight years ago. She'd overheard and understood at least that much.

She closed her eyes as she sank onto a kitchen chair. She wasn't sure what she should do. She might be able to sneak upstairs and hide in her bedroom until the argument was over. She might be safe there.

But if Glen saw her. . . .

She shivered again. She didn't want to think what he might do to her if he thought she'd been eavesdropping from the kitchen. He was becoming more violent with each passing day. And he and Mark had started drinking that afternoon and had kept at it throughout the evening. Whiskey always made Glen less predictable and more likely to lose his temper with her.

She heard the sound of shattering glass and felt tears burning her eyes. She'd worked so long and so hard to make the parlor pretty. She'd scrimped and saved to buy or make all the nice things. Rose had worked hard, too.

"I said to get the hell out!"

Virginia stared at the closed door, alarmed by how close her husband's voice sounded. He must be standing in the hall, just beyond the kitchen.

A moment later, she heard the front door slam, followed by footsteps on the stairs, and then the slamming of the bedroom door. Finally, the house grew dreadfully silent. The silence was almost worse because she didn't know what would come next. She knew Glen wouldn't stay upstairs for long. He would be down, and then what would he want from her?

She should have listened to Rose. She should have gone away with her daughter when she'd first heard Glen was out of prison. She should have thrown a few things in a carpetbag and gone as far as she could go.

But what could she do outside of Homestead? This was her home. This was her boardinghouse, her only way to earn a living. This was her life, and Glen was her husband. He only treated her this way because she wasn't a good wife. If she could learn how to please him. . . .

"I told you to get out. What are you doin' back here?"

Virginia started at the sound of Glen's outraged voice. She couldn't understand what Mark replied. Hesitantly, she went to the kitchen door and pushed it open, peeking through the opening.

The two men stood at the top of the stairs. Glen's face was blotched by rage and the effects of the whiskey. His hands were closed into meaty fists.

"You get out," Glen ordered, "and don't come sniffin' round here no more."

"I won't tell anyone where it's stashed. I'm your son. I just want—"

"I know what you want, you bastard." With a furious swing, Glen smashed his fist into Mark's jaw.

Arms flailing madly, Mark tried to regain his balance, but it was useless. He fell backward, striking his head against the stairs with a mighty crack, then tumbling over again until he landed at the base.

Thump.

Virginia suspected her son was dead by the way he lay in a crumpled mass. There was something unnatural about the position.

"Come over here."

She glanced up and saw Glen staring at her. "Come *over* here," he ordered again.

Trembling, she moved forward as he descended the stairs. Glen shoved at Mark's body with the toe of his boot. Seeing no movement, he stepped over his son and grabbed Virginia by her wrist.

"You're goin' for the doctor, and you're gonna tell him you saw Mark trip an' fall down the stairs. You got that?" He waited for her to nod, then continued. "You tell him I've been feelin' poorly an' was in our bedroom when it happened. The boy had just been up to see me and was leavin' when it happened. Just lost his footing an' fell down the stairs." His grip tightened. "You understand?"

She nodded again.

He released her wrist, only to clap his hand around her neck, pressing tightly against her throat, cutting off her air. "You make sure you don't forget the way it happened."

"I . . . I won't. I won't forget."

"Good. Now get goin'."

Hank stretched his long legs out in front of the chair. The house was peaceful, now that the two young'uns were in bed. He glanced across the living room at Doris. She was sitting beside the lamp, sewing on one of Sarah's dresses, a basket of mending on the floor beside her.

"Dorie, I'm going to retire, just as soon as the town can hire a new sheriff," he announced into the silence.

Doris set her mending down in her lap and

stared at him as if he'd suddenly sprouted an extra head.

"I'm too old for this work. Job needs a younger man."

"Are you serious?"

"Dang right, I'm serious. And about time, too. I'm no spring chicken. First time we have any *real* trouble in this town, I could have my hands full." He stretched and sighed. "No, it's time I passed on this badge to a younger man."

"I think I've heard this tune before." Doris threaded a needle as she spoke. "You're as strong and hale as many a man half your age. What would you do if you weren't working?"

"I'd build that new house down along the river and then I'd go fishing."

She smiled at him, then resumed her sewing without another comment.

She didn't believe him. She didn't think he'd give up sheriffing. She'd said so to him more than once. Well, she was wrong. He'd worked hard all his life. He'd been a lawman longer than many men lived. It was time he collected a little reward for himself.

Yes, a house in the river canyon. That was just what he wanted.

A loud rapping interrupted his daydream before it could get started. "Sheriff! Sheriff!"

He rose instantly and went to open the door. Virginia Townsend stood on the other side. Tears streaked her cheeks, and her face was as white as a sheet.

"Mrs. Townsend, what is it?"

"It's Mark. He's fallen down the stairs. He's hurt. He's hurt real bad. He may be . . . he may be dead. I went for Doc Varney, but he's not in. I don't know what else to do. Please, help me."

Doris pushed her way past Hank and wrapped one arm around the other woman's shoulders. "Of course we'll help."

"Where's your husband, Mrs. Townsend?" Hank asked.

It didn't seem possible, but she seemed to grow even more pale. "He's sick," she answered quickly. "Real sick. Been in his bed all day."

"Hank, you'd better go right over there. I'll see if I can find out where the doctor is."

He nodded as he reached for his hat. "I'll do what I can till Doc comes." He stepped through the door. "Let's go, Mrs. Townsend."

It wasn't far from the McLeod home to the boardinghouse, and the two of them reached it in short order. Hank didn't wait for Virginia to open the door for him. Instead, he led the way.

Dressed in his nightshirt and robe, Glen appeared out of the parlor. When he saw Hank, his gaze hardened. "Where's the doctor? My boy needs a doctor."

Hank stepped past him and dropped to one knee beside the body. He felt Mark's throat for a pulse. There wasn't any. He stood slowly and turned around. "He doesn't need a doctor any longer."

Virginia staggered, as if she would faint. Hank moved quickly to support her, then solicitously escorted her to the nearest chair.

"I'm sorry," he said softly. "Real sorry." He straightened and looked over his shoulder at Glen. "What happened?"

"I don't know. I was in my room." Glen wiped his brow with the sleeve of his robe. "I ain't been feelin' right, an' today I took to my bed. Mark came up to see me. We talked a few minutes an' then he left. Next thing I knew, Virginia started yellin' an' sayin' Mark was hurt. Minute I looked at him, I sent her for the doc."

Hank wasn't a suspicious man by nature, but it was hard for him to believe anything that came out of Glen Townsend's mouth. Still, Mark was his son. What reason would Glen have to lie?

Hank turned back to Virginia, bending low to take hold of her hand. "Can you tell me what happened?"

"He just...." She darted a glance at her husband. "He just slipped and fell. I . . . I think he'd been drinking."

When weren't the Townsend men drinking? Hank wondered.

He turned away from Virginia for a second time. "Well, we can't just leave him lyin' there like that. Tell me which room I should take him to." He crossed to Mark's body, bent over, and lifted him off the floor.

"The room at the top of the stairs," Virginia said. "And . . . thank you, Sheriff."

The easy camaraderie Rose had felt with Michael up on the mountainside didn't vanish entirely with their return home. Remnants of it remained right up until the moment Michael announced it was time for him to retire for the night.

"Yes," Rose replied, "I guess it is that time, isn't it?"

"Allow me to see you upstairs," he said with a gallant bow. When he straightened, he offered her his arm, along with a charming smile.

Suddenly, she felt awkward and unsure. She remembered all too well the way she'd felt when he'd touched her. In truth, it was almost as if she could *still* feel his touch. It made her insides turn soft and warm just thinking about it.

"Rose?"

She glanced toward the kitchen. "Maybe I should check on Duchess one more time."

"And wake her up? Don't you dare." He motioned her forward with a jerk of his head. "Come on. It's late."

She was being silly, she decided as she turned to put out the lamp.

Just as the light flickered and died, a loud knock resounded at the door. Rose's gaze darted to her husband's dark silhouette. A sixth sense told her the knock meant trouble.

Michael stepped forward and opened the door. "Mrs. McLeod?"

"May I speak to Rose, Mr. Rafferty? There's been an accident over at the boardinghouse."

Rose felt an icy chill. "Ma? Is it Ma?" she asked as she hurried to the door, unconsciously grabbing hold of Michael's arm.

Doris McLeod shook her head. "No, dear. It's not your mother. It's Mark. He's fallen and broken his neck." Her voice lowered. "I'm afraid he's dead."

It surprised her, the sharp sadness she felt. Perhaps it was for what she'd never shared with Mark rather than for what they had shared.

"I think you're mother needs you, Rose," Doris continued. "She's quite beside herself with grief."

"Yes. Yes, of course. I'll come right away." She glanced up at Michael.

"I'll come with you," he said softly.

"Perhaps you shouldn't," Rose said. "You're still not completely well and—"

"I'm well enough to be with my wife when she needs me."

His words and the strength behind them sent a strange quiver coursing through her. With only what moonlight could creep beyond the porch and through the open door, she stared up at Michael. She felt a curious sense of relief, knowing he would be with her.

He placed his hand over hers, where it still

gripped his arm. "Whatever you need from me, I'll do."

"Thanks," she whispered.

Then, together, they followed Doris McLeod to the boardinghouse.

Chapter Twenty-Six

The next week passed in a blur for Rose. It wasn't mourning for her brother that consumed her days and nights. It was worry over her mother. Virginia's grief bordered on insanity.

After Mark's burial, Virginia locked herself into his old bedroom and refused to come out. Rose braved her father's foul moods and drunken insults to sit beside her mother's bed for long hours every day, coaxing her to eat, bringing her hot cups of tea and cold glasses of lemonade.

Michael returned to work at the hotel site across the street from the boardinghouse, and several times each day, he crossed that street to ask about Rose and Virginia. Rose didn't have the words to tell him how much his concern meant to her.

* * *

It was midafternoon, ten days after Mark's death. The day was hot for June, and there wasn't even a hint of a breeze to stir the curtains that bordered the open window.

Rose sat in the chair beside her mother's bed, reading to her from one of her favorite books.

"He'll see us all dead," Virginia said unexpectedly, her gaze locked on the ceiling as usual.

Rose paused in her reading. "What?"

"It's my fault. All my fault."

"Ma, what are you talking about?" She leaned forward.

"It's the drink." Virginia turned her head on her pillow. "I wasn't the best mother to you, Rose, and I'm sorry 'bout that."

"Oh, Ma. . . ."

Virginia's eyes filled with tears. "I wanted Mark t' be the sort of man I could be proud of, but he had too much of his pa in him. The drink and the meanness. I should've known it'd come to this."

"I don't understand, Ma. Come to what?"

Suddenly, her mother rolled over onto her side, turning her back to Rose. "You go away. You leave me be. If he thinks I've been sayin' things I shouldn't. . . ." She covered her face with her hands.

"Ma, why don't you come home with me just until you're feeling better?"

"No!" Virginia sat up, her eyes wide with alarm. "No, I can't leave! This is my home. I won't be taken from it."

Rose laid a hand on her mother's arm. "Of

311

course not. No one's going to take you from it." She stood and applied gentle pressure to Virginia's shoulders. "You lie back now and try to get some sleep."

Hesitantly, the older woman obeyed.

Rose waited until her mother's breathing became even; then she left the room and went downstairs. She was glad her father was nowhere in sight. She didn't feel like dealing with him right now.

Stepping outside, she leaned her shoulder against one of the posts that supported the porch awning. Her gaze moved across the street to the large, two-story building that was quickly taking shape. Michael stood near the rear of the hotel, calling instructions up to a workman who was standing at the top of a tall ladder.

She felt oddly content, just looking at him. She thought of all the tender, considerate things he'd done ever since they'd learned of her brother's death. He'd been there for her in a hundred different ways.

I'm falling in love with him.

She sat down on the step, too shaken by her discovery to waste time walking to the porch bench. She was afraid her legs wouldn't carry her that far.

In love with him?

She stared at the object of her thoughts, watching Michael as he moved with those long, confident strides of his. She hadn't realized before now how much she enjoyed looking at him. He was a strong man, yet he'd never used that strength to threaten or hurt her. She'd seen him angry, but he'd never allowed his anger to control him.

As those thoughts ran through her mind, she saw Duchess get up from her place in the shade and amble after Michael. She scratched at his pant leg, begging for attention. Absently, while he talked to another of his workmen, Michael bent low and scratched the puppy behind her ear.

Could Rose be in love with him?

There was so much to lose. What if she were wrong about him? What would he do if he drank too much? What would he do if *she* did something that truly angered him? Could she trust him to go on loving her even then? Could she trust him not to hurt her?

And once she admitted she loved him, she would never be free. She would be his wife forever, to do with as he pleased. Her life would belong to Michael rather than to herself.

Was loving Michael worth the risk?

She thought of Virginia, lying upstairs in Mark's old bedroom, curled up on the bed, afraid of her husband's anger, afraid of life itself. If Rose made a mistake, if she was wrong about Michael, could that be her future?

As if he knew she was thinking about him, Michael turned and looked in her direction. She saw him smile. Then he leaned down, picked up Duchess, and started across the street. Before he reached her, she rose to her feet, one hand gripping the post.

What if I can't stop myself from falling in love with you? she wondered, looking into his eyes of blue. *What if it's already too late?*

Michael couldn't help noticing the weariness that was stamped on Rose's face. It made his heart ache, knowing she was hurting. He felt helpless, frustrated that he couldn't do something more for her.

"How's your mother?" he asked.

Rose shrugged. "The same."

"I think it's time you got some rest. First you were up all hours taking care of me. Now you're wearing yourself out taking care of your mother. Let Mrs. McLeod or Mrs. Barber sit with her. They've both offered."

"I can't," she answered with a sigh.

"Yes, you can, and I think you should do it. *Now.*"

He saw the way she stiffened, as if he'd struck her instead of simply speaking forcefully. This wasn't going to be easy, he realized.

He set Duchess down and watched as she scampered up the steps to scratch at her mistress's skirt, begging for Rose's attention the way she'd begged for his only minutes before. Rose knelt on the porch floor and accepted the puppy's lavish attentions. She laughed softly when Duchess licked her face.

Michael lowered himself onto the step below her. "Rose. . . ."

She met his gaze. Her smile vanished, replaced by something much closer to panic. "I'm afraid, Michael."

"I know you are."

"It's too hard."

"No, it isn't. You can trust me."

"How do I know? How can I be sure?"

"Try me and see." He took hold of her hand. "I love you, Rose. Nothing's going to change that."

She stared into his eyes for a long time before pulling her hand free and rising. He stood, too.

"I'll be home to fix your supper," she whispered, then turned and went inside.

Michael stared at the closed door. What could he do to help? He had to do something.

He swung his gaze toward the Pony Saloon. Rose's mother was afraid; that much was clear. And from what Michael had witnessed in the past, she had reason to be. He somehow doubted this had as much to do with her dead son as it did with her husband.

He made his decision quickly. With long, ground-eating strides, he headed for the saloon. He knew he would find his father-in-law there, nursing a bottle of cheap whiskey, and he wasn't disappointed.

He walked straight up to the table, pulled out a chair, and sat down across from Glen Townsend.

"What do you want?" the man asked.

"I want to make a deal with you, Townsend."

His eyes narrowed suspiciously. "What sort of deal?"

"How would you like to make five hundred dollars?"

"Doin' what?"

"Sell me the Long Bow Valley Room and Board."

Glen snorted. "It's worth more than that."

"No, it isn't." Michael leaned his forearms on the table. "It isn't worth that now, and it'll be worth even less when the hotel opens. I can undercut whatever price the boardinghouse charges. I can do it for as long as it takes. You know I can. And I will as long as you hold any claim to it or live there."

"What're you talkin' about? You gonna throw me an' my wife out—"

"Not Mrs. Townsend. Just you." He leaned forward and lowered his voice. "I can have the money for you tomorrow, Townsend. You just sign your name to a piece of paper and move out, and I'll give you five hundred dollars." He reached into his pocket and pulled out twenty dollars, tossing the bills onto the table. "That's just a bonus if you agree to it tonight."

Glen stared at the money lying on the scratched table surface.

"Oh, there *is* one more condition."

The older man glanced up. "What?"

"You stay away from Mrs. Townsend from now on, just as you stay away from Rose.

You don't talk to her. You don't go to the
boardinghouse. You don't ever ask her for
money again."

Glen was angry, but he was also greedy.
His gaze returned to the money on the table
between them as he considered Michael's offer.
Greed won out. "A thousand. I'll do it for a
thousand dollars."

"Seven fifty," Michael countered. "That's my
last offer. I won't make it again." He stood
up.

"You've got yourself a deal." Glen slapped the
palm of his hand against the table and barked a
laugh. "You're an idiot, Rafferty. That hotel o'
yours ain't gonna make you a plug nickel, and
now you've bought yourself the boardinghouse
to boot." He took a quick drink of whiskey, then
wiped his mouth with his sleeve. "And 'cause
I know you're a gentleman an' won't go back
on your word, I'll let you in on a little secret."
It was his turn to lower his voice. "I wasn't
plannin' on stayin' in this two-bit town much
longer anyway." He laughed again.

Michael didn't let his face reveal his thoughts.
It didn't matter to him that Glen wasn't
planning on staying in Homestead. As far
as he was concerned, it was seven hundred
and fifty dollars well spent if he stayed away
from Virginia and Rose until he left town. The
boardinghouse had little to do with it.

And Michael would make sure he did stay
away.

He shoved his chair up to the table. "You get your things together tonight and be out in the morning. I'll meet you at the bank at ten o'clock."

"I'll be there, Rafferty. I'll be there."

Chapter Twenty-Seven

Stratus clouds, stained pink against a pewter sky, drifted above the mountain peaks as Rose hurried home from the boardinghouse. When she opened the door, she could hear the sizzle and pop of meat frying on the stove. Normally, the odors wafting from the kitchen would have been tantalizing, but she wasn't feeling hungry at the moment.

"Michael?"

He appeared in the doorway to the kitchen, Rose's apron tied around his waist.

"Is it true?" she demanded.

"Is what true?"

"You've bought the boardinghouse?"

He nodded, looking pleased. "It's true. I was hoping to tell you myself."

"What on earth were you thinking?" Her voice rose to a shout. Her hands were clenched into fists at her sides, and her entire body quivered with rage. "What will Ma do now? It was her home."

"Wait a minute. Your ma's not going to have to do anything. The place is hers."

"But Pa said—"

"Never mind what your pa said." He crossed the parlor in several quick strides. "I bought it so your mother would always have a home. I told your father to pack up and get out. Did he?"

"Yes, he. . . ." She stared up at him, standing so close before her. "He left. He moved into Mark's old room above the saloon." As an afterthought, she added, "Mrs. Barber said she'd stay with Ma tonight."

Michael reached out and brushed wisps of hair off her forehead. "Good. I'm glad she's not alone."

"Why did you do it, Michael?"

"For you." He drew another step closer. He tipped her chin upward with an index finger. "I did it for you, Rose. I'd do anything for you."

She knew he was going to kiss her. Her insides went all aflutter and her heart started to hammer in her chest. Her gaze seemed riveted to his mouth. She was unable to look away, unable to step away. He didn't hold her there. He wasn't even touching her except for his finger beneath her chin. Yet she was powerless to move. She could only stand and wait for his mouth to brush against hers.

And, at last, it did.

She wrapped her arms around his neck and gave herself over to his kisses, savoring the taste of him as she opened her mouth and allowed his tongue entry.

Her senses reeled. She felt both weak and strong. It was too much like a dream and yet more real than anything she'd ever felt.

"Rose," he whispered against her lips, "I love you."

No, don't speak. Don't say it.

She captured his mouth once again with hers, in order to keep him silent. She wanted to feel the fire of his kisses, wanted to drown in his arms. She didn't want to think of what it might mean. To her. To him. To them.

Michael lifted his head slightly away from hers. "Are you hungry? I've got steaks—"

"I'm not hungry."

"Good."

With a swift but gentle movement, he had her cradled in his arms, his mouth once again delighting hers. Her eyes were closed, but she knew when he carried her into the kitchen to pull the frying pan from the stove top. She felt him taking the stairs two at a time and guessed that it was to his room that he carried her.

There was still a faint light coming through the bedroom window, enough to let her see his face when he laid her on the bed and straightened above her. He stood motionless, looking down at her, as if waiting for something. She didn't know what. She didn't care what. She only knew she felt a terrible loss now that she was out of his arms.

"Michael. . . ." she whispered.

She saw him free the buttons on his shirt, then pull the garment over his head. His chest was bare beneath it. She longed to touch his skin, to feel the surprising silkiness of the dark golden hair that grew there. She remembered bathing him when he was sick, but this was different. The touching would be different.

He took hold of her hands and pulled her upright, then sat on the edge of the bed. Slowly, deliberately, he pulled the pins from her hair, causing it to fall like a cloud around her shoulders.

The feel of his fingers on her head, in her hair, caused the breath to catch in her throat. His touch was gentle, caring.

"You're so very beautiful," he whispered.

So are you.

His mouth returned to hers as his fingers nimbly freed the buttons and hooks of her blouse. A moment later, she felt cool air caress the bared flesh of her shoulders and arms.

She gasped when he touched her breasts through the thin fabric of her chemise. With his fingertips, he traced feather-light circles around them, the circles growing smaller with each revolution until he was stroking the sensitive nipples.

His hands continued their sweet torture as his mouth trailed kisses down the length of her throat. She allowed her head to fall back so she might enjoy the feeling even more. She gripped his upper arms to keep herself from falling away. She seemed to have no strength of her own.

Later, she wouldn't be sure when or how he had disrobed them. It seemed that he never stopped kissing her, never stopped caressing her, never moved away from her. And yet, he must have done so, for suddenly she realized they were reclining on the bed, their bodies entirely naked. They were naked and touching, and it was wonderful.

He suckled her breast and she gasped. He stroked her thigh and she moaned. He made her imagine things, made her want things, that she had never imagined nor wanted before. He played her body like a great musician might play an instrument, drawing forth a melody that was both beautiful and haunting.

Drawn as tight as a lariat on a wild horse, Rose felt as if she would shatter. Her flesh was heated, her breathing ragged. She ached in a wonderful, terrible way. She wanted it to stop now. She wanted it to go on forever.

Michael covered her body with his, supporting most of his weight on his elbows and knees. He kissed her eyelids, her forehead, and the tip of her nose before whispering, "I don't want to hurt you, Rose."

Instinctively, she raised her hips off the bed, pressing herself against his strange hardness. A moan escaped her throat.

"Rose, there'll be pain. Only the first time, but—"

"I don't care," she replied, meaning it. "Please. . . ."

He was right. There was pain. But she ignored it as he slowly initiated her into a private loving she hadn't dreamed existed, and soon it was forgotten.

He didn't speak, didn't command, yet she followed him as if he had done so, rising to meet his sinuous thrusts, matching his movements with her own. She delighted in the feel of his breath in her hair, the sound of her name upon his lips. She could feel his strength, yet felt no fear.

They were man and wife, two people made one, and Rose understood the concept as she'd never understood anything before.

A keening pleasure consumed her, and a tiny cry escaped her throat. She felt him plunge deeply inside her, felt his body shudder, heard his corresponding moan, so like her own.

For a time, the world stood still. There was nothing, no one besides these two. There was nothing but the feel of Michael's arms about her, his kisses, his caresses. There was nothing but the love he'd shared with her this night. Nothing but Michael. . . .

Bathed in the moonlight that now spilled through the bedroom window, they lay on their sides, their arms wrapped around each other, her cheek pressed against his chest, his chin resting on her head.

Michael wondered if Rose had fallen asleep. She hadn't stirred in the longest time. He took pleasure in the simple sound of her steady breathing, knowing she must have learned to trust him, at least a little, to be able to remain in his arms even now.

"How did you get this scar?" she whispered, her finger suddenly trailing along his ribs.

"I thought you were asleep."

"Mmm. Maybe for a little while." She traced the scar again. "How did it happen?"

"Dillon and I took a silver tray from the butler's pantry and used it to slide down the staircase. We crashed at the bottom. Broke an expensive vase. Mrs. Jergens, our housekeeper, was not pleased." He laughed softly at the memory.

"Tell me about your family. Where you come from. Everything."

"Everything?" He smiled. "Well, where do I start?" He was silent a moment as he stared at the woman beside him, wishing he could see her better than the moonlight allowed.

When the silence stretched out unbroken, she said, "Start at the beginning."

At the beginning. . . . He envisioned his father and stepmother, Dillon and the children, Mrs. Jergens and Mr. Harvey, the butler. He imagined the Rafferty home and the Palace Hotels.

They were his family, his home, his past, and the memories were bittersweet.

"I guess that would be when my father came to America from Ireland. He was poor, had nothing at all, except for a willingness to work hard and a dream to make something of himself. He made his way across the country to California and began mining for gold."

Michael felt a pulling at his heart as the memories multiplied, some good, some not so good.

"John Thomas, my father, was one of the lucky ones. He managed to find enough gold to buy his dream. He built a hotel fit for kings and queens. He called it the Palace Hotel."

His jaw clenched, as if resisting the continuation of the story, but he went on. It was time he went on.

"For a number of years, my father kept a mistress, an Irish woman of common birth. Like my father." He paused. "Funny, I never asked what her name was." Again he paused. "When he met my mother, a woman whose family was from the cream of American society, he knew he wanted to marry her. He had great plans for the Palace Hotel in San Francisco, and she was a part of those great plans. Three days before his marriage, he gave his mistress some money and sent her away."

Michael pictured his father—handsome, proud, determined, ambitious. He wondered if John Thomas might have loved his mistress.

He wondered if it had been easy for him to be rid of her or if he might have suffered from what he'd done. Michael had never asked him. He wondered why.

Rose's hand began a gentle stroking of his back, as if she sensed the story wasn't easy in its telling.

"I was born nine months to the day after their wedding. My mother died shortly thereafter. Mrs. Jergens, the housekeeper, was my mother in those early years. I traveled with John Thomas as he began building other Palace Hotels. Denver. Chicago. New York. It was quite an experience for a young boy."

"But you were lonely," Rose whispered. It wasn't a question.

He considered her comment a moment. He was mildly surprised to discover it was true. "Yes, I guess I was."

"Go on," she encouraged.

Michael held her a little tighter. "I guess my father must have been lonely, too. I remember how different he seemed after he met Kathleen O'Hara. They married the year I turned ten. Five months later, Dillon came to live with us."

"Dillon? But I thought—"

"That he was my brother? He is. My half brother, born to my father's mistress after he sent her away. Dillon's birthday is just a few days later than mine. His mother sent him to my father when she knew she was dying."

"Oh, Michael. . . ."

"I didn't find out the truth until we were sixteen. After that, I resented him."

"Oh, Michael," she whispered again.

He shook his head. "There wasn't any reason for it. I didn't feel the same way about my other brothers and sister, the children born to my father and Kathleen. But I resented Dillon. I resented every bit of affection John Thomas showed to him, every one of his successes in school and in business, everything that went right for him."

He stopped speaking, not wanting to look at those things again. He'd put his thoughts on paper. He'd sent his letters. He'd done what he could to put the past behind him. This wasn't a night for old memories. This was a night of new beginnings.

"You don't feel that way anymore, do you." Again, her words were more statement of fact than question.

He kissed the top of her head. "No, I don't feel that way anymore." Then, to change the subject, he touched a small line of puckered flesh on her arm. "Now it's your turn. Tell me how you got *your* scar."

"I used to fight with Mark a lot," she answered without hesitation. "When I was seven, he shoved me into a tree. There was a broken branch with a sharp point. Doc Varney had to give me five stitches."

He kissed her hair again, wishing he could

make her memories happier ones, hoping he could make her future all that he wanted it to be. "I'll bet you've been fighting someone most of your life."

"Most of it."

"You don't have to fight anymore." He nuzzled her earlobe.

He heard a whispering sigh.

"You *can* believe me, Rose."

She raised her head and looked up at him. In the soft moonlight, he could see her gaze searching his face, looking for answers. He knew she was afraid, understood her fears. She'd never had anyone to trust. He wanted to be that someone.

Before she could say anything, he pulled her cheek back against his chest. "It's all right, Rose. You don't have to say anything. Everything will be better from now on. I promise."

Chapter Twenty-Eight

Rose was in the mercantile the next morning when the news arrived in Homestead.

"The railroad's comin'!"

Within a matter of minutes, it seemed that every citizen of the town was packed into the store, voices buzzing excitedly.

"This will mean more to us than statehood," Doc Varney proclaimed. "Think how much faster I can get medical supplies when they're needed."

"Be a whole sight easier to ship our crops to market, too," Ted Wesley stated.

Emma Barber could scarcely contain her exhilaration. "The town'll grow faster than ever. Business will boom for certain. Everyone of us'll benefit."

Rose caught sight of Michael at that moment. Standing just inside the door, he was watching her with a secret sort of smile, his gaze gentle and loving. It made her feel all strange inside, flooding her with memories of their night together, making her forget those around her or what was happening.

Slowly, he made his way through the crowd. Her pulse quickened as she watched him drawing near. She wanted to look away from him, to deny the emotions that swelled inside her breast. She didn't want him to see, didn't want him to know what he had come to mean to her. She wanted to convince herself—and Michael, too—that what had happened between them was simply a satisfying of a physical hunger, nothing more.

When he reached her, he said, "Big news for Homestead."

That was when she remembered it. She pictured the two of them on the parlor floor, bent over the blueprints of the hotel. She remembered their laughter.

"Do you want me to give away trade secrets?"

"Yes!"

"How can I be sure you won't tell anyone?"

"Because, sir, I am your wife."

She remembered their sudden awkwardness. She remembered wondering what it would be like to love and be loved.

"This was your secret, wasn't it?" she said, trying to forget the longing that filled her heart.

He raised an eyebrow, as if he didn't understand her meaning.

"This is why you knew the hotel would succeed."

He grinned. "You found me out."

"Will it make as much difference as they say?"

"It will make even more than they imagine." His arm went around her shoulders, and he drew her close against his side.

She shouldn't have felt so safe and secure within the circle of his arms, but she did. She knew it was dangerous to let herself start caring, but she couldn't help it. She knew the day would come when her heart would be broken, when Michael would realize he didn't love her, *couldn't* love her, and then it would be over. After all, they had nothing in common. He was from a rich and privileged family. She was the daughter of a lawbreaking drunkard. He should be married to someone like Lillian Overhart, a refined young woman who belonged in society. Rose was just a small-town girl with few refinements and fewer illusions of what life had to offer.

One year. Their marriage was to last only one year. Rose knew she couldn't, shouldn't, count on anything more than that. She also knew she was beginning to want much more.

With effort, she returned her attention to those around her. The townsfolk were planning a celebration for that very night. Before long, the women were scurrying from the mercantile, on their way to their individual homes to bake their favorite dishes for that night's festivities.

Rose went, too, needing at least a little while away from Michael so he couldn't guess what she was feeling in her heart.

That evening, Addie Rider stepped through the wide doorway into Doc Varney's barn. Her eyes swept over the enclosure as memories swarmed around her, ghosts of gatherings of the past.

She remembered well the first community festivity she'd attended here. Like tonight, it had been a barn dance—the Homestead Harvest Dance. Just as tonight, the hard-packed dirt floor had been swept clean, and the air had smelled of fresh hay and straw. Long tables covered with white cloths and platters and bowls of food had lined a wall, just as now. Even the Chinese lanterns hanging from the rafters had looked the same.

She glanced toward the makeshift riser at the far end, where the musicians were already playing a foot-stomping tune.

"Remember our first dance?" Will asked as he joined her in the doorway.

Addie nodded. "I remember it well." She glanced at him. "I remember everything about that night."

He kissed her temple, then whispered, "So do I. Especially how you looked in the red glow from the fireplace, your nightgown lying at your feet."

She lightly slapped his shoulder as her cheeks

flamed with color. "Shh! What if someone hears you?"

"You think they don't know I like to make love to my wife?" Will chuckled.

Despite herself, she smiled.

"Care to dance with me, Mrs. Rider?" he asked, the twinkle still in his eyes.

"I'd love to, Mr. Rider," she answered and stepped into his waiting arms.

Dancing with Will was as magical tonight as it had been nearly ten years before. While the music played, there were only the two of them. She didn't need to worry about their children or the ranch or anything else. There were just this night and love.

Silently, she sent up a quick prayer of thanks to God for bringing her to Homestead all those years ago. Her heart spilled over with joy and gratitude for all the love she had known with this man.

When the music stopped, Will took hold of her elbow and guided her toward the refreshments, where Rose Rafferty served them each a cup of punch. They chatted amiably with Emma Barber and Doris McLeod and Zoe Potter as they sipped their drinks and looked around at all their friends and neighbors.

Once again, Addie sent up a silent prayer of thanks, this time for all of these people who had come to mean so much to her through the years. So many of them were more than friends and neighbors. They were like family to her.

Music started again, and Addie glanced
toward the dance floor just as Yancy put his
hand in the small of Lark's back and began to
dance with her. She felt Will stiffen. She waited
anxiously to see what he would do. After several
seconds had passed and he hadn't moved from
her side, she dared a glance up at him.

She didn't see anger or indignation. What
she saw was resignation. She knew then that
Will had finally admitted to himself that Lark
had fallen in love, that he couldn't fight the
inevitable, that he would never again be the
apple of his daughter's eye. Lark had grown
up, and she was moving away from him, into
a life of her own.

Addie slipped her hand into his and squeezed
it. Will looked down at her. She offered him
a tender smile that told him she understood.
Then, in unison, they returned their gazes to
Lark and Yancy.

At that moment, Yancy Jones couldn't care
less what other folks thought of him. What
mattered was what Lark thought, and right
now, she was looking at him as if he was as
handsome as a new rope on a thirty-dollar
pony, half again as tall as a bull buffalo, and
as wise as a tree full of owls. Her luminous
round eyes never wavered from his face as he
whirled her around the barn, her long dress
popping like the crack of a whip.

It wasn't as if he didn't know he should

have refused when she'd sauntered up and asked him to dance. He told himself he'd only agreed to save her from embarrassment since she'd asked him in front of a whole passel of cowpokes standing outside, smoking their rolled cigarettes. Truth was, he couldn't have said no, not when she'd looked at him with hunger in those blackstrap-colored eyes of hers. When she did that, he was as helpless as a cow in quicksand.

But maybe it wasn't such a bad thing, the two of them dancing together like this. It let every other man in Long Bow Valley know that Yancy Jones had staked his claim. Lark Rider wasn't available for courting anymore.

A half smile curved one corner of his mouth. Two more weeks and he'd have his hundred dollars for Mr. Stanford at the First Bank of Homestead and the old Hadley place would be the new Jones place. With Michael Rafferty's generous wages and the long hours he'd been putting in, both on the hotel construction and at the mill, Yancy had already been able to place orders for fencing materials and some furniture for the house. Not much. Just enough to get him by. It was a long ways from being suitable for Lark Rider to live in.

The music stopped. For a moment, Yancy stood in the middle of the crowded barn, his arms still holding Lark.

"Yance?" There was a world of wanting in the way she spoke his name.

He wanted to tell her he loved her. He wanted to march right over to her pa and tell him the two of them were gettin' hitched and that was final. He wanted to hold her and kiss her and make love to her from the second the sun went down till it came up again.

But the time wasn't right. He didn't own his own place, hadn't stocked it with horses or cattle, didn't have much more than a bed and a chair inside the house he lived in. He'd yet to prove himself worthy of Lark to Will Rider and the rest of the town or even to himself.

No, the time wasn't right to do what she was wordlessly asking him to do.

"Oh, Yancy," she whispered breathlessly, tears welling up.

He surprised himself with how quickly he turned and, still holding her by one hand, pulled Lark across the barn and through the doorway, past the group of men enjoying their cigars and cigarettes beneath the star-studded heavens, and into the mass of tethered horses, buggies, and wagons.

He stopped just as abruptly as he'd begun, this time pulling her up tightly against him and kissing her as he'd been aching to do for longer than he cared to think about. It had been far too many weeks since she'd led him into that grove of cottonwoods and aspens and offered her lips to him, and Yancy felt like a starving man faced with a sumptuous banquet. He intended to indulge and to hell with the repercussions.

* * *

Rose watched as her friend was whisked out of the barn.

"Looks like Yancy's as much in love as I am," Michael said softly, leaning close to her ear as he spoke.

A shiver ran up her spine in response.

"I think it's time for you and me to dance, Mrs. Rafferty. You've been working behind that punch bowl all evening, and it's time someone else helped out."

"But I. . . ."

Much as she'd seen Yancy do, Michael took hold of her hand and led her toward the other couples who were dancing. She tried to work up her anger, tried to tell herself he was being domineering and demanding again, but it didn't work this time. The truth was, she wanted to dance with him.

She slipped into his embrace as if she'd been doing it for years. He guided her around the floor in time to the music so expertly that he made her feel graceful and refined, even though she knew full well she had two left feet.

Unable to keep herself from it, she turned her eyes up toward his. He was watching her with a look that made her insides turn soft and warm.

She wondered if he would make love to her again that night.

"Rafferty!"

Rose was stopped as much by her father's

voice as by Michael's arms as he shielded her with his body, deftly moving her to stand behind him. She leaned slightly to one side in order to see around him.

"You knew about this, didn't you?" Glen swayed drunkenly as he shook his fist at Michael. "The railroad. You knew when you bought the boardinghouse."

The music stopped. The crowd quieted around them.

"I don't think this is the time to discuss business, Mr. Townsend," Michael returned in an even tone.

"What the hell do I care what you think? You ain't gettin' away with it." He swung wildly in Michael's direction.

His hand still on Rose's arm, as if to reassure himself of her safety, Michael adroitly side-stepped his assailant's fist.

Before Glen could gather himself for another attack, the sheriff appeared, grabbing Glen by his wrist and hauling it up behind his back, eliciting a cry of protest.

"That's enough of that for one evening," Hank said. "I think you'd better come over to the jail and sleep this off."

"I'm not the one you should be arrestin', Sheriff. It's him. It's that son of a bitch who had his way with my girl an' stole the boardin'house from me."

Rose heard a gasp from those around her and felt many pairs of eyes turn her way.

339

Michael took a quick stride forward and grabbed Glen by the lapel, jerking him away from Hank and lifting him nearly off his feet. "Say what you want about me, Townsend, but be careful what you say about my wife. Now, you let these good people know that what you implied wasn't true before the sheriff has to arrest me for breaking your stinking neck."

Rose could feel her husband's fury, and she could witness the terror in her father's face.

"Tell them," Michael said again, tightening his grip on Glen's collar.

"Michael. . . ." the sheriff warned.

"Tell them." His tone, though softer, carried an even deeper threat.

"It ain't," Glen managed to say, his voice a coarse whisper. "It ain't true."

Michael nodded. "Thank you. Now let me tell *you* something. I happen to love your daughter, and I won't allow you or anyone else to hurt her. Do I make myself clear, Townsend?"

Glen nodded frantically.

"Good." Michael shoved her father back toward the waiting sheriff. Then he brushed his shirtfront as if to rid himself of filth before turning toward Rose. "I believe this was our dance." As he took her into his arms again, he glanced toward the musicians, who quickly began playing a song.

Rose was only vaguely aware of Hank taking her father away, only slightly aware of the other couples who joined them again in a waltz. She

340

was too busy staring up at her husband and hearing his words echoing over and over again in her head.

I happen to love your daughter, and I won't allow you or anyone else to hurt her.

He meant it. He loved her.

But will it last?

Rose was afraid to believe it could. Nothing good had ever lasted for Rose. She was so afraid this wouldn't either.

But she wanted to believe. She wanted desperately to believe his love would last.

If only she could be sure.

Chapter Twenty-Nine

Will wasn't surprised to see Yancy riding his gray stallion into the yard of the Rocking R the next afternoon. In fact, he'd expected him to come even earlier in the day.

He stepped down from the porch, squinting his eyes against the bright sunlight as he waited for his future son-in-law to arrive.

Yancy stopped his horse about half-a-dozen yards away from where Will stood. He touched the brim of his Stetson. "Mr. Rider."

"Yancy."

The cowboy dismounted. "I've come to talk to you about Lark."

"I know."

"Guess you already know that I'm in love with her and am askin' for your permission to make her my wife."

"Yes, I know."

Yancy cleared his throat nervously.

Will knew even more than the younger man

had told him. He knew that Yancy was working two jobs as well as repairing the old farmhouse at the east end of the valley. He knew that Yancy not only worked hard, but did his best at any task assigned to him. He knew that Yancy was honest and determined, and he knew, deep in his heart, that Yancy would love and cherish Lark, just as she deserved.

He suppressed a sudden smile. No point making this easier on the man. As he recalled, he'd been mighty nervous himself when he'd proposed to Addie.

"I love Lark, Mr. Rider, and I mean to provide her a good home. I don't pretend that I'll be able to give her what she's had here. At least not real soon. But I'll see that she's never in want, and I'll see that she's happy."

"I see," Will replied softly.

"I'm buyin' the old Hadley place and fixin' up the house. I've got me a job at the sawmill to see us through until I can buy me some cattle and a few horses to work 'em."

"Hmm."

Yancy stepped forward, his expression deadly earnest. "Mr. Rider, I'm askin' for your permission. I hope you'll give it 'cause I don't mean to go away. I'm gonna stay right here, no matter what."

"I see. Well then, I don't suppose it would do me much good to say no. But it's up to Lark whether or not she wants to marry you. You'll have to ask her yourself."

343

Yancy seemed stunned speechless by Will's reply.

Will turned and glanced up at Lark's window. He saw the sudden closing of the curtains and grinned to himself. "I imagine she knows you're here and is waitin' to see what you came for." He looked at Yancy again, then held out his hand. "Good luck."

The cowboy took hold of the proffered hand and shook it. "Thanks, Mr. Rider."

"Just don't ever call me Pa," he continued with false gruffness.

Yancy actually chuckled. "No, sir. I wouldn't think of it."

Will jerked his head toward the house. "Get on inside. You'll feel better when the asking is behind you."

He watched the younger man step up onto the porch and knock on the door; then he looked one more time up at his daughter's window.

The place was sure going to seem strange once she was gone.

Rose was hanging laundry out to dry when Lark came galloping Dark Feather down the road to Homestead. Lark must have seen her standing near the clothesline, for she turned the little mare abruptly, slowing her just soon enough to prevent a cloud of dust from covering the newly washed bedsheets. Rose knew at once that something wonderful had happened, judging by her friend's joyous expression.

Lark hopped down from the saddle. "We're engaged!" she shouted, then threw herself into Rose's arms. "Yancy asked me to marry him, and I said yes!" She backed away and twirled in a circle, her arms thrust heavenward. "Oh, I'm so happy I could burst!"

Rose laughed aloud. "Calm down a minute and tell me about it."

Her friend stopped spinning and grasped Rose by both hands, drawing her toward the shade of the tree where they dropped to the ground. "Yancy rode out to the ranch today. He told Papa he wanted to ask for my hand, and Papa said he could. Do you believe it? After Papa was so stubborn and all. He even *punched* Yancy before we went to Boise, just because he kissed me, and now he actually seems happy about it. We're going to get married in September. Mother has all sorts of ideas for the wedding and the dress. Oh, Rose, I can hardly wait."

Rose didn't try to say anything. She simply smiled, knowing her friend well enough to wait until her outburst had run its course.

"Yancy even has his own place now. Did you know that? I went out there once when he wasn't home, just to see what it was like. It's small and plain, but I can fix it up really nice. And we'll be all alone out there with no one to bother us. He can kiss me all night long if he wants to and no one can tell him to stop."

Rose thought of Michael's kisses and what they led to, and her stomach tumbled. They'd made love again last night, and it had been even more glorious than the first time. She'd clung to him silently, long after the loving was over, wishing time would stand still and she would never be forced to leave his arms.

"What's it like, Rose?" Lark whispered.

She blinked, bringing her attention back to her friend. "I'm sorry. What did you say?"

"What's it like? You know. When you're . . . well, when you . . . you know what I mean."

Rose felt the heat rising in her cheeks. She looked down at her hands as she plucked blades of grass from the earth. "It's very . . . special," she replied softly.

"Rose. . . ." There was a note of surprise in Lark's voice.

She didn't look up.

"You love him, don't you? You're not just pretending anymore."

It wasn't really a question, but Rose nodded slowly in reply.

"Oh, Rose. . . ." Lark took hold of her by one hand. "I'm so very glad for you. You deserve to be happy." She leaned forward and kissed Rose's cheek.

She wished she were as sure of her own happiness as Lark seemed to be. She didn't want to think beyond the next year, for that was where sorrow awaited her.

Lark flopped backward onto the ground, her

346

hands tucked beneath her head, her eyes staring up at the cloudless blue sky. "Remember when we used to come sit in the shade of these trees and talk and share our hopes and dreams? I was so shy and afraid back then. I scarcely talked to anyone but you. Remember?"

It was hard to believe that was ever true.

"You were always fighting Mark because he was saying mean things about me. Remember how he used to call me a—" Abruptly, Lark sat up. Her eyes widened, lost their sparkle. Her voice was a breathless whisper. "Rose, what if he doesn't know?"

"Know what?" Rose asked, confused by her friend's sudden change of mood.

"What if Yancy doesn't know about . . . about my real father? That he was half Sioux Indian."

"It won't matter to him."

"But what if it does?"

Rose remembered well the way her brother had tortured Lark about her Indian heritage, always calling her a breed and telling her nobody liked her because of it. For a while, other children and even some adults had sided with Mark, but eventually it didn't matter to most folks. She doubted they even remembered that Lark wasn't actually Will and Addie Rider's natural daughter, let alone that she was part Indian.

"I'll have to tell him," Lark said softly. Tears filled her eyes. "Why didn't I think of this before?"

Robin Lee Hatcher

Rose put her arms around her friend and hugged her close. "Because it doesn't matter. It doesn't matter at all."

Lark had never been as afraid as she was now. She didn't ride Dark Feather very hard or fast on her way to Yancy's place. She wasn't in as great a hurry as she'd been earlier this afternoon.

She saw Yancy before he saw her. He was digging postholes, his muscles straining, his arms moving in a steady rhythm as he scooped the dirt up and tossed it into a pile.

She wished she could be as certain of Yancy's feelings as Rose had been, but Lark remembered too well the way some people had treated her after her parents died, both at the orphanage and here in Homestead. She knew that many otherwise respectable, seemingly open-minded people could be prejudiced against those who were different. She'd heard the slurs and insults often enough.

Yancy was working without a shirt, and his torso was covered with a sheen of sweat. She didn't think she'd ever seen a man look so fine without a shirt on as Yancy did. He'd thought her pretty before. He'd told her so. Would he still think her pretty when she told him the truth?

Yancy raised an arm to wipe his forehead. As he did so, he saw her riding toward him. His mouth turned up in a pleased grin as he reached for his shirt and put it on. By the time she'd pulled her mare to a halt, he was ready to help her to the ground.

"I didn't expect to see you again today," he said before kissing her on the lips. "Does your pa know you're here?"

"I . . . I needed to tell you something before . . . before Mother goes any further with the wedding plans."

His smile immediately disappeared. "What's wrong?"

She took a deep breath. A sick knot had formed in her stomach, and her knees felt weak. Even her voice quivered. "There's something you don't know about me, Yancy. I . . . I never thought about it before, but. . . ."

He took hold of her upper arms, forcing her to look at him. "What is it, Lark? Don't go worryin' me like this."

Once started, the words tumbled out of her mouth quickly. "Yancy, if you marry me, you've got a right to know our children will be part Sioux Indian. My grandmother was full Lakota Sioux. Will Rider is really my uncle. He and Addie adopted me when I was eight years old. I suppose most folks around here have forgotten where I came from or just never knew, but I couldn't let you marry me without knowing." She stopped as abruptly as she'd begun, waiting for his reaction, wanting it and dreading it at the same time.

His expression softened as he drew her

against his chest, wrapping her in his arms. With his mouth near her ear, he said, "Did you really think it'd matter?"

She nodded as tears spilled over, running down her cheeks to dampen his shirt.

"Lark, I figure I'm the luckiest man west o' the Mississippi. I hope we have us enough kids to start our own school, and I'm gonna love each and every one of 'em, especially if they look like their ma." He kissed the crown of her head. "I've been workin' the range near on half my life. I knew you didn't get your looks from Will or Addie, and I figured out the rest on my own."

"And you don't care?" she whispered.

"Care? Yeah, I cared. I cared that I wasn't good enough for you. I'm still not, but I'm not about to let you go now. It don't matter what excuse you come up with to call off the weddin'. We're gettin' married come September."

Finally, she was able to raise her head and look at him. She could see the truth in his eyes. He *really* didn't care. He meant every word he said.

"Oh, Yance, I love you so."

"I reckon you better, 'cause I sure as heck love you." He cradled her face with his callused hands. "And don't you ever doubt it again."

He kissed her, just the way she liked to be kissed. The kind of kiss that took her breath clean away and left her feeling as limp and useless as a rag doll. He kissed her until her insides felt all strange and yearning and her outsides all hot and tingly. He kissed her until he'd stolen the last shreds of doubt from her mind, the last scrap of fear from her heart.

And by the time he was finished kissing her, Lark's only thought was how far off September still was.

Chapter Thirty

Michael looked up from the papers in his hands, glancing across the room at Rose. The lamp cast a soft yellow glow over her, gilding the chestnut hair that fell in a smooth cascade about her shoulders. He liked it when she wore her hair down.

The past week since the barn dance had been one of the best of his life. Folks were treating him like a respected and longtime resident of the town, rather than a stranger. The hotel construction was coming along right on schedule. Furnishings for the hotel were expected to arrive this week. And every night Rose went up those stairs with him and into his bedroom.

He marveled at the contentment he felt as he sat in the small parlor, observing his wife while she mended the shirt he'd torn on a nail the day before. The house was quiet except for the ticking of the clock on a nearby table. The only sounds carried on the soft June breeze through the open window were the rustle of leaves stirring in the trees and an occasional *jug-o-rum* of a bullfrog.

He should be feeling restless, he thought as he listened to the soft country sounds. He *would* have felt restless just a couple of months ago. If he'd never come to Homestead, he would be dining in the opulent homes of friends, attending social gatherings and hob-nobbing with San Francisco society instead of sitting in this quiet parlor, watching a beautiful woman mending his shirt. If he'd never come to Homestead, he would, more than likely, be discussing business deals at this very moment in smoke-filled rooms, oblivious to the din of voices all around him.

The miracle was he didn't feel restless. He felt relaxed, content. For the most part, he felt happier than he'd ever been in his life. There was only one thing that he needed to complete his happiness. He wanted Rose to admit she loved him.

What, he wondered, would he have to do to teach her to trust him? How did he touch a heart that was so closely guarded?

Rose set the mending in her lap and rubbed her eyes with the pads of her fingers. When she lowered her hands, she glanced his way to find him watching her. For a moment, she simply stared at him in return.

Michael wondered what she was thinking

353

behind those beautiful hazel eyes.

"I'm tired," she said at last. "I think I'll go to bed."

Instantaneously, he pictured her in his bed, the sheets and bedcovers rumpled, her lush body naked. Desire burned in his loins.

"Me, too," he whispered, his voice husky with restrained passion.

He wondered at her power to excite him so easily. He was no stranger to the sexual pleasures to be found in a woman's arms, but he had never felt this all-consuming hunger before. He never seemed to get enough of Rose, no matter how many times he made love to her. Even after a week of loving, his appetite for her had not waned. In fact, it seemed to increase with every passing day.

They rose from their chairs simultaneously. The room was no longer silent. It seemed to crackle with fervent, unspoken emotions.

Michael knew, even as he stepped forward to draw Rose into his impassioned embrace, that she was giving him her body willingly, but still had a tight rein on her heart. He hoped one day she would give him both.

Later—much later—Rose listened to her husband's even breathing and knew that, at last, he slept. Carefully, so as not to awaken him, she slipped from his embrace and out of the bed. She pulled her nightgown over her head, then padded on bare feet to the window.

The night sky above was the color of ink, dotted by thousands of stars but without even a sliver of moon. The earth below was covered in a blanket of darkness, all in varying shades of black.

For one of the few times in Rose's life, she felt safe and secure. More importantly, she felt loved, cherished, wanted. She knew these were momentary feelings. Michael would eventually go away just as her pa had eventually returned. The fragile happiness she had found would vanish like a wisp of smoke in a strong wind.

But not yet. Not just yet.

The following day, the stagecoach rolled into Homestead right on schedule. The cloud of dust that had chased it for many miles caught up with its prey, then whirled down the street on its own, leaving those in its wake coughing and blinking their eyes.

"We're here, folks," the driver shouted as he hopped down from his perch. He yanked open the door. "Welcome to Homestead."

John Thomas Rafferty stepped out first. His sharp eyes made a quick appraisal of the town; then he turned and assisted his wife from the coach. Kathleen was followed by Joseph, Colin, Sean, and Fianna.

John Thomas cast one more glance about him before saying, "We'll find us a place to stay first. Then I'll seek out Michael."

355

"*We'll* seek out Michael," Kathleen replied firmly.

He narrowed his eyes, but he didn't bother to argue with her. He would have been wasting his time to do so. He could tell by the look in her green eyes.

John Thomas found the driver behind the coach, where he was unloading their luggage. "Can you recommend a good place to stay?"

"Only one place in Homestead till the hotel is finished. That's the boardinghouse." He jerked his head to one side. "Down that way."

"Thank you, sir. We appreciate your help."

"Come along, children," Kathleen said softly.

The family crossed the street, then followed the uneven boardwalk past the livery and blacksmith shop, a saloon with a false front, and a barbershop and bathhouse. Before they reached it, they could see the sign for the Long Bow Valley Room and Board. They could also see the new hotel under construction just across the street.

John Thomas slowed his steps as he stared at the two-story building taking shape. "The boy has lost his mind," he murmured to himself.

"Or fallen in love," his wife added as they stopped walking altogether.

He glanced at Kathleen. "No man gives up a fortune to live in a town like this just for love."

"It's not as if he's destitute, J.T. Michael has acquired a sizable worth of his own. He doesn't need your business to survive."

"Nonsense. He's wanted nothing more than Palace Hotels since he was six years old. Why do you think he's fought Dillon every step of the way? He wants the hotels."

Kathleen's smile was tolerant. "And what about his wife?"

"No doubt she's a fortune-hunting strumpet who will leave him if offered the right incentives."

"Or perhaps she actually loves Michael."

John Thomas gave a derisive grunt.

"I don't think you read one word of his letter after the part about his remaining in Homestead to run this hotel."

What she said was close to the truth, but he wasn't about to admit it. He'd come to Homestead to talk some sense into his eldest son. The last thing he needed was a mother filled with lots of romantic notions. He hadn't even wanted to bring her with him, but Kathleen always seemed to manage to get her own way. John Thomas just couldn't seem to say no to her.

As if she'd read his thoughts, she smiled, tightening her grip on his arm and leaning forward to kiss his cheek. "You really are a terrible impostor, John Thomas Rafferty," she whispered near his ear, "and I love you for it."

Michael was seated at the kitchen table, eating his lunch, when the knock sounded at the door.

"I'll get it," Rose told him as she left the room.

He heard the door open. There was a moment of silence before a man said, "I'm looking for Michael Rafferty." Another pause. "I'm his father."

Michael rose quickly to his feet. He hadn't expected this. He'd expected a letter, perhaps even a telegram. But not this.

Kathleen's voice reached his ears before he could head for the door. "And you must be Rose. I'm Kathleen Rafferty, Michael's stepmother."

In a few long strides, Michael reached the doorway. "Father. Kathleen. I didn't expect—"

"What on earth *did* you expect us to do when we learned you were married?" Kathleen stepped forward and gave him a warm hug and a kiss on the cheek. Then she whispered, "I can see why you married her, Michael. She's lovely."

He returned Kathleen's embrace, but it was his father's reaction he was awaiting. He was surprised by the confused emotions that surged through him. Old angers. Insecurities. Hopes and expectations. Admiration. Disappointments.

"May I come in?" John Thomas asked.

"Of course." Michael motioned toward the sofa. "Please."

He could see the way his father looked about him. For a moment, he saw the house through his father's eyes. Michael wondered if he was crazy to give up what he'd had in San Francisco, to give up the life of opulence, of travel, of society balls and charity suppers, of hardheaded business dealings.

Then he looked at Rose, and everything fell back into place.

Michael put his arm around her shoulders. Leaning down, he touched his forehead to hers. "They're going to love you," he said softly.

Rose wasn't so sure about that. She'd seen the way Michael's father had looked at her, had looked at the home she'd made for her husband. The older man's disapproval was palpable.

"Come on." Michael moved them toward the chairs that sat opposite the sofa. After Rose was seated, he drew the other chair over close to hers, sat down, then reached for her hand. Looking at his parents, he said, "I guess the news of my marriage came as somewhat of a surprise."

"It was," John Thomas responded. "But not as much as your other announcement."

Rose glanced sideways at her husband. What was his father referring to? What other announcement?

"I expect you've changed your mind by this time," John Thomas continued.

"No. I haven't."

"But to give up everything you've ever worked for. . . ." Michael's father shook his head. "It's because of this thing with Dillon, isn't it? Well, perhaps Kathleen was right. I should have found another way to settle things. Come back to San Francisco and we'll discuss it."

Rose was growing more and more confused. And frightened.

"Palace Hotels needs you, Michael. And you need them. You'll never be satisfied living in the territories, running a small hotel."

Michael's hand tightened on hers, but his gaze was glued to the man opposite him. "You're wrong, Father. Palace Hotels doesn't need me. You're going to be around for a long time to come, and when you retire, Dillon or Joseph or Colin or Sean can take over. And you're wrong about something else, too. I *can* be happy living here, running a small hotel. I'm happy now, happier than I ever knew I could be. Maybe if I get tired of it, I'll buy some land and raise cattle. I've got friends here who can help me get the hang of being a cowboy." Michael turned his head and looked straight into Rose's eyes. "I guess whatever we do is up to Rose and me to decide."

Her heart hammered with frightening intensity.

"You see, Father, I found something more important than building a successful hotel. I found Rose."

His image swam before her as she fought unwelcome tears. The wall she'd so carefully constructed to shield her heart was crumbling about her. She felt stripped, exposed, unprotected.

But she couldn't stop herself from loving him. Not now. Not even forever.

Chapter Thirty-One

Rose stood before the mirror, staring at her reflection. She couldn't believe the woman she saw in the glass was really Rose Townsend.

A wisp of a smile curved her mouth. Perhaps she wasn't Rose Townsend. Perhaps the woman in the mirror was Rose Rafferty.

The striped dress of dark blue satin and fawn silk net had arrived on yesterday's stage, along with more than a dozen other dresses, all of them of the latest fashion, all of them more expensive than anything she'd ever owned before. They'd been delivered to the house shortly after Michael's parents had returned to the boardinghouse.

Michael had watched her open the parcels, eagerly awaiting her response to each and every one of the gowns. And there were other things besides. Frilly undergarments. Matching gloves, parasols, and purses. Shoes made of satin and kid; real shoes, not boots with buttons to be hooked and unhooked. Silk stockings in various shades. Hats with ribbons and plumes, even fur.

"Why, Michael?" she'd asked, holding one of the dresses against her bosom while staring at the bounty spread on the floor before her.

"Because, my dear, you're lovely, and you deserve lovely things."

Lord, how she'd wanted to give in to the tenderness in his voice. How very much she'd wanted to believe him. Wanted to believe him still.

She blinked away the memory, bringing her attention back to the young woman in the mirror. She hadn't time for woolgathering. Not today. She was to prepare tonight's supper for Michael's entire family over at the boardinghouse. It had been Michael's idea. He wanted to show his father what a successful restaurant the hotel would have with Rose in charge.

She wondered how her mother was doing with a house full of Raffertys. Rose thought Virginia's health and mental state had improved some since Michael had purchased the boardinghouse and put her father out. But there was still a haunted look in Virginia's eyes that made Rose uneasy. How would her mother cope with Michael's family, especially his father?

She felt a shiver run through her as she

remembered the way John Thomas Rafferty had looked at her yesterday. At best, he held her in contempt.

She took a deep breath. *You'll not be frightened of him,* she silently scolded herself. *You're every bit as good as he is, for all his money and power.*

She lifted her chin and straightened her shoulders. She was going to do Michael proud by fixing the best meal John Thomas, Kathleen, and their children had ever eaten. She owed Michael that much after all he'd given her.

And because she loved him.

But she wouldn't allow herself to think about that now. It didn't bear thinking about. If she thought about it, she would have to admit to herself that she wasn't every bit as good as John Thomas Rafferty, and she wasn't good enough for his son.

Rose turned away from the mirror and walked resolutely out of the bedroom and down the stairs. Her pace didn't slow as she passed the hotel site, not even when she saw Michael showing his father around. She walked on toward the mercantile, ticking off the things she would need to prepare the meal she had in mind.

She was concentrating so hard she didn't see her pa until it was too late. By that time, he'd grabbed hold of her arm and hauled her into the shadowed alleyway between the saloon and the livery.

"Pa!" she whispered as his fingers pinched into her arm.

"Well, at least you remember who I am to ya."

She recoiled from the smell of whiskey on his breath. Memories of his strength and the way he used it when he was drunk swarmed over her, but she didn't let fear find its way into her voice. "Let go," she demanded firmly. "You're hurting me."

He didn't obey. Instead, his grip tightened. "You think you're somethin' with that rich husband o' yours, don't ya? Look at ya, all gussied up like some fancy woman. Well, you just watch your step, girly, 'cause I'm still your pa." He yanked her toward him, leaning his face down toward hers. "It's only 'cause I don't aim t' stay in this town that he's gettin' away with takin' what's mine. Stole the boardin'house from me; that's what he did. And you helped him cheat me outta it."

"The boardinghouse was never yours. Ma's paid for it with her own pain and sweat. It belongs to her."

"You watch your mouth," he growled, "or you might be the next brat to fall down a flight o' stairs." Then he shoved her away from him.

Her eyes widened, and her breathing quickened. "What are you saying?"

"You just watch yourself, Rose." He pointed at her. "An' keep an eye on that man o' yours, too." Then he stumbled drunkenly away.

Rose leaned against the wall of the livery, a new fear stirring in her heart. Was he saying what she thought he was saying? Had he done something to Mark?

He could have. She knew he was capable of it. She'd always believed it was her pa who'd killed Tom McLeod and set the sawmill ablaze the night he'd left Homestead. But would he kill his own son? No. No, he couldn't have. Even her pa wouldn't do that.

You just watch yourself, Rose. An' keep an eye on that man o' yours, too.

She shuddered. If anything happened to Michael. . . .

Michael was proud of what had been accomplished in the weeks since he'd arrived in Homestead. He showed it all to his father without hesitation or apology. No, it wasn't a Palace Hotel, but it was *his* hotel. He had designed it, and he knew it would succeed. It would be important to the people of Homestead. His friends. His neighbors.

John Thomas's approval came grudgingly, but it was there all the same.

"You've done a fine job, son. You've proven your point. Now it's time to come home."

"I thought I'd made myself clear yesterday. I don't intend to come back. Rose and I are quite happy here."

"But don't you—"

"Father," he interrupted, placing a hand on

the older man's shoulder, "I'm not doing this out of anger or spite or revenge. It's my choice. It's what I want to do. I discovered I didn't care much for the man I'd become. But here. . . ." He gestured toward the town. "Here I've found something better. Here *I'm* better."

John Thomas stared at him a moment, then shook his head. "I don't understand."

"Stay here awhile. You will." Michael glanced across the street at the boardinghouse. "And give Rose a chance, too," he added.

His father scowled. "You haven't told us how you met her or what caused you to marry so quickly."

"I met her at the boardinghouse when I came to Homestead. I married her so quickly because . . . because it seemed the right thing to do. And it was."

"You really think you're in love with the girl?"

Michael's voice hardened as he turned a steady gaze on his father. "I don't *think* it. I *know* it."

John Thomas looked as if he would try to dispute Michael's statement, then pressed his mouth together to hold back the words.

Michael breathed a silent sigh of relief. He didn't want to argue with his father. Especially not about Rose. "Let me show you the dining area," he said, then led the way.

Rose worked alone in the boardinghouse kitchen. She had refused both her mother's and Kathleen Rafferty's offers of help. Tonight's meal was something she wanted to do alone. It was important she did it alone. She had something to prove—to herself, to Michael, to his family.

Besides, the solitude gave her time to think about her confrontation with her pa earlier in the day. After some careful reasoning, she'd decided she needn't fear his threats. Michael was more than capable of taking care of himself. He'd dealt quite handily with Glen Townsend on several other occasions. Besides, her pa had said he didn't plan to stay in Homestead. She just hoped he would go soon.

With the back of her hand, she pushed stray wisps of hair away from her face. The kitchen was warm this late in the afternoon. Perspiration beaded her forehead. She could have done with a moment outside in the shade of the poplars, but there was still too much to be done before supper.

Still, she had to admit she'd accomplished a great deal already, and she was pleased. Potatoes were boiling on the stove and a fine cut of beef was roasting in the oven, along with carrots and slices of onions. Two pies cooled on the windowsill, along with some freshly baked bread.

She wished it were later in the season. She would have loved to serve some fresh apples or cherries from the orchards that thrived down along the Snake River.

She heard the kitchen door open behind her as she removed the potatoes from the stove. "I told you to relax, Ma. I'll take care of supper tonight."

"So she told me."

Rose almost dropped the kettle. She set it down quickly, then turned to face her father-in-law. "Mr. Rafferty. You surprised me." She wiped the sweat from her brow with the back of her hand; then, embarrassed, she dried her hand on her apron.

"Smells good," he commented as he moved forward into the center of the kitchen, stopping at the table.

"Thank you."

John Thomas cleared his throat before saying, "Young woman, I believe my son is making a grave mistake that he will one day regret. However, he doesn't seem inclined to listen to his father's reasoning at the moment. I'm hoping I might engage your cooperation."

A knot formed in her stomach. She no longer felt the heat of the kitchen. Instead, she felt a chill of trepidation seeping through her veins.

"What is it you want from me, sir?" she asked softly, dreading his reply.

"I think you know. I think that's why you married my son. Will five thousand dollars be adequate?"

"Five thousand dollars?" She felt desperately short of breath. "For what?"

"Why, to leave my son, of course."

All her anxieties, all her fears, all her uncertainties seemed to pile up and explode. They showed themselves in a spurt of temper. "I didn't marry your son for his money, Mr. Rafferty, and I surely don't want any of *yours*." She stepped forward, stopping opposite him, only the table between them. "I wasn't looking to be married when Michael Rafferty came to Homestead. In fact, a husband was the *last* thing I ever wanted. He'll tell you that himself. All I wanted was to leave here, to get away, go anywhere. But then . . . but then Michael married me. He's been nothing but good to me, and I won't do anything to . . . to hurt or . . . or betray him. It'll have to be him who tells me to go away. I won't do it for you or for your money."

She stopped abruptly. She could feel herself shaking, but she hoped it didn't show. She didn't want this man to think it was fear that made her quake.

Or maybe it *was* fear. Fear of the truth.

John Thomas watched her in silence for what seemed an interminably long time. Finally, he inclined his head toward her. "I believe I may have judged you unfairly, Rose. I beg your forgiveness."

Her strength left her like air from a punctured balloon. She grabbed onto the back of the chair pushed up to the table, praying her legs would continue to hold her upright.

The truth was, she thought Mr. Rafferty was

right. She, too, thought Michael was making
a mistake he would one day regret. She was
certain Michael would, indeed, one day tire of
her and send her on her way. He would want to
return to his real life. He would want to return
to San Francisco and Palace Hotels and a wife
like Lillian Overhart. What affection he felt for
Rose would not last. It couldn't.

But she wasn't ready just yet for the inevitable. Not just yet.

"You won't mention this conversation to my
son?" John Thomas asked softly.

"No, sir, I won't."

"Thank you." Then he left the kitchen.

I'm not ready yet, she thought again. *Not just
yet. Oh, Michael, why did you have to make me
love you? Why did you have to make me want
you forever?*

John Thomas was unusually quiet as he and
Kathleen prepared to retire for the night. In
fact, he'd been unusually quiet throughout the
evening.

"I thought supper was delicious," Kathleen
said as she ran the brush over her thick auburn
hair, watching his reflection in the mirror.

"Yes. Yes, it was." He stared out the window
at the street below.

She twisted on the dressing-table stool.
"J.T. . . . . tell me what's troubling you."

He turned and met her gaze. "You know how
Michael's letter said he was ashamed of some of

the things he'd done to gain control of Palace Hotels?"

"Yes."

"Well, I've done something I'm ashamed of in order to take him back to Palace Hotels." He raked one hand through his sand-colored hair.

"Whatever it is, Rose won't hold it against you. She loves him, and she'll forgive you because you're his father."

He raised an eyebrow, silently questioning how she knew it was Rose he was talking about.

Kathleen wore a gentle smile as she rose from the stool and crossed the room, her silk wrap whispering about her ankles. She didn't stop until her arms were around her husband, her head pressed against his chest. "I know you well, John Thomas Rafferty. You are bullheaded and determined to have your own way. You've always fought for what was best for your children and for me. Problem is, you don't always know what's best for us. Michael knows what he needs this time. You've raised him to have a good head on his shoulders and a kind heart besides. He'll use them both well."

"Hmm." His arms tightened around her.

"Don't worry, J.T. I have a feeling about the two of them, just as I had a feeling about the two of us the day we met."

He stroked her hair. "It's a miracle you ever fell in love with me."

"And isn't it grand that miracles can happen to the likes of us?"

He laughed softly. Then, allowing the return of the Irish brogue he'd worked so hard to eliminate over the years, he said, "Aye, that it is, Katy love. That it is."

Michael didn't make love to Rose that night. It wasn't because he didn't *want* to make love to her. He *always* wanted to make love to her. But she seemed so very fragile tonight. He wanted to ask her what was wrong, but he wasn't sure he wanted to hear her answer.

Lying in their bed, he drew Rose into his embrace, pulling her against his chest. He kissed the top of her head and stroked her back.

Maybe he didn't need to ask her what was wrong. Maybe he already knew.

It didn't have anything to do with his family, although he suspected that something had happened between Rose and his father. John Thomas's initial attitude toward Rose had been less than accepting and barely more than cordial. That had changed this evening. By the time Michael and Rose had left the boardinghouse, he'd known Rose had won over John Thomas as thoroughly as she'd won Michael himself.

It didn't have anything to do with her own family, although he suspected that Glen Townsend would continue to cause her grief

Robin Lee Hatcher

whenever the opportunity arose. Glen had just better make certain Michael never learned of it.

But then, he didn't doubt for a moment that Rose could do an admirable job of holding her own with either of those two men, despite the intelligence of one and the brute strength of the other. She was a fighter, his Rose. She'd had to be. She'd been fighting most of her life.

But Michael wanted her to quit fighting now. He especially didn't want her to fight him. He wanted her to trust him, to trust her own feelings for him. He wanted her to say the words aloud. He wanted her to tell him she loved him.

You will tell me one day, he thought as he caressed her hair. *Somehow I'll make you admit to loving me. And I'll wait as long as it takes.*

Chapter Thirty-Two

The next week was the most confusing of Rose Rafferty's life. Michael's family, it turned out, was a noisy, fun-loving group who thrived on laughter and more than a fair share of practical jokes. They showed their emotions openly, hugging and kissing each other with some frequency, and it didn't take long for them to include Rose in their candid displays of affection. They made the boardinghouse come alive as it never had before. Even Virginia came out of her shell a little, easing Rose's worries.

Rose felt awkward around the Rafferty family at first, especially around John Thomas. But her father-in-law seemed to have forgotten that he'd offered her money to leave Michael. In fact, she began to wonder if she'd simply imagined the exchange in the boardinghouse kitchen. There were times, in fact, that she looked at him and saw what a father could be, if a child was lucky.

375

Little by little, Rose began to feel a part of the Rafferty family. They seduced her with their stories of Michael's childhood and tales of his triumphs in the world of business. They charmed her with their protectiveness, with the way they squabbled amongst themselves, yet would brook no criticism by others. They teased and joked with her, treating her as if she'd always been one of them.

And, for his part, Michael continued to treat her with love and tenderness, chipping away at her fears, wearing down the last shreds of her defenses. Against her better judgment, she began to believe in a love that lasted, not just for people like Kathleen and John Thomas, but for someone like her. She began to believe that Michael could love her, not just now but for all the tomorrows to come. She began to believe that she could have the happiness that had always eluded her, if only she would reach out and take it.

She began to believe in Michael.

"Where are you taking me?" Rose asked for the fifth time as the buggy bumped along the road.

"You'll just have to wait and see," Michael answered.

She smiled, wondering what his surprise was all about, even as she enjoyed the suspense.

She'd been in the kitchen of the board-inghouse helping her mother and Kathleen prepare the noon meal, when Michael had walked into the room, grabbed her by the wrist, announced that Rose and he would be missing lunch, then led her out to the buggy that waited by the gate.

"What on earth are you doing?" she'd asked as he lifted her onto the seat.

"I'm tired of sharing you with my family," he'd answered as he joined her in the buggy and picked up the reins. "I want an afternoon all to ourselves." He'd looked over at her and winked, smiling mysteriously. "Besides, I've got a surprise for you."

Of course, she wasn't completely in the dark about their destination. The trail they were following led up to the ridge where they'd picnicked the day he'd presented her with Duchess. But she couldn't imagine what his surprise might be. There weren't any packages in the back of the buggy, no more wicker baskets under the seat. He obviously wasn't giving her another puppy or more hats and shoes and dresses.

Michael flicked the reins against the horse's back as they started up the incline. "Close your eyes," he said without looking at her.

She obeyed, feeling a silly excitement over the entire adventure. No one had ever attempted to give her a surprise, let alone whisk her away from her chores.

As the buggy moved from the shade of the trees into the clearing of the ridge, she felt the warmth of the sun upon her face. "Can I open my eyes?"

"No, not yet."

They slowed, then stopped. The buggy rocked as Michael hopped down. She listened to the crunch of pebbles beneath his boots as he walked around to her side.

"Keep 'em closed," he reminded as his hands closed around her waist, lifting her to the ground.

His kiss was completely unexpected. Her heart jumped, and her breath quickened, just as it always did when he kissed her. Then his arm swept beneath her knees and lifted her feet off the ground. She clung to him, enjoying the taste of his mouth, the feel of his arms cradling her against him.

She opened her eyes and gazed up at him as he lifted his mouth from hers. "What was that for?" she whispered.

"Just because I love you, Mrs. Rafferty." He grinned. "Now, close your eyes again."

"Michael—"

"Close them."

"But—"

"Humor me."

With a sigh, she did as she was asked. She laid her head against his shoulder as he carried her across the clearing. To be honest, she didn't care where he was taking her or why.

He stopped walking. His lips brushed her hair. "I know your birthday isn't for another

three months, but I couldn't wait until then."
He set her on her feet, then turned her to face
away from him. "Open your eyes, Rose."

She opened them.

"You're not ten anymore, but I hope. . . ." His
voice drifted into silence.

Rose stepped toward the beautiful golden
horse that was tethered to an aspen. The horse
bobbed its head, then pawed the ground. Rose
touched the animal's neck, at the same time
glancing behind her.

"He's yours," Michael said, answering her
silent question.

"Mine?" She looked at the gelding again.

"Now you can go riding with Lark whenever
you want."

How could he have known? How could he
see into those secret corners of her heart, those
old hurts, those buried hopes and dreams?
Somehow, he understood the child who'd felt
so different from everyone else, the girl who
had no one to love her, the young woman who
worked so hard and had so little. She'd denied
ever wanting a horse, and yet he'd guessed the
truth, guessed that she'd wanted one still, just
as he'd understood about the puppy.

His hands closed over her shoulders. "I want
to give you whatever will make you happy,
Rose. Tell me what you want, and I'll get it
for you. Name it and it's yours."

"He's beautiful," Rose said softly, her voice
thick with emotion.

Michael turned her toward him. "But not as beautiful as you." He cradled her face with the palms of his hands. "Nothing is as beautiful as you, Rose." He kissed her, a kiss as sweet as dew in the morning, as gentle as a summer breeze.

I love you, Michael.

She wanted to tell him. She wanted to say it aloud. She wanted to announce it to the world. But the words caught in her throat, words too foreign, too strange to be uttered. So she told him the way she felt in other ways, the only way she knew how.

It would be late afternoon before they returned to Homestead.

Michael glanced at his wife, seated beside him. She, in turn, was twisted around to look behind her at the gelding, which was tied to the back of the buggy.

"I just can't get over that he's really mine," she said, catching him watching her. "I can't wait to ride out to the Rocking R and show him to Lark."

"Just so long as I'm with you. Maybe next Sunday after church."

"But I don't want to wait until Sunday."

"He's still a little green, Rose, and you aren't exactly an experienced horsewoman." He recognized the stubborn set of her chin. "Promise me you won't take him out without me. Not until you're both familiar with each other."

She looked from him to the horse. She seemed to be considering his request. He was fairly certain she would agree with him. After all, things had been going incredibly well between them. There was no reason for her not to comply with this simple request.

That was when he saw him, standing on the porch of their house. He recognized him even before the buggy left the road. Rose must have felt his sudden tension. She turned forward on the seat. She didn't ask it aloud, but he felt her questioning gaze.

"It's Dillon," he replied.

His brother stepped down from the porch. His dark hair was tousled, his clothes dusty, his face closed, revealing nothing.

Michael pulled in on the reins, drawing the horse to a stop. Without comment, he passed the reins to Rose and stepped down from the buggy.

"Dillon."

"Hello, Michael." His brother cracked a half smile. "Not an easy trek here from Newton. I had a devil of a time getting here as fast as I did."

Damn, it was good to see him. It was good to see his grin, good to feel he wasn't his enemy. He wondered if Dillon felt the same.

"I hear tell the family's here."

Michael nodded. "Yes. They arrived a week ago."

"John Thomas accept your decision?"

"I think he has."

"Are you sure it's what you want?"

"I'm sure."

Dillon glanced toward the buggy, where Rose was waiting. "I never thought you'd let pleasure get in the way of business, but now I understand why you changed your mind." He stepped forward, his smile broadening. Dillon Rafferty had always had a charming way with the ladies. "You must be Rose. I'm your brother, Dillon." He took her by the hand and helped her down from the buggy.

Rose glanced from Dillon to Michael and back again. "It's amazing," she said.

Dillon chuckled and leaned close to Rose's ear. "I used to put boot black in his hair so it looked like mine. Folks thought we were twins . . . unless he rubbed up against something." He winked at her. "But as we got older, it became clear I was by far the more handsome of the two."

Michael didn't know whether to laugh with Dillon or hit him.

His brother looked at him, and his smile immediately faded. "I'm glad you wrote to me, Michael. The past few months have given me a chance to think through a lot of things. Lots of things are clearer now. John Thomas wasn't all wrong to send us off to prove ourselves." He shoved out his hand. "I've missed . . . well, I've missed you. Let's forget what came between us."

Michael felt a swelling of emotion in his chest. He grabbed Dillon's proffered hand, giving it a couple of hearty pumps. Then, realizing that wasn't enough, he yanked his brother forward and hugged him fiercely. When they stepped back, each held the other by the shoulders.

"I've a lot to make up to you," Michael admitted.

"No more than I have to you. Let's just put it behind us." He jerked his head toward Rose. "For now, I think I'd like to get acquainted with my new sister." Dillon grinned again, that irrepressible grin that had always spelled mischief.

"Just remember she's *my* wife," Michael warned, only half joking.

Dillon Rafferty was as charming a reprobate as Rose had ever known. He had the same sparkle, the same enjoyment for living that all the Raffertys exhibited. But she liked Dillon best. Perhaps it was his uncanny resemblance to Michael. Or perhaps it was because she knew how much her husband loved his half brother.

That evening, as she quietly observed the two men, listening to their stories, watching as they mended bridges once burned, Rose knew a moment of envy, wishing she might have had a brother who'd loved her as these two loved each other.

And then she realized that she'd been given that chance. Dillon was her brother now. Dillon and Joseph and Colin and Sean were all her brothers. She even had a sister in young Fianna. Because of Michael, she could have a family who loved her.

Her gaze turned to her husband. He had given her so much she'd never had before—an adorable puppy, a beautiful horse, a pleasant home, pretty dresses, freedom, and now a family—but most of all, he'd given her love.

She was truly the luckiest woman alive.

Chapter Thirty-Three

July 3, 1890—Statehood!

The word swept through Homestead like a brushfire. For all their talk that the railroad had meant more, the citizens of Long Bow Valley turned out for a celebration that wouldn't soon be forgotten.

They came on horseback. They came in their buggies and their wagons. They came on foot. They came with elderly parents who were bent with age and with infants carried in their mothers' arms. They came alone, in pairs, and in bunches—parents and children, married and single. They came with blankets and picnic baskets, fiddles and bows.

They came to celebrate and celebrate they did.

Except for the bartender and the hurdy-gurdy girls, Glen sat alone in the Pony Saloon. He could hear the cheerful sounds coming from the grounds of the Homestead Community Church. Laughter and gaiety. But he wasn't feeling much like either of them. Murder was more what he had in mind.

He'd received the telegram at noon today, bearing the bad news. Quinn Tracy had skipped the country. Glen didn't need to go to Wyoming to know the money was gone from where they'd stashed it eight years ago. His double-dealing partner had left him with nothing for all those years he'd spent in prison. Quinn had taken it all and gone to South America—alone.

All his life, Glen had gotten the short end of the stick. He'd worked hard. He'd provided for that sniveling wife of his and the two brats she'd borne. Hadn't he brought Virginia to Homestead as she'd wanted? Hadn't he built her that damned boardinghouse? Hadn't he labored at the sawmill and kept food on the table? Damn right, he had. And where had it gotten him?

He had nothin'. Virginia had the boarding-house, and Rose had her rich husband, and he had nothin'.

He poured another swig of whiskey down his throat, enjoying the burning sensation.

By God, he should've known Rafferty owned the Palace Hotels. He should've guessed. Look what he stood to inherit when that old man of his died. Rose would be livin' in style, and Glen would still have nothin'.

Seven hundred and fifty dollars. That's all

he'd gotten for the grief of raising that thankless brat of a girl with her sassy mouth and defiant ways. She'd never treated him with the respect a pa deserved. Always was high and mighty. He should have given her a few more smacks with his belt. Damn it, if he shouldn't have.

"Bring me another bottle, Grady," he called to the bartender.

How much money did he have left? he wondered. Two fifty maybe. Where had the other five hundred dollars gone?

Whiskey, sure. He'd bought plenty of whiskey, but what about the rest? He'd lost a fair amount in some games of cards. He'd used some to rent the room above the saloon, paying plenty more for it than it was worth. He'd had to use more in order to eat at the restaurant every day.

Two fifty. What could he do with just two hundred and fifty dollars? It would be gone before he knew it. He hadn't worried about it before now. After all, he'd had plenty more waiting for him in Wyoming. Or, at least, he'd thought he had. But it wasn't there anymore, and it wouldn't take Glen long to be left with nothin' once again.

Rage began to build inside him. He closed his hand into a fist, longing to be able to work out his anger, his frustration. He looked at the three saloon girls sitting at a table near the stairs. Opal was the closest any of them came to being pretty.

"Come here, Opal," he said with a jerk of his head.

She glanced at the two other women, hesitating.

"Come over here, I said."

Her reluctance made him angry. Damn her all to hell! He had money to pay for her services, and she had darn well act as if she liked it or he'd make her regret it.

The townsfolk spread blankets on the ground and served up a bounty of food. They dined on fried chicken, sliced ham, potatoes, baked beans, and breads. There were cookies and cakes and pies and puddings. They drank sweet punch and hot tea. Everyone shared the bounty with neighbors. For this night, the townspeople all shared the same hopes and dreams.

And so they celebrated.

Virginia watched the festivities from the window of her second-story bedroom. She felt an odd detachment from it all, as if she were viewing the scene from a distance much greater than that which separated the boardinghouse from the church.

She knew them all, all those people gathered in the field beside the church. She'd known many of them for more than a decade. She'd watched their children grow up and begin families of their own. They were her friends and her neighbors, yet she felt a stranger to them all.

Rose was down there. Rose and her husband and all of his family. Rose was happy at last, and Virginia was glad. Heaven knew, Virginia had never given the girl a single moment of happiness. Not that she hadn't wanted to. She just couldn't.

But at least now, when Virginia died, she could go knowing Rose had found something special.

She thought about death and dying a lot these days, just as she had when Mark and Rose were babies and Glen had lived with them. Every time he'd hit her, every time he'd dragged her unwillingly into his bed, she'd wished she could die. She'd wanted the release death would bring.

For nearly ten years, she'd been satisfied with living day to day, relieved to have the fear taken from her. But now it was back. Now Glen was back.

Virginia closed her eyes. She hoped God would see fit to let her into heaven when her time came. She'd been a sorry excuse for a mother. She'd even witnessed Glen murdering their son and hadn't said a word, just because she was afraid. She was a coward and always had been when it came to Glen.

Glen. . . . He was out there, somewhere. Her husband of more than twenty-five years. He was out there, and he knew she'd seen him kill Mark, and she knew he would do the same to her if he wanted to. And so she stayed inside the boardinghouse, hiding, afraid, a coward to the bitter end, just wishing she could die.

But at least Rose had found love and happiness. If Virginia died tomorrow, she would be glad for that.

As night fell, the women of Long Bow Valley put away the leftover food while the men gathered wood and built a bonfire in the center of the open field. Fiddles and mouth organs appeared, and the musicians commenced to play lively, foot-stomping tunes. Ted Wesley's baritone voice shouted commands to the dancing couples.

It was a magical, wonderful night.

Sarah McLeod imagined she was in a majestic English ballroom instead of an open field under the stars. She imagined the people dancing were lords and ladies rather than simple country folk. She pretended her grandfather was a duke and her grandmother a duchess, and all the townsfolk were their subjects. It was a grand dream.

"Sarah! Sarah! They're gonna start the fireworks."

She let out a lengthy sigh as she was drawn back to reality.

"Don't be provincial, Tommy," she told her little brother in a lofty tone.

Of course, she wasn't entirely sure what provincial meant, but she liked the sound of it. It was a word she'd recently added to her vocabulary after reading it in a magazine. She knew it would be important that she have a large vocabulary when she traveled the world and became friends with lords and ladies and American millionaires.

"Come on, Sarah," Tommy repeated, this time pulling on his sister's arm.

"All right. I'm coming." She jerked free, but got to her feet and followed him across the street, where everyone was spreading blankets away from the bonfire.

She saw Rose Rafferty with her new husband and all his family from San Francisco. She'd heard her grandma talking to Mrs. Barber, saying that Rose wasn't going to leave Homestead and go to San Francisco after all. That she and Mr. Rafferty were going to settle right here. Sarah thought Rose must have lost her mind.

Everyone knew Mr. Rafferty was rich. She'd heard the gossip, same as everyone else. Mr. Rafferty could've taken Rose anywhere, but she was choosing to stay right here. Mrs. Barber said it was 'cause Rose had fallen in love.

Sarah wrinkled her nose. Love was all right, she supposed, but she wanted a whole lot more out of life than just a husband and a bunch of babies. As soon as she was old enough, she was going to leave Homestead and go just as far away as she could get. She was going to see the world—London, Rome, Paris. Maybe she'd become a famous actress or an opera singer.

Reverend Jacobs said she had a mighty fine singing voice.

And when she did get around to getting married, it wasn't going to be to some farmer or sheriff in a place like Homestead, Idaho. She was going to marry a duke or an earl or maybe even a prince.

She closed her eyes, drifting back into one of her favorite fairy tales.

Rose leaned into the crook of Michael's arm, resting her head against his shoulder. She enjoyed the warmth of his body against hers, enjoyed the way they fitted together so perfectly, as if they'd been made for each other.

Michael stroked her hair with his hand. "Homestead's going to become an important link for logging and mining in these mountains, once the railroad comes in here. The town's going to grow. We probably ought to think of buying up some land now, while we still can."

She turned her head, looking at him. "Do you really mean to stay here? Are you sure you won't want to go back to San Francisco?"

"Why? Do you want to leave Homestead?"

She thought about that for a moment. *Would* she rather leave Homestead? There weren't a lot of happy memories associated with it. Yet, when she thought about leaving. . . .

"Look at that sky," Michael whispered, drawing her even closer to him. "The sky's not the same in California. Mountains either."

She wasn't sure he was telling her the truth. She suspected the sky was the same everywhere, that mountains were mountains. Still, this was home. This was *her* sky, and these were *her* mountains.

A rocket shot upward and burst into a shower of blue and white sparkles, startling her from her reverie. The ground shook and the noise was deafening as charge after charge was set off, the fireworks shooting up into the sky to challenge the stars.

A sense of joy seemed to explode within her with the same brilliance. She felt a burst of courage.

"I love you, Michael," she said aloud, but the words were lost in the din of the night.

She knew he hadn't heard her, but that was all right. There would be other times to tell him, other opportunities to say the words. It was enough for now to know she'd spoken them, that she'd set the words loose, given them life.

There was something different about Rose tonight. Michael wasn't certain what it was. He only knew something had changed between them.

The bedroom window was open to the cool night air. Even now, long after the last rocket had exploded against the star-studded sky and the bonfire had been doused, the ashes stirred, there was a lingering smell of sulfur and wood smoke in the air. A nearly full moon had crept over the peaks of the mountains and now shed its light into their bedroom.

Rose stood with her back to the window, the moonlight spilling around her. Michael watched as she removed the pins from her hair and let it fall over her shoulders. Slowly, almost deliberately, she removed her dress, her stockings. She lingered over each item, prolonging the sweet torture he was feeling.

They had made love many times in the past couple of weeks. Yesterday, they had even made love outdoors in the middle of the day, right up there on the ridge. He thought he had learned everything there was to know about her body.

But tonight it seemed very new to him, new and sweet and seductive.

His desire intensified.

Finally, she stood before him, completely bereft of clothing. She didn't move, didn't try to slip beneath the covers on the bed. She simply stood there and waited for him.

His mouth was dry. His pulse pounded in his temples. He wanted to touch her, caress her, possess her.

Slowly, he crossed the bedroom. He cradled her face in his hands and tipped her head so he could savor her lips. When he felt her hands at his waistband, he sucked in his breath, controlling the urge to take her quickly.

Although his head couldn't put it into words,

his heart felt what she was doing. She was giving him something she'd never given him before. She was doing more than making love to him. She was offering him her trust, her heart, her love.

Rose disrobed him with the same slow deliberateness with which she'd removed her own clothes. Michael felt as if he were on fire, and he welcomed the feel of the cool night air on his fevered skin.

When their clothes lay in disarray around their feet, Rose placed the palms of her hands against his tense abdomen, then moved them slowly upward, over his chest and shoulders, not stopping until her fingers were laced behind his neck. Finally, she drew herself up against him, standing on tiptoe, and kissed him until they were both breathless.

Michael groaned as his hands moved to cup her buttocks and draw her ever tighter against his hardened member. Released from their kiss, she sighed, her breath tickling the skin of his neck.

She looked up at him. "Love me, Michael," she whispered.

"I do love you, Rose."

He slipped an arm beneath her knees, sweeping her feet up off the floor, and carried her to their bed. On sheets made warm by their passions, they each sought to bring the other delight—kissing, touching, stroking.

And later, when their soft cries of pleasure

had faded into the night, he said the words again, "I do love you, Rose."

Exhausted, he fell asleep at once, too quickly to hear her whispered reply, "And I love you."

Chapter Thirty-Four

Rose awakened just before dawn, her heart singing with joy, her body quickened by emotions too wonderful, too foreign to name. She felt a strange energy that made her restless, even though she knew she should be exhausted after so few hours of sleep.

She gathered her clothes off the floor, where they'd fallen last night as she'd disrobed for Michael. She blushed as she remembered her boldness. Then, on silent feet, she made her way downstairs, where she dressed in the kitchen.

She thought about stoking the fire in the oven and baking something, then discarded the notion. The day was more than likely going to be warm. She didn't need to heat up the kitchen so early.

She opened the back door, letting in a rush of fresh morning air and an excited puppy.

Unfastening the rope that held the gold-and-white dog captive at night, Rose lifted Duchess into her arms, then leaned against the door-jamb and watched as the sky above faded from black to gray, the stars winking out one by one.

Duchess began to wiggle impatiently. "All right. All right," Rose muttered, setting the dog on the floor. "You're getting too big to hold like that anyway. Come on. Let's go for a walk."

The path led them to the shed, where the two horses were sheltered, Michael's tall roan and Rose's flaxen-maned gelding. Duchess tried to scramble through the stall railing, but Rose grabbed her just in time.

"I think you'd be sorry," she whispered to the rambunctious pup.

At that moment, the golden gelding thrust his head over the stall and nuzzled the puppy in her arms.

"Look. You're both the same color." She stroked the horse's neck. "I think I'll call you Duke. Every duchess should have one, I suppose."

He bobbed his head as if he'd understood, and Rose laughed, the overwhelming sense of joy returning, bubbling over.

"You know what I'd like to do," she said to Duke in a conspiratorial tone. "I'd like to go for a ride. I'd like you and me to become friends."

And why shouldn't she? He was hers, after all.

Michael had warned her that he was still a bit green, but Duke certainly looked calm enough. Yesterday, up on the ridge, after they'd made love—she felt a blush rising in her cheeks at the memory—Michael had set her on Duke's back and she'd ridden the horse for a short while. Duke had seemed completely well mannered and not the least bit green or difficult to manage.

The more she thought about it, the more she wanted to take the horse for a ride. She wanted to make all those silly girlhood dreams come true. She wanted to feel the wind in her hair. She wanted to gallop across the grassy fields, maybe even let him soar over a bubbling brook.

She shook her head. She supposed galloping and soaring would have to wait until she'd become a little more confident. But she was certainly capable of riding out to Lark's ranch and showing her horse to her friend.

Her decision made, Rose set about bridling and saddling the animal. Luckily, Lark had shown her several times how to cinch a saddle, and the lessons had stuck with her. Not that Rose didn't have several false starts. She did. Even once she'd managed to do it exactly as she remembered, she wouldn't have sworn she'd done it right.

She supposed she would find out if the saddle

suddenly slipped sideways and dumped her on the ground.

Miraculously enough, the saddle didn't slip a bit, even though it took Rose several attempts to pull herself up onto it. Then, her skirts tucked in an indisputably unladylike fashion around her legs, she guided Duke out of the shed and down the road toward the Rocking R, Duchess trotting along beside them.

Still half asleep, Michael stretched out his arm . . . and found an empty spot where Rose should have been. He opened his eyes, squinting against the morning light that was brightening the bedroom.

He moaned softly. He'd given the work crew the day off. He didn't have to be over at the hotel site at the crack of dawn for a change. He had hoped to spend a good portion of the day in bed with his wife.

He thought of last night and smiled. Even the very first time they'd made love, more than two weeks before, Rose had been a passionate participant, and that hadn't changed. But last night had been different. He sensed she'd given him something more than just physical pleasure, and he wanted to pursue just what that something more might be.

Still squinting against the light, he braced himself on one elbow and glanced about the room. Her clothes were gone from the floor, which meant Rose was up and dressed.

He grunted a protest as he sat up, running his fingers through his hair, pushing it back from his face. He sniffed the air experimentally. Breakfast wasn't ready, he decided.

Well, he could simply lie back and wait for her to come check on him or he could get up and go find her. But who knew how long it would be before she decided he'd been in bed too long? She might decide he deserved to stay there all day.

He did, he thought, but not alone.

He tossed aside the bedcovers and slid to the edge of the mattress, lowering his legs over the side. He stood in the center of the room and dressed quickly, then checked the bedroom across the hall, which was empty, and finally went downstairs. She wasn't in the parlor or kitchen.

Michael frowned. Where could she have gone off to so early in the morning? Maybe she was down at the privy, he decided. He opened the back door. Duchess's rope lay near the step, but neither puppy nor mistress was in sight. If Rose were visiting the outhouse, Duchess would have been waiting near the privy door.

Looking for Rose wasn't exactly how he'd expected to spend his day off. She obviously had found some reason to go out, probably over to the boardinghouse. And if that was where she was, they'd both be spending the rest of the day in his family's company, rather than nestled in the bed upstairs as he'd hoped.

Robin Lee Hatcher

Letting out an aggrieved sigh, Michael started down the path to the shed, deciding he might as well take care of his morning chores before he went searching for Rose.

It was her own fault, of course. She'd kept an unwilling Duke at a sedate pace for what seemed a terribly long time. And then she simply hadn't been able to stop herself. She'd loosened the reins and tapped her heels against the horse's golden sides and let him have his head.

She wasn't quite sure when the exhilarating gallop had become uncontrollable. It was probably when the spirited gelding left the main road and lit out across the fields. The thundering hooves had seemed to grow louder and louder. The ground had sped past at an unbelievable pace.

Even then she hadn't been frightened. Not really. She'd clung to the saddle horn and leaned into the wind and told herself just how wonderful it was.

Wonderful . . . until Duke jumped over that blasted bubbling brook she'd imagined earlier. Her seat parted company with the leather of the saddle. When she came down, the horse was no longer beneath her.

She hit the ground with a thump. The wind rushed from her lungs with a whoof. The earth spun beneath her, and black dots blotted her vision until she could see nothing at all.

She had no idea how long she'd lain there, unconscious. She was awakened by Duchess's tongue on her face. At first she wondered what the pup was doing in her bedroom. Reality came back to her slowly—and more than a little painfully. Once she'd opened her eyes and remembered where she was and how she'd gotten there, she pushed herself upright, wincing at the pain that made itself known in several parts of her body.

She had a bump on the side of her head. Her right arm and cheek were scratched, and her hip felt bruised. Nothing too disastrous, but painful all the same. Then she tried to stand.

She let out a cry as she sank back to the ground. Blinking away the spontaneous tears, she lifted her skirt and stared at the thorn in the bottom of her bare foot. She yanked the prickly object free, tossing it aside with an unladylike observation. Then she looked around for some sign of her missing shoe, but it was nowhere to be seen.

Now what? she wondered. Duke was nowhere in sight so she couldn't hope to find him and ride back to town. That meant she would have to walk, and that wasn't going to be much fun with a sore foot and only one shoe.

It would have been difficult for Michael to describe what he felt when he saw her sitting near that stream, her dress torn and dirty, her face and arm scratched, her skirt hiked up to her knees so she could stare at her feet.

She looked up, saw him, and smiled.

Relief. That would describe what he felt. Relief that she was obviously all right. Pure, unmitigated relief.

That feeling was followed by a protective fury.

"What the hell did you think you were doing?" he demanded as he dismounted.

Her smile disappeared. "I was riding my horse."

"I told you not to go riding alone. Didn't I tell you that?" He knelt beside her. "Didn't I tell you that just two days ago?"

She scowled at him, but Michael was too wound up with worry and anger to see it.

"Do you know what might have happened to you out here? You could have broken your fool neck. I'm lucky I found you as soon as I did. I never would've bought you that horse if I'd thought you'd do something this crazy."

"I have every right to go riding if I want to."

"Not until I know you and that horse are suited for each other, you don't. Now, let me have a look at that foot. What's wrong with it? Did you sprain it?"

She jerked it away from him. "*Don't* touch me."

What was the matter with her? he wondered. "I've got to see how badly you're hurt."

"It's nothing but a few scratches. I'll be fine

just as soon as you find Duke and we can go back to town."

"I'll look for . . . *Duke* . . . later." He rose to his feet and leaned down to pick her up.

She glared at him, her body tense, her expression stubborn. "I'm not budging from this spot until you find my horse."

"Damn it, Rose Rafferty," he snapped at her. "You're hurt and you need to see the doctor. I'm not going to leave you sitting here while I traipse around the country looking for that horse. I've a good mind to give him back to Chad Turner and tell him to shoot him for the damage he's caused."

She threw a clump of dirt at him. "Don't you dare! Don't you dare hurt that horse!"

He was completely at the end of his patience. He reached down and whisked her up into his arms, then turned toward his horse. "Come on, Duchess," he called to the pup.

"Put me down, Michael," Rose demanded while trying to wriggle free of his arms.

He had a good mind to plop her down in the cold running stream. If she hadn't been hurt. . . .

"Put me down!" There was a new note of panic in her voice. "Put me down, I tell you!"

Suddenly, he remembered the way she'd looked when they'd argued on their wedding day, as if she'd expected him to strike her. It had been clear to him even then that a blow was how she thought every argument ended.

But he hadn't ever hit her. He'd never even threatened to hit her. In truth, they hadn't really argued since their wedding day. He'd been trying hard to show her how much he loved her, to prove that she could trust him. Maybe he'd been trying too hard.

He lowered her feet to the ground, but kept his hands on her shoulders, giving her gentle support. She tried to pull away from him, but he didn't allow it.

"No, you don't, Rose Rafferty," he said in a low voice. "Being in love doesn't mean never arguing or never having differing opinions. It doesn't mean we're not ever going to disagree or fight. It sure doesn't mean I won't ever raise my voice to you. I'm not going to spend the rest of my life tiptoeing around you. I was worried, and it made me angry that you'd done something foolish. And when I'm angry, I sometimes yell. I don't imagine today will be the last time I yell at you, either." He paused, drew in a deep breath, and let it out in a sigh. "I'm sorry for what I said about the horse. It wasn't his fault. It was yours." Again he paused. "But even when I'm angry, even when it's your fault, I'll never hurt you, Rose. Not ever."

She looked up and met his gaze.

"You sit down and wait here with Duchess and think about what I said. I'll go find your horse."

Chapter Thirty-Five

Rose did think about what Michael had said. She thought about it while she waited for him to find Duke. She thought about it during the ride home. She thought about it while he helped her change out of her clothes and cleanse her wounds, and after he put her to bed for the rest of the day.

Most of all, she thought about how often he'd said he loved her in the past few weeks. It was time, she decided, that she expect the good instead of the bad. He wasn't going to hurt her. He would never hurt her, no matter what she said or did. Even when her silence had forced him to marry her, he hadn't hurt her. He could have, but he hadn't.

He loved her, and she loved him. They were married. They would always be married. Their future stretched before them, the years full and happy. At last, she understood just what a wonderful gift he'd given her.

She wanted to tell Michael she understood. She wanted to tell him she loved him. Not against the explosion of rockets. Not while he was asleep. She wanted to look him in the face and tell him she loved him more than life itself. That she would love him forever and then some.

Rose tossed the sheet aside and got out of bed. She went downstairs, calling his name, but he wasn't there. She found a note on the table.

I've taken the family out to the Rocking R. John Thomas wanted to see the Rider ranch before returning to California. Stay in bed and get your rest. Don't prepare supper. We'll all dine at the restaurant tonight.
Love, Michael

She wished he'd asked her to go along. She wasn't so fragile that a few bumps and scratches would keep her in bed all day. For a brief moment, she considered saddling up Duke and riding out to the ranch, but reason asserted itself almost immediately. The Rocking R had been her destination this morning, and look what had happened. She might be able to stand another tumble from her horse, but she didn't want another lecture from her husband.

She chuckled, taking illogical pleasure from the memory of him scolding her. She'd never had anyone worry about her whereabouts enough to come looking for her, and she had to admit, now that she didn't have her back up, that he was extraordinarily handsome when he was angry.

With nothing else to do, she returned upstairs and donned one of her new dresses. She brushed her hair and fastened it back with combs, allowing it to fall loose down her back. Then she set out for the boardinghouse and a quiet visit with her mother. Perhaps it would brighten Virginia's spirits to know that Rose had fallen in love.

Hank McLeod read the telegram, a frown drawing his thick, gray brows together. Glen Townsend and Jack Adams were suspected in the murders of two men in Colorado, shortly after their release from prison. Two horses had been taken. Both wore the brand of the Broken Arrow Ranch.

Hank remembered the unsavory fellow who had returned to Homestead with Glen. The sheriff didn't doubt for a moment that either Mad Jack or Glen could have had something to do with the murders.

And it would be easy enough to find out. All he had to do was check the brand on Glen's horse.

He grabbed his hat from the peg near the door and stepped out onto the boardwalk. Just as he did so, a series of loud bangs

erupted down the street. He turned toward
the noise, his body alert. Then he relaxed. It
was only some boys setting off firecrackers for
the Fourth of July.

He dragged in a deep breath and let it out.
It sure as heck was time for him to retire. No
sheriff worth his salt would mistake the sound
of firecrackers for gunfire.

With long strides, he headed for the livery
stables.

Except for the animals, the barn was empty.
Like most folks, Chad Turner was taking a
holiday. If Hank were retired, he could be
enjoying a day off, too. He could be spending
it by the river, catching a string full of rainbow
trout for their supper.

One by one, he checked the horses in their
stalls. He checked them all, even if he recognized them as someone else's horse. Finally,
he reached Glen's horse. He stepped into the
stall and turned the animal's side toward the
dim light coming through the open door. The
horse pranced nervously as more firecrackers
were set off in the street.

"Easy, boy," Hank muttered.

There it was. The broken arrow on his left
hind thigh.

Hank tipped his Stetson back on his head.
Damnation! More than a decade of relative
peace. Nothing much more to do than put
a man in jail to sober up after an evening
of generous imbibing. And now he had a

murderer living above the saloon.

Hank should have retired before now. He sure as heck should have retired before now.

Glen didn't know if it was providence or dumb luck that drew him to the livery stables that afternoon. But when he saw Hank McLeod checking the brand on his horse's hip, he knew his sojourn in Homestead was over. It didn't matter now that he had little money and nowhere to go.

"Hold it right there, McLeod," he said, drawing his gun. "Get your hands up where I can see 'em."

Hank looked toward him. "You're only makin' it worse for yourself, Townsend. Put that away."

"I'm not goin' back to prison. Not for somethin' I didn't do."

"You didn't kill those men?"

"No, I didn't. Mad Jack did it. Wasn't nothin' I could do to stop him." Not that he'd tried, he ended with a mental shrug. "Come on out in the open. And get your hands up where I can see 'em like I told you."

The sheriff opened the stall door and stepped out, his hands up in the air. His gaze never left Glen, not even for a second.

Glen felt sweat trickling down the sides of his face. It was damn hot in this barn.

He jumped as firecrackers erupted out in the street, glancing nervously over his shoulder, then back at the sheriff. He had to decide what

411

he was going to do with Hank, and he had to decide soon.

Virginia squeezed Rose's hand with her own. "I'm glad you're so happy, child. I wish at least part of it was my doin'."

"But it is, Ma. You told me not to throw away my chance for something better. You told me my marriage didn't have to be like yours. It's because of you I tried to get along with Michael when I was sure our marriage would never work." She leaned forward. "Oh, Ma, you don't have to be afraid anymore. Pa will leave Homestead soon. There's nothing to keep him here. And Michael has ordered him to stay away from the boardinghouse."

"Your pa won't leave. I know too much."

Rose felt a tiny shiver of alarm. "What do you know?"

Virginia shook her head as she dropped her gaze to the floor. "Too much. I just know too much."

"Ma. . . ."

"I've not been a good mother to you. I'm sorry, Rose. I'm more sorry than you'll ever know." She stood. "I'm tired and I'm gonna lay down before the Raffertys all come back and the house is full of noise again." She headed for the stairs. "You see yourself out."

Rose sat in the parlor for some time, listening to the ticking of the clock and wishing she knew what to do for her mother. Virginia had never been a particularly strong woman, and she'd retreated into herself since Glen's return from prison. If only Rose knew how to help her. . . .

With a sigh, she rose from the sofa and went to the front door. She still didn't feel much like going home, nor did she feel like waiting there alone for Michael's return. Again, she considered riding Duke out to the Rider ranch, and again, she discarded the idea.

She stood outside on the porch for several minutes before deciding to walk down to Zoe's Restaurant. Maybe she'd have herself a piece of pie along with some of Zoe's friendly conversation.

Several school-aged boys ran down the street, shouting and laughing, and a few seconds later, another string of firecrackers rattled the air. Rose jumped, even though she'd known what was coming. She'd better get used to it, she thought. The racket would doubtlessly continue until well after dark.

She was just passing the livery stable's door when two loud bangs erupted inside. She heard the frightened cry of the horses.

If those boys were lighting firecrackers in the livery, Chad Turner would flay them alive.

She stepped inside. "Who's in here?" she demanded.

Before her eyes could adjust to the dim light of the stables, she felt strong fingers clasp her wrist and drag her arm up behind her back.

413

"Don't you say a word," a gruff voice whispered in her ear.

"Pa?"

She would have turned and looked at him, but that was when she saw Sheriff McLeod, lying next to one of the stalls. There was blood on his head, more on his shirt.

"Dear God. . . ."

Her father jerked her arm. "He had it comin'. And if you don't keep your mouth shut, you'll get the same thing."

"Is he—"

"Never could stand that family. Workin' for his son when it was me that kept that mill goin'. Tom McLeod was as big a fool as his old man."

Icy terror seeped through her veins. "You killed him, too, didn't you?"

"That's a mighty stupid question, girly, and I don't think you wanna know the answer." He pushed her toward the stalls. "You and me are gonna saddle up a couple of horses and get out of here. And if you don't cause me too much trouble an' that husband o' yours is willin' to pay the price, you just might live longer than your brother."

Rose knew then. She knew without a doubt. He'd killed Mark, just as he'd killed Tom and Hank McLeod. He'd kill her, too, if she wasn't careful.

She tried not to let her fear reveal itself in her voice. "They'll come looking for you. Someone

414

else must have heard the shots."

He merely laughed as he wrapped a gag around her mouth, then tied her hands behind her back, securing her to a post. Once he was certain she couldn't escape or cry for help, he strode over to the sheriff's inert body, dragged him into an empty stall, and covered him with straw.

Her father was right to laugh at her declaration. Even she had thought the sound she'd heard was firecrackers. By this time, everybody in Homestead had grown accustomed to hearing the bangs and pops, mixed with children's laughter. No one would wonder about the two loud bangs that had killed Hank McLeod. They'd sounded no different from the others.

If Chad didn't find Hank's body tonight when he came to feed the livestock, Rose might not ever be found.

She didn't fool herself. Her father wouldn't keep her alive any longer than he thought it served his best interests. If she became a hindrance to him rather than a means of gain, he would fire one of those bullets into her head without so much as a blink of an eye.

Michael was eager to return from the Rider ranch and get home to Rose. Even though he knew she hadn't been badly hurt in her fall from the horse, he didn't stop worrying about her. If it weren't that John Thomas had announced yesterday it was time for the family to return to

San Francisco, Michael would have postponed his promise to take them all out to the Rocking R and spent the day pampering his wife.

Of course, she didn't deserve pampering after the stunt she'd pulled this morning, he reminded himself. But there was no anger left in him. All that truly mattered was that she was okay.

He remembered the furious glare she'd given him. Rose hadn't cared much for being ordered around or yelled at. Chances were she was still angry with him. She hadn't said two words from the moment he'd returned with Duke to the moment he'd left the house to take his parents and siblings out to the Rocking R. He hoped he hadn't opened a breach that would be too difficult to mend.

As soon as Michael reached the house, he bounded up the stairs to check on Rose. She wasn't in their bedroom. He checked the rest of the house, but it was empty. He opened the back door. Duchess was still on her leash. He was quite certain Rose wouldn't have the audacity to take Duke for another ride, but just to be certain, he went out to the shed to check. The gelding was in his stall, just as he was supposed to be.

Michael shook his head. To think he'd expected her to obey him and stay in bed. He should have known better. She probably was over at the boardinghouse right this minute, telling John Thomas about her wild ride that morning and informing him that his son was an overbearing brute who couldn't hold his temper.

Returning to the house, he grabbed his hat, plopped it down on his head, and started off for the boardinghouse, never dreaming that anything could be wrong.

Chapter Thirty-Six

Michael had talked to a good portion of the townsfolk, asking about his wife, before he heard the news that Hank McLeod had been discovered in the livery stables, suffering from gunshot wounds.

By the time Michael—and most of the rest of the town—reached the livery, the doctor was already there, tending to the injured man's shoulder. Doris McLeod knelt near her husband's head, gently stroking his gray hair, which was streaked with blood from a head wound.

When Hank saw Michael, he weakly motioned him forward. "Glen . . . Townsend. . . ." he whispered as Michael knelt beside him. The sheriff's voice was barely audible, coarse and raspy, but he still had enough strength to lift his right hand and grab hold of Michael's shirt. "He killed . . . my boy. . . . He. . . ."

Michael wasn't sure what Hank was talking

about. He hadn't known the man had a son.

"Took . . . Rose. . . ."

Cold fingers of dread closed around his heart. "Townsend took Rose?"

Hank nodded.

"How long ago? Where?"

The sheriff didn't answer. His eyelids had drifted closed, and Michael could tell the man was beyond hearing.

"I'll spread the word," Chad Turner said from behind him. "We can have a posse together in no time. Don't worry. We'll find her."

Still staring down at the sheriff, Michael said, "If he's hurt her, I'll hunt him down if it takes me the rest of my life. So help me God, I will."

He straightened and left the livery stables without another word. Walking with long, determined strides, he headed for his home, his horse, and his gun.

For the first hour, Rose was terrified. She clung to the saddle horn, her wrists bound together, and prayed she wouldn't fall from the saddle. She wasn't sure what her father would do if she delayed his flight from Homestead.

By the second hour, she marveled that no one had noticed her leaving town with her father. Had everyone, except the children, stayed inside on this hot Fourth of July? Was there no one who would think it odd for her to go riding with Glen Townsend? Perhaps not.

People saw what they wanted to see. Maybe most folks didn't realize how cruel her father had been, could be, was.

By the third hour, she'd decided she wasn't going to cower before him. She'd fought her pa in her own way before, but he'd still had the power to make her do whatever he'd wanted. She'd given him that power because she'd been afraid of him. She wouldn't let him use her own fear to manipulate her. Not ever again.

"Why are you doing this, Pa?" she called ahead to him as the horses picked their way along the trail that followed the frothy, swift-flowing river. "Why are you taking me with you?"

"Because, little girly, that husband o' yours owes me, and if he wants you back, he's gonna have to pay plenty."

She began sawing her wrists back and forth, trying to loosen the rope that bound her. She studied the passing countryside. If she were to get free, she wondered, could she make it back to Homestead on her own? At least she wouldn't get lost. Not as long as she followed the river.

"How do you know he'll even want me back?" she asked, as much to irritate him as anything else. "Michael didn't want to marry me, you know. You forced him to. He'll probably be glad to be rid of me."

"Oh, he'll want you back. A man doesn't go

to the trouble he has for you for somethin' he don't want."

"If you mean the boardinghouse, he did that for himself. He wants a monopoly on visitors passing through Homestead. He's interested in making money. That's all."

"I should've burned the place down before I let him have it."

"That's what you did to the sawmill, wasn't it? You killed Tom McLeod for the money in the safe, and then you set fire to the mill."

Glen glanced back at her. He was silent for a long time before answering, "You're too smart for your own good, girly."

A sick knot tightened in her belly. She'd known it was true. All those years ago, she'd been certain that was what had happened, but she'd been too afraid to speak up and tell someone. Now, because of her timidity, Hank McLeod was dead, just like his son.

Her pa faced forward again. "You better hope your husband's willin' to come through with enough money to get me out of the country."

She understood his unspoken threat. She knew too much. If her pa couldn't escape, he'd have to kill her to keep her from talking. But he'd probably kill her anyway, so what difference did it make?

"How can you ask him for ransom if you're where he can't give it to you? Why are we going so far away?"

"You ask too many questions. Shut up and let me think."

Yes, he planned to kill her. She could hear it in his voice. He didn't have any intention of turning her over to Michael. Hank McLeod was dead. She was the only one who knew it was Glen who had shot the sheriff. Her pa wasn't about to turn her loose to point a finger in his direction.

Dear Lord, she prayed silently, don't let it end like this. Not like this.

Yancy Jones rode beside Michael. Dillon and John Thomas followed up in the rear. Every man in Long Bow Valley was saddled up and looking for Rose by this time. Michael's group was following the river canyon.

Michael was thankful for Yancy's presence. The cowboy's experienced eyes had recognized signs of recent travel—two horses, moving fast—giving Michael hope that they were following the right trail.

The four men rode hard, not speaking. What, after all, was there to say?

Dusk came early to the deep river canyon. The tree-filled mountains, rising sharply on either side, cut off the sunlight long before sundown brought darkness to the valley to the north.

As the day waned, so did the heat. The temperature dropped surprisingly fast. Rose shivered and longed for something warmer to wear, but knew it would be useless to complain. Her pa wouldn't care how cold she was.

When darkness came—an inky blackness that made it impossible to see more than a foot or two ahead—Glen was finally forced to stop. "Get down an' rest. We'll wait until the moon comes up, then move on."

Her wrists still bound despite her efforts to slip free, Rose clumsily slid from the saddle. Her knees crumpled as soon as her feet touched the ground, and only her grip on the saddle horn kept her from falling down completely. She felt all of her bumps and bruises from that morning's fall, plus a few new aches as well. She forced herself to breathe slowly, steadily, waiting for the strength to return to her legs before letting go of the saddle.

The sounds of the night seemed strange, almost eerie. The rushing river tumbling over boulders. The hoot of an owl. The rustle of forest animals as they moved through the trees and underbrush. The distant howl of a coyote, the answering cry of another.

"Best stay by your horse," Glen said to her. "Don't want you turnin' into dinner for a mountain lion."

Rose subdued a shiver of fear. Her pa expected her to be afraid. He *wanted* her to be afraid. But surely nothing out there could be more dangerous than what she faced right here. If she could just get away from him, if she could find some place to hide. . . .

"Pa, I need you to untie my hands."

He laughed, and the sound startled her. He'd moved closer, and she hadn't seen him, hadn't known he was there.

Steadying herself, allowing no anxiety to creep into her voice, she said, "I've got to relieve myself, and I can't do it with my hands tied. Even *you* can understand that."

He grunted.

She held her breath, waiting, hoping.

Just a couple of steps brought him up to her. His vision at night was obviously better than hers. The realization made her question the plan that was slowly forming in her head. But what other choice did she have? She wasn't going to let him use her to take money from Michael, and she wasn't going to let him hurt her either.

He grabbed hold of her arm. She felt the cold blade of a knife against her skin. Then the rope fell away from her wrists. Prickles of pain shot up her arm, and she rubbed the raw flesh, trying to ease the soreness.

"No need to look for a tree," Glen warned as she took a step away from him. "You can just do what you must right here by the trail."

"I'm not stupid enough to try to run," she retorted. "You're the brave man with a gun."

"Don't sass me, girly, or you'll be sorry you did."

Rose moved a few more steps down the trail,

then stepped off to one side. With fingers made clumsy by fear, she wrestled with the satin tie of her petticoat, but finally it was free, sliding down to pool at her feet. As quietly as possible, she stepped out of it, picked it up, and held it behind her back.

"Hurry up over there," her pa snapped impatiently.

"I'm hurrying."

Her eyes had adjusted a little more to the darkness. She could make out the rump of her horse. She thought her father stood between the two horses, holding them both by the reins. She prayed she was right. She would only get one chance.

She moved forward, holding her breath, until she was close enough to do some good. Then, with a shriek, she whirled the white petticoat over her head. She struck the rear of her horse, then sent the petticoat flying at both of the horses' heads. The animals reared up, terrified squeals shattering the once peaceful night.

Rose didn't wait to see what happened next. She tripped, stumbled, and slid her way down the steep bank to the river. There she ran as best she could, crouching low, her heart thundering in her ears. She hoped the sound of her footsteps was covered by the rush of the water.

Dark skeletons of trees and brush reached out to scratch at her face and arms. The river splashed over rocks, splattering her, making her seem twice as cold. She felt starved for air, yet didn't dare open her mouth to drag in more for fear she would give herself away.

She felt her strength draining fast, but fear kept her going. She tripped once, nearly falling face first into the water. Only a desperate grab for an anchor saved her. She lay there holding on to the bush long after the danger of drowning was past.

She listened, wondering if her pa had heard her fall, wondering if she'd cried out and didn't know it. But the same rushing water that covered her sounds also covered those of her father. She didn't know if he was following her. And if he was, she wouldn't know until it was too late.

She picked herself up and continued on. She had to find shelter before the full moon came up and illuminated the river canyon almost as bright as day.

"Michael, we've gotta stop," Yancy said. "It's too dangerous for the horses. We can't see what's in front of our faces. Townsend can't be movin' either. Not till the moon's up."

Michael dismounted. "I'll go on on foot then. You bring my horse. Catch up with me when you can."

"Michael, be reasonable," his father said.

"I can't be reasonable!" he shouted back. "He's got Rose. Now, you all stay here with the horses. We may need them later."

He didn't say *why* they might need them, but the thought was there in the back of his mind. They might need them to carry out Rose's body. Glen had killed before. He could kill again. It wouldn't bother him that Rose was his own daughter.

Michael yanked the rifle from its scabbard. He wasn't an expert with firearms, but he knew how to use them. And he wouldn't hesitate to use them if Glen Townsend had harmed Rose.

He set off at a jog, his eyes narrowed, his concentration centered on the trail before him. He listened to the sounds of the river off to his right, using it to guide him when sight wasn't enough.

He wasn't certain how far he might have traveled before he had to slow down and take a rest. If he hadn't stopped, perhaps he wouldn't have heard the distant squeal of frightened horses. At least, that was what he thought it was.

Rose, he mouthed silently, then started off again, praying he was in time.

Chapter Thirty-Seven

Like an unwelcome omen, the moon crested the eastern ridge of mountains. It shed its brilliant white light over trees and rocks, forest and river. It made the night nearly as bright as day.

Except shadows were deeper . . . and so was fear.

Rose pressed herself against the tree trunk, her legs drawn tightly against her chest. She saw her father riding down the trail in her direction. She could have sworn she could see the rage in his eyes. He carried his revolver in his hand. If he saw her, he would kill her. She didn't doubt it for a moment.

Suddenly, he jerked back on the reins, stopping his horse. Her heart began to race.

Then Glen jumped down from the saddle and waved at his horse, turning it back up the trail the way he'd come from. He crouched by the side of the trail and waited.

She followed the direction of his gaze. This time her heart nearly stopped. It was Michael. It was Michael, and he didn't know Glen was waiting there for him.

She didn't think about what she was doing. She simply reacted, jumping out of her hiding space and shouting, "Michael, look out!"

She wasn't sure if she felt the bullet graze her arm first or if she heard the sound of its report. She only knew that she was suddenly tumbling backward, rolling down the steep bank to the river waiting below.

Michael saw Glen dash for the spot where Rose had disappeared. He began running, too, but Glen was too close. He got there first and vanished down the side of the riverbank.

Michael kept running, hoping, praying. *God, take me instead. Don't let her die.*

He paused at the top of the decline. In an instant, his gaze found Rose lying at her father's feet. But Glen was uninterested in her. His attention—and his revolver—were pointed directly at Michael.

"Don't move, Rafferty," he warned.

Michael froze in place.

"Put down your rifle. Real slow like."

He did it, all the while mentally commanding Rose to move, to somehow let him know she was alive. *Move, damn it! Please move.*

But she didn't move. Her body was completely still.

"Now the revolver. Just unfasten the gun belt

and let it drop. No sudden moves."

"Why don't you just shoot me now, Townsend, and get it over with?" he asked as he loosened the buckle.

"Because I think your old man would pay good money to get you back alive." He nudged Rose with the toe of his boot. "I don't think you'll pay anything for her now."

Rage boiled in Michael's chest, but he didn't let it take control. He didn't care if he died. Not with Rose gone. But he'd be damned if he was going to die without taking Glen Townsend with him. So he focused his attention on Glen's every action. The man would make a mistake, and when he did, Michael would make his move.

Some sixth sense kept Rose still until she had completely regained consciousness. She became aware of Glen's voice first. Then she heard Michael's.

She knew without opening her eyes that her pa had his gun trained on her husband. She knew he wouldn't hesitate to shoot him. She controlled her breathing and lay as still as death, listening, waiting.

"No point leaving her here like this," Glen said, pressing the toe of his boot against her stomach. "Might as well let the fish have her." He gave her a little push.

"No!" Michael yelled.

She grabbed her father's leg and jerked with all her strength just as the gun exploded. She opened her eyes in time to see Michael flying through the air toward Glen. As he rammed into the older man, Glen's leg was wrenched from Rose's grip, and the two men fell into the tumbling, racing river.

"Michael!" She scrambled to her feet. "Michael!"

She saw the two of them bob to the surface once, then disappear again.

"Michael!"

She began running along the bank, searching the river frantically for any sign of them.

She wasn't aware of the thundering hoofbeats until the noise seemed to surround her. She stopped, not knowing whether to be frightened or relieved, and glanced up toward the trail and the three horsemen.

Dillon jumped from the saddle and raced down the bank to reach her. Dillon, who looked so much like Michael. The pain in her heart was unbearable.

"Michael," she gasped, grabbing Dillon by the arm. "He's in the river. Pa shot at him. I don't know if he's hit. We've got to find him. He might be hurt."

"Where's Townsend?" Yancy shouted from the trail above.

"He's in the river, too."

"Stay here," Dillon ordered, forcing her to sit down. "Don't move until we come back." He ran up the incline.

"Like hell I will," she returned, hopping to her

feet and scrambling up after him. "I'm going with you." She grabbed the reins to Michael's roan, clambered up into the saddle, and lit out in front of the others.

No one was going to keep her away from Michael again.

Michael and Glen struggled with each other and with the water, refusing to let go or give up, even as the river sucked them beneath the frothy surface again and again.

Michael knew Rose was alive, and he was determined to get back to her, but he wasn't going to let her father escape to ever hurt her again. He managed to get his hands around Glen's throat, pressing his thumbs against his windpipe. Glen scratched and clawed at him, dragging them both underwater again.

Michael lost his grip on Glen's neck, but still managed to hold on to his shirt. His lungs felt as if they would burst before he managed to surface. He hauled Glen toward him, ready to clasp his hands around his neck a second time, when the river slammed them against a submerged boulder, tearing them apart.

The wind rushed out of Michael's lungs as his body rolled over the boulder and plunged over a sharp fall in the river. It took every ounce of his remaining strength to swim toward shore. Several times, he thought he wouldn't make it. Several times, he had a hold on a branch or rock or chunk of earth, only to have himself torn away from it by the power of the river.

Finally, when he knew he had few chances left, he managed to grab hold and hang on. Gasping and coughing, he dragged himself halfway onto the bank.

He closed his eyes, exhaustion making it impossible to move any farther. But he had to move. He had to get back to Rose. Only his body wouldn't obey his mental commands.

Rose wasn't sure how she knew it was Michael.

The bend in the river was shaded from the bright moonlight. Shadow upon shadow cast everything in shades of gray and black. The form along the river's edge looked like nothing more than another large, dark rock that littered the bank.

And yet she knew she'd found him.

She pulled hard on the reins, causing the roan to slide to a stop on his hind legs and his head to fly up in the air. Before the horse had gathered himself, Rose was out of the saddle and sliding her way down to the water's edge.

"Michael." She fell to her knees. "Michael." She reached for his arms and tried to pull him out of the water.

"I'm all right, Rose," he said breathlessly.

"Oh, Michael." The tears came unexpectedly, running down her cheeks. Tears of relief. Tears of joy.

She pulled on him again, this time drawing

his head into her lap and rolling him onto his back so she could see his face, so she could be sure he was all right.

Michael, I love you, she thought, but her throat was too tight for speech, her emotions too great to be put into words. Her tears continued to flow unabated.

He opened his eyes and stared at her as if he'd heard her private thoughts. She was vaguely aware of his father and brother and Yancy arriving, but she paid them no heed, her attention captured by the way Michael watched her.

"I've never seen you cry," he said, a tender note of surprise in his voice.

"I never do," she managed to say.

He pulled himself out of the river and stood, then reached down and drew her up to him. "You're okay? He didn't hurt you?" he asked softly.

She nodded, then shook her head.

He kissed her hair, kissed her forehead, her eyelids, her nose, her mouth. "I thought I'd lost you."

"I'm here. I'm all right." She returned his kiss and finally said the words for all to hear. "I love you, Michael. I'll love you forever."

Chapter Thirty-Eight

They returned to Homestead with the sunrise, Rose cradled in Michael's arms, her father's body draped across the saddle of his horse. Yancy had found Glen, drowned and battered by the river, several miles down from the spot where Michael had dragged himself ashore.

Michael took Rose home—and it seemed that most of the town was there waiting for them.

Virginia was there. "It's my fault. If I'd only said somethin'. . . ."

"No, Ma, it wasn't your fault. It's just the way he was. You couldn't have stopped him. I love you, Ma."

Doc Varney was there. "Hank McLeod's going to be just fine. He's as ornery as he ever was, and it's going to be no easy task to keep him in bed as long as he should be there. You don't worry about him, Rose. You just take care of yourself."

Lark was there. "I'd have never forgiven you

if you weren't here to stand up at my wedding with me, Rose Rafferty."

Zoe Potter and her daughters, Emma and Stanley Barber, the reverend and his wife, Vince Stanford, and more. All the people Rose had known most of her life, all there because of her, because they'd been worried about her, because they'd been searching for her. Their concern, and the commotion that went with it, was rather overwhelming, and it seemed an eternity before they departed, leaving her alone with her husband at last.

When the last of the well-wishers were gone and the door closed behind them, Michael took hold of Rose's hand and led her up the stairs to their bedroom. Exhaustion made each step an effort.

Tenderly, he wrapped her in his arms and held her close against him. His clothes were stiff and scratchy from his episode in the river, but Rose didn't mind. She didn't mind anything as long as Michael was holding her.

They didn't move for the longest time, just stood there, hanging on for dear life. She could feel the steady beating of his heart as she pressed her head against his chest. She could feel the tautness of his muscles beneath her hands on his back. She knew this man, knew his heart, his body. She knew him so well she'd become a part of him. Above all else, she loved him.

He kissed the crown of her head, then tipped

her chin with the tip of one finger, forcing her to look up at him. "I expect you know that I mean to renege on our agreement." He leaned low and kissed her mouth, kissed it long and leisurely and thoroughly.

Her heart was pounding in her ears by the time he was through. She took in several deep breaths of air before asking, "What agreement?"

"That our marriage would be one in name only." His fingers began to loosen the fastenings of her bodice.

She laughed, a low, seductive sound in her throat. "I think that agreement was broken weeks ago."

He joined her soft laughter as he pushed her bodice off her shoulders. Seconds later, her dress lay in a puddle around her feet. Her exhaustion seemed to have slipped away with her clothes, her body awakened by his touch.

"There was more to our agreement than this," he whispered as his hands gently cradled her breasts and his lips skimmed over her neck.

"What?" She had no idea what he was talking about. Her mind seemed to turn soft along with the rest of her body as he continued to caress her, kiss her, undress her.

"A year won't be long enough." He laid her back on the bed. When he joined her, he'd shed his clothes. "Not nearly long enough." He claimed her mouth for another breath-stealing kiss.

He pulled his lips from hers and raised himself on his elbows, allowing cool air to slip between their bodies, raising gooseflesh on his skin.

Rose opened her eyes and gazed up at him. "A year?"

"I want forever. Promise me forever, Rose."

She stared up at the man she'd grown to love. Eyes the blue of a summer sky. Hair the color of spun gold. A face more perfect than any she'd ever known. Her Greek god. Her own knight in shining armor.

Rose lifted her fingers and caressed the side of his face. "Even forever won't be long enough."

Author's Note

Dear Reader:

Writing a series of related books such as the *Americana Series* is an interesting experience for me as a writer. When I began *Where The Heart Is,* the first book in the series, I wasn't entirely certain who would be the central characters in subsequent books. It quickly became apparent that Rose, whose childhood was so unhappy, deserved a forever kind of love. I hope you feel she found it in *Forever, Rose.*

It was less apparent who the heroine of the third book would be, but I soon knew it had to be Sarah, a little girl who had lost both her parents when she was so young, a child with hopes and dreams beyond the world she knows. Perhaps it was because there's a part of me in Sarah. I lost my father when I was an infant, so I know what a void it leaves in a young girl's life. And I, too, was a dreamer who longed for experiences beyond the tiny circle of my own world. (Which, no doubt, is why I became a writer.)

Remember When, available in the fall of 1994, is the story of a young woman who longs for experiences far from Homestead and a man who has seen the face of war and wants nothing more than to return to the peace and safety of the home he left behind.

Sarah McLeod, in 1899, is restless and anxious to leave, but she is needed to take care of her elderly grandfather, the grandfather who so lovingly raised her from a toddler. Still, she dreams of beautiful, exciting, exotic places, perhaps even marrying an English lord and living the rest of her life in a castle. She's certain her destiny is far away from dull little Homestead.

Jeremiah Wesley, in contrast, has been away from Homestead for fourteen years. He's seen a great deal of the country, even other parts of the world, and he found many of them less than beautiful, exciting, or exotic. Recovered from wounds suffered in the Spanish-American War, Jeremiah is seeking a place for his emotions to heal as well. Homestead seems the perfect sanctuary.

Sarah was seven years old the last time she saw Jeremiah Wesley, and she has no reason to expect that his return can change the course of her dreams.

Or maybe it can. . . .

I hope you'll look for the third book in the *Americana Series, Remember When,* in the fall of 1994.

I do enjoy hearing from readers. If you'd like an autographed bookmark, please send a #10 self-addressed, stamped envelope to me at the address listed below. If you would like to be added to my mailing list to receive periodic information on future releases, please let me know.

Wishing you love and luck,

Robin Lee Hatcher
PO Box 4722
Boise, ID 83711-4722

LINDA WINSTEAD

From the moment Dillon feasts his eyes on the raven-haired beauty, Grace Cavanaugh, he knows she is trouble. Sharp-tongued and stubborn, with a flawless complexion and a priceless wardrobe, Grace certainly doesn't belong on a Western ranch. But that's what Dillon calls home, and as long as the lovely orphan is his charge, that's where they'll stay.

But Grace Cavanaugh has learned the hard way that men can't be trusted. Not for all the diamonds and rubies in England will she give herself to any man. But when Dillon walks into her life he changes all the rules. Suddenly the unapproachable ice princess finds herself melting at his simplest touch, and wondering what she'll have to do to convince him that their love is the most precious gem of all.

_4223-1 $5.50 US/$6.50 CAN

Love, Cherish Me — Rebecca Brandewyne

The man in black shows his hand: five black spades. Storm
Lesconflair knows what this means—she now belongs to him.
The close heat of the saloon flushes her skin as she feels the
half-breed's eyes travel over her body. Her father's plantation
house in New Orleans suddenly seems but a dream, while the
handsome stranger before her is all too real. Dawn is breaking
outside as the man who won her rises and walks through the
swinging doors. She follows him out into the growing light,
only vaguely aware that she has become his forever, never
guessing that he has also become hers.

___52302-7 $5.99 US/$6.99 CAN

"Each new Connie Mason book is a prize!"
—Heather Graham, bestselling author of
A Magical Christmas

Love Me With Fury. When her stagecoach is ambushed on the Texas frontier, Ariel Leland fears for her life. But even more frightening is Jess Wilder, a virile bounty hunter who has devoted his life to finding the hellcat responsible for his brother's murder—and now he has her. But Ariel's proud spirit and naive beauty erupt a firestorm of need in him—transforming his lust for vengeance into a love that must be fulfilled at any cost.

___52215-2 $5.50 US/$6.50 CAN

Pure Temptation. Fresh off the boat from Ireland, Moira O'Toole isn't fool enough to believe in legends or naive enough to trust a rake. Yet after an accident lands her in Graystoke Manor, she finds herself haunted, harried, and hopelessly charmed by Black Jack Graystoke and his exquisite promise of pure temptation.

___4041-7 $5.99 US/$6.99 CAN

THE IMPOSTOR
ELAINE FOX

Melisande St. Clair knows who she is and what she wants, and when Flynn Patrick steps out of the water and into her life, she knows that his is the face of which she's dreamt. But when she is forced to travel with the handsome stranger, he claims he is from another time and makes suggestions that are hardly proper for a nineteenth-century lady. Although she believes no one could mistake him for an English gentleman, the Duke of Merestun swears that Flynn is his long-lost son. Suddenly, Flynn seems a prince, and all Melisande's desires lie within reach. But what is the truth? All Melisande knows is that she senses no artifice in his touch—and as she fights to remain aloof to the passion that burns in his fiery kiss, she wonders which of them is truly . . . the impostor.

___4523-0 $5.50 US/$6.50 CAN

Dorchester Publishing Co., Inc.
P.O. Box 6640
Wayne, PA 19087-8640

Please add $1.75 for shipping and handling for the first book and $.50 for each book thereafter. NY, NYC, and PA residents, please add appropriate sales tax. No cash, stamps, or C.O.D.s. All orders shipped within 6 weeks via postal service book rate. Canadian orders require $2.00 extra postage and must be paid in U.S. dollars through a U.S. banking facility.

Name_____
Address_____
City_____State_____Zip_____
I have enclosed $_____ in payment for the checked book(s).
Payment <u>must</u> accompany all orders. ❑ Please send a free catalog.
        CHECK OUT OUR WEBSITE! www.dorchesterpub.com